THE MINISTRY

—

Praised by critics . . .

'The most talked-about debut of 2024 . . . The combination of whimsy and high seriousness works brilliantly'
Sunday Times, The 18 best novels of the year

'With a thoroughly offbeat love story at its heart and subtly interwoven musings on the UK's imperial legacy, it's fast moving and riotously entertaining, a genre-busting blend of wit and wonder'
Observer, 10 best new novelists

'*The Ministry of Time* pulls historical figures into the near future, where inevitable romantic entanglements complicate a mysterious governmental project'
New York Times, Books of the year

'Smart, funny and moving, this debut has been the hit of the year'
Guardian, Books of the year

'An addictive sci-fi romantic comedy . . . exciting, fun and a good old-fashioned page turner that you'll recommend to all your friends'
i Paper, Books of the year

'Simply adorable . . . It's the book I have recommended to friends with the most success'
Spectator, Books of the year

'This is extraordinary writing, with unforgettable characters and a spine-tingling love affair, and manages to be both a serious look at the weight of history and an absolute riot. A true original'   *i Paper*

'Intelligent and witty . . . a clever, funny yarn that breathes fresh air into time-travel novels, postcolonial narratives and romance stories alike . . . a sparkling delight'   *Observer*

'Fizzing with sharp one-liners about everything from Tinder to e-scooters, the novel is also a thoughtful meditation on imperialism and immigration'   *Guardian*

'A powerfully drawn love story, an insider's takedown of murky bureaucracy, an action thriller . . . It's a fun ride'

Evening Standard

'Bradley's utterly winning book is a result of violating not so much the laws of physics as the boundaries of genre. Imagine if *The Time Traveler's Wife* had an affair with *A Gentleman in Moscow* . . . Readers, I envy you: There's a smart, witty novel in your future'   *Washington Post*

'History collides delightfully with contemporaneity'

Times Literary Supplement

'A delightfully audacious screwball comedy'   *i-D*

'Comedy, betrayal and romance collide in a story that explores everything from climate change and colonialism to friendship, hope and forgiveness. Start backing out of your weekend plans now . . .'   *Stylist*

'Outrageously brilliant'

Eleanor Catton, author of *Birnam Wood*

'Bradley writes with the maximalist confidence of P. G. Wodehouse, but also with the page-turning pining of Sally Rooney. It's thought-provoking and horribly clever – but it also made me laugh out loud'

Alice Winn, author of *In Memoriam*

'An ecstatic celebration of fiction in all its vehement, ungovernable, mutinous glory'

Megha Majumdar, author of *A Burning*

'A fantastic debut: conceptually brilliant, really funny, genuinely moving, written in the most exquisite language and with a wonderful articulation of the knotty complexities of a mixed-race heritage'

Mark Haddon, author of
The Curious Incident of the Dog in the Night-Time

'Sly and illusionless in its use of history, lovely in its sentences, warm – no, hotter than that – in its characterisation, devastating in its denouement. A weird, kind, clever, heartsick little time bomb of a book'   Francis Spufford, author of *Golden Hill*

'A feast of a novel – singular, alarming and (above all) incredibly sexy. An astonishingly assured debut'

Julia Armfield, author of *Our Wives Under the Sea*

'What a stunning and remarkable wonder . . . *The Ministry of Time* is the most vibe-forward book I have ever read'

Vanessa Chan, author of *The Storm We Made*

. . . championed by readers.

'I'm almost tempted to write a novel-length review of how much I love this'   Alexical, Amazon reviewer

'This is an inventive, futuristic tale that is worth all the international hype'   Kate, Dymocks bookshops

'I genuinely have not fallen in love with a fictional character this hard in a very long time'

Yasmeen, Waterstones bookseller

'I couldn't love this book more . . . Read it and fall in love (again and again and again)'

Forum Books

'Completely original . . . I finished the book in record time and immediately read it again to fully savour its many layers and quirks'   Eleanor, Amazon reviewer

'Phenomenal, brilliant, superb! There are not enough words in any language to describe how wonderful this book is'

Lauren, Harry Hartog bookshops

'*The Ministry of Time* fell into my lap at just the right time and gave me all I could want. Loved it'

Kim, Waterstones reviewer

'A treasure of a book . . . We're all Graham Gore girlies now!'

Phlox Books

Kaliane Bradley is a British-Cambodian writer and editor based in London. Her short stories have appeared in *Electric Literature*, *Catapult*, *Somesuch Stories* and *The Willowherb Review*, among others. She was the winner of the 2022 *Harper's Bazaar* Short Story Prize and the 2022 V.S. Pritchett Short Story Prize. *The Ministry of Time* is her first novel.

THE
MINISTRY
OF TIME

KALIANE BRADLEY

Sceptre

First published in Great Britain in 2024 by Sceptre
An imprint of Hodder & Stoughton Limited
An Hachette UK company

This paperback edition published in 2025

The authorised representative in the EEA is Hachette Ireland,
8 Castlecourt Centre, Dublin 15, D15 XTP3, Ireland (email: info@hbgi.ie)

1

9191-008 Photographic negative of Lieutenant Graham Gore (Commander)
© National Maritime Museum, Greenwich, London
Sketches by Graham Gore © Scott Polar Research Institute
Map designed by Barking Dog Art

A CIP catalogue record for this title is available from the British Library

Paperback ISBN 9781399726368
ebook ISBN 9781399726375

Typeset in Sabon MT by
Palimpsest Book Production Ltd, Falkirk, Stirlingshire

Printed and bound in Great Britain by Clays Ltd, Elcograf S.p.A.

Hodder & Stoughton policy is to use papers that are natural, renewable
and recyclable products and made from wood grown in sustainable forests.
The logging and manufacturing processes are expected to conform
to the environmental regulations of the country of origin.

Hodder & Stoughton Limited
Carmelite House
50 Victoria Embankment
London EC4Y 0DZ

www.sceptrebooks.co.uk

for my parents

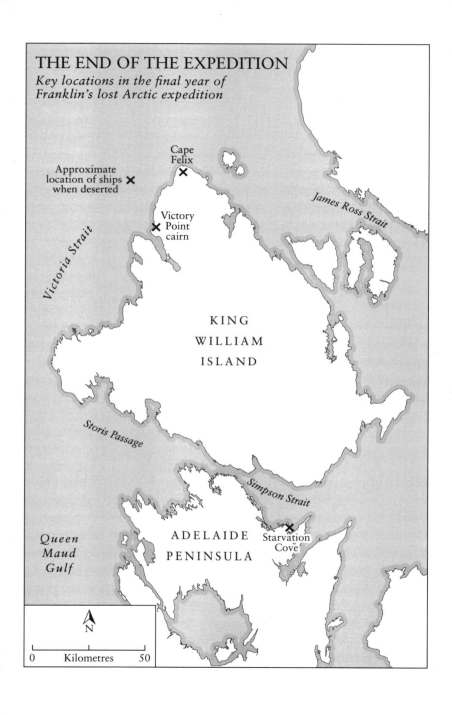

THE END OF THE EXPEDITION

*Key locations in the final year of
Franklin's lost Arctic expedition*

Cape
Felix ✕

Approximate
location of ships ✕
when deserted

James Ross Strait

Victory
Point ✕
cairn

Victoria Strait

KING

WILLIAM

ISLAND

Storis Passage

Simpson Strait

*Queen
Maud
Gulf*

ADELAIDE

PENINSULA

Starvation
Cove ✕

⌃
N

0   Kilometres   50

I

Perhaps he'll die this time.

He finds this doesn't worry him. Maybe because he's so cold he has a drunkard's grip on his mind. When thoughts come, they're translucent, free-swimming medusae. As the Arctic wind bites at his hands and feet, his thoughts slop against his skull. They'll be the last thing to freeze over.

He knows he is walking, though he can no longer feel it. The ice in front of him bounces and retreats, so he must be moving forward. He has a gun across his back, a bag across his front. Their weight is both meaningless and Sisyphean.

He is in a good mood. If his lips were not beyond sensation, he would whistle.

In the distance, he hears the boom of cannon fire. Three in a row, like a sneeze. The ship is signalling.

Chapter One

The interviewer said my name, which made my thoughts clip. I don't say my name, not even in my head. She'd said it correctly, which people generally don't.

'I'm Adela,' she said. She had an eye-patch and blonde hair the same colour and texture as hay. 'I'm the Vice-Secretary.'

'Of . . . ?'

'Have a seat.'

This was my sixth round of interviews. The job I was interviewing for was an internal posting. It had been marked 'Security Clearance Required' because it was gauche to use the Top Secret stamps on paperwork with salary bands. I'd never been cleared to this security level, hence why no one would tell me what the job was. As it paid almost triple my current salary, I was happy to taste ignorance. I'd had to produce squeaky-clean grades in first aid, Safeguarding Vulnerable People, and the Home Office's Life in the UK test to get this far. I knew that I would be working closely with a refugee or refugees of high interest status and particular needs, but I didn't know from whence they were fleeing. I'd assumed politically important defectors from Russia or China.

Adela, Vice-Secretary of God knows what, tucked a blonde strand behind her ear with an audible crunch.

'Your mother was a refugee, wasn't she?' she said, which is a demented way to begin a job interview.

'Yes, ma'am.'

'Cambodia,' she said.

'Yes, ma'am.'

I'd been asked this question a couple of times over the course of the interview process. Usually people asked it with an upward lilt, expecting me to correct them, because no one's from Cambodia. You don't *look* Cambodian, one early clown had said to me, then glowed like a pilot light because the interview was being recorded for staff monitoring and training purposes. He'd get a warning for that one. People say this to me a lot, and what they mean is: you look like one of the late-entering forms of white – Spanish maybe – and also like you're not dragging a genocide around, which is good because that sort of thing makes people uncomfortable.

There was no genocide-adjacent follow-up. (Any family still there *understanding moue*? Do you ever visit *sympathetic smile*? Beautiful country *darkening with tears* when I visited *visible on lower lid* they were so friendly . . .) Adela just nodded. I wondered if she'd go for the rare fourth option and pronounce the country dirty.

'She would never refer to herself as a refugee, or even a former refugee,' I added. 'It's been quite weird to hear people say that.'

'The people you will be working with are also unlikely to use the term. We prefer "expat". In answer to your question, I'm the Vice-Secretary of Expatriation.'

'And they are expats from . . . ?'

'History.'

'Sorry?'

Adela shrugged. 'We have time-travel,' she said, like

someone describing the coffee machine. 'Welcome to the Ministry.'

*

Anyone who has ever watched a film with time-travel, or read a book with time-travel, or dissociated on a delayed public transport vehicle considering the concept of time-travel, will know that the moment you start to think about the physics of it, you are in a crock of shit. How does it work? How *can* it work? I exist at the beginning and end of this account simultaneously, which is a kind of time-travel, and I'm here to tell you: don't worry about it. All you need to know is that in your near future, the British government developed the means to travel through time but had not yet experimented with doing it.

In order to avoid the chaos inherent in changing the course of history – if 'history' could be considered a cohesive and singular chronological narrative, another crock of shit – it was agreed that it would be necessary to extract people from historical warzones, natural disasters and epidemics. These expatriates to the twenty-first century would have died in their own timelines anyway. Removing them from the past ought not to impact the future.

No one had any idea what travelling through time might do to the human body. So the second reason that it was important to pick people who would have died in their own timelines is that they might well die in ours, like deep-sea fish brought up to the beach. Perhaps there were only so many epochs the human nervous system could stand. If they got the temporal equivalent of the bends and sluiced into grey-and-pink jelly in a Ministry laboratory, at least it wouldn't be, statistically speaking, murder.

Assuming that the 'expats' survived, that meant they would

be people, which is a complicating factor. When dealing with refugees, especially en masse, it's better not to think of them as people. It messes with the paperwork. Nevertheless, when the expats were considered from a human rights perspective, they fit the Home Office criteria for asylum seekers. It would be ethically sparse to assess nothing but the physiological effects of time-travel. To know whether they had truly adjusted to the future, the expats needed to live in it, monitored by a full-time companion, which was, it transpired, the job I'd successfully interviewed for. They called us bridges, I think because 'assistant' was below our pay grades.

Language has gone on a long walk from the nineteenth century. 'Sensible' used to mean 'sensitive'. 'Gay' used to mean 'jolly'. 'Lunatic asylum' and 'asylum seeker' both use the same basic meaning of 'asylum': an inviolable place of refuge and safety.

We were told we were bringing the expats to safety. We refused to see the blood and hair on the floor of the madhouse.

*

I was thrilled to get the job. I'd plateaued where I was, in the Languages department of the Ministry of Defence. I worked as a translator-consultant specialising in Southeast Asia, specifically Cambodia. I'd learned the languages I translated from at university. Despite my mother speaking Khmer to us at home, I hadn't retained it through my formative years. I came to my heritage as a foreigner.

I liked my Languages job well enough, but I'd wanted to become a field agent, and after failing the field exams twice I was at a bit of a loss for career trajectory. It wasn't what my parents had had in mind for me. When I was a very small child, my mother made her ambitions known. She wanted me to be

Prime Minister. As Prime Minister, I would 'do something' about British foreign policy and I would also take my parents to fancy governmental dinners. I would have a chauffeur. (My mother was a reluctant driver; the chauffeur was important.) Regrettably she also drilled the karmic repercussions of gossip and lying into me – the fourth Buddhist precept is unambiguous on this – and thus at the age of eight my political career was over before it began.

My younger sister was a far more skilled dissembler. I was dutiful with language and she was evasive, pugnacious with it. This is why I became a translator and she became a writer – or at least she tried to become a writer and became a copy-editor. I was paid considerably more than her and my parents understood what my job was, so I would say that karma worked in my favour. My sister would say something along the lines of: go fuck yourself. But I know she means it in a friendly way, probably.

*

Even on the very day we were to meet the expats, we were still arguing about the word 'expat'.

'If they're refugees,' said Simellia, one of the other bridges, 'then we should call them refugees. They're not moving to a summer cottage in Provence.'

'They will not necessarily think of *themselves* as refugees,' said Vice-Secretary Adela.

'Has anyone asked them what they think?'

'They see themselves as kidnap victims, mostly. Nineteen-sixteen thinks he's behind enemy lines. Sixteen-sixty-five thinks she's dead.'

'And they're being released to us *today*?'

'The Wellness team think their adjustment will be negatively impacted if they're held on the wards any longer,' said Adela, dry as a filing system.

We – or rather, Simellia and Adela – were having this argument in one of the Ministry's interminable rooms: pebble-coloured with lights embedded in the ceiling, modular in a way that suggested opening a door would lead to another identical space, and then another, and then another. Rooms like this are designed to encourage bureaucracy.

This was supposed to be the final direct briefing of the five bridges: Simellia, Ralph, Ivan, Ed, and me. We'd all gone through a six-round interview process that put the metaphorical drill to our back teeth and bored. *Have you now, or ever, been convicted of or otherwise implicated in any activity that might undermine your security status?* Then nine months of preparation. The endless working groups and background checks. The construction of shell jobs in our old departments (Defence, Diplomatic, Home Office). Now we were here, in a room where the electricity was audible in the lightbulbs, about to make history.

'Don't you think,' said Simellia, 'that throwing them into the world when they think they're in the afterlife or on the Western Front might impede their adjustment? I ask both as a psychologist and a person with a normal level of empathy.'

Adela shrugged.

'It might. But this country has never accepted expatriates from history before. They might die of genetic mutations within the year.'

'Should we expect that?' I asked, alarmed.

'We don't know what to expect. That's why you have this job.'

*

The chamber the Ministry had prepared for the handover had an air of antique ceremony: wood panels, oil paintings, high ceiling. It had rather more éclat than the modular rooms. I think someone on the administration team with a sense of drama had arranged the move. In its style and in the particular way the windows flattened the sunlight, the room had probably remained unchanged since the nineteenth century. My handler, Quentin, was already there. He looked bilious, which is how excitement shows on some people.

Two agents led my expat through the door at the other end of the room before I'd adjusted to knowing he was coming.

He was pale, drawn. They'd clipped his hair so short that his curls were flattened. He turned his head to look around the room and I saw an imposing nose in profile, like a hothouse flower growing out of his face. It was strikingly attractive and strikingly large. He had a kind of resplendent excess of feature that made him look hyperreal.

He stood very straight and eyed my handler. Something about me had made him look and then look away.

I stepped forward and his eyeline shifted.

'Commander Gore?'

'Yes.'

'I'm your bridge.'

*

Graham Gore (Commander, RN; c.1809–c.1847) had been in the twenty-first century for five weeks, though, like the other expats, he'd only been lucid for a handful of those days. The extraction process had merited a fortnight of hospitalisation. Two of the original seven expats had died because of it, and only five remained. He'd been treated for pneumonia, for severe frostbite, for the early stages of scurvy, and two broken toes on which he had been blithely walking. Lacerations too, from a taser – he'd shot at two of the team members who'd come to expatriate him, and a third was forced to fire.

He'd attempted to flee the Ministry wards three times and had to be sedated. After he'd stopped fighting back, he'd gone through a ground-zero orientation with the psychologists and the Victorianists. For ease of adjustment, the expats were only given immediate, applicable knowledge. He came to me knowing the basics about the electric grid, the internal combustion engine and the plumbing system. He didn't know about the World or Cold Wars, the sexual liberation of the 1960s, or the war on terror. They had started by telling him about the dismantling of the British Empire and it hadn't gone down well.

The Ministry had arranged a car to take us to the house. He knew, theoretically, about cars, but it was his first time in one. He stared through the window, pallid with what I assumed was wonder.

'If you have any questions,' I said, 'please feel free to ask. I appreciate that this is a lot to take in.'

'I am delighted to discover that, even in the future, the English have not lost the art of ironic understatement,' he said, without looking at me.

He had a mole on his throat, close to his earlobe. The only existing daguerreotype of him showed him in 1840s fashion, with a high cravat. I stared at the mole.

'This is London?' he asked, finally.

'Yes.'

'How many people live here now?'

'Nearly nine million.'

He sat back and shut his eyes.

'That's far too large a number to be real,' he murmured. 'I am going to forget that you told me.'

*

The house that the Ministry had provided was a late Victorian redbrick, originally designed for local workers. Gore would have seen them built, if he'd lived into his eighties. As it was, he was thirty-seven years old, and had not experienced crinolines, *A Tale of Two Cities* or the enfranchisement of the working classes.

He got out of the car and looked up and down the street with the weariness of a man who has travelled across the continent and is yet to find his hotel. I hopped out after him. I tried to see what he could see. He would ask questions about the cars parked on the street, perhaps, or the streetlamps.

'Do you have keys?' he asked. 'Or do doors operate by magic passwords now?'

'No, I have—'

'Open sesame,' he said darkly to the letterbox.

Inside, I told him I would make tea. He said he would like, with my permission, to look at the house. I gave it. He made a swift tour. He trod firmly, as if he expected resistance. When he came back to the kitchen-diner and leant against the doorjamb, I seized up painfully. Stage-fright, but also the shock of his impossible presence catching up with me. The more he was there – and he kept on being there – the more I felt like I was elbowing my way out of my body. A narrative-altering thing was happening to me, that I was experiencing all over, and I was trying to view myself from the outside to make sense of it. I chased a tea bag to the rim of a mug.

'We are to – co-habit?' he said.

'Yes. Every expat has a bridge for a year. We're here to help you adjust to your new life.'

He folded his arms and regarded me. His eyes were hazel, scrawled faintly with green, and thickly lashed. They were both striking and uncommunicative.

'You are an unmarried woman?' he asked.

'Yes. It's not an improper arrangement, in this century. Once you're deemed able to enter the community, outside of the Ministry or to anyone not involved in the project, you should refer to me as your housemate.'

'"Housemate",' he repeated, disdainfully. 'What does this word imply?'

'That we are two unpartnered people, sharing the cost of the rent on a house, and are not romantically involved.'

He looked relieved.

'Well, regardless of the custom, I'm not certain it's a decent arrangement,' he said. 'But if you've allowed nine million people to live here, perhaps it's a necessity.'

'Mm. Beside your elbow is a white box with a handle. It's a refrigerator – a fridge, we call it. Could you open the door and take out the milk, please?'

He opened the fridge and stared inside.

'An ice box,' he said, interested.

'Pretty much. Powered by electricity. I think electricity has been explained to you—'

'Yes. I am also aware that the earth revolves around the sun. To save you a little time.'

He opened a crisper.

'Carrots still exist, then. Cabbage too. How will I recognise milk? I'm hoping you will tell me that you still use milk from cows.'

'We do. Small bottle, top shelf, blue lid.'

He hooked his finger into the handle and brought it to me.

'Maid's got the day off?'

'No maid. No cook, either. We do most things for ourselves.'

'Ah,' he said, and paled.

*

He was introduced to the washing machine, the gas cooker, the radio, the vacuum cleaner.

'Here are your maids,' he said.

'You're not wrong.'

'Where are the thousand-league boots?'

'We don't have those yet.'

'Invisibility cloak? Sun-resistant wings of Icarus?'

'Likewise.'

He smiled. 'You have enslaved the power of lightning,' he said, 'and you've used it to avoid the tedium of hiring help.'

'Well,' I said, and I launched into a pre-planned speech about class mobility and domestic labour, touching on the minimum wage, the size of an average household, and women in the workforce. It took a full five minutes of talking and by the end I'd moved into the same tremulous liquid register I used to use for pleading with my parents for a curfew extension.

When I was finished, all he said was, 'A dramatic fall in employment following the "First" World War?'

'Ah.'

'Maybe you can explain that to me tomorrow.'

This is everything I remember about my earliest hours with him. We separated and spent the fading day bobbing shyly around one another like clots in a lava lamp. I was expecting him to have a time-travel-induced psychotic break and perhaps chew or fold me with murderous intent. Mostly he touched things, with a compulsive brushing motion I was later to learn was because of permanent nerve damage from frostbite. He flushed the toilet fifteen times in a row, silent as a windhover while the cistern refilled, which could have been wonder or embarrassment. At hour two, we tried to sit in the same room. I looked up when he breathed in sharply through his nose to see him pulling his fingers away from a lightbulb in the lamp. He retreated to his bedroom for a while, and I went to sit on the back porch. It was a mild spring evening. Idiot-eyed wood pigeons lumbered across the lawn, belly-deep in clover.

Upstairs, I heard a cautious woodwind polonaise strike up, waver and cease. A few moments later, his tread in the kitchen. The pigeons took off, their wings making a noise like swallowed laughter.

'Did the Ministry provide the flute?' he asked the back of my head.

'Yes. I told them it might be grounding for you.'

'Oh. Thank you. You – knew I played the flute?'

'A couple of extant letters from you and referring to you mention it.'

'Did you read the letters that mentioned my mania for arson and my lurid history of backstreet goose-wrestling?'

I turned around and stared at him.

'A joke,' he supplied.

'Ah. Are there going to be a lot of those?'

'It depends on how often you spring on me such statements as "I have read your personal letters". May I join you?'

'Please.'

He sat down beside me, keeping a space of about a foot between our bodies. The neighbourhood made its noises, which all sounded like something else. The wind in the trees sounded like rushing water. The squirrels chattered like children. Distant conversation recalled the clatter of pebbles underfoot. I felt I should have been translating them for him, as if he didn't know about trees.

He was drumming his fingers on the porch. 'I suppose,' he said carefully, 'that your era has evolved past such tasteless vices as tobacco?'

'You arrived about fifteen years too late. It's going out of fashion. I've got some good news for you though.'

I got up – he turned his head, so as not to have my bare calves in his eyeline – fetched a packet of cigarettes and a lighter from a drawer in the kitchen, and came back.

'Here. Something else I got the Ministry to lay on. Cigarettes more or less replaced cigars in the twentieth century.'

'Thank you. I'm sure I will adapt.'

He busied himself with working out how to remove the plastic film – which he put carefully away in his pocket – flicking the zippo, and frowning at the warning label. I stared at the lawn and felt like I was manually operating my lungs.

A few seconds later, he exhaled with obvious relief.

'Better?'

'It embarrasses me to convey just how much better. Hm. In my time, well-bred young ladies did not indulge in tobacco. But I note that a great deal has changed. Hemlines, for example. Do you smoke?'

'No . . .'

He smiled directly into my face for the first time. His dimples notched his cheeks like a pair of speech marks.

'What an interesting tone. Did you used to smoke?'

'Yes.'

'Did you stop because all cigarette packets carry this garish warning?'

'More or less. As I said, smoking is very out of fashion now, because we've discovered how unhealthy it is. Damn it. Could I have one, please?'

His dimples, and his smile, had vanished on 'damn'. I suppose as far as he was concerned, I might as well have said 'fuck'. I wondered what was going to happen when I did eventually say 'fuck', which I did at least five times a day. Nevertheless, he proffered the packet, and then lit my cigarette with anachronistic gallantry.

We smoked in silence for a while. At some point, he raised a finger to the sky.

'What is that?'

'That's a plane. An aeroplane, to give it its full name. It's a – well. A ship of the sky.'

'There are people in there?'

'Probably around a hundred.'

'In that little arrow?'

He watched it, squinting along the cigarette.

'How high up is it?'

'Six miles or so.'

'I thought so. Well, well. You *have* done something interesting with your enslaved lightning. It must be flying very fast.'

'Yes. A flight from London to New York takes eight hours.'

He coughed suddenly, bringing up a mouthful of smoke. 'Uh – I want you to stop telling me things for a moment, please,' he said. 'That's . . . quite enough for today.'

He ground the cigarette out on the porch. 'Eight hours,' he murmured. 'No tides in the sky, I suppose.'

*

That night, I slept with unpleasant lightness, my brain balanced on unconsciousness like an insect's foot on the meniscus of a pond. I didn't so much wake up as give up on sleep.

Outside on the landing there was a huge tongue-shaped shadow, stretching from the closed bathroom door to my bedroom. I put my foot in it and it went *squelch*.

'Commander Gore?'

'Ah,' came a muffled voice from behind the door. 'Good morning.'

The bathroom door swung open, guiltily.

Gore was already fully dressed and sitting on the edge of the bath, smoking. The bottom of the bath had a low tide mark of cigarette ash and soap scum. Two cigarettes were crushed out in the soap dish.

As I would discover, this would become his habit: rising early, bathing, ashing in the tub. He could not be persuaded to sleep in, use the shower – which he disliked and intimated was 'unhygienic' – or ash in the ashtrays I would pointedly leave on the edge of the bath. He would be embarrassed by the sight of my razor, shave with a cut-throat blade, and insist on separate soaps.

All this was to come. On that first morning, there was Gore chain-smoking and a bleeding water supply line. The toilet's cistern lay on the floor, gleaming like a slain whale. A vile smell was seeping up from the floor.

'I was trying to see how it worked,' he said diffidently.

'I see.'

'I fear I may have got carried away.'

Gore was an officer from the dusk of the Age of Sail, not an engineer. I'm sure he knew plenty about ship's rigging but he'd probably never handled an instrument more technologically complex than a sextant. Men in their right minds are not usually overcome with a mania for pulling the plumbing apart. I suggested he might like to wash his hands at the sink downstairs, and I could, perhaps, call a plumber, and we could, potentially, take a constitutional walk on the nearby heath.

He gave this due consideration over the stub end of the cigarette.

'Yes, I would like that,' he said finally.

'We'll go downstairs and wash our hands first.'

'It was clear water,' he said, grinding out the cigarette. His face was averted from mine, but I could see the mole on his throat lay on pinkening skin.

'Well. Germs.'

'"Germs"?'

'Hm. Bacteria. Very, very tiny creatures which live in – everything, really. Only visible through a microscope. The bad ones spread disease. Cholera, typhoid, dysentery.'

I might as well have named the Father, the Son and the Holy Spirit for the look of alarmed amazement that came over Gore's face. He looked down at his hands, and then slowly extended his arms, holding them away from his body like a pair of rabid rats.

*

He took some comfort from the phrase 'fresh air', at least, once we'd stepped out onto the heath. He was far more impressed by germ theory than he had been by electricity. By the time we'd crossed the first of the early-morning dogwalkers, I was enthusiastically describing the cause of tooth cavities, with hand motions.

'I don't think it's very polite of you to say there are germs in my mouth.'

'There are germs in *everyone's* mouths.'

'Speak for yourself.'

'There'll be germs on your shoes and under your nails. It's just how the world works. An aseptic environment is. Well. It's a dead one.'

'I won't be participating.'

'You don't have a choice!'

'I will write a strongly worded letter of complaint.'

We walked a little further. The colour was starting to return to his cheeks, though around his eyes I could see score marks of strain and insomnia. When he saw me scrutinising him, he raised his eyebrows and I tried a cautious smile.

'Careful,' he said. 'Your germs are showing.'

'Well!'

We got croissants and tea from a food truck set up by the children's park. These concepts were either familiar to him, or explicable from context, and we managed our walking breakfast with no further revelation.

'I've been told there are other, uh, expats,' he said eventually.

'Yes. There are five of you.'

'Who are they, please?'

'There's a woman from 1665, who was extracted from the Great Plague of London. Uh. A man – a lieutenant, I believe – from 1645, Battle of Naseby. He fought back harder even than you. There's an army captain – 1916. Battle of the Somme. Someone from Robespierre's Paris, 1793, she's got quite the psych profile.'

'You didn't "extract" anyone else from the expedition?'

'No.'

'May I ask why not?'

'Well, this is an experimental project. We wanted to pull individuals from across as wide a range of time periods as possible.'

'And you chose me, rather than, say, Captain Fitzjames?'

I blinked up at him, surprised. 'Yes. We had documentary evidence that you – you'd left the expedition—'

'That I'd died.'

'Uh. Yes.'

'How did I die?'

'They didn't say. You were referred to as "the late Commander Gore".'

'Who are "they"?'

'Captain Fitzjames, Captain Crozier. Co-leading the expedition after the death of Sir John Franklin.'

We'd fallen into a languid, patrolling step, and he'd gone cool.

'Captain Fitzjames spoke very highly of you,' I ventured. '"A man of great stability of character, a very good officer, and the sweetest of tempers."'

That, at last, brought his dimples out.

'He wrote his memoirs on his return, then?' Gore said, amused.

'Ah. Commander Gore.'

'Hm?'

'I think I should – could we sit down? On that bench over there.'

He pulled up the swing of his step so abruptly that I kicked myself in the ankle trying to stop.

'You are about to tell me something happened to Captain Fitzjames,' he said.

'Let's sit down. Here.'

'What happened?' he asked. The dimples had gone. Apparently I did not get them for very long.

'Something happened to – everyone.'

'What do you mean?' he asked, a touch impatiently.

'The expedition was lost.'

'Lost?'

'In the Arctic. No one returned.'

'There were 126 men in two of the most powerful ships in the Service,' he said. 'You are telling me not one returned to England? Captain Crozier? He'd been to Antarctica—'

'No one survived. I'm sorry. I thought you'd been told at the Ministry.'

He stared at me. The green rings in his eyes turned the colour of shined chestnuts when he canted his head.

'Tell me,' he said slowly, 'what happened. Once I – left.'

'So. Yes. Right. Uh. We picked you up in 1847, from Cape Felix. We knew a summer camp had existed there, but we weren't sure what it was—'

'It was a magnetic observatory. It doubled as a base for the hunting parties too.'

'Right, okay. So, we knew that the camp had been abandoned in a hurry. When the site was found in 1859, there was all this abandoned equipment. Tents. Scientific instruments. Bearskins. Historians were never sure why, but we thought—'

'Surely it was because of you,' he said, comprehension breaking on his face. 'The – flash of lightning, I thought it was. Then that – doorway of blue light.'

'Yes.'

'I saw figures in the doorway. There was an . . . enormous net . . . which hurt.'

'I'm sorry. We couldn't send people through the portal – we didn't know what would happen to them. I think the net was steel-linked? To stop you, uh, cutting yourself free.'

More staring. I hurriedly added, 'We weren't sure that we were the cause of your men abandoning the camp until we did it. It's one of the "great mysteries", ha, so we thought we might as well take our chances that it was us and—'

'Did your people kill everyone?' he asked. His voice was strangely mild, but there was a crimson rash prickling across his cheeks. 'I know my officers. Knew them. They would have come out after me. Sent a party after me.'

'I'm sure they did come after you, but the portal would have closed by then.'

'How did they die, then?'

'Well. The sea never thawed. The two ships stayed trapped in the pack ice. By winter 1847 the expedition had lost nine officers and fifteen men. I don't know how many of them died while you were still—'

'Freddy – Mr Des Voeux – and I had left a note for the Admiralty on King William Land. In a cairn at Victory Point. It contained—'

'Yes, the expedition found your note in April 1848. Crozier and Fitzjames updated it to say they'd abandoned the ships and that the whole crew were planning to march south to Back's Fish River. King William Island is, er, it's an island, by the way.'

He turned away from me and tugged the cigarette packet from his coat pocket.

'Back's Fish River was eight hundred miles away,' he said eventually.

'Yes. They didn't make it. They starved to death on the march down.'

'All of them?'

'All of them.'

'I can't imagine Captain Fitzjames dying of something so morbid as starvation. Or Harry Goodsir? He was one of the cleverest men I'd ever—'

'All of them. I'm very sorry.'

He stared out over the heath and exhaled slowly.

'It appears I was spared a wretched death,' he said.

'I'm sor— you're welcome?'

'How long did it take?'

'Inuit testimony suggests a small group of men returned to the ships and survived a fourth winter. But everyone was dead by 1850.'

'What is an "Inuit" testimony?'

'Er. You called them "Esquimaux". It's correct to call them Inuit.'

To my surprise, he flushed deeply and flinched. He looked disproportionately guilty – Victorians didn't have political correctness – but all he said was, 'The Admiralty sent no rescue parties?'

'The Admiralty sent several. Lady Franklin financed a number as well. But they all went in the wrong directions.'

He shut his eyes and blew a feather of smoke at the sky. 'The greatest expedition of our age,' he said. There was nothing in his voice – no anger, no sadness, no irony. Nothing.

*

Later that day, he said, 'I apologise for my reaction. It was – something of a shock, but one I should have borne with greater stoicism. After all, we knew what we'd signed up for. I hope you didn't feel that I was in a temper at you.'

'No. I'm only sorry you received the story so disjointedly.'

He stood back and looked at me. If he were another sort of man, I would have called this look a once-over. But there wasn't enough heat in it to be a once-over. He was simply looking at me, head to toe, for the first time.

'Why are you my bridge?' he asked. 'Why did they not assign an officer of some sort? The secrecy of this, ah, *project*, as you call it, was impressed on me at length while I was . . . recovering.'

'I suppose I *am* an officer, sort of. A professional, anyway. I worked in the Languages department as a translator-consultant. My area of expertise is mainland Southeast Asia.'

'I see,' he said. 'Actually, I don't see. What does all that mean?'

'I'm cleared to Top Secret and I've worked with – displaced people. The Ministry's original intention was to have the expats co-habiting with therapists, but in the end they felt it made more sense for you to have . . . a friend.'

He stared at me blankly and I blushed, because even to me it sounded like I was pleading. I added, 'I already knew a lot about you. I'd read about the expedition. They've written books and books about it. Roald Amundsen, the guy who discovered the North and South Pole, did it because he was obsessed with John Franklin's expedition. He—'

'You have the advantage of me,' he said.

'I do, yes.'

The dimples came out for that. Not very mirthfully, but they did come out.

'And who found the Northwest Passage?' he asked. '*That* was our original intention.'

'Robert McClure, in 1850.'

'Robbie?!'

'Yes. He found it when he came out after you on one of the search expeditions. He told the Inuit he was looking for a "lost brother". As you're the only expedition member he knew personally, I always assumed—'

'Oh,' he said.

I stopped talking. He'd said 'oh' as if I'd pushed a needle through his clothes. All these people were history to me but still felt alive to him. The queasiness of his discomposure dropped the floor out of the room. I was so embarrassed that I automatically took the cigarette he offered me, even though I had, as I've said, given up smoking years beforehand.

*

The more I got to know him, the more I discovered Gore was the most entirely realised person I'd ever met. In his own time, he had liked hunting, sketching, flute-playing (he was very good at this) and the company of other people. Hunting was out of the question, and socialising was limited by order of the Ministry. By the end of the first week he was visibly going bonkers with no one but me to talk to.

'When will I meet the other expats?'

'Soon—'

'Am I to be idle for this entire year? You do still *have* a naval service?'

'We expected you would need more time to adjust—'

'Is the sea still wet? Can one still float ships upon it?'

The first thing to slow him down was the capaciousness of streaming services. Specifically, Spotify. I ran him briefly through the evolution of the phonograph – which he might have lived to see had he not perished in the 1840s – the turn-table, the cassette player, the CD, MP3s, before landing on music streaming services.

'Any music? Any performances, any time, whensoever you wish it?'

'Well, not any, but it's a very large library.'

We were sitting beside one another on the sofa, a Ministry-issue laptop on my knees. He liked the laptop, as a concept. He was cautiously interested in Google and Wikipedia, but the difficulty of finding letters on the keyboard had hobbled his curiosity. He had already remarked on how unnerving he found my ability to type at speed without looking.

'Will you please instruct the machine to play Bach's Sonata in E-flat major?'

I hit play on the first version Spotify suggested.

We settled back, if 'settle' is the right word for the stiff, wary way we offset one another's weight on the cushions. After a while, he covered his eyes with his hands.

'And one can simply . . . repeat it. Infinitely,' he mumbled.

'Yep. Would you like it again?'

'No. I don't think it's very respectful.'

'Shall I put on something else?'

'Yes,' he said, not moving. 'Instruct the machine to play something that you prefer.'

It didn't seem like it would be kind to play Kate Bush. I put on Franck's Sonata in A major.

'When was this written?'

'I'm not certain of the exact date. The 1880s, I think? After you – after your – afterwards.'

'My sister Anne would have loved this. She was a great fan of sentimental violin.'

I looked away. When the music finished, he said, in a thick voice, 'I'm going to go for a walk.'

He left and didn't return for several hours. The air turned sharp and cool. Oily clouds were piling up in the sky. A storm was coming. I was fretful and couldn't stay in one room for longer than a few minutes. It had occurred to me only after he shut the door that I wasn't allowed to let him out of my sight yet.

When he returned, he blew in like the weather. His jaw was set, which I had started to understand was a sign of enormous agitation.

'This city is so crowded,' he said, standing in the hallway in his coat and boots. 'Worse even than when I was last here.

There are buildings everywhere. No horizons. Only buildings and people as far as the eye can see, and great metal towers strung with rope. Huge grey roads, covered in metallic traffic. There's no space here. How can you breathe? Is all of England like this? The entire world?'

'London is a capital city. Of course it's crowded. There are still empty places.'

Behind my back, my fist was spasmodically clenching and releasing.

'Where? I would like to go somewhere where I don't feel as if I'm in a microscope's slide.'

'Uh. There are currently movement restrictions on all expats. You must have been told. You can't leave the boundary lines.'

He stared at me, unseeing.

'I'm going to have a bath,' he said, finally.

*

While I still worked in Languages, I'd been employed as the primary translator on a project between the trade department and a pan-ASEAN forestry commission. I'd had a gristly time translating *internally displaced person*, which, during this project, referred to people who had been forced to leave their villages because of logging work – hard to explain, because some other people, often from the same villages, had achieved economic stability and long-term employment because of the logging work. *Progress*, that was another tricky thing to translate.

I'd sat with the term *internally displaced person* until I'd broken it down semantically. I was wrestling with a ghost meaning: a person whose interiority was at odds with their exteriority, who was internally (in themselves) displaced. I was thinking about my mother, who persistently carried her lost homeland jostling inside her like a basket of vegetables.

Gore was internally displaced in this way. I could sometimes see him regarding the modern world as if through a telescope. He stood forever on the deck of a ship somewhere in the early 1800s. He must have done it even in his own era, coming down from the ports to note with alarm that women were wearing their sleeves wide again, that some European country had declared war on another again, while he was months or years away at sea. He told me stories as if he was trying to catch himself in amber. Just like my mother, though I didn't tell him that.

I told him about the forestry commission, and he listened keenly.

'You were quite important,' he suggested.

'No need to flatter me. I was just a translator.'

'One never understands one's use but through the opinion of others. Take the Aden expedition. That was a triumph, and my captain insisted I be promoted to first luff as if I'd had a major hand in it.'

I smiled at his knuckles. We'd been briefed on *teaching moments*, where we might find the values of the expats didn't align with those of modern, multicultural Britain. For Gore, Control had identified the conquest of Aden and the First Opium War. *Avoid confrontational or oppositional language. Avoid being drawn into conversations about personal value systems.* In January 1839, the British decided to acquire the port of Aden, which was part of the sultanate of Lahej. It was a useful port on the trade route to the Far East. So far as I understood the British Empire, other people's countries were useful or negligible but rarely conceived of as autonomous. The Empire regarded the world the way my dad regards the elastic bands that the postman drops on his round: *This is handy, it's just lying here, now it's mine.*

'Did you have a major hand at Aden then?' I asked, like a coward.

'Modesty is a virtue and I must warn you that I am a very virtuous man.'

'I should warn you that these days, blowing up an Arabian port because you want to claim it for the Empire is generally frowned upon.'

'But intervening in the trade commission of another country, in order to increase the trade advantage of the Kingdom, is considered diplomatic.'

'Well,' I said, and I was about to protest that it had been an *environmental* intervention, even though it would mean having to explain *environmental*, when I saw that he was regarding me with something approaching admiration, and I stopped.

I should say that my face does a good impression of whiteness, late-entering or not. I didn't know how to tell Gore that I'd been tricking him, feature by feature. I wasn't sure I was ready to. He'd made, as people do, an assumption about me that left me room to manoeuvre. Later, when he found out the truth – as people do – he'd be unbalanced by his own mistake. Another person's unguardedness in that moment can be very useful, interpersonally, as long as you don't soften. There is language I could use about this if I were the melodramatic type: *behind enemy lines*, for example, or *double agent*. My sister might use these terms, or she might call me a fraud.

Besides, I'd read both of his extant letters. He'd written to his father to say that he was pleased with the outcome at Aden. A hundred and fifty Arabs died in the battle and the British didn't sustain a single casualty. It was a bloodbath.

'Your job sounds very interesting,' he said. 'How did you get it?'

*

Gore wouldn't watch television. He seemed to find it a tasteless invention.

'You can send dioramas through the ether,' he said, 'and you've used it to show people at their most wretched.'

'No one's forcing you to watch *EastEnders*.'

'Any child or unmarried woman of virtue might engage the machine and be faced with lurid examples of criminal behaviour.'

'No one's making you watch *Midsomer Murders* either.'

'Or deformed monstrosities against the will of God—'

'What?'

'*Sesame Street*,' he said. Then he had to busy himself with looking through his pockets for his cigarettes, his tongue tenting his cheek as he tried not to laugh.

Finally, at a loss for anything else to do, he began to pick over the bookshelves. I hit an early win with Arthur Conan Doyle. I tried giving him the Aubrey–Maturin series, starting with *Master and Commander*, but he found them upsettingly nostalgic. He liked *Great Expectations* but made it less than a fifth of the way through *Bleak House*. I suggested the Brontës and I might as well have told him to pick up and read a pigeon. He had no patience for Henry James but he liked Jack London. Out of curiosity, I tried him on Hemingway, which he pronounced 'shocking' and read in the bath.

One day, on a whim, I gave him *Rogue Male* by Geoffrey Household. It was the literary equivalent of playing with fire – I'd delayed my explanations of the World Wars, much less given context about why an unnamed English crack shot and sportsman would want to try shooting a European dictator in the 1930s. But he'd complained so much about not being able to hunt that I thought the premise might entertain him.

A day or so later, I got the email that officially launched the next segment of the project.

'Commander Gore?'

'Hm?'

'I have some good news. The Ministry want us to go in next week.' He did not look up. 'Oh. You've not got very far with *Rogue Male*, then.'

'Oh,' he said, 'I finished it. And then I started it again.'

II

Gore hauls himself aboard the ship, met by the mittened hands and mufflered faces of the watch. The ship, trapped in sea ice, tilts queasily to one side where the frozen waves have shoved against the hull. Below deck — so sealed from the elements and so thick with bodies that the air is warm — Gore finds the crew in the rare, humid grip of a hurry. Captain Fitzjames has convened an emergency command meeting.

He hands off his bag to the officers' steward and insists on attending the meeting, trying to shake the ice-dementia. He knows without consulting a glass that his mouth is corpsey blue.

In sick bay, Stanley, the ship's surgeon, asks him for the date.

'Twenty-fourth July 1847,' he says, after too thick a pause.

'You want a firmness of diction,' mutters the doctor. He does not say *you're slurring*, not to an officer. Gore tries a smile. Fissures teem along his lips. But no one orders him not to attend the emergency meeting.

It is held in the Great Cabin of *Erebus*, a desperately unhaunted room. Sir John Franklin had died here, succumbing to age and the climate, more than a month before. His avuncular ghost has failed to manifest. James Fitzjames, his commander and now captain of *Erebus*, lives in the Cabin like an orphan locked in a crypt.

Captain Crozier of *Terror*, the expedition's new leader, has sent

Lieutenant Irving over to *Erebus*. He is a shy man with heavy whiskers and an unhappy habit of quoting scripture at sailors.

'I'm afraid,' says Irving, 'that it isn't good news.'

'The rations,' Fairholme cuts in. Fairholme is the third lieutenant of *Erebus*, a big bouncing man who towers over most of the other officers. Now he cringes, putting Gore in mind of a Great Dane caught stealing food.

'With yours too,' sighs Irving. 'God has seen fit to test us in our resolution. But His ways are not our ways, and the wiseness of the world is as foolishness to——'

Gore puts his palm down flat on the mahogany table. Gently, but with finality. The drone of Irving's voice bespeaks panic: that of a preacher pleading with the weather.

'James,' he says.

He means Fairholme — he wouldn't presume to address Captain Fitzjames by his Christian name in a command meeting — but it is Fitzjames who answers.

'It's the tinned rations,' Fitzjames says. 'Some of them have been found to be inedible. More so than usual,' he adds, smiling faintly. 'Rotted. On both ships, so they must have been defective when we shipped out, rather than attributable to some noxious influence on the journey.'

Gore lifts his hand. He's left a smear on the table the colour of tamarind flesh. There is a sour, steady pain in his palm that he briefly misunderstands as a taste.

'How many of the tins?' he asks.

Fitzjames doesn't answer. He is seated in Sir John's place. His curls have lost their gloss but they still flash a troubling copper.

'Was there much game, Graham?' he asks instead.

Gore considers the weight of the sack he'd carried, which had felt so meaningful. 'Three partridges,' he says, 'and a boatswain gull too far off to hit. Nothing else. Not even tracks.'

'In four and a half hours?'

'Was I gone that long?'

They fall silent again. This had once been a convivial wardroom. A story couldn't start that wasn't met with an opposing tale, like an arch bridge made of chatter. But even speaking the obvious is like massaging wax from granite these days. The persistent grieving and shrieking of the wood of the ice-locked ship robs them of sleep and silence between paragraphs; without those fallow periods, all speech is feeble.

'We don't have rations to see both ships' companies through a third year,' says Fitzjames. 'Is Captain Crozier of an accord?'

'Yes, sir,' says Irving miserably.

Fitzjames drums his fingers on the table. Like Fairholme, he is a big man, set like a cathedral, but his face is boyish when he is worried. His parentage is a mystery; he is rumoured illegitimate; presumably he spent much time worried as a child and now his face returns to it.

'Two-thirds rations?' he says.

'Captain Crozier's suggestion is that we reduce to two-thirds, yes, sir.'

At this, Stanley leans in. He is a fussy, short-tempered, handsome man who does not enjoy his job. 'I must impress upon the meeting that the *debility* that wracks those in the sick bay will doubtless find ample footholds should we reduce the men's rations.'

'And if we do not reduce the rations, the men will starve to death instead,' says Fitzjames. 'I'd like to get as many of them back to England as possible when the ice breaks up. This is the compromise we must make.'

Gore is looking at his left palm. The sour pain is still there, seeping through the bandages. So is the blood, but it seems melodramatic to observe this.

'And if the ice doesn't break up?' he asks mildly.

The ice outside shifts — the Arctic stammering its jaws as a cat does when it sees a bird. The ship's cat died in convulsions during their second winter. Gore had liked that cat. He'd become quite attached to it, especially as his dog had died in the first spring.

Creak, crack. The ship bellows in agony.

Chapter Two

We took the London Underground into the Ministry. I gave him foam earplugs.

In fact the Tube journey didn't faze him, even before he put the earplugs in. But I was forced to explain a joke used on an advert for a mattress provider, which in turn required me to explain the concept of 'dating' – not a subject I would have liked to broach when it was necessary to shout above the sound of the train. The expression on his face, once I'd outlined the fundamentals as pertaining to the advert, suggested that he wished that he hadn't asked.

Once we arrived at the Ministry, an escort of subtly armed suits took him to meet the other expats. I was expecting he'd go through a group therapy session, but Gore was in a sunny mood so he must have been envisaging something closer to a salon.

I sloped up to see Quentin, my handler. The handlers had offices in one of the Ministry's inner sanctums. They were all glass-walled and made me feel like a lacklustre fish in an aquarium.

Quentin treated me with an impatient familiarity, as if we were both sticky and were leaving streaks on one another. He was a former field agent. I couldn't decide if his job as my handler was proof that he had been a good or bad one.

'Hi, Quentin.'

'Ah. London's notorious toilet exploder.'

'Okay, well.'

'No, honestly, I'm glad it wasn't anything more serious. Has he exhibited any other violent tendencies?'

'It wasn't violent. It didn't even wake me up. It was just very thorough.'

'Any sign of cognitive impairment?'

'Mm. When the Wellness team released him, I was told he'd been informed about the fate of the expedition. He didn't know anything. He'd assumed they'd survived.'

'Ah. That's . . . a problem. He *was* told. Three times. The first two times were followed by his second and third escape attempts. Both times he was . . . disorientated. Seemed a bit damaged in transit. When he didn't make a break for it the third time, we assumed it had sunk in.'

'Has this happened to any of the other expats?'

'Nineteen-sixteen keeps asking when he's going to be sent back to the front. Can't keep it in his head that the war's been over for a century. Anything else? Depressive or manic bouts?'

'He's the calmest man I've ever met.'

'Nice for you. All right, I'll raise it with the Vice-Secretary. Might be a good idea to get the expats in an MRI scanner. Keep a close eye on any changes in his behaviour. Report any signs of physical or mental deterioration immediately.'

'What'll happen if they start going insane?'

Quentin grimaced. 'Back on the wards,' he said, evasively. 'If the effects of time-travel severely impact their *quality of life*, they're better off in an – an *enclosed* environment where they can be – cared for.'

We let that sit on the table between us.

I said, 'Did you get my email about the budget? And getting a cleaner? Not a Ministry "cleaner". Someone who does the hoovering.'

'You can't make him clean?'

'He thinks it's inappropriate for people of "our class" to scrub floors. I tried to explain that I've never had a cleaner in my life, and my mother had *been* a cleaner. No luck. It took him half a day to get his head around the fact I have a degree, but now he thinks I'm Professor Emeritus. You know he went to sea at the age of eleven?'

'He's made quite an impression on you,' said my handler drily.

'We've been in one another's pockets for two weeks. Hard for him not to.'

'Is there not enough leeway in your current budget?'

'Not at the rate he's going through cigarettes.'

'You should discourage that.'

'What? And impact his *quality of life*?'

That got a cool laugh. 'Touché. I'll look into it.'

*

After I met with Quentin, I went to the bridge meeting chaired by Vice-Secretary Adela, who didn't improve with familiarity. She was a small, tough, wiry woman who put me in mind of an elegant alligator. Since joining the time-travel project, I'd learned she was a former field agent – one of the old school – and had lost her eye in Beirut in 2006. Her dashing black eye-patch almost distracted from her face, which had an uncanny architecture that suggested reconstructive rather than cosmetic surgery.

The bridges were all wound up. No one else's expat had had a polite nervous breakdown and dissected a toilet, but the other bridges described an expat trying to address God through Radio 3, another picking a fight with a parked car.

'Complex PTSD,' said Simellia, 'is—'

'Complex,' said Adela. 'Thanks for your input. Given their histories, mental trauma is to be anticipated. I remind you that we are interested in the actual feasibility of taking a human body through time. Our concern is if the process of time-travel has major implications for the expat or the expat's surroundings.'

'Can we send them back?' asked Ivan. 'I'm asking on behalf of my expat, not because—'

'No.'

'Why not? Ma'am,' Ivan added.

'We can't risk the temporal repercussions,' said Adela. 'They are supposed to be dead. As long as they're here, it's functionally as if they *are* dead in their own time. Again, I must emphasise, you are focused on the long-term prognoses of the expats in our era. Your remits really could not be clearer.'

'What happens if they survive?' I asked.

'Then you will have the lovely warm glow of having contributed to a humanitarian project.'

'And if they die?'

'Then you will have contributed to a scientific project. Atoms unsuccessfully split and so on.'

'If they survive, what will we do with the door?' asked Simellia.

'The use of the door is not your concern,' said Adela, all honey-coated arsenic. 'It is no one's concern until we have established that it can be used at all. You will earn your place in the history books, Simellia, as long as we can guarantee that history continues.'

*

I walked down to the central lobby with Simellia, who'd left the meeting room like a diver kicking free of a kraken. Simellia's expat was Captain Arthur Reginald-Smyth, who'd been extracted from the Battle of the Somme. The expatriation team who'd fetched him had said it was the worst pick-up – more viscera than the Battle of Naseby, more howling than the guillotines. When the door closed one agent had a human eyeball clinging to a crease in her combats. The force of a mortar explosion had bounced it through the portal.

'How's it all going?' I asked her.

Simellia proffered a look that was all eyebrow. 'Oh, it's going. We can certainly say that it's *going*.'

I matched her pace. Simellia was a little older than me, but far more senior. Before she'd joined the project, she'd held a director's position in the Behavioural Science department. I was somewhat in awe of her, and I translated this into artificial bolshiness, because I imagined her a woman impatient with another woman's self-deprecation. As we walked, I kept hearing the wet cluck of my foot unsticking from the sole of my brogues.

'Did you notice that Adela's face has changed again?' asked Simellia.

'Yeah. I don't know what fillers she's using but I think they're alive. Swear to God her cheekbones were on the move.'

'She's an interesting woman,' said Simellia, which could have meant anything. I tried another topic.

'Bets on Home Office absorption?'

'What's that?'

'If they make it through the year without dying of a time-travel disease then the Ministry falls under the Home Office. Cross-historical immigration is still immigration. I'd put a fifty on it.'

One of Simellia's eyebrows did something semaphoric. 'I

don't think we'll be bringing over enough of them to require Home Office manpower.'

'England's closed, is it?'

'Yeah, hostile era policy.'

'Fuck off back to the Dark Ages if you don't like it.'

Simellia emitted an enigmatic smile. 'There's your boy,' she said.

We'd arrived in the central lobby. Gore was standing in a shaft of sunlight, staring up at the steel-and-glass ceiling. He looked dazzled into boyishness by the half-sky of the building's skull.

'A snaky-hipped lady-killer,' said Simellia drily. I laughed. 'I'll see you at the next working group,' she added.

'Sure. See you.'

I clucked across the shining floor until I reached his side. He looked down at me and said, mildly, 'Someone told me off for trying to smoke indoors.'

'Yeah, you can't do that in this era.'

'Send me back to the Arctic.'

'Ha!'

We went for lunch at a small bistro near the Ministry. Gore came from an era of *service à la française*, private dining rooms and putting everything into jelly. When I began to explain, in tones of motherly patience, how twenty-first-century restaurants operated, he said, 'I've eaten kangaroo on the uninhabited shores of the Albert River. I understand how a knife and fork work. Please sit down.'

He pulled out the chair for me, then settled back and regarded the menu with exploratory interest. I don't think I was wrong – it's just that he approached all uncertainty as a challenge. I couldn't remember my first time in a restaurant as an unsupervised adult, but I could vividly remember my first time ordering a drink in a bar that I was too young to be in. I ordered a pint of Guinness because it was what my dad drank. It tasted like angry Marmite, I hated it, and I didn't order anything else for many years because I'd got served that one time and didn't want to break my streak.

'What are the other expats like?' I asked.

'Overwhelmed. The pair from the seventeenth century loathe one another. I suspect the young lady – Margaret something-or-other – has blossomed under the appalling liberties of your age, and Lieutenant Cardingham does not approve. I found Captain Reginald-Smyth very sympathetic, however. He reminds me of Lieutenant Irving.'

'How so?'

'Soft-spoken, shy, awash in a grand quantity of private torment.'

This made me laugh, even though I knew the expatriation eyeball story. I didn't ask him if the captain had explained the First World War, or maybe he'd been told and then failed to retain the information. I didn't know to what extent his brain, behind that broad white forehead, had been shaken and bruised like an overripe peach.

Our food arrived and he speared a falafel speculatively on the end of his fork.

'I thought it might be a good thing to make a proper friend of him,' Gore continued. 'He said he would arrange for his bridge to take us to –' here he raised his eyebrows – '*a public house*. I am looking forward to seeing what visions of sin this era has concocted for the humble tavern.'

'Wow. Maybe you'll go somewhere with Sky Sports.'

'I refuse to find out what that is.'

'And you'll meet Simellia.'

'Is that the name of his bridge?'

'Yes. She's an interesting woman. You'll like her,' I said, with no idea at all if he would like her. 'So. Captain Reginald-Smyth. You're currying favour with your superiors?'

He took a bite of falafel and gave me a dimpled smile while he chewed. He swallowed and said, 'A Royal Navy commander has the equivalent army rank of Lieutenant-Colonel. I outrank everyone. I don't think Lieutenant Cardingham much likes that, either.'

*

Back at the house I was still struggling to think of as 'home', Gore shyly asked me if I would also 'come for a drink'. He had done well, at lunch, to hide his deep embarrassment over my payment of the bill (with a Ministry expense card); he was adjusting with gold-star alacrity in recognising that it wouldn't be a reputation-detonating act for a respectable woman to be seen in a *public house* in the company of bachelors.

In response, I made a non-committal noise. Nineteen-sixteen – Reginald-Smyth – was not a well man. I was told he'd wept in the street the first time he'd heard a car backfire. He'd picked up the use of a modern washing machine very quickly, and compulsively washed his sheets. Simellia thought it might have something to do with survivor's guilt manifesting in the anxiety that the (long-dead) lice that plagued him on the Western Front had followed him to the future. Either way, I wasn't sure if I ought to burden him with a third face to which he had to play polite. I emailed Simellia to ask for her opinion and she suggested we meet for a pre-drink drink to discuss the having of drinks.

The next evening, I went to meet her at the pub she had suggested, an old-fashioned watering hole close to the Ministry, poky and bizarrely fuggy and upholstered in leather. It was like being inside the elbow of a patched jumper. There was only one other customer, sitting in the corner, lugubriously posting crisps into his mouth. The drinks menu was a hand-scrawled chalkboard over the bar. At a squint, it appeared my choices included mmllmmT, suaaúug and wwij.

'Can I get a half of Guinness?'

The young man behind the bar, who was polishing a glass hammily, gave me an encouraging smile.

'Right you are.'

He poured it as if he was an extra in *Casablanca*. *Do you actually like your job?* I wanted to ask him, but instead I crept to a corner table and drank some of the establishment's finest angry Marmite.

While I was waiting, I started work on a core report. Bridges had to file core reports on a weekly basis, via their handlers, to Control. There was a separate protocol for alerting Control to time-travel emergencies, such as our expats turning inside out, but it involved such an unwieldy number of codes and permissions that Quentin had told me just to ring him if Gore began to play hopscotch between dimensions. He'd even given me his personal number for the purpose, which was excitingly unauthorised.

CORE REPORT: 1847
(Graham Gore, 'Franklin Expedition')

Standard [x]
Special measures [ ]

If this report includes cross-expatriate material, please indicate expatriate

1645 (Thomas Cardingham, 'Battle of Naseby') [ ]

1665 (Margaret Kemble, 'Great Plague of London') [ ]

1793 (Anne Spencer, 'French Revolution') [ ]

1916 (Arthur Reginald-Smyth, 'Battle of the Somme') [x]

Observations on subject's physiology/physical appearance

On closer examination, blushes easily. Not previously noticeable because he speaks so calmly. As per last week's report, face shows evidence of broken sleep or sleeplessness (dark circles, puffy eyes). No longer bolts meals as if he's been starving in the Arctic for years, though still very quiet and intense around desserts. No weight gain; I'd value the opportunity to discuss nutrition plans with the Wellness team. No further discomfiture with clothing. Some chapping at knuckles and backs of hands which may be eczema or may be due to over-cautious hand-washing; please could the Wellness team tackle the subject of germs in a non-inflammatory manner.

Observations on subject's mental state

Calm, pleasant. Adjusting well. Has demonstrated levity, humour. Keen to befriend other expats (especially 1916). Recent report from Wellness team (see email of 14th April) appeared to suggest that bridge work has failed to create a foundation for meaningful therapeutic work. May I counter that asking 1847 about his relationship

with his mother when he has been almost
continuously at sea since he was 11 is an
unproductive place to start. **FLAG TO CONTROL***
His short-term memory has shown some signs of
damage or deterioration, particularly re:
information imparted on his arrival—

'What a charming picture of conscientiousness,' said a voice above me.

'Simellia! Hello.'

Simellia looked, as always, chic. She often wore architectural jackets and skirts in stained-glass tones and their palette improved the room. She was unlikely to get called 'miss'. She would probably be 'ma'am' if the lad behind the bar knew what was good for him. She came back with a glass of chilled red wine, which I hadn't realised was a drink you could get on purpose.

'Do you think the guy at that table is a spy?' I asked.

Simellia flicked her eyes to him. 'No,' she said. 'He's an alcoholic. The boy behind the bar is, though.'

'Yeah? Is it the way he's wiping down surfaces like he's being choreographed?'

'It's that apron. That's a costume if I ever saw one. Also, Ralph trained him. Back in Defence.'

I coughed at my half-pint. Ralph, a snide and etiolated former field agent, was my least favourite bridge. He had somehow managed to get assigned the only young woman expat.

'Wait. Kidding?'

'No. Apparently it was very awkward when Ralph came in here for a lunchtime gallon of Merlot and spotted him. He's part of Defence's tracking team. You know they don't much like the fact that the Ministry is a separate institution. They thought the time-door ought to fall under their remit.'

'Forgive me my density, Simellia, but if you know this place is run by spies, why are we drinking here?'

'Because I want to see what happens.'

'Oh. Wow.'

'Now drink your beer and look suspicious.'

I laughed and the spy carefully did not look round. 'Okay,' I said, 'okay, let me pop my shirt collar. How's this? Hang on, let me hunch up a bit. How's *this*?'

'Great. You look like you're about to sell me dirty magazines from out of your raincoat, and you're not even wearing a raincoat.'

She took a sip of her wine and adjusted my shirt collar to a more furtive angle. 'You know what he'll write about us anyway,' she said calmly, 'no matter what we do or how we dress. "The biracial woman and the Black woman who work at the Ministry."'

I straightened my shoulders hurriedly. 'Ah. Well. Of course, I have the privilege of passing as white—'

I paused. I find that people usually want to tell me whether they agree with this assessment or not. Simellia, however, waited for the end of my sentence.

'—so he'll have to write about my pornographic raincoat instead,' I finished lamely. 'Er. How are you finding the, er – the whole— Is he all right, your expat?'

'He used the word "negro" until I stopped him, but I don't think he meant it with two Gs, if that's what you're asking me. How's your expat managing the news of your miscegenation?'

I took a big swig of Guinness. 'Well. He isn't. I haven't told him.'

Simellia nodded slowly, as if I'd asked her to do some long division. When she next spoke, I could hear a smooth change in register from backchat to professional counsellor. 'I

47

understand why you've held off discussing it until now,' she said. 'But I don't advise leaving it much longer. It's psychologically important – for both of you – that you're able to inhabit your identity, and that he's able to accept you gracefully and wholeheartedly. We mustn't adjust for *them*. They are here to adjust to *the world*. A person at a time. That's how you do it.'

'Do "it"?'

'Make a new world.'

She had a soft light in her eye, a sudden distance in her gaze. Gosh, I thought, she really believes it.

Personally, I believed that I had the bridge job because I was an exception, and not a rule. If I'd got it by lionising my marginalisation, peeling back my layers to show the grid of my veins, I wouldn't have put it past the Ministry to use the layout against me at a later date. Never tell a workplace or a lover anything that might cause them to terminate your relationship until you're ready to leave. I try not to give too many context clues early on and I didn't like to draw attention to little harms. Why would I want to point out the places where my flesh was soft, my organs vulnerable? If my white friend casually called sushi 'exotic', couldn't I be pleased she was eating something other than unseasoned red meat? Anyway, I could be a little exotic – just enough to bring up in my annual appraisals if a raise or title change was under discussion.

The spy behind the bar, who had been conspicuously checking the till and polishing already-gleaming glasses, put some music on. Simellia brightened up.

'Hey! "Electric Boogie"!'

'Eh?'

She laughed. Simellia smiled all the time but she almost never laughed, so I remember this moment clearly. I suddenly saw how much of a façade was the elegant, highly efficient government professional – behind which was someone who, maybe, had too many texts from a wayward sibling that she hadn't dealt with, someone who was giving up on dating for the fifth time in as many years, someone who had to smother her impatience when Drunk Elephant-shopping beauty evangelists tried to explain the miracle moisture properties of cocoa butter to her. Before, I hadn't really been aware that other Simellia was there, but now, I felt her barricades.

'It's very funny to me that anyone can get to aunty age and not know what "Electric Boogie" is,' she said. 'You don't know the electric slide?'

'Excuse me. Aunty who? Ralph's protégé called me "miss".'

'Get up.'

'What?'

'I'm going to teach you.'

'Simellia. In the *pub*? What will the boy put in his report to Defence?'

'He'll put, "The biracial woman and the Black woman who work at the Ministry". Trust me on this.'

*

In the end, we decided that Captain Reginald-Smyth's first time in a pub and first public get-together with another expat would be overwhelming enough without adding a new bridge. So on the evening Gore was out with the two of them, I sat with some friends in their grey-and-yellow kitchen with a bottle of mid-price wine. I spent the visit pretending to be normal – I was in fact contractually obliged to do this – but my entire being was wired to wonder what he was doing, what he was seeing, what he was asking. When I burned my tongue on the pizza my friend had heated in the oven, I bizarrely imagined that somewhere, he had burned his tongue in symbiotic sympathy.

The Ministry provided purportedly voluntary therapy sessions for all bridges, as our work was emotionally involved and psychologically taxing. I hadn't signed up. I felt that human connection shouldn't be professionally managed, or that I was somehow qualified for personal pain given a family history of pain. Fear and tragedy wallpapered my life. When I was twelve years old, I'd sat at the dining table with my mother, peeling the skins off garlic for her. She was telling me about one of her sisters, who had been beautiful and married rich. They'd killed her, of course – the cadres who sacked Phnom Penh – and she mused out loud, *'I wonder if they raped her before they shot her?'* *Yes*, thought twelve-year-old me seriously, *I wonder if they did?* And I would always be a twelve-year-old who had wondered that about her aunt at the dining table. An underrated symptom of inherited trauma is how socially awkward it is to live with.

When I got back to the house, I found an open packet of cigarettes at the dining table and settled in to smoke one, listening to my mind bleat. He returned about halfway through the cigarette.

'Commander Gore?'

'Good evening. After-dinner smoke?'

'Mm. My friends aren't smokers and they don't know I've relapsed.'

'Ah. I will keep your secret.'

He spoke with grave clarity, slightly louder than usual. He was drunk, and hiding it well. If I wasn't co-habiting with him, if my pay cheque wasn't dependent on recording his every move, I might not have noticed.

He opened the narrow drawer that contained bottles of spirits.

They rattled lushly. The Ministry had resisted providing these, but as I kept pointing out, he'd been in the Royal Navy at the height of the rum ration years; no doubt he drank.

He selected a whiskey, wandered to the freezer, then paused. 'Will you join me?'

'No, I – actually yes please.'

I was also quite drunk, but he'd never offered me anything stronger than tea before.

He came to the table with two iced glasses and the entire bottle, which he set down in front of me. I slid the cigarettes across to him and he lit one briskly.

'We must get a decanter. I feel like a lushington, pouring from a bottle. Here.'

'Thank you. Did you have a nice time?'

'Yes. I like Arthur.'

'And his bridge?'

'I like her too. She is a negress—'

I choked. 'Uh. We don't use that word any more. We just say "Black". As an adjective. You would say, "she is a Black woman".'

'That sounds rather rude. Or brusque, somehow. "Negro" is derogatory?'

'People will assume you're racist.'

'"Racist"?'

'Oh. Uh. That you have prejudices against people of other races.'

He frowned. 'Does not every race have this?' he asked. 'Having exposure, in the main, to the customs and habits of their own race, and being unfamiliar with the customs of others?'

'Well. In this era we try to look beyond a person's race and consider them by their merits alone.'

'We?'

'The Ministry, for example. The civil service is an equal opportunities employer.'

He murmured *equal opportunities employer* back to himself and I flushed so deeply I could feel it smearing across my sternum. He said, 'She is a doctor. Of the mind. I forget the term—'

'Psychiatrist? Psychotherapist?'

'The latter, I think . . . But she said she was the only person of her race in the entire department. Not only the sole *Black*, as you say, bridge, but the only Black . . . mind doctor . . . in the . . . mind doctor squadron.'

'Oh, yeah, Kooks and Killers is super white. Obviously, at intake, there are fewer Black candidates, you know, structural reasons, uh, it starts at school, even, there are barriers in their way from the start, and then by the time they're school leavers, university leavers, uh . . . It's an ongoing process. We've only had about fifty years of thinking about it seriously, and every generation sees that the last one wasn't doing enough. They'll probably find us criminal in a century or so.'

I stammered this out hurriedly. Simellia felt so present that she might as well have been there, invigilating our conversation. Gore was pondering his whiskey, and nothing I'd said would have made sense to him, but I wanted to get a good mark from Simellia for my anti-racism (totally normal to want, totally possible to achieve).

Gore stared into his glass, turning his wrist to give the ice cube a tour of the perimeter.

'"Kooks and Killers"?' he said at last.

My shoulders unknotted.

'Ha. Ministry nickname for the Behavioural Science department.'

He raised his eyebrows at the ice in his glass, tipped it back and forth. I pulled a second cigarette and he lit it for me with automatic politeness.

At length, he said, 'When I was a younger man, I spent some time on the Preventative Squadron. It was set up to suppress the West African slave trade.'

He threw back half his whiskey, set it down. 'I was thinking about the *Rosa*. That was captured when I was . . . five-and-twenty. On Christmas Day, I remember that distinctly. It was flying under Spanish colours, with some three hundred – mm – *Africans* aboard. I was on the *Despatch*, under Commander Daniell. We brought them to the port at Barbados. At that time, I was quite thick with the assistant surgeon, John Lancaster. We were of an age, and he was excellent company. He spoke Spanish, which none of the other officers did. He was determined to make me eat a coconut. Have you ever eaten a coconut?'

'I have.'

'I'd never experienced a fruit that fought back so hard against being eaten. Where was I? Yes. Commander Daniell and the chief surgeon went ashore in February, and left me as Acting-Lieutenant, just as the *Rosa*'s case was being tried. John and I had to go aboard and count the negr— captives. They'd been provided with such provisions as they needed, and confined to the ship, along with the *Rosa*'s crew, for the duration of their detention. But they couldn't leave the ship, you see, and . . .'

He stopped, drank the other half of his whiskey, then reached for the bottle.

'I was, I think, a little giddy with my own power. I had never been handed the command of a ship, regardless that it was docked, regardless that its captain would return soon enough. Riding beside that giddiness was the dread weight of responsibility. When I saw the captives, I recognised that their berthing was – inadequate. That they had undoubtedly suffered greatly, and were exhausted and sick. Two had died since we captured the *Rosa*. But my chief thought was, *I had better get this headcount right*. Or perhaps I might have thought, briefly, *poor wretches*. But there was more obligation than Christian compassion in my heart. Whether I saw men, or women, or children . . .'

He trailed off.

'You're thinking about Simellia.'

'I've had Black seamen under my command. That's a different thing. Those unfortunates in the hold . . . I don't know . . . Would she have behaved so pleasantly towards me, had she known that I'd looked at them and seen a tally?'

'She's familiar with the era.'

He nodded, rather gloomily, and lifted his glass to his mouth again. This time, he didn't drink, but regarded me over the lip.

'I hope you do not mind me making this observation,' he said. 'But I think I am right in saying you are not, yourself, wholly an Englishwoman.'

'Well done,' I said, as neutrally as I could. 'What gave it away? Shape of my eyes?'

'The colour of your mouth.'

The ice hit the bottom of my glass with a frigid knock. I'd never heard that one before.

*

He didn't like twenty-first-century language. 'Victorian' was his greatest descriptive enemy, and to be fair I'd heard people apply the word miscellaneously to any period 1710–1916. But much of what I thought of as quintessentially 'Victorian' was in his future and, to him, gargantuan, disproportionate, ungentlemanly, unpious. He didn't understand my use of the term 'classical music', which meant something to do with formal Classicism to him and meant, to me, that it had violins. He hated 'text' as a verb, 'sex' as an act, 'tomato' as a salad product. One afternoon he came in from a walk and asked me, very thoughtfully, 'Some charming young women – out on the heath – addressed me quite boisterously – what is a "dilf"?'

It goes without saying that he called me half-caste. Perhaps it goes without saying that it took a while for me to correct him. I'd used it myself, before I learned not to. People forget how recent an invention 'mixed-race' is, and by the time I was at the Ministry, we weren't even supposed to write that. We were supposed to write 'people with a mixed ethnic background'.

I'd taken my time correcting him because I wasn't sure what I meant to myself. 'Mixed-race' people don't technically belong to either of their heritage spaces, but they don't necessarily belong in a 'mixed-race' space either – there's too much flex in the term. I used to think every mixed-race person was an island, composed of a population of one. Maybe that's because the Cambodian diaspora is so small here, or maybe it's because I wanted, wilfully, to be an exception.

Graham used other words too, not wrong, exactly, but not right, like 'your people', or 'your culture'. When I said, in a wincingly tight voice, that we had the same people and culture, he replied, mildly, 'But I don't think that we do.' Then came the image searches about Cambodia, on food and dress and customs. I had to do those for him, in the early days, because he still didn't know how, and the English-language internet was not on my side. *Exotic, friendly, conservative, resilient.* The way he couched his questions, too, was imperfect. I had to correct 'ancestor' for 'grandparent', 'sacred' for 'polite', 'tribal leaders' for 'farmers'. Eventually he asked if he would meet my family, eyes full of hopeful curiosity. This was forbidden, but I reluctantly showed him a picture of my parents and sister on my personal phone, the screen supernovaed with cracks. He pointed at my sister, beaming. 'Oh! There's two of you!' he said in a voice so full of naked delight that I hurriedly put the phone away.

One of the many hypotheses coagulating in these early days of time-travel was that language informed experience – that we did not simply describe, but create our world through language, like Adam in the Garden of Eden calling a spade a spade or whatever happens in Genesis. At its heart, the theory promised that the raw stuff of the universe could be carved into a clausal household, populated by an extended family of concepts. In retrospect, we might have devoted more time to explaining to the expats why they couldn't use what were now considered slurs. Some of them never really got the hang of this.

The expats, loose as dust in narrative time, were schooled mercilessly in description. According to the hypothesis, the more accurate their vocabulary, the more likely they would temporally adjust. *Assimilate* is actually the word we used – they would *assimilate* if they said 'phone' instead of 'unholy device' or 'car' instead of 'horseless carriage' – but we meant *survive*. The bridges were expected to be day-by-day dictionaries. For the expats, Simellia and I were contextually so unusual that we were asked more questions ('Will your women's brains not overheat?', Sixteen-forty-five; 'When did you throw off your chains for these – how do you call them – "pantsuits"?', Seventeen-ninety-three). I was discomfited by this stilted forbearance of our sex and our skin. It's not that I wanted to be someone like Ralph, any more than I wanted to develop a crust, but I'd fondly imagined authority as an equaliser.

Twice a week, we would sit the expats in a room with a comfortable chair, a desk, a screen, and a pot of tea. The tea was not essential to the experiment but they were more inclined to cooperate if they were given nice tea with a china cup and saucer – even Sixteen-forty-five and Sixteen-sixty-five, who didn't have the manufactured appetite for it. Embarrassing stuff, something for a *Punch* cartoon about Englishness, but it worked.

The bridge would sit behind a two-way mirror with the members of the Wellness team running the experiment. We'd stand and watch as images from twenty-first-century life appeared on the screen in front of the expat, who would then describe aloud what they could see. Anachronisms, malapropisms and total ignorance would be noted but not pointed out; it was up to the bridge to *actively correct* them in future daily routines.

To begin with, the language experiment had a chilly, near-sensual thrill. There's something vengeful about agreeing on an interpretation. Set your narrative as canon and in a tiny way you have pried your death out of time, as long as the narrative is recalled by someone else. I certainly understood better why people became writers, and why jealous lovers force so many false confessions, and why the British history curriculum looks the way that it does.

But after the first few sessions, the Voight-Kampff neo-noir charm of the language experiment wore off and it became boring for bridge and expat alike. Gore played up. He started describing the images on screen via caricature – what a mermaid would say about a coffee shop, for example. It charmed me and I resented his ability to play drawing room games in the laboratory. I had limited experience of charm – that twinkly old-fashioned thing that afflicts the eccentric – and my brusque defences against similar attributes (flirtation, civility, servility) didn't work, because Gore's charm was undirected. I might as well have tried to catch fog in a jar. And he'd go on and on: Anne Boleyn discovering off-the-rack fashion, a horse in an Apple Store. He was funny, that was the problem. Funny men are bad for the health. Please just tell us what *you* can see, someone from the Wellness team would wheedle over the microphone, and Gore would coal up his Victorianisms until I was chewing at my fingers.

One pedantic Tuesday he was placed in front of a screen which showed a blonde, frowning, female soldier in combat fatigues, carrying a machine gun and kneeling in the undergrowth. He went quiet and considered her for a while over the rim of his teacup.

'Commander Gore?' prompted the operator from the Wellness team.

He turned to face us and sighed.

'A woman in the workplace,' he said.

The operator laughed, though she shouldn't have, and covered her embarrassment by giving me a thumbs-up. I only saw it out of the corner of my eye because I was trying to meet Gore's and to remember if I'd told him that the mirror was two-way.

*

In the first couple of months, I watched him fill out with attributes like a daguerreotype developing. Take Sunday mornings. One Sunday, I rose before ten (unusual) and wandered the kitchen, too unfocused by the clementine-sweet spring sun to consider breakfast. He came through the front door while I was gazing blankly at the kettle.

'Good morning.'

'Morning. Have you been out for a walk?'

'No. To church.'

I felt strangely embarrassed, as if he had just told me that he spent his Sunday mornings at a soft play centre. He smiled at me and said, 'I have noted the dreadful secularism of this age. You may assume a less guilty expression.'

He went for long walks and came back with sketches of pylons and dismantled gasometers: black ink, exacting and melancholy, with a fastidiousness of line I recognised from his archived sketches of ships. I wondered if he saw glorious visions of industry or broken metal monsters. Perhaps he saw nothing but shapes. He gave me the best of his gasometer sketches and I put it up in the tiny office.

At the insistence of the Wellness team, the Ministry granted the expats access to the staff gyms and pools. Gore took up boxing, often with Sixteen-forty-five, Lieutenant Thomas Cardingham. I understand some well-meaning numpty on the Wellness team had tried to persuade them to join the fencing troupe (currently comprising a total of one member, viz, the numpty), as they were both familiar with sword warfare. Cardingham, when presented with a foil, laughed so hard that his nose dripped. Gore was more polite – Gore's weapon of choice was charm – but I'm told he mentioned the Battle of Navarino and some graphic stuff about disembowelment. Neither of the men were classically trained fencers. They just knew how to kill someone with a sword. The numpty let the matter drop.

Gore couldn't understand the simultaneity of stacks of meat in supermarkets and our anxiety around hunting. Someone on the Wellness team taught the expats the term *quality of life* and somehow, grumbling about his inability to hunt and the paucity of countryside to hunt in, he parlayed the term into an air rifle.

I came down one morning to find he'd killed all the squirrels in the garden. He'd piled them in a grotesque furry cairn.

'What the *hell*!'

'There is no need to swear. I have heard you talk to them in the roughest way about the lawn, so I thought I would despatch them.'

'They're dead!'

'Of course they are. I'm a very good shot. How do you feel about pigeons?'

'Leave the pigeons alone!'

'As you please. Would you like these? You could make a lovely hat.'

'No!'

Later, at dinner – a now-unidentifiable meat he had char-coaled into submission, limp green beans – he said: 'I think it would improve my *quality of life* if we got a dog.'

The expats weren't allowed pets. They were detained at the generosity of His Majesty's Government and could not, them-selves, take on a caring burden. Wear and tear, also, of the furniture; an insinuation, never expressed before them, that they might die of mutations and leave the animal parentless. I murmured, 'It's quite a small house for a dog.'

'They are only so big,' he said, indicating with his hands the dimensions of a very large dog.

'Where would it sleep?'

'Where he lay down.'

He'd had a dog on the expedition, I knew, a black Labrador so ancient that a number of letters from the other expedition members remarked on the animal's decrepitude. It must have died, along with all of the men he'd served with. I said, with the intent to get off dangerous ground, 'Cats are smaller.'

'We do not need a cat,' he said. 'A little creature who sleeps for hours and plays with her prey? We already have you.'

I almost pushed a green bean into my lungs. He watched me,

let me bar my shaking throat with my fingers, gargling vegetable, before he poured me water.

Gore was bored, that much was clear. Despite the amenities and pleasures of the twenty-first century, he was bored. He had been handed a plush-lined life, with time to read, to pursue thoughts to their phantasmagoric end, to take in whole seasons at the British Film Institute, to walk for miles, to master sonatas and paint to his heart's content. He did not need to work, to exchange the sweat of his brow or the creak of his mind for board and bed. And yet, he was bored of having no purpose. He was getting bored of everything. I was afraid that he was getting bored of me.

*

Towards the end of May, the expats were summoned for MRI scans. We took the Tube to the Ministry together.

The medical staff hustled me into the observation room while they prepared him for his scan. Three men were already waiting at the controls. One was a radiographer I'd seen around the Ministry. Another, tall and tanned with peppery hair, was in uniform with brigadier's pips.

The third man was the Secretary for Expatriation. He had a presence as mild as salad and the beautiful crow's feet of someone who could afford to age attractively. He seemed like he shouldn't have the job – not just that of Secretary of Expatriation, but any job at all – as jobs are not very chic. I expect he had been given it because someone's father knew someone else's father. Although I was a bridge and therefore a key member of the project, I'd had barely any contact with him. Adela acted as de facto rod and crown.

'Mr Secretary,' I said.

He turned pleasantries onto me. The Brigadier, who was already standing very straight, stood a little straighter.

'Ah,' said the Secretary, 'have you met—?'

'Ma'am,' said the Brigadier. He had an exquisite broadcaster plum I thought had died out in the seventies. 'You are Commander Gore's bridge?'

'Yes, sir.'

'Congratulations on your new role. Where were you before? Special Branch?'

'No, sir. Support ops.'

'Behavioural Science?'

'Languages.'

'I will watch your career with interest,' said the Brigadier.

I disliked him instantly. He said it like he was chewing on it.

Lying inside the scanner, Gore said, over the intercom, 'This is like being inside a gun's barrel.'

'Just relax, sir,' said the radiographer.

'I'm horizontal. I'm as relaxed as I can be. Can you read my thoughts with this machine?'

'No, not at all.'

'Oh, in which case, I am very relaxed. And I can assure you that I'm thinking friendly things towards you.'

After he'd been barked at by the magnets, Gore came through to the observation room. The Brigadier's uniform had an incredible, immediate effect. Gore snapped, rather coldly, to attention.

'At ease, commander,' said the Brigadier. 'I am just on my way out.'

'Sir.'

Even the Secretary relaxed once the Brigadier had left. 'Defence deputation,' he said to me confidingly. 'Big brother watching over little brother, you know.'

Gore said, 'May I confirm that I am a miracle of medicine?'

'We'll get the results in a week or so, but I don't think you should be troubled,' said the radiographer. 'Here. No significant abnormalities that I can see.'

'Oh, you truly can't see my thoughts . . .'

'Sorry to disappoint!'

The next expat up for scanning was Arthur Reginald-Smyth, who arrived bridgeless and did not look quite as blasé; in fact he looked green. He was a tall man, with close-cropped hair and a fine clean jaw. He had to remove a signet ring from his finger before he lay down, and once he lay down, his hands began to shake.

'Just relax, please, sir,' said the radiographer. 'I can assure you that you're in safe hands.'

Gore leant down over the radiographer and said, into the microphone, 'It's great fun, Sixteen, you'll get a dag of your thoughts.'

'You won't—'

'Forty-seven?' said Reginald-Smyth, in a hoarse, anxious voice. 'Is that you? What are you doing there?'

'Reading your thoughts, old chap. That was a very nasty one. I've never seen such obscenities. Good grief. *How* many sugars do you take in your tea?'

Reginald-Smyth's hands had stopped shaking. 'Someone needs to put you back on a bally boat,' he said, almost amused.

'We're going to begin now, captain,' said the radiographer. 'You may find the machine a little noisy . . .'

'Oh!'

'It's all right, sir.'

'Oh God!'

'Good thought you had there,' Gore said. 'Something about, hmm, elephants. Waltzing elephants.'

'It sounds like bloody tank fire!'

'Which may also be the noise of waltzing elephants. Having not had the pleasure of meeting one, let alone dancing with one, I can't confirm.'

Reginald-Smyth's bunched fists uncurled with an effort. 'I can't imagine you dancing,' he said, with a shaky attempt at humour.

'According to this wonderful map we have of your thoughts, that is exactly what you are imagining.'

'Oh, shut up.'

'We really can't see anything you're thinking,' said the radiographer, but he was grinning.

'You tell that to Forty-seven,' said the captain, then, 'Jesus,' tightly, through his teeth, as the MRI scanner thudded again.

'We don't have to stay for the . . . results, or anything?' I asked the radiographer.

'Oh, no, not at all.'

'If you'd like to return home, I can make my own way back,' Gore said to me.

'Oh. Right then.'

He gave me a broad, pleasant smile, then patted the radiographer on the shoulder and began to calm Reginald-Smyth down again. There was a loosening in his demeanour, the unfurling of some pennant that I hadn't realised had been coiled and tucked. But of course – he was an officer of a bachelor service, who had spent most of his life at sea. He had missed the company of other men.

*

I stepped through the front door in a mournful mood. My breath was shallow. My stomach was airy, empty. Every time I thought about him, I felt as if I was overstretching a pulled muscle, but in my mind. I decided I would email the Wellness team, immediately, and arrange to begin therapy.

But I couldn't write the email. My fingers seemed magnetically charged to repulse the keys of my laptop. I had a shower and unloaded the dishwasher. I tried to read. Words slipped up.

In the end, I opened the drawer in the bottom of my bedside table and pulled out a tin that once held a fountain pen. I had most of an eighth and some rolling papers. I disembowelled one of his cigarettes for the tobacco and rolled a loose, sloppy joint with my magnetically repulsive fingers before going to sit on the back porch. A stupid wood pigeon made its idiot way through the clover.

'Hello, pigeon. You don't know it, but I saved your life.'

Coo, coo.

I heard his key in the front door.

'Hall-oo.'

'Hello. Big pigeon here don'ttryandshootit.'

'Is something wrong with that cigarette? Smells odd.'

'Ah. Ahaha. No. Captain okay?'

'He had a horrible time but it ended soon enough. We had to talk Miss Kemble through it afterwards. We weren't sure what experience she'd had that might compare to the machine. Arthur thought a stage coach journey in a very narrow coach? In any event she called us both plague sores and said that she understood it to be an instrument that paints pictures of the brain using the power of magnets.'

'Ha!'

'She's very unusual. She reminds me of you.'

'Is that good?'

He smiled. 'What *is* the matter with that cigarette?'

'Promise not to tell anyone at the Ministry?'

'Oh. *Forbidden* tobacco. Full of germs.'

'It's called – well, cannabis. But it's got a lot of names. It was legalised a few years ago and now it's very uncool.'

'What does it do?'

'Would you like to try?'

He raised an eyebrow, but came to join me on the porch. The pigeon, who had seen what happened to the squirrels, took off.

'You have to inhale it. Properly. If it makes you cough – there.'

'Erk.'

'Try again.'

'Erk.'

He handed the joint back to me, his eyes watering, and fumbled for his cigarettes. Languid spring heat papered the garden. We smoked companionably in the dimming light. The pigeon came back and eyed us both, in case our constituent parts had collapsed into bird seed.

'What would you call the colour on that fowl? Lilac?'

'Lilac?'

'On – there. Is that lilac? Lavender?'

'What?'

'What?'

'What?'

We stared at one another. Then we creased towards one another and began to giggle helplessly.

I retreated inside to make a pot of tea. He found a packet of unopened chocolate digestives. We settled in to demolish them.

'I think we should get a dog.'

'Mm. No.'

'We should have had this stuff in the Navy.'

'Chocolate biscuits or weed?'

'Both. "Weed"? That sounds very whimsical. Something that fairies put in their pipes.'

'If the Royal Navy had a weed ration in the Age of Sail, your Arctic journey would have ended up in Rio de Janeiro.'

'Good!'

This made us both start honking weakly again.

'Well, I'm glad you've found *something* about the twenty-first century that you approve of, commander.'

He smiled, dimples curving. 'I think, as we are "housemates", and also, I hope, friends, that you should call me Graham.'

*

'Who is "Auntie"?' he asked me, the next morning. He'd come down from his bath barefoot, with his hair still damp – another first. His curls had grown back in.

'I'm going to need more context.'

'After you returned home yesterday, the Brigadier came back to see Arthur. They had a conversation about television, which Arthur seems to think is a wonderful invention. The Brigadier mentioned "Auntie's output".'

'Oh. It's a *very* old nickname for the BBC. Hasn't been in use since the sixties, I think. The nineteen-sixties, I mean. How odd. He asked me if I'd been part of Special Branch too. Can't remember the last time I heard someone call counter-terrorism "Special Branch". Well, maybe it's not so weird. The top brass all live in the past anyway.'

'As it ever was. Why "Auntie"?'

'It was considered very staid and fussily benevolent. You know. Educational programming for the beloved workforce.'

'In the nineteen-sixties? And one could smoke indoors?'

'Yes.'

'Why was I not taken there? Did the fashionable still wear hats? I notice that only the very religious appear to preserve this decorum.'

'Fashion,' I muttered. I pulled out my phone, Googled a picture of a girl in a sixties miniskirt, and held it up to him. He blushed with his face on mute.

'Well, that looks very unhealthy,' he said.

Much later that day, he asked, 'What is the handheld machine called, the one that projects a white, filmy grid with information on it?'

'A filmy—? It wasn't a smartphone?'

'No. It was quite a different shape, and the projection stood out from it. Here. I made a sketch from memory.'

'. . . I don't know what this is. Where did you see it?'

'Outside the Ministry. There was a person waiting by the staff entrance and projecting it into the air.'

'That's. Hm. I don't know what that is. You're certain that's what you saw?'

'Yes. It was projecting.'

I leant over the table and stared at his sketch, or at least, I affected to. Really, I was looking at the willow line of his lashes, curving downwards as he frowned at the drawing.

III

Gore lies in his cabin and considers his palm.

Debility, Stanley had said. Well, they all knew what that meant. *Scurvy*. Men ruptured by melancholy, bleeding from their hairlines. Teeth loose in the head as a blown rose's petals. Weeping for home — more so than usual. Aching at the joints. The smell of an orange, it's said, could drive a *debilitated* man to derangement. The word 'Mother' is like a lance to the ribs. Old wounds reopen.

He stretches his fingers wide, as if trying to span an octave on a pianoforte. Hot, dark pain gels the bandages together.

This old wound, formerly healed, he'd received in Australia with Captain Stokes. A gun had exploded in his hands. They were rowing up a river in the captain's gig, charting its course. The cockatoos they'd spotted on the opposite bank were so dense as to be cloud-like, billowing from tree to tree. He'd taken up his fowling piece and sighted along the barrel.

'Bird for dinner,' said one of the men.

'If Gore doesn't miss,' said Stokes.

'I don't miss.'

After that, there's a gap in his memory. There was a thunderous report. He's sure he saw a bird drop. Then the sky, hysterically blue. He was on his back in the bottom of the boat. It seemed like his hand hurt, but he wasn't sure. It felt wet. He sat up. Stokes was blanched, reaching for him with shaking hands.

'*Killed the bird*,' Gore had remarked quietly. Stokes had started laughing.

He misses Stokes. He misses Australia. He'd like to feel the amniotic swelter of the continent's interior. He can't even summon the memory of what it was like to be comfortably warm, let alone perishingly hot. He misses newness, freshness. He'd like to look at a tree or pick his way through undergrowth. Even accidentally giving himself a digestive complaint by eating the wrong berry seems like a lark from this position. There's nothing here but the most barren and desolate country imaginable. He supposes he'd like to see his family too, in New South Wales, but he doesn't dwell on that, the same way he doesn't examine the wound in his palm.

He shifts on the narrow bunk. He's thinner these days. His hipbones are real architectural features. His skeleton has become navigable below his skin, which he dislikes, because he doesn't like to think overmuch about his body, in case it remembers him and begins to make demands. But he has always been thin. No use in lamenting that God did not see fit to build him in the Apollonian mould of James Fitzjames and James Fairholme.

No use, either, in lamenting the day's poor takings. He'll go out again tomorrow and find bigger game. The last time he was in the North, he killed a reindeer on his hands and knees. The beast was served at Christmas dinner. He'd been six-and-twenty at the time. Robert McClure had been a mate alongside him. Still handsome then, Robbie. His hairline just beginning its uphill scarper. Those big sad blue eyes when Captain Back raised a glass to give the Sunday toast for absent friends. Robbie, who never wrote, who would have heard the news about the expedition in a months-old newspaper on whatever godforsaken Canadian station he'd been tossed on. Absent friends indeed.

Yes, tomorrow Gore will go out hunting again. One thing God has granted him is an excellent aim. He is very good at killing things. Things, sometimes people. He pulls a trigger and knows himself loved.

Chapter Three

I grew up in a house full of paperwork. My bedroom had a shifting floor of invoices and parking ticket disputes, some of them older than me. There was documentation for long-cancelled magazine subscriptions, savings funds since drained, school reports full of pleasures to have in class. My mother, a British citizen, had a Cambodian passport wedged in the bottom of a drawer. The picture in it showed a young woman with black hair cut in a beautiful helmet. I never knew this woman, though my mother thought of her with pity and a little scorn. There were things the young woman forgot to do, or didn't think were necessary, and my mother had to live with her mistakes for the rest of her life.

My family lived inside proof of ourselves like crabs in shells. It could be suffocating – literally: the dust, the dry rustle in the summer heat. But no one was going to tell us what we weren't entitled to or had failed to file. Not with duplicates, *'your supervisor in copy'*.

Growing up in a house like that made me obsessive about archiving. It made me an excellent civil servant and my sister a meticulous copy-editor. I adored the world in a reducible format. There wasn't a man so special that he might not one day find himself in a footnote or one of my green hanging files. With my hand over the archives, I had control over the system. It didn't matter that it was only the filing system. It was control, and that was what I wanted.

It's surprising, then, that I allowed Graham's drawing of the projection device to enter my files as a joke, like a coin minted 70 BC. I thought it was a form of juvenilia, drawn in his earliest years as a modern man, something to remind him of on a significant anniversary of his arrival here; and not, as it would turn out to be, a red letter from another era.

*

By the start of that summer, Graham was practically a native of the era. He wore button-ups and was clean-shaven to his cheekbones. He had a preferred washing-machine cycle. Most mornings he rose – hours before me – and went for a run. He would sometimes wake me up with a juicy smoker's wheeze on his return to the house. He started giving me custody of his cigarettes and enforced a pre-dinner smoking ban.

There were other times when it felt as if Graham deliberately disliked the twenty-first century, as if assimilation was a form of treachery to his past. I was prickly and defensive about this; I could not look at why directly. I heard the way I spoke to him about it: *adjustment, reasonable, citizen, responsibility, values.* He blew a lot of pensive cigarette smoke at me.

I couldn't make him interested in films. He would often fall asleep if I showed him something after dinner; he could sleep through *The Blues Brothers* as easily as he could *The Third Man*. Later, I learned his lack of interest in cinema was as baffling to the other expats as it was to me. They all regarded it as my era's greatest artistic achievement. (Even later than this,

Sixteen-sixty-five – Margaret Kemble – would persuade him to watch *1917* with her and he would be shocked into wakefulness. 'Poor Arthur,' he would tell me. 'I had no idea.')

He was, however, enamoured of the concept of endless music, disseminated into any room. It was how he started to learn to type, carefully pecking in the names of symphonies and taking a full minute to find the letter 'M'. He said that, in his own time, he had hunted and drilled and drawn up watches to a fragmented gurgle of internal music, like Joan of Arc with a Walkman; now, at last, he could play the music he had always half remembered.

He listened to a lot of Bach, which I enjoyed, and Mozart, which I tolerated. He liked Tchaikovsky, didn't mind Elgar, was intrigued by Vaughan Williams and Purcell, but couldn't stand Stravinsky. Having failed with film, I tried pop music. I tested some early rock'n'roll on him and he shrugged; I experimented with eighties power ballads and he was exasperatingly polite about it. My attempts to interest him in non-orchestral music fell on deaf ears until he suddenly, inexplicably, independently developed a liking for Motown.

Once a week, the expats were examined for empathy and the bridges were examined for honesty – or so the joke ran. Another hypothesis about time-travel was that it might reduce a person's capacity to feel compassion. Forcibly removed to a new epoch, meeting all places and people therein as foreign, would lead the expats to defensively 'other' the people around them; worse still, these 'others' could not be psychologically processed because the expat hadn't experienced a normative passing of historical time. The empathy theory drew on sleep science. When we sleep, we enter the hadal valley of REM, and through our dreams we process the day's events. But people with disrupted, non-linear sleep cycles – for example, people suffering from PTSD, whose excessively high levels of noradrenaline blocked REM-level dreams – couldn't enter deep sleep to process their memories and chemically defang them, so their recollections of unprocessed violence and fear leaked into their waking world. Just as the right continuous conditions were required to experience good sleep, the right continuous conditions were required to experience temporal actuality with the requisite level of empathy.

Thus, on a weekly basis, the expats were subjected to tests designed to trigger empathy or disgust, and scrutinised. The first tests were conducted in the laboratory booths but they resembled the Ministry hospital wards so strongly that the expats had tremendous anxiety reactions and it was difficult to get serviceable data from them. Graham, for example, kept asking to be excused for a smoke – heart rate elevated – and struggled to focus on the tests – eyes moving rapidly. I once found him the sole occupant of the fifth-floor smoking area (a pigeon-shit-encrusted balcony), methodically shredding a filter of a finished cigarette. I watched him for a while, interested in the way that only his fingers moved. Most people ripple with surplus motion unless they are concentrating, but Graham only ever moved the parts of him that he wanted to move.

In the end, we converted one of the wood-panelled rooms in the Ministry into a 'library' where the tests would be conducted. The Secretary for Expatriation personally paid for the addition of dozens of leatherbound volumes of Enlightenment-era science and travel to the shelves. One of the administrators, who had a Master's degree in art history, bought some framed Canaletto prints on the tech supply budget, which caused a brief fracas, but the Secretary liked those too so it got signed off.

After that, the 'empathy exams' returned more useful results – though there were other issues. A controversial test used pictures of soldiers from the First World War, caved and razed by new weapons. The disruption was terrible. Nineteen-sixteen had to be sedated. The other expats were horrified too. Even Sixteen-forty-five and Graham, who had fought in large-scale battles, were laid out by the ultramodern scope of the harm. They began to resist the exams psychologically, spoiling our hard-won data. It was agreed that we'd delay introducing them to Hiroshima, Auschwitz and the Twin Towers. Control promised to provide a timeline for the revelations, but it hadn't materialised.

As to the bridge 'honesty exams', these were like something out of a 1960s Cold War spy thriller. It involved a polygraph and everything. Operators squished on electroencephalograms and asked us about how we were feeling. Unlike the Ministry-funded therapy, these sessions were mandatory. Our progress was charted against an enormous file sustained by Control – although where they came up with their benchmarks was anyone's guess.

Adela was always present at the honesty exams, often intervening in them. I got the impression that she was listening to offstage prompts that only she could hear, being the only one among us who was aware she was on a stage, and was trying to chivvy us along the right course of action.

One day she asked me, 'How would you describe your work?'

'Meaningful,' I said promptly. (This was a regular question.)

'Anything else?'

'Challenging. Unusual.'

'Anything else?'

'Uh. Sometimes I feel like I'm a bit in the dark? Like. What *are* we going to do with the time-door if it works?'

'Would you say that you found your work erotic?' asked Adela.

The operator sucked his teeth and made some rapid notes about whatever my readings had just done. I don't think he expected the question any more than I did. I visualised sinking backwards into black mud.

'No,' I said, very placidly.

'Are you sure?'

'I don't know, ma'am, am I?'

Adela smiled with about a third of her mouth. Her face had changed again. She looked pinched and hungry, and hauntingly as if her skin was held in place by a bulldog clip at the back of her skull.

'No. You're not,' she said. 'I don't need to look at your readings to check that.'

'I suppose it depends on what you mean by "erotic".'

'No. It doesn't. What do you think of Commander Gore?'

'I think he's an interesting man.'

Adela looked at my readings and increased the percentage of her smile. 'That will do. Unhook her, Aaron.'

Not all of my job was this confrontational. Going through Graham's proficiencies with Quentin was fun. Today my overgrown son told a man on an e-scooter he was riding a coward's vehicle. Today my overgrown son tore off his headphones and gave me a blow-by-blow account of the opening of Tutankhamun's tomb because he'd been listening to a podcast about Ancient Egypt. Today my overgrown son put metal in the microwave, *deliberately*, even though I had *told* him *not* to do that, because he wanted to see what would happen. We'd sit there trying to decide if his actions demonstrated alienation or acclimatisation. Often I thought that they demonstrated that he was Graham Gore. I began to think of him as his own benchmark, which was dangerous. Adela had spotted something in me that I hadn't, not yet, and if I'd been less charmed by my own levity then I might have been moved to wonder why she wasn't trying to stop me.

I gave Quentin Graham's drawing at one of our regular meetings. I thought that he would find it as charming as I had.

'What do you reckon he actually saw?' I said. 'Game console? Stroboscope? My money's on a handheld umbrella that opened fast enough to startle him, by the way.'

But Quentin gawked at the drawing – his complexion growing fungal – then crumpled it in his fist and shoved it up his sleeve. He smacked at his desktop keyboard until, on the other end of the office, the belligerent laser printer started up. He pulled me over to it.

'Why are you printing the Wikipedia page for –' I craned my head – 'the Cretaceous–Paleogene extinction event?'

'Because this printer is noisy,' hissed Quentin, 'and I'm fairly sure all of the offices are bugged.'

I smiled at him. 'Are you sure, Quentin?'

The printer hummed itself into silence. Quentin's mouth writhed about under his nose. 'Am I sure about what?' he said, with strained lightness.

Far from wondering if I should have looked at the sketch more carefully, I thought about the semaphore flags of weakness visible in the facial muscles. Contractually, we could not be signed off from the time-travel project; we could only, mysteriously, be 'reassigned' by Control. I've seen people burn out – not with drama and defiance but with the damp blue despair of something being cooked off for disposal – and I've seen how such a fire spreads to others if it isn't contained. I patted Quentin on the shoulder, and told him to keep the drawing if he liked.

*

Graham continued to acclimatise to the concept of me. 'You seem very busy,' he might say, almost shyly, watching me rattle at the laptop. Or: 'That looks complicated,' and sound both teasing and wistful. He would nearly always follow up with a story that began, 'When I was sailing with Captain Ringsabell, on the HMS *Youshouldhaveheardofthis*.' I don't think he was boasting, but rather trying to find a way to relate to me, a permutation of womanhood rendered sexless by authority. I came to understand that this bothered me, and I felt embarrassed about that, as if I'd been caught complaining that men on the street had stopped catcalling.

The Ministry provided the house we lived in, and we didn't pay rent or bills. I finally had a savings account that looked like it might withstand a life emergency rather than crumple at a dentistry bill. I was in the economic bracket my parents had hoped I might enter, and having been brought up so thriftily among so many 30-day guarantee receipts, I had no idea what to do with the cash. So I bought a hand-sewn bag in the shape of a hen. It was the sort of purchase that would force him to recognise my girlishness, which I was, by this time, desperate for him to acknowledge.

I showed him the bag, distracting him from his seventh or eighth re-read of *Rogue Male*.

'Look. Chicken bag.'

'I see that even in the future, women remain fascinated by impractical accessories.'

'It's not impractical. It's a bag.'

'Nothing will fit inside it. I do not think it could even carry this book.'

'I can put a coin purse in it. See.'

I reached inside the hen and pulled out the coin purse that

came with it. It was in the shape of a small yellow chick. He smiled.

'I've changed my mind,' he said. 'I think chicken bag is very good.'

What to do with money? Social media was full of stories of mothers keeping sewing kits in biscuit tins and filling childhoods with biscuit-related working-class/immigrant malaise. I'd laughed at all of them, of course, because they were aimed at people like me. Making do ceases to be habitual and becomes a matter of conscience. *My mother had been a cleaner,* I'd told Quentin, and I'd never had a cleaner until Graham refused to mop and I had to ask Quentin for one, because my own mother, *my own mother—!* What was I handwringing about? Sorrow, I suppose, that my parents hadn't had easier lives. I kept thinking: I should save. I expected that it could all be taken from me. But wasn't I safe? Wasn't I Ministry?

*

It didn't take us long to dash up against another issue with acclimatisation, which was that the expats didn't make sense to each other, either. Nineteen-sixteen was as incomprehensible to Sixteen-forty-five as I was. Everyone was paddling in their own era-locked pool of loneliness.

Ed – Seventeen-ninety-three's bridge – had a romantic solution: once or twice a week, the expats should all cook and eat together, temporarily commandeering one of the canteens for the purpose. This would encourage bonding. He cited sociological essays about immigrant community restaurants, oral traditions and the ancient banquet, the genesis of *homo sapiens* as hunter-gatherers, the creation of the supper club. He sent an email with so many attachments that I immediately deleted it and emailed Quentin for the highlights. *People like to eat dinners that are nice, often together*, Quentin wrote back.

I went along to one of the earliest dinners, chicken bag slung over my shoulder. Bridges tended not to eat at the Ministry canteen with administrative staff and the operators on the Wellness team – the office-based employees – and the decorous hostility with which the paper-pushers met me was adorable. When I got to the kitchen itself, the first thing I saw was Graham leaning down to light a cigarette on the gas ring, his curls dangerously close to the hob. We'd had to disable smoke detectors in every Ministry room that Graham used. If he couldn't have a cigarette, he'd throw whatever experiment he was strapped into.

'Forty-seven! Mark your thatch! Or are you that frantic for martyrdom at the pyre?'

Graham straightened up, cigarette between his lips, and beamed.

Directly in the light of his smile was a small woman, barely five foot, perhaps twenty-seven years old, and so beautiful that light seemed to obey unique physics around her body. She had strawberry-blonde hair and was wearing an apron that said KISS THE COOK.

I wedged myself into his sightline and he brightened further.

'Oh! A little cat has come in for her supper. Have you met Margaret Kemble? Sixty-five, this is my bridge.'

I turned. Sixteen-sixty-five – Margaret Kemble – gave me a broad grin.

'Good e'en. This clodpole lodges with you? I am sorry for your trouble. A drink?'

I took a few seconds to parse her accent – unplaceable, because it had been extinct for a couple of centuries. 'Er,' I said, 'yes, please—'

'She'll get excitable about the garnish,' said Graham. 'It will be like drinking a salad.'

'Sauce! I'll boil your ears. Take that devil's finger out of your mouth and find some parsley.'

'Isn't she charming?' said Graham, ashing into a small bowl and earning more archaic insults. ('Noddy! Heron-faced fool!') He'd gone rose pink. It struck me that he might be flirting with Margaret, in a yank-the-ponytail sort of way. The realisation came on like indigestion. I stepped between them again.

'Are you helping?' I asked him.

'Yes,' said Graham, at the same time Margaret thundered, '*No.*' She put a glass down in front of me – ice, water, an oily suggestion of cordial, and, sure enough, some fussy edible garnishes. I blinked at it and then at Margaret, who smiled.

'I wit the miracle of fresh water is commonplace for you,' she said, at a normal volume. 'But I've got up this vessel in a holy-day habit, as merits its purity. 'Tis a miracle to me.'

'Oh, of c-course,' I stuttered. 'Well, really it's a miracle for us too. The UN reckon we're three years away from the first large-scale water war. Er, has "UN" been explained to you? Sorry. It looks very nice.'

Margaret patted my hand with hers. She had small, pretty hands. I'd never thought of hands as being pretty before. My brain was crunching with the effort of accommodating the variegated categories of Margaret's attractiveness, which I had begun to block from Graham with my shoulders. 'Drink your tap-juice,' she said kindly. Behind me, Graham laughed.

'You'll make the dinner smell of cigarettes,' I snapped at him.

'Oh, that's all right. I smoke so many I cannot, in fact, taste anything else.'

'I will *mash* you,' said Margaret. 'Bate your breath and fetch me parsley!'

Graham said, 'Hm!' and pulled hard on his cigarette. He wandered off with the expansive air of a man who might pick up some parsley, not because he has been told to, but because that might be a jolly thing to do en route to his next footloose and fancy-free destination. I watched him go.

'Do you, er, like cooking?' I asked Margaret.

'No,' said Margaret. She shrugged at my expression. 'An I forsake this duty,' she said, 'we'll sicken. Forty-seven thinks tobacco is an herb. But womenfolk were cordoned at the stove for centuries. The men mun take lessons.'

'Ah,' I said. 'Well. We're trying.'

'My bridge mislikes such banter withal. But he is a dry old crocodile.'

I grinned at her. 'Ralph? Yeah, that's a fair descriptor.'

'From him have I learned much language, but the lessons are mithered and troublesome to hold. What is a "feminist killjoy"?'

'Er—'

'Have they a base? Mayhap a uniform? If not, I will design it. Ah, you laugh! But would we not look well in thigh-boots and tabards broidered with FEMINIST KILLJOY? It sends a sturdy message.'

She pulled a modern face – crowded with punchline, the sort you see on stand-up comedy specials. I had the sense she'd learned the face and figured the Ministry and its employees as an audience, which suggested an instinct for camouflage that I hadn't expected. I tried to look at her more closely, but her glamour got in the way.

'There is some joy I'd passing love to kill,' Margaret said. 'Have you met Lieutenant Cardingham?'

She jerked her chin towards a corner. Graham, a bouquet of parsley wilting in his hand, was talking to a handsome man of thirty or so, not more than five foot five, with striking cheekbones and a trim, tawny beard. His hair was long and wavy. In deference to contemporary fashion, he had pulled it into a bun, but more than any other expat I'd seen, Sixteen-forty-five – Thomas Cardingham – looked like he'd time-travelled recently. Whatever Graham was saying to him was tickling his fancy, because he threw his head back and guffawed in a way that stifled the sound in the room.

'They like each other well,' said Margaret quietly, 'but i'faith, he will not speak to me or Mistress Spencer. He called me a stale and Mistress Spencer a natural.'

'That's bad,' I hazarded. (Later I would look these up in the Ministry online cross-era dictionary and discover 'sex worker' and 'mentally disabled person'.) 'He's very striking, isn't he?'

'Aye, as is a poison toadstool.'

The doors of the canteen swung again. I looked up, hoping to see Simellia with Nineteen-sixteen, but was surprised by the sight of the Brigadier.

He hesitated a moment, taking in the uniformed (and armed) operational staff supervising the supper, then nodded stiffly at no one in particular. Despite being out of uniform, he looked oddly formal, as if he was the sole person in serif font. He was a much less convincing spy for Defence than the boy in the pub had been, and I found myself looking for the tell-tale bulge of a gun in his jacket.

'He looks suspicious,' I said.

'Hungry,' said Margaret. 'Discomfortable man! Sometimes he comes with his varlet and they sup together i'th'corner.'

The Brigadier drifted closer. He did look hungry. He looked like I did as a student when I ate nothing but buttered toast and apples. He turned the white of used candlewax when Margaret opened the oven to better squint at her roast potatoes.

'That smells delicious,' he said slowly. 'Ah . . . Sixteen-sixty-five? My . . . colleague Salese will be joining us.'

''Tis all the same to me, sir,' said Margaret, 'though I fear this cod will grow legs and walk afore *my* "colleague" returns with my parsley.'

The Brigadier looked me up and down, presumably for his report. 'Is your chicken all right?' he asked.

I cleared my throat. Chicken bag was slightly agape to accommodate the novel I was reading.

'These hardbacks are too big,' I said. 'I could use this one to brain a badger. Do you . . . read much, sir?'

'I have some favourites,' said the Brigadier. He had shifted to watching Margaret slap fillets of cod into a dish of flour, to astonishingly cloudy effect. 'Elizabeth Bowen. Evelyn Waugh. Graham Greene.'

'The English Catholics?'

He looked back into my face. He looked much too intensely, and I felt his gaze sting my pores. 'I suppose they were,' he said. 'But I think of them as war writers. It's my specialism. The war.'

'How . . . interesting,' I said. 'Do you have a favourite? Author. Not war.'

'Graham Greene,' he said. 'He wrote a superb 1943 novel that I think of often. Have you read it? *The Ministry of Fear.*'

*

We had our hellheight heatwave soon after – four days at forty-three degrees centigrade, cooler and shorter than the previous year's heatwave. Despite that, the chief meteorologist handed down a sentence of three months' tropical heats, so the summer water ration was reinstated. Graham's baths dropped to inches.

Because we lived in a government-owned residence, there were also restrictions on how long we could have the air conditioning on. Graham picked at this, irritating and irritated.

'You're lucky we've got air con at all.'

'But why would the government punish its own workers?'

'We're supposed to be aiming for carbon neutrality. We're way the fuck off, like way off the targets, but every little bit helps, apparently.'

'What?'

'Never mind. Look, it's *all* government-owned residences. Council houses have an automatic limit on air con and energy use too.'

'What?' he said again, but in the itchy-voiced way of someone who doesn't want an answer and is speaking as a distraction from self-flensing.

Movement was anathema. I slept, mostly, naked and poaching in my sweat. The water ration forced Graham to switch finally to thirty-second showers. I didn't see him for the whole of the heatwave. We left our bedroom doors open with the intention of letting the air circulate – though the air hung like an executed corpse – and said lacklustre things about making a salad to each other from our separate cells.

You'll have lived through heatwaves by now, and you'll know that they make time go utterly Dalí clocks. I was always semi-conscious, whereas Graham had spasms of insomnia. I know he often lay on the carpet rather than on his bed, because his voice issued at floor level. I could hear him praying at night. That was difficult, like feeling his tongue in my ear. We had patchy conversations at 3 a.m., in our overlapping shadows of wakefulness.

'The garden is dead,' he might say, apropos of nothing, after hours of breeze-blocked silence.

'It'll come round.'

'Can you see the moon?'

'Yes. There's a reflection on the tarmac. I think the tarmac's melted.'

'It's a handsome moon tonight.'

'We've gone there. To the moon.'

'Oh.'

On the last night – the bleeder night, they were called, because of how many people had nosebleeds – the temperature dropped fast and I felt my first breeze in four days. It must have stirred him too. Towards dawn, I heard him say, 'My England wasn't like this.'

*

I needed to distract him. Any melancholia he exhibited would be my business. In fact it would be my failing.

I had never owned a bike that was not second-hand and coming apart. Brakes were more of an ideological pursuit than a mechanism. So I bought a brand-new bike, cycled it home from the shop, and wheeled it into the kitchen. He was at the table, staring glumly at his cigarettes. A half-filled spatial reasoning test was open at his elbow – the Ministry's latest line of expat questioning.

He looked up.

'Oh. A velocipede.'

'Bicycle. Bike for short. They're good for getting around. Isn't it lovely?'

'It looks like a torture device. They were not popular in my time. Unhealthy, I think, not something you would like to take over cobblestones. Though we did not have these . . . what are these called?'

'Tyres. They're made of rubber and filled with air, as a cushion. Stop ringing my bell.'

'Will you not be flattened by a car?'

'Yeah, it's a risk, especially in this city, but I could be flattened by a car when I'm just walking around.'

'I have seen people on them. It appears very dangerous.'

He said this with interest. He had a gleam in his eye. I said, 'The closest I've ever got to flying is going downhill on a bike when I'm drunk.'

'*Very* dangerous.'

'Want a go?'

'Yes.'

*

I bought a second bike. His legs were longer than mine. I expensed it and let Quentin deal with it.

We walked up to the heath one afternoon. He gripped the handlebars tightly, and frowned when the bike wobbled over the pavement.

'It's as bad as a horse.'

'Can you ride? Horses, I mean?'

'With careful inter-species negotiation.'

'Ha.'

'If I'd wanted to have some great animal look at me with its teeth and step on my feet, I'd have joined the Army and made the acquaintance of some colonels.'

'Ha!'

We strolled up the side of a slight incline. It was a sultry summer day. The sky looked like tissue paper and the heath lay swooning in the sun. Insects made their opinions known.

'Right. So. I know this looks counter-intuitive, but you catch your balance and you just . . . go.'

He got on. One foot scrabbled for the pedal. He fell off.

'Ow.'

'Don't worry about the pedals for now. Just focus on getting your balance. We're at the top of a hill, see? So if you just let the momentum take you . . .'

He got on. He moved about a metre. He fell off.

'Ow. Will you mount yours, and give a demonstration of how this is supposed to work, please?'

I swung my leg over my bike. Since living with Graham, I'd started wearing skirts with hemlines that fell below the knee, so this was a performance.

'Very unladylike.'

'Don't worry, my womb is firmly strapped in.'

He flushed from his forehead to his throat, but continued, in his usual mild voice, 'And would Artemis be so kind as to demonstrate the driving of her team?'

I pushed off and sailed down the incline. I didn't even need to pedal. Warm wind tugged my hair. I touched the brakes lightly and grazed to a halt.

Behind me, I heard, 'Oh *da*— dear.'

I looked. He'd fallen off again.

I stumped my bike back round and cycled up towards him. He was lying on his back, one arm thrown across his eyes.

'Hello.'

'I would like to remind you that I am an officer of the Royal Navy.'

'You're on the floor is what you are.'

'My captain commended me for gallantry at Aden.'

'On the floor. With the bugs.'

'You say children learn to ride these things?'

'Yep. Little ones.'

He flung his arm off his eyes and stared at the sky. 'I'm too old for this,' he muttered.

I started to ride around him in slow circles. He propped himself up on his elbows and regarded me balefully.

'You are a little annoying, aren't you?'

'No, I'm a *lot* annoying. Watch *this* – wheeeeee . . .'

I whizzed back down the hill. Behind me, he said, 'Huh!' I counted to five and I knew that I'd judged right. Nothing made him work harder than the sense that he was getting irritated. He simply refused to be irritated. He would learn to ride a bike so that he could go back to being 'a man of great stability of character' as soon as possible.

He whooshed past me with a 'Ha!'

'Yes, very good,' I shouted after him. Now you need to pull on the brakes. Pull on the brakes! *Pull on the—*'

*

A few days later, when the heat had dropped to a mild twenty-nine degrees, we cycled to Westminster. I'd suggested an easier, shorter route to a quieter destination, and he'd said, 'Why?' so we went to Westminster. He was nearly run over twice and it put him in a good mood. He was really going native if he knew how to best the London traffic.

'What have you done to the Thames?' he demanded.

'You did it, actually. The Victorians. Cleaned it up and – embanked it, I think the word is? Congratulations for missing the Great Stink of 1858.'

'"The Victorians". You know, Queen Victoria was on the throne for less than a third of my life.'

'Pretty significant third, though. Got your commission. Got that very foxy daguerreotype taken.'

'I assume, by "foxy", you are referring to the size of my snout in that portrait.'

'"Foxy" in this context means – eh – alluring.'

'Can you swim?'

'What?'

'If I push you in the river, will it be murder?'

We cycled across the river, past the Globe, and had lunch at the Anchor, a pub which had stood on the site since 1616 and was one of the few London establishments familiar to all of the expats. It had low ceilings, paned windows in scarlet frames, and coffee-brown wooden beams. I could call it 'quintessential' without feeling too ridiculous.

We'd been co-habiting for five months and had never been in a pub together before. I don't think he'd ever been out with a woman one on one in his own time. I'm not certain he had even had women friends. He found the whole thing very daring and mischievous and kept smiling at me as if we were getting away with a visionary practical joke.

'Smugglers used to drink here,' he said. 'In my day.'

'Tourists drink here now.'

'Am I a tourist?'

'I suppose you are, in a way. How are you finding our fair city?'

'Underdressed,' said the man wearing trousers and a shirt in micro-mini-everything weather.

We had battered fish'n'chips, another grand British tradition that he predated by two decades. 'I don't know what you mean most of the time when you talk about "Victorians",' he'd once said to me. 'I don't recognise anything "Victorian" about this city. It's like Ancient Rome at its most orgiastic. A war would see you right.' He seemed to be serious.

I started telling him about my mother's disappointment when she first arrived in England and ordered fried fish, expecting pan-fried mudfish and receiving a lump of oily white cod in a crusted parcel. 'I sympathise,' he murmured. He used his knife to lift a chip suspiciously. I pushed the ketchup at him.

'There was an inn, close to where we set sail,' he said, 'called the White Hart, where Lieutenant Hodgson made himself terribly unwell eating periwinkles.'

'I promise that ketchup won't give you food poisoning. Probably the winkles had cholera or something, which we don't have any more, and certainly not in condiments.'

'Hmm.'

I started tapping at my phone, which was, incidentally, an instrument he hated.

'Put that machine away. We are lunching.'

'I was looking up the White Hart in Greenhithe. It's called the Sir John Franklin now.'

His cutlery clattered on his plate.

'Ah. Sorry. What a thing for me to bring up at lunch.'

'There's no need to apologise.'

He put down his knife and fork carefully, and stared at his fish.

'You can't bring them here. As you brought me.'

'No. I've not been involved with the technological part of the project, but I'm told this isn't possible.'

'Yes. I do not mean to make you repeat yourself.' (He had asked twice before if he could be returned to the same spot.)

'I know you feel . . . sorry for them.'

'I feel responsible for them. I was the third most senior officer after Sir John passed on. And I was with them for two and a half years. They were decent, deserving men. I wish you could have known them.'

'Yes. So do I.'

'I cannot imagine – what you say happened. That they walked, and starved. Left the bodies where they fell. I knew those men. They had good souls.'

He passed his hand across his forehead, then shielded his eyes, head bowed.

'Sometimes, when I see something that strikes me, I imagine trying to explain it to the wardroom. Radios, for example. I think they would have been tickled by those. Or feminism. They'd have found that very good fun too.'

'Unusual use of the word "fun", but I'll allow it.'

He unfolded his arms to bother his peas with his fork tines.

'Your heatwave,' he said.

'It wasn't *my* heatwave. It was a multi-national responsibility. But yes. The heatwave.'

'You said it was caused by historic . . . emissions? Pollution?'

'Yes. Fossil fuels and so forth.'

'Can you go back and stop it from happening?'

*

The bridges were due to have a six-month progress meeting with the Vice-Secretary, but Ralph called it early.

Adela took bridge meetings in a soundproofed room deep in the Ministry's chest. She always arrived first and we'd find her sitting at the top of a long table like a mannequin awaiting the gift of demonic possession. But this time I arrived a quarter of an hour early and she wasn't there.

I trotted down the corridor to the nearest kitchen. Kitchens in restricted areas are farcical, by the way. All paperwork that enters restricted areas has to be accounted for, which means that if people put post-its on their lunches, e.g. SANDRA'S DON'T TOUCH PLEASE, they had to be stamped with *Unclassified*. The project's operators and administrators couldn't even start a ping-pong league without getting Secretary approval – which they did, and which the bridges were explicitly not invited to join.

Adela was standing at the sink and anarchically disobeying the water ration by running her wrists under cold water. She looked unwell, but God alone knows how her plastic surgeon thought she was supposed to look.

'Ma'am.'

'Oh. You're early. How unlike you.'

'Could I ask a question about the time-door?'

'No.'

'If the expats survive, are we going to experiment with using time-travel to change history?'

Adela turned the water off then ran her thumb along the spigot, her finger squeaking on the metal.

'You misunderstand how history works,' she said. 'History is not a series of causes and effects which may be changed like switching trains on a track. It is a narrative agreement about what has happened, and what is happening. I am astonished you have worked in the civil service for as long as you have without understanding that.'

'So we're not going back in time to strangle baby Hitler.'

'You're a stupid girl.'

'Yes, ma'am.'

'History is what we need to happen. You talk about changing history, but you're trying to change the future. It's an important semantic differentiation in this field.'

Adela's hands were already dry by the time she'd delivered this splendid work of didactics, but she scrunched a paper towel and pulled open the under-sink cupboard to drop it in the bin. As she did, she revealed a frill of paper edges. They were in a distinctive procedural green, with black seals. I recognised them because they were the files which the bridges used to deliver their core reports on the expats – the observations that we'd been told were so vital. The seals weren't broken. Adela had thrown them into the bin without reading them.

*

'Congratulations,' she said to us at the meeting. 'They've all made it through half a year without dying. I'll save the briefing for the end of the session, as several of you have asked me to attach Urgent Business to the agenda.'

Adela talked to us as if we were pissing lavishly all over her time. Why she applied for the position of Vice-Secretary, or how she got it, was a mystery. She didn't enjoy the prestige, as the Secretary did, and she seemed bizarrely overworked for the proxy boss of a project in its pilot stage.

Ed said, 'Thanks Adela. I think we should reconsider post-bridge year goals. I appreciate that this year is intended to give the expats the skills to live independently in this era, but I think they would benefit from extended, structured contact—'

'Noted,' said Adela. 'We'll return to the matter in three months.'

'That doesn't give us much—'

'That's the Secretary's decision. Simellia?'

'I'd like to raise what I believe is a labour issue,' said Simellia. Adela unnerved Simellia too; she hadn't made a single super-fluous noise or movement, with the perspicacity of a prey animal.

'Speak.'

'Much of the data gathered from the expats is contributing directly to the time-travel project, but they're making a significant contribution to other schemes. I'm thinking of the History of Britain project in particular, and DfE analytics. They're essentially working as consultants for the archivists, especially Eighteen-forty-seven and Nineteen-sixteen—'

'Excuse me,' said Ralph, loudly. 'I called this meeting early because I have an *immediate* problem.'

I tried to catch Simellia's eyes to roll mine, but she'd powered down. Ralph was the only bridge she did this with. She'd once told me it was because she couldn't even find the energy to despise him.

Ralph was another former old-school field agent – a dinosaur, really. He was stiff as a train track with a thin, awful, manta ray mouth. For some ungodly reason he had been assigned Margaret Kemble. I expect he thought he'd get a nice old-fashioned girl who'd read him Donne and do the laundry.

'I find myself in a position I am *eminently* unqualified to handle,' Ralph continued. 'It's about Sixteen-sixty-five's . . . predilections.'

*

Graham was already home that afternoon. He'd had a 'day off', a telling term that bolstered Simellia's labour argument, and had spent it at the Tate Modern with the other expats, trying to understand contemporary art.

'I have some *questions* for you,' he said severely as I came through the door.

'Well, I have some questions for you.'

'Oh?'

'About Miss Kemble.'

He emptied his face of all expression.

'Yes?'

'Well,' I said. 'Did you know that she's a lesbian?'

'This is a sitting-down conversation, isn't it?' said Graham. 'Oh dear . . . what a revelatory day I'm having . . .'

He made two cups of tea. A packet of cigarettes fell out of the cupboard where we kept the cups and he shoved it into the bread bin.

'A lesbian,' I said, 'is a woman who is only attracted to other women.'

'Attracted to . . . ?'

'You know what I mean. Come on. You were in the Navy, I'm sure you've come across the concept of – I'm not even sure what word you were using – homosexuality?'

'No . . . ?'

'Carnal and romantic desire for members of your own sex.'

Graham put his mug down. He was blushing in that water-colour way that I found so beguiling and I caught up with what I was looking at: an isolated man who had just discovered that a woman with whom he was spending a lot of time would never be interested in him. I frowned, and he frowned, and we were frowning into our tea.

'I think this era ascribes too much importance to what people consider of themselves in private,' he said, very coolly. 'What you are referring to, as far as the Service was concerned, was – well – it was punished harshly, if you were caught. But to make an identity out of a set of habits does not strike me as wise or even very useful.'

'We think about it differently these days.'

'Evidently.'

For the rest of the day, Graham treated me as if my recipe

had been changed and my flavour was unpleasant. He cut restlessly around the rooms, running his fingers along the spines of books. I should have used this as a *teaching moment* that would improve Margaret Kemble's *quality of life* but I was hurt in a manner I couldn't examine.

It was my turn to cook. I made the dish I thought was most likely to symbolically kill a Victorian child with the ingredients I had to hand, which was mapo tofu with a belligerent amount of garlic and mala. It had an effect, though not the quasi-fatal one I anticipated. He stopped morbing and started touching his lower lip with amazement. He had a second helping.

Afterwards, he fetched his cigarettes from the bread bin and lit one, pushing the packet across to me with the edge of his hand. I watched him get down half a cigarette in silence.

'You told me that Robert McClure discovered the Northwest Passage,' he said at last.

'Yes. You knew him. From Sir George Back's Frozen Strait expedition.'

'A dreadful expedition. Did you know we had to wrap *Terror* in chains to stop her falling apart on the journey home? The officers had to help pump out the seawater. No one got more than four hours of sleep at a time, and the ship screaming all the while. To say nothing of the ten months trapped in pack ice—'

'I know.'

'Mm. Well. When we made port at Lough Swilly – in sinking condition – they couldn't find temporary lodgings for everyone. He and I had to share a room. I don't know how much you know about Robbie—'

'Grim and opportunistic. Well, don't pull that face. History records and all that. He almost killed himself and all his men on the expedition where he found the Passage.'

Graham blew smoke out through his nose reflectively. 'I see,' he said. 'I'm not sure it's fair to call him "grim", though you wouldn't be the first to say it. He was a severe disciplinarian, it's true. Held grudges. But he was a very lonely person. Romantic, too, which made his loneliness worse.'

'He went out after you twice. He must have been lonely.'

Graham had reached the end of his cigarette, but he kept pulling at it restlessly.

'He said he'd never go back,' he said. 'In Lough Swilly he – I think he really believed we'd die out there, which I never did, and – well. He clung to me. Every night. And wept.'

He ground out the cigarette and said, quickly, 'I was posted to the *Modeste* two months later and I never saw him again. So when you say that he came out after me—'

I waited. He absently touched one of the curls by his ear. But his colour was quite cool. Drained, even.

'He was very lonely,' Graham repeated.

I didn't write the story up in my weekly report. I couldn't tell what it was supposed to mean. Whether he was giving me an excuse or giving me an example.

*

It was around this time that different parts of the project started to individually, in tandem and at random, get on my fucking nerves.

I was lightly haunted – at the level of a chronic but manageable digestive complaint – by the memory of those 'vital' files in the bin, seals unbroken. But Adela didn't issue any new orders. The bridges kept turning in their core reports and the experiments kept running. Given how much of our working day the data collection took, we all assumed that the time-travel project was running to the stated purpose. Every day I had to record his heart rate, his blood pressure, his temperature; every day a written record of what he wore, what he ate, how much exercise he took; every week checking progress against the imaginary benchmarks set by Control, *use of phone, use of transport, use of media* and the assessment of how harmful or useful each medium was; all the time the corrective tests for vocabulary and habit; novelistic observations on his character and temperament. It seemed that the job continued. I suppose if you switch on your lights and boil your kettle with energy provided by a nuclear power station, you don't spend much time reflecting on the fact that the atom had originally been split to kill cities.

Not long afterwards, I received three emails in a row: first, from the Wellness team, indicating that there were irregularities with the results of some of the medical scans done on the expats; then a second from the Secretary for Expatriation, denying the existence of irregularities and demanding forgetfulness of the first email; then a third heavy-handed message reminding its recipient list of the consequences of breaking the contract of the Official Secrets Act as it pertained to our work.

Graham hadn't exhibited any behaviour more eccentric than usual, but as he was a difficult man to read, I didn't know whether I was witnessing a series of neurological events. He'd lain motionless in the garden for two hours, on a wet and putrid night, to shoot a fox, and pulled out one of his own rotting teeth (he showed it to me afterwards; it was the colour of a tombstone, caped with gelatinous red): was this Victorian, or was this 'irregularities'?

I called my handler.

'Quentin. Accepting as I do that you're unlikely to tell me what the fuck is going on: what the fuck is going on?'

'Seventeen-ninety-three has stopped showing up on scanners.'

'What?'

'Did you call me from your work phone?'

'I – yes? This is a work matter?'

He hung up.

I got off my chair and sat on the floor, chewing at the skin around the nail of my thumb. Anne Spencer (Seventeen-ninety-three) had been picked up from Paris. Her husband, a Frenchman, had already been guillotined. At the bridge meetings, Ed reported that she was responding badly to expatriation. I had understood this to mean she was mentally unwell. Now it seemed he'd been referring to the physical effects of time-travel.

I opened my contacts on my work phone, wrote Quentin's personal number on the back of my hand, and cycled some five miles to a phone box. The phone box only accepted contactless payment cards. I called the phone box a bastard and cycled another mile until I found one that still took coins.

'Quentin. I'm on a payphone. Costs like a quid now. I used to phone home from school for twenty pee.'

'Right.'

'You need to tell me what's happening.'

'Seventeen-ninety-three isn't showing up on scanners any more. Body scanners. Metal detectors and things. We put her through another set of MRI scans and they're coming out blank.'

'I don't understand.'

'Neither do we. She's been recalled to the Ministry. Her bridge is stood down.'

'Does this have anything to do with Commander Gore?'

'I don't know. I hope not. I have to say, he's not really the most important thing on my mind right now. Listen, did he tell you anything else about that device he sketched? Who was holding it? What they looked like? What they were facing?'

I'd barely thought about the sketch since I'd handed it off.

'Quentin,' I said, 'you're not talking about the – the glorified Nintendo console?'

That was a mistake – a pebble flicked at the scalp of an avalanche, though I didn't know it yet. Quentin swallowed sharply. He must have been pressing the phone to his face, because the sound was large and liquid, the sort of noise someone makes when they're trying to choke down tears.

'Are you even aware—' he began, then broke off and barked, 'Do you hear clicking?'

'Um. Could be the payphone?'

Another stressed, oesophageal noise. 'This line isn't secure,' said Quentin. 'For God's sake. Hang up.'

*

I hope you will forgive me. I couldn't take him seriously. I thought the high stakes of the project – the potential of the universe to eat its own tail and swallow us for dessert – had made him hysterical, paranoid. I didn't need him to embroil me in a conspiracy theory. The fact that I lived with a Victorian naval officer was astonishing enough for me. I hung up the phone, heard my coins splash against other coins – the phone box was in use. What had other people needed it for, I wondered? An adulterous tryst, a whispered plea to the Samaritans? In an era of mobile phones, there were only a few things that mouthpiece would have heard. Love and endings. Panicked calls to the emergency services: *Please, please, I don't know if he's breathing. I don't know if he'll make it.*

IV

It is cold the next day. Of course it is cold the next day. They are in the Arctic. But they sometimes have days of glorious sunshine. The stewards hang the laundry on ropes outstretched from the rigging. At least one man aboard *Erebus* has red flannel underwear. (Gore, taking McClure's decade-old advice, wears leather breeches beneath wool.)

The sunny days also induce snow-blindness, as the summer rays bounce up from the ice like a tossed knife. The broad emptiness of the landscape (seascape rather — they are locked in pack ice) makes sound and movement travel weirdly. Taking a daily constitutional around the ship is to risk hallucination, to see hoards of assassins and phantom guests where a tin or a boot lies lumpen.

Today the weather is overcast and grumbling. Gore sets out over the frozen sea for King William Land by himself. He prefers this to hunting in company. He becomes, along the hallowing earth, a moving point of muscle and sinew, quite clean of thoughts. If he sees a quarry, he does not re-enter his body. He bends all his thoughts to the bullet. If there was someone with him, he'd have to remember he was fully inhabited by Graham Gore.

On the 1836 Frozen Strait expedition he'd once spent ten hours on the ice, hoping to bag a seal (they had an unsporting habit of sinking once killed). This crazed feat of endurance had rendered him snow-blind, which was the only thing that persuaded him back to the ship. That was ten years ago, of course. He's older now. He's been behind cannons at sieges, he's had dysentery, his back aches in the mornings. He tends to return to *Erebus* when his body reminds him that they're the same person.

On land, he shoots two brace of partridges, slack feathered pouches that will barely thicken a soup. He keeps walking, intending to meet the next hillock, which always promises to be the highest until he attains it. No caribou, no musk oxen. Not even wolves enliven his natural history studies. He can't feel his feet. Each step has the unnatural pressure of blows in dreams. Perverse to admit it but he rather enjoys this. He'll pay for it later, swelling like a waterlogged corpse when the frostnip kicks in.

It's thirst that sends him homewards. He runs out of water within a couple of hours. When he takes a pull of brandy from the flask, the freezing metal skims off a haze of skin. It is summer, he is lucky. If he'd tried drinking from a metal container in January, he'd have a divot in his lip.

The frozen waves are piled against the shore of King William Land like the walls of a collapsing temple. He has to use the pick to let himself down the other side, scrambling for footholds with his numb feet. He's seen etchings of the Arctic in the *Illustrated London News*. Flat. A washed sheet landscape beneath a grey sky. But the Northern seas are full of teeth. They're crazy with pressure ridges and treacherous drifts. It will take him more than an hour to reach the ships, though the distance would take perhaps twenty minutes at a brisk walk across a lawn.

The sky lowers itself to the earth as he toils across the floes. A storm is coming, squeezing the visibility out of the air.

Gore notes this dispassionately. Either he'll make it back to the ship or he won't. He would like to survive until he can have a cup of cocoa, but he takes care not to visualise the cocoa too indulgently.

Fitzjames had once asked him how he could approach life-threatening peril and minor annoyances with the same mildness and he'd shrugged.

'It doesn't improve my mood to catastrophise, so I don't.'

'And what about hope? Have you ever been in love, Graham?' Fitzjames had asked. 'Ever lived for the bestowment of a fair smile?'

'Ah, love, life's greatest catastrophe.'

The wind picks up. The gelid light hurts his eyes. He pulls back even from thinking about his cup of cocoa and sets his mind exactly on top of his head. One foot in front of the other. Swing, push. Swing, push.

He is in this frame of mind — mindlessness rather — when he sees a dark shape crouching by a black disk. A seal hole in the ice. The dark shape moves very slightly. A stretch, perhaps — the energy is languid — though his eyes are too far gone to be sure. He is aiming his gun before his mind knows he is aiming.

The gun lets go its bullet with a sonorous bark. There's a cry across the ice. A broken noise. Terribly, terribly human.

*

Chapter Four

Towards the end of the summer, two important things occurred.

The first thing. We were on our bikes and had stopped at some traffic lights when a motorbike sped across the road in front of us, a midnight-blue metal blur. We were cycling home from an exhibition at the Natural History Museum. The motorbike was the first thing to distract him from the theory of evolution, about which he had produced some exceedingly early-Victorian opinions.

He said, 'Now *there's* a good reason to invent the internal combustion engine. Why is it so much faster than a delivery motorbike?'

'Different type of bike, I guess.'

'And it is breaking no laws?'

'No . . .'

'How fast can it go?'

'Now look. You've only just learned how to ride a bike!'

'Did Bellerophon, on seeing Pegasus, say, "Oh, no thank you, terrestrial horses will be sufficient?"'

I emailed Quentin – *guess what he wants now* – and my email bounced back. The address autofilled and had always worked before. I tried several different iterations of Ministry email domains. None of them delivered.

While I was biting the skin off my thumb and re-reading the Undeliverable notice, I got a phone call on my work phone from an unknown number. All phones assigned to the project had private, protected numbers and there was no way it could have been a spam call, or even a casual one. I picked up. On the other end was the Vice-Secretary for Expatriation.

'Good afternoon,' Adela said.

Her voice was quiet as cloth. She told me that my email had been forwarded to the finance department for approval, as Quentin was currently 'unavailable'.

'Where is—'

'Are you enjoying your work?' she asked me. She sounded like she was reading from an autocue that had been placed just beyond comfortable distance. It occurred to me this might be a delicately offered threat. I mumbled that I was very happy to be part of the project.

After I hung up – a varnish of sweat in the palm of my hand – I opened my work laptop. Theoretically, I knew that my internal emails were monitored, but I'd only sent those messages ten minutes beforehand, for Christ's sake. I deleted the harmless Google account I had been using in a Chrome browser, then I deleted the browser.

It wasn't punishment I feared, so much as the disempowering effect of punishment. Every step in my career had been towards becoming the monitor rather than the monitored. It wasn't that I didn't have moral qualms, but I felt there was something sophomoric, unpragmatic, about raising personal qualms in the jaws of the state machine. And so, in the back of my mind, an hourglass turned.

*

The second important thing that happened was: the movement restrictions on the expats were conditionally lifted. If they could pass an examination, set by Control, and demonstrate sufficient familiarity with the twenty-first century, then they had leave to travel within mainland Britain.

Another time-travel hypothesis from the early days of the project was that the dimensions of time and space were linked, not inextricably but like a lymphatic and circulatory system. Both were needed for the universe to function in a way hospitable to human survival, and both could be fatally damaged at discrete points while the rest of the 'system' appeared to function. We needed to see the expats move through broader geographical space without atomising into the scenery (or the scenery atomising around them) to know for sure that the twenty-first century had accepted their presence.

The expats were envisioned as either foreign bodies against which the universe might launch an immune attack, or cells that could be recognised and incorporated by the 'systems' into the body of the world. We used, once again, the word *assimilation*, but instead of *survival* we meant a sort of sublimation, a permeable boundary between the individual and the world they'd entered. To belong, the hypothesis suggested, is to have a stake in the status quo.

So I was anxious about Graham's disdain for the twenty-first century, because never mind that I felt rejected by it, I was worried that the universe would feel the atemporal sting of his contempt and take him away. '*My England wasn't like this,*' he'd told me – but this was the natural evolution of his England. *I* was the natural evolution. I was his lens if he would only raise me and look with me.

*

Graham told me that when the conditional lift of the movement restrictions was announced to the expats, they'd started 'wagging their tails'.

'Oh yes? Are you insinuating that you were exempt from tail-wagging?'

'I was very restrained. I only jumped up and licked the man's face a *little*.'

He pronounced this 'leetle', with great tartness and vinegar. My nose went numb.

I persuaded Graham to use the tiny office, in which I ordinarily worked, to cram for the test. The Ministry gave no indication of what format the test would take, or what manner of questions would be asked, or tasks set. I thought this was unfair, and suggested as much to him.

'Oh, it's not so different from the lieutenants' examinations. One had an idea of what one was expected to know, and the written portion was tolerable, but the oral portion depended on the mood of the men in front of you . . .'

'Were you nervous?'

'No. I was cocky, if you still use that word. I don't think you would have much liked me at nineteen.'

We were having this conversation in the office. It was a tiny, south-facing room, stuffy in the August heat. In deference to the weather, he had rolled up his shirtsleeves, and the erotic charge of his bare forearms was giving me a headache. There were two pale brown beauty marks on the inside of his left arm, and a flimsy net of pink scars in the palm of his left hand. He filled the room like a horizon.

At thirty-seven, he was only a little less cocky than he was at nineteen, but more adept at hiding it. He had made friends with a couple of the range masters and quartermasters at the Ministry, and occasionally went down to the shooting ranges to unnerve the junior field agents by besting them in target practice. By the time of the examination, he was also cramming the Highway Code, determined as he was to get on a motorbike and make mischief outside the boundary lines. He was spending more time at the Ministry, getting under people's feet and asking questions, in that mild, impossible, imperturbable way of his. I had the feeling that I thought must afflict parents when their children start to grow apart and answer back. He was moving outside my observation, graduating from my guidance, fitting this new plastic world around him.

*

The sunlight became acerbic. At midday it shone down vertically, so that, when I ventured onto the pavement, I walked into a world burned clean of shadows. I missed the shadows and the long English rains.

The expats were still struggling. Graham moved into crisis management mode, though I'm sure he thought of it as keeping up his crew's morale. With the permission of Control, and with the help of administrative staff, he organised a series of lecture-soirées. On Tuesday evenings, a member of the Ministry would give a lecture on contemporary British culture, and then we'd all eat sandwiches with the crusts cut off and drink lemonade and rum punch. On Thursday evenings, one of the expats would give a short presentation on something that interested them, and then we'd all eat bits of ham with cocktail forks and drink tepid beer and lukewarm Coca-Cola. It freed Margaret from doing all the cooking for the group dinners, which was, by the way, what had happened.

The Ministry lectures were, to a sentence, dreadful. Control handed down a series of pre-written presentations and they were so didactic as to be oppressive. They made me read a lecture on multiculturalism, the bastards, leaving blanks for *insert own experience here*. I gave it in a monotone without lifting my eyes from the page then drank 250ml of white wine at a quaff; Simellia gently clinked her full glass against my empty, her jaw set (she'd been asked to deliver a lecture on post-war migration from former colonies and the Windrush generation). Control's lectures were nakedly about getting the narrative right. In their much-edited correctness, their placid-voiced hectoring, they bankrupted the energy in the room. Ideas are frictional, factional entities which wilt when pinned to flow-charts. Ideas have to cause problems before they cause solutions.

The expats did much better. Contrary to what the simple-minded among us had expected, they did not give presentations on their eras. Margaret, who had responded far better than Graham to the magic of cinema, amazed us by putting together an actual PowerPoint presentation about why Charlie Chaplin 'appears a fool but is verily a philosopher'. Cardingham climbed the podium with soldierly grace, fixed us with a sneer and, in language even more obscure than Margaret's, delivered a summary of the Manson murders which was also, somehow, a deranged excoriation of vegetarianism. (His bridge Ivan was pulled into an emergency meeting the next day.)

Arthur Reginald-Smyth's presentation was the talk of the Ministry. Reginald-Smyth was in his mid-thirties and quite hand-some, in a washed-out, wipe-clean Anglo-Saxon way. He was over six foot tall but held himself as if he thought he should be shorter. He had a faint rhotic impediment, and his 'R's flattened into 'W's, which may be why his presentation went the way it did.

'Thank you all for coming,' he said. 'I'm afraid I'm a rotten public speaker, and so I won't be speaking this evening.'

There was an embarrassed silence, then: 'Shame!' yelled Margaret from the audience. 'Fie! Rhubarb, rhubarb! And diverse other curses!'

I flinched, but Reginald-Smyth smiled and made a sort of cheerful fidgeting gesture, a bad actor ostentatiously preparing for his next line. There was a smattering of laughter as the audience realised they weren't about to watch an unwell man humiliate himself by running away. How strange that it hadn't occurred to me that the expats might be friends with each other, regardless of what I was doing.

'Er, Simellia,' said Reginald-Smyth, 'could you . . . ?'

Simellia was leaning against the wall, by the door that led to the lecture theatre. She swung open the door with a fun little nudge of her hips, reached outside and pulled something in. It was a Casio keyboard, on wheels. Another amused, appreciative murmur ran round the auditorium. She helped Arthur lift it onto the stage.

'Um, Forty-seven . . .' said Reginald-Smyth.

Graham unfolded and ambled with studied nonchalance to the stage. He was holding what I briefly mistook for an épée but was in fact his flute. He leapt lithely up, beside Reginald-Smyth, who was glowing rose and trying hard not to corpse.

'We are going to offer you *eine kleine*, er, "disco".'

'We have rehearsed a little,' said Graham, 'but not, I would say, copiously.'

'We'd be telling you a tall one if we said "copiously",' said Reginald-Smyth.

'Indeed. Or, in fact, "well".'

'Yes. We have not rehearsed well, or much. We are fairly dreadful.'

'We are,' Graham confirmed solemnly. 'Godspeed to you all.'

They launched into a hornpipe, one that I'd heard Graham

occasionally playing in the morning around the hour that he thought I should get out of bed (I didn't), but after a few bars the song morphed into a Jackson 5 song. They were very good. 'Rhubarb!' Margaret shouted again. There was more laughter. I felt, through the floor, a dozen feet begin to tap.

Simellia slid onto the seat next to me. 'Hi,' she whispered.

'Hey. You're not going to ask me to dance, are you?'

'Well, now you mention it . . .'

In fact there were a couple of members of the operative and administrative staffs hopping about in front of the stage, very young people who had been selected and fast-tracked from degrees at Oxford and Cambridge into the Ministry. I wondered how scary their NDAs were. One of them looked like he'd heard the term 'throwing shapes' and was trying out some interpretative mime to realise it.

Simellia, in all other matters a restrained woman, couldn't resist a wiggle to a tune. She shoulder-bopped in her chair. I side-eyed her. 'Did you know about this?' I whisper-demanded.

'Not until the last minute. They've been rehearsing in secret in a spare office. They came and found me yesterday, after my catch-up with my handler, to ask for help setting up.'

'Mm,' I said.

'They are likely to have asked me instead of you because they both know me, and the situation is not a reflection on your relationship with Eighteen-forty-seven,' said Simellia, who, in addition to being in thrall to rhythm, was also in thrall to doing best-practice at me.

'Uh huh.'

'You should both come over some time. We could play board games.'

'You do *not* want to play board games with me. I ruin every Christmas with Risk. Julius Seize-Her, my family call me. There isn't a single board game you could name that I couldn't suck the fun out of.'

'*Shall* we dance?' said Simellia, who had been watching the makeshift dancefloor all through this intimate and vulnerable confession.

'No.'

'Come on. It'll be nice for Arthur.'

'*No.* Oh *God.*'

Simellia pulled me by the elbow towards where the back office staff were gyrating and started doing what I can only describe as cool-mum-at-a-concert swaying. 'Yeah, get in, ladies!' yelled Ivan, earning an indelible presence on my shitlist. I looked wildly around, because there was nowhere in the room to look at that wasn't, alas, in the room, which meant I was still in the room. I was in Graham's sightline and I wanted to be eaten alive by a shark from the feet up.

'Oh, who's that?' I said desperately.

Simellia did an outrageous winding thing to follow my gaze. 'You've not met Salese?'

'No. Or if I have – mind my feet! – I don't remember.'

The person I was referring to was lurking at the far edge of the auditorium, with hair the colour of wet earth under moonlight and a pinched, unhappy expression. I don't think Salese could have looked more disapproving if we'd all started sucking at each other's fleshly parts and chanting 'Hail Satan!' The Brigadier was standing beside Salese. They were speaking, heads close together. They looked as if they were in an invisible bell-jar of gloom which blocked out the room's miniature festivities.

'They make me sad,' murmured Simellia.

'They weird me out.'

'Yes, that too.'

Each presentation was half an hour long, so the nightmare was over before I started wondering whether I should suggest the electric slide. 'Well done,' said Simellia. 'You almost looked like you were about to start enjoying yourself.'

'For the most part, Simellia, I bow to your good judgement, but around anything with a rhythm you seem to think we're in a musical.'

'There is no revolution without joy,' said Simellia. She'd switched back to her reflective counsellor voice and seemed to be about to impart a life lesson. I wondered how many times she'd advised the radicalised teenagers she worked with in Kooks and Killers to keep a list of things they were grateful for, though I recognised the thought as spiteful.

'Oh, I don't know about that,' I said. 'I'd ask Seventeen-ninety-three about revolutions and the joy therein. Anyway, what revolution? We work for the government.'

Graham and Reginald-Smyth had clambered down from the stage and were standing just at the periphery of our conversation.

'Good lecture,' I said. 'Unique.'

'You did wonderfully,' said Simellia.

'Thank you,' murmured Reginald-Smyth. 'The, er, the old light-fantastic tripping was much appreciated.'

'Yes, *tripping* is how I'd put it,' said Simellia. I moved slightly sideways to jab her in her ribs.

I said, 'Cambodia holds the Guinness World Record for the largest Madison dance in the world, I'll have you know. I mean, I wasn't there. But I'm claiming it.'

'That's jolly nice,' said Reginald-Smyth. 'What's a Madison?'

'What's a Guinness?' asked Graham.

'The Madison is a line dance. It got very popular in Cambodia in the 1960s and never stopped being popular. Well, except during the— Anyway, my parents had a couple of Madison dances at their wedding, I'm told. My mother's great at dancing. When she was a little girl she wanted to learn traditional folk dance but she was sent to a lycée in Phnom Penh and it wasn't on the curriculum, *quelle surprise*.'

'A lycée?' Reginald-Smyth echoed politely. During my speech he had looked more at sea than perhaps even Graham had been as a lifelong career sailor.

'A French school. Cambodia used to be a French protectorate. My grandfather was in politics and he wanted her to be *évoluée*. Evolved. To the French system.'

Neither the Victorian nor the Edwardian seemed surprised by this, though Simellia breathed deeply through her nose.

Graham and Reginald-Smyth wandered off to get their fair share of the room's congratulations. Simellia said, 'My mother liked a party too. She used to organise the Easter ball for our church.' She had turned to look at the clock on the far wall, so I couldn't see her expression, but I heard the way her voice shivered on the past tense. '*Évoluée*,' she muttered. 'Remind me to lend you my Frantz Fanon.'

'I won't. Another do-good second-gen whose mother used to party, huh? Does this country have a factory setting for them or what?'

'Well, we've both got eldest-daughter disease,' said Simellia, turning back to me. 'My siblings went in other directions. My brother's in the music business and my sister makes fancy cakes. They call me the Cop. Every time I ring up my brother he goes, "Hello officer." When he was a bit younger he used to call me Babylon but he stopped when I threatened to tell his producer he'd gone to private school.'

I laughed and let Simellia slip her arm through mine. I was thinking: two siblings, dead mother, no mention of her dad as yet. Put that in the file and remember it. And I was thinking: why is it always the eldest daughters?

I never did read the Fanon, though I don't think I would have understood it. I didn't understand that my value system – my great inheritance – was a system, rather than a far point on a neutral, empirical line that represented *progress*. Things were easier for me than for my mother; things were easier for me than for my father; my drugs were cleaner, my goods were abundant, my rights were enshrined. Was this not *progress*? I struggled with the same bafflement over *history*, which I still understood in rigid, narratively linear terms. I should have listened more carefully to Adela about history. I know Adela would say the same.

*

I travelled in with Graham for his acclimatisation examination, in hopes of seeing Quentin, whose phone no longer connected. We'd both become habitual cyclist-commuters, but on that day, we took the Tube, imagining it would be less sweaty. Foolish, guileless us. The Tube was a sauna in August. For the examination, he had put on a suit (sixties-style, slim-cut, painfully becoming). He was suffering.

'If I expire, will you bury me at sea?'

'I promise. Irish? Channel? Atlantic?'

'Arctic,' he said, maudlin. 'At least it's cooler there.'

'Take your jacket off.'

'Believe me when I say that you do not want me to take my jacket off.'

I wished him luck at the staff entrance and watched him pass a handkerchief over his sweat-damp curls. I walked up to Quentin's office, but it was empty. Not even a laptop charger remained. I put my head around the aquarium door of another handler (formerly a member of the intelligence services, assigned to Thomas Cardingham's team).

'Sadavir!'

'Hey! How are you doing? Heard your expat's taking the exam today?'

'Yep! He's . . . confident, I think.'

'Seems he's adjusting well. Idiosyncratically, but well.'

'He killed all the squirrels in the garden. And he won't watch TV.'

'Uppity bastard.'

'Ha!'

'Could be worse. Our boy's mainly interested in Minecraft and sex workers. It's been a real fucking pain to get that squared on the budget.'

'Ah yeah, I can imagine. Quentin's been on at me to get Eighteen-forty-seven to cut down on smoking.'

'How is Quentin? I heard he was reassigned.'

'Is that what's happened?'

Sadavir frowned and stood up. For a moment I thought he was about to reprimand me for losing track of my handler – which surely was my handler's responsibility, not mine – but I realised he was directing the frown over my shoulder. I turned.

'I hope I am not disturbing you.'

The Brigadier stood in the doorway, accompanied by Salese.

'Can we help you, sir?' Sadavir asked, stepping in front of me.

'I'm looking for the Vice-Secretary. I have heard there have been some issues with one of your free travellers.'

'Do you mean the expats?'

'Yes,' said Salese quickly, 'that's meant. We rec see her.'

'We would like to see her,' the Brigadier said.

I tried to catch Sadavir's eye but he was looking between the Brigadier and Salese.

'I hope you understand why I am asking, sir,' he said, 'but could I see some identification?'

The Brigadier pulled a Ministry-issue ID card from his pocket and handed it to Sadavir. He was looking worse than when I last saw him – he had that ineffable air of someone who has to boil hot water on his stove for bathing, which was surely incompatible with his rank. He saw me staring and I lowered my eyes.

Sadavir handed the ID back. 'Vice-Secretary Adela is in a Control meeting,' he said carefully, 'and so, of course, none of us know where she is exactly. But yes, the meeting is about Seventeen-ninety-three proving the space-time hypothesis right. The twenty-first century appears to be rejecting her. This *was* in the reports to Defence, sir,' he added reproachfully.

'Oh, it's not the century, it's the soul,' said the Brigadier. 'Her "hereness" and "thereness" have no consistency, no continency, and she is beginning to slip out of time. It is unusually accelerated in Seventeen-ninety-three. She does not even try to bring her "thereness" in line, you see. Because she is grieving, and grief will always take one out of time.'

Sadavir looked worried. 'Is that what Defence think?' he said. 'Have you told the Vice-Secretary?'

'I'm afraid I've only ever met the Secretary,' said the Brigadier. 'But I would very much like to meet Vice-Secretary Adela.'

He considered me again, cold and curious. I felt a boyishness around him – not playfulness or youthfulness, of which he had neither – rather the quality of his focus, which was as intense as a child experimenting dispassionately with the limbs of a pet, to see how far they turned before they broke.

*

I went home and, on arrival, checked my emails. As with a driving test – or the lieutenants' exam – the acclimatisation exam results were delivered immediately. Graham had passed.

I cycled up to the nice grocery store to buy a bottle of champagne, pausing on the way home for a soft-serve ice cream. I sat on the bench to lick the ripple into a mound and think about the Brigadier. A man of bivouac experience, I felt; there was something disturbingly makeshift about both him and Salese, as if they'd been dropped behind enemy lines and were mimicking familiarity while waiting for the right moment to cut a throat.

Despite the group dinners, despite the empathy exams and the language tests and the jolly little flat with Ed, the jolliest and youngest of the bridges, the Ministry had more or less agreed that Anne Spencer – Seventeen-ninety-three – was a failed experiment and probably dying. Her blank MRI scan was one of many examples Ed had glumly filed of her body failing to register with modern technology before he was stood down. She was invisible in recorded time to all things but the naked eye. The Brigadier's contention that this invisibility was internally rather than externally wrought was interesting. It might bring a new facet to identity politics: 'What time are you?' 'Are you multi-temporal or stuck in a time warp?' Or maybe a mismatch of internal and external experiences of time was more like carrying cancerous cells. 'Do you have the time?' we could ask, and mean 'Do you think you'll survive?'

I finished my ice cream and watched the evening slide around. The sun started slipping off the sky and breezes patchworked the air. By the time I'd cycled back, Graham had returned. He had stacked several ice cube trays and was taking them upstairs.

'Congratulations!'

'Thank you!'

'Bought this to celebrate.'

'What a kind thought.'

'Where are you taking those ice cubes?'

'I am going to have the coldest bath that modern technology can muster.'

'If I put this in the freezer for fifteen minutes, do you want a glass in the bath? I can leave it outside the door.'

'You are a dreadful decadent. Yes please. I am also going to smoke half a packet of cigarettes, I think. One after the other.'

'They gave you a grilling then?'

'Apparently I can pass as an eccentric. I suggested that somewhere like Scotland, Arthur and I might simply pass as Englishmen. One of the panel was a Scotsman, and I think he liked that.'

When I brought the glass up – stoppering the rest of the bottle for dinner – I could hear Graham singing 'I love to steal awhile away', occasionally muffled by his drags on a cigarette. Water plashed against the tub. He dropped to humming and presumably soaping. I slid quietly to the floor and leant my head against the wall. I wasn't going to see a Ministry therapist. I knew I should and I knew I wouldn't.

*

The following week, we had Margaret and Captain Reginald-Smyth over for dinner. Graham decided to make a spaghetti bolognese, as we both reasoned that it was easy, delightful, and modern.

With the exception of naval rations meted out during Discovery Service expeditions, cooked over campfires and valued for their fuel rather their flavour, Graham had never so much as heated a bowl of soup before arriving in the twenty-first century. On ships there were cooks and officers' stewards; at home, on the few occasions he was at home, there were women. Nevertheless, he had taken to cooking in a way he had failed to take to television or texting or the use of deodorants ('I bathe *every day*,' he'd said to me with hurt dignity). Tonight, he hummed with a busyness that hardly shielded nervousness. He burned the onions and automatically reached for his cigarettes. I took them away – I didn't want ashy bolognese – and he accused me of 'nanny-stating' him, a turn of phrase I found very alarming because I certainly hadn't taught it to him. Where was he picking this stuff up?

The doorbell rang while the sauce was reducing. He handed me the wooden spoon and went to answer the door.

'Hello Sixteen, hello Sixty-five. Welcome.'

'Forty-seven!' exclaimed Margaret. 'This is a bold adventure! I arrived on a "bus".'

'Evening, Forty-seven,' I heard Reginald-Smyth say. 'That smells nice.'

'Kind of you to say so. I'm afraid I'm going to have to get you both very drunk. I'm not much of a cook.'

He brought them into the kitchen.

Margaret was wearing high-waisted cerulean bell bottoms and a white blouse clocked with lace. She looked like a disco goddess, an astonishing concoction given that she was only barely older than the piano, never mind the synth.

'Hello,' I said, stunned.

'Hello!' she said, in her unplaceable accent, and surged into my arms. She beamed up at me and I must have swallowed loud enough for my throat to click in her ear, because she said, 'Am I mistaken? I have seen folk do greet each other like this. Though Forty-seven will not let me.'

'No, no, this is fine. Feel free to stay here. I'll have his hug for him.'

Reginald-Smyth ('Call me Arthur') forwent the hug and shyly shook my hand. 'Ripping to see you,' he murmured. He pronounced this in a way that was close to 'whipping' and I saw Graham suppress a twinkle.

I dropped the wooden spoon back into the pan and said, 'Would you like a martini? It's the only drink I know how to mix. This is a classy household.'

'"Classy"?' asked Margaret.

'Fine and noble, here applied mockingly,' said Arthur. 'As you should know of any household that contains Forty-seven.'

'Belike I'll be fluent after a "classy" martini.'

'I like those trousers,' I said to her.

'Many thanks! I do like the zipper – see?' She demonstrated unzipping her pockets. 'The time I might have saved on trussing myself in stays had I but a single zipper . . . Did you have the zipper?'

'No,' said Graham.

'No, though they were coming into use in my time.'

'They are a goodly invention.'

'A little . . . dangerous, sometimes,' said Arthur carefully. 'Dependent on their placement.' He caught Graham's eye and they grinned sheepishly at each other.

Graham forgot to put the spaghetti on and Margaret started hiccuping at the first mouthful of her martini. The men smoked copiously in our not overlarge kitchen and I'd forgotten to wash up all the matching plates. Nevertheless, the little party was very pleasant. I opened a bottle of wine (Margaret couldn't finish her martini) and we toasted the only thing we could all agree was good about twenty-first-century Britain: music when you damn well wanted it.

They were friends, I saw – not incidentally, but real friends. Margaret had tried to befriend Anne Spencer, but had been thwarted by her reticence and by what Margaret called her 'sorrows'. Margaret loathed Cardingham, and Arthur stiffly referred to him as a 'difficult chap'. This interested me, as Graham often boxed with him.

'He is a pizzle-headed doorknob,' said Margaret.

'Very colourful,' said Graham. 'But he is as stranded as we all.'

'I don't know, Forty-seven,' said Arthur. 'I don't particularly want to spend my rescued life around him.'

'He mun be returned to the cowpat whence they dragged him. How do you stand him, Gray?'

'One develops a great deal of patience at sea.'

'You make the Navy sound like the priesthood,' said Arthur. 'Hmm.'

Arthur was happy and flushed. He was one of those unusual extroverts who have all the attributes of an introvert, save that they like being around other people. He had a gift for gentleness too, one of the rarest virtues in any gender and especially in the kind of man Arthur was supposed to be. I eased some biography out of him: half-decent public school; Classics at Oxford, where he'd had a lot of fun and failed his exams; retraining as a doctor.

'Came a cropper there too,' he added.

'Not good with wiggly internals and so on?' I asked.

'No, I qualified all right. But I didn't much care for the other chaps. Brutish breed. The profession makes a man hard in the heart, or it did in my time. They get rather superior. You can't be superior about other people's pain. I threw that in after a few years. Started over in the Raj, some school fellow of my father got me a job. Oversaw the building of some unwanted railways, which benefitted nobody but the company. Dreadful stuff. I was transferred to our London office about six months before Germany invaded Belgium.'

I saw Graham's eyebrow quirk in a rascally way as he did the maths. 'You became a captain *extremely* quickly, Sixteen. Found your forte?'

Arthur grimaced. I saw his hand shiver momentarily on his glass and then he swallowed everything in it with a wet click. 'Promotion was – fast – in the war,' he said shortly.

He added that he probably would have been happy as a teacher or a vicar but he'd come from the sort of family where the former was an embarrassment and the latter a punchline. I filed these desires away as 'professionalised fatherhood'; some days later, taking a long lunchtime walk around Bloomsbury with Simellia, she described Arthur as having 'a deeply moral sense of his duty of care' and I felt ashamed of my absent-minded cruelty to someone I had liked.

Margaret, incidentally, listened to the men talk about their careers with a suffused urgency that only I noticed. In her own era, she'd slept in the room next to the one where she had been born. She thought Scotland was far-flung and semi-barbaric. When we came round to talking about my time working as a translator in Cambodia, I felt her attention all over me like a flannel. I may have talked slightly too much.

How the topic of weed came up I couldn't remember – probably during one of the vigorous debates about what the twenty-first century had genuinely improved, which in the opinion of the expats was a mixed bag. I was shortly handing my grinder and papers to Graham (who was far more adept at rolling).

Meeting Margaret made me vivid and receptive. Sentences weighed more. I kept a half-conscious catalogue of where the men were looking. I've seen people deal with this in different ways. By 'this': I mean power. I mean magnetism. I try to absorb it. Within twenty minutes Margaret and I were planning a girls-take-Soho night out, which necessitated me explaining the history of Soho, the concept of clubbing, the genre R'n'B, the club night R'n'She, and dancing. I hadn't been clubbing since I was an assistant in Languages. No matter.

'I know a little of the pavane and the jig . . . but if there will be only women . . .'

'You really don't need to worry about that. You just sort of . . . throw yourself around. And wiggle.'

'I would like to be "thrown",' she said wistfully.

'Here. I'll teach you the electric slide.'

'I say, that looks fun,' said Arthur. 'What's it called? The electrical slide . . .' He was swaying and his oddly seductive rhotacism had intensified. Graham pinched the joint out of his fingers.

'Don't encourage them, Sixteen. I'm going to open another bottle of wine.'

'I've had enough of the polka. I want to learn the electrical slide.'

'What manner of dance is a polka?' asked Margaret, breathlessly, mid-slide.

'Ask Forty-seven to teach you. I think they had it in his time.'

'I will not be press-ganged into dancing, thank you,' Graham said, and slid with the bottle of wine off to the left.

'Hey! You *can* dance!'

'Such matters are between myself and God,' he said gravely. 'Oh, stop frowning, Sixty-five. Arthur, will you please lead her in a polka, if you can still stand.'

Arthur got up and we exchanged a sort of maddened, camp, bowing exchange of Margaret between us, but as soon as she was gathered into Arthur's arms, I started to laugh helplessly. Margaret barely came to his shoulder.

'Oh . . . oh God . . . you look like a handsome giraffe . . . and his tiny rabbit wife . . . ahaha haa . . . God . . .'

'You take her, Forty-seven.'

'Excuse me!'

'Here.'

'I don't dance. I took up the flute *especially*, in order that no one would ask me.'

'In this age, musicians are imprinted inside music boxes, and there is no need for the band to keep time,' said Margaret. 'You will instruct me in the polka, or I will step on your toes.'

'I think "feminism" has gone to your head. Ow!'

'May I have this dance?' Arthur asked me.

Graham had never, even pulling out my chair in restaurants, even handing me plates in the kitchen, deliberately touched me. It was strange to see him handle Margaret. My heart was careening in a way that felt inextricable from a *good time*. I pulled up to Arthur.

'I'll teach you some swing dance,' I said. 'I had a terrible ex-boyfriend who was very into lindy hop, and he used to drag me out to lessons with him, so I have to pass the talent on like a curse.'

'I understood at least half of those words. I've known men like that. Who lead one in a merry dance.'

I looked at Arthur thoughtfully. I had accidentally caught his eye a number of times that evening. On reflection, every time it had happened, it was because our glances had both been resting on Graham.

At the other end of the kitchen, I heard Graham saying, 'Your *other* left.'

'Go to! Why do you not instruct more levelly?'

'Why do you keep trying to lead? No, Sixty-five, your *other* other left.'

'You are a terrible teacher.'

'I don't dance. Ow!'

Arthur, by contrast, danced beautifully. He dipped me and I bent like a reed. He spun me and I was, with such satisfaction, spun.

'Why, captain. You've got fresh and funky before.'

'My dear lady, we invented the "fresh" and the "funky".'

There must have been something in our movement, or the music, that triggered a memory of the trenches – or something else, an agony in Arthur that was unrelated to the brief bloody corridor of the war. We'd finished the joint long enough ago that it can't have been the vertigo-nausea of a bad reaction. Whatever it was, it came over him like a caul. Without any warning, he blanched, and I felt a slick cold sweat transfer from his palm to my waist.

'Arthur?' I said, at the same time Graham said, 'Sixteen?'

Arthur passed a shaking hand across his forehead. His breath was coming in short bursts.

'Oh . . . For – give – mm—'

'It's too warm in here,' said Graham. He'd drawn Arthur from my grasp and was steering him towards the kitchen door. 'Let's sit outside and have a cigarette. I need to rest my feet. Maggie flattened them.'

Arthur wheezed in a way that passed as a laugh. He was high-shouldered and skittish in Graham's careful grip, and then he was suddenly slumped against him, his face turned against Graham's ear.

'Tobacco deprivation is very dangerous,' said Graham.

'I'm – sor—'

'Be careful of the step.'

I felt Margaret squirrel her hand into mine. Graham shot me a look – in fact, a Look – and the weight of its exchange pulled my heart upwards. I asked Margaret if she had been introduced to the phenomenon of modern make-up and took her up to my room.

As soon as she stepped in, I started making a tally of the evidence of unbeauty. There was a chair whose seat was filled with clothes too dirty for the wardrobe but too clean for the washing basket. My bedside table sprouted two water glasses and a mug. Dust crouched on the skirting boards and in the seams of my chest of drawers. When a woman is as impossibly attractive as Margaret, the mediocrity shed by a woman like me bustles around her like a horde of pigeons. Or so I thought, at that time. Truthfully, I'd been foxed by how beautiful she was. I felt a complicated anguish when I saw her little besocked toes treadling the carpet.

Margaret appeared unaware of any of these concerns. She didn't even glance at herself in the mirror. She gave me an interested grin as I pulled out my lipsticks.

'Oh! What manner of material makes this colour?'

'I have no idea.'

'I do not think I have seen such colour. 'Tis very dramatic.'

'Yeah. I'm actually not sure why I own blue lipstick. Here, try this pink. It doesn't suit me, it makes me look a bit green.'

'It matches with my pustules,' she said sadly. (She had a bijou constellation of acne across her forehead and cheeks. She made acne look chic.)

'Oh. Well, there's foundation for that. Look . . .'

I'd stopped wearing it – I was, at the time, thinking of the way my face might be received by a Victorian who didn't approve of cosmetics – but I demonstrated the coverage of my sole foundation. Margaret was amazed by the smoothness of its application and the faithfulness of its shade. She drew an arrow with it on her cheek. On her fair skin, it looked like clay. We started giggling.

By and by, the drink and the weed overtook us. We took the conversation to a horizontal position, struggling as we both were with articulation and uprightness. We lay face to face on the bed, woozy and languid. I had an obscure sense that I had won something, though whether from Margaret, off Graham or within myself I wasn't sure.

'You're pretty,' I said.

'*You* are "pretty".'

'Feel a bit tired.'

'Mmm. Are you Graham's mistress?'

'Mmf. No. God. No. Just his bridge.'

'Oh,' she said, and fell asleep.

I began to doze. I didn't know how much time passed, but I came to when I heard his voice.

'. . . check on Maggie and the moggy.'

The door to my bedroom creaked.

'Your bridge is very kind. Strange, though, for a bridge.'

'She's a strange woman. Ah.'

'Oh. Leave them, Gray. Poor things.'

'The degeneracy of this era. They have not even taken down their hair.'

The door grumbled shut and I fell back into a doze. Margaret was snoring lightly, like a puppy being squeezed. The door reopened and I surfaced to vague consciousness. I felt a wave of cool air, and then a gentle warmth. He had spread a blanket over the pair of us.

The next morning, Margaret and I woke up with no voices. We crept downstairs together, for tea and toast. When we got to the kitchen, we found that the men had done the washing up.

*

Autumn set in like a decorative inlay. The trees wilted and dropped leaves. Leaden clouds enamelled the sky and the wind picked up all over the city.

Graham and Arthur had decided to go to Scotland for the stag season – partly so that they could experience a domestic flight. They flew to Aberdeen, watched by the Ministry. They were shadowed by field agents, but once the pair got to the tiny Highlands town where they were staying, the Ministry had to call the shadows off. The town was the sort of quiet, close-knit place where the locals were wary of suspicious characters with no obvious purpose.

All the expats had phones, paid for (and tapped) by the Ministry. Graham had switched his own phone on a total of three times in the seven months he had been in the twenty-first century. I was therefore unsurprised when, about half an hour after their plane landed, I got a call from Arthur's phone.

'Hi, Arthur!'

'It's me. Sixteen is clinging to a wall.'

'Oh! Hello. How was your first flight?'

'It was both extraordinary and terribly mundane. Though I'm afraid Arthur and I nearly broke one another's hands during take-off.'

'Ha! Did your ears pop?'

'Yes! Very strange. But the aeroplane took us above the clouds! They were beneath us like a mattress. They looked almost solid.'

'Fun fact, the average cloud weighs about five hundred and fifty-one tons.'

'That *is* a fun fact.'

'You didn't have any trouble at the airport?'

'The machine that reads bodies stopped working when I passed through it.'

'Reads . . . ? Oh, the body scanner. It didn't go off?'

'Some airport officer had to manhandle me to ensure I was not carrying weapons. In full view of everyone! My honour has been impugned.'

'Oh dear. Now you're spoiled.'

'No one will ever take me as a wife.'

'I'm so sorry for your loss.'

'Somehow I will bear it stoically. Now, I must go, because if I don't smoke a cigarette soon, I am going to bite through a wall.'

After the call, I turned on my laptop to check the Teams channel – me, Quentin, Control, the Wellness team and the administrative staff assigned to Expat Eighteen-forty-seven. The field agents had already filed an alert about the body scanner failing to 'read' Graham. Recommend returning expats to base, one of the agents had written. I thought about the boyish grin on Graham's face when he came home after passing the exam, his high-spirited singing in the bath. I typed fast.

Overcorrecting out of cautiousness will be as damaging to his adjustment as forcing him home. His 'readability' has not, hitherto, been a cause of concern.

Then, in the private conversation with Quentin: he's gone thru the scanners at the staff entrance with no problem, right? most of the time.

Quentin's status was invisible. It had been for a while.

In the main channel, a member of Graham's Wellness team was agreeing with me. His 'read' rate average is 86% and has been since records started. By far the highest of all the expats. We don't want to risk alienating him and impacting that average.

Records started two weeks ago, the agent typed.

Several people started typing, but stopped when Adela – whose status was also invisible – dropped:

ACCORDING TO YOUR REPORT 1916 FOLLOWED 1847 AND WAS TEMPORARILY UNREADABLE, SUBSEQUENTLY READABLE. SUGGESTS DELIBerate attempts to test readability. Do not interfere. Expats will be monitored on their return.

The conversation ended there. Adela could do barking over a meeting even over text. 'Thank you,' I said out loud. I slammed the laptop shut.

After that, I drifted through the house like a purposeless balloon. In truth I was purposeless: my job for the bridge year was to watch him, and he was not there to be watched.

I went into his room. He was a neat man, used to the limited space of a cabin at sea, and there wasn't much to see. I sat on the very edge of the bed. It was a double, and I knew from past conversations that he slept like a dropped twig at one far end of it, accustomed as he was to ships' berths. I didn't rummage through his drawers for his journal, or sketches, or push my face into his clothes. I acted as if watched by an invisible audience, who were checking for signs of mania.

*

A few days after he and Arthur had left England, Simellia paid me an unannounced visit. She came in the wake of a new project-wide working group on 'readability' and the Brigadier's concepts of 'hereness' and 'thereness'.

This was a development of such significance that the Secretary had been forced to chair a working group, announcing (glassy of voice and face) that while bridge work wasn't changing, the

Wellness team would be 'running some tests' on the expats, monitoring 'vitals and responses' under 'standard and stressor conditions'. 'Sounds a bit MK-Ultra,' I'd ventured. 'Unprecedented in the history of the world, et cetera,' he'd told the air to the left of my head.

'Oh, Simellia, hi.'

'Hello. Hope I'm not disturbing you. I wanted to see how you were doing since Quentin's reassignment.'

'Yes – of course – come in—'

I put the kettle on and made a performance of biscuits. The air around us flexed with expectation. I said: 'Can't believe we're dealing with the long dark time-travel of the soul, or whatever Defence think "thereness" is. Quite a change from Kooks and Killers, eh?'

'We tend not to use that nickname in the department.'

I winced. She added, not unkindly, 'You know how it is. I'm sure you're tired of people making jokes about Google Translate.'

'I suppose so. Builder's okay?'

'Yes, thanks. Am I right in thinking that your grandfather was a governor of the rainforests in Cambodia or something like that?'

I made an audible syllable of surprise, which was drowned out by the kettle. I was always on amber alert, minimum, when people asked about my heritage with any taxonomic specificity. I never knew what they were hoping to do with it. My sister described these interactions as 'microaggressions', as if she didn't talk about her Cambodian heritage at every possible opportunity. I probably had her latest essay, published in an online magazine the previous week, about the psychic horror of passing as white, to blame for Simellia's question. My sister and I shared the same bizarre Eurasian double-barrelled surname so we were easy to link. I sometimes wondered if my sister had decided to develop daddy issues about our long-dead Cambodian grandfather because our father was a nice, quiet white guy who liked afternoon naps, making long lists and curating complete sets of things (stamps, DVDs, limited edition fountain pens) – he was not someone you could have an interesting and publishable psychological complex about.

'Er, my grandfather was governor of Siem Reap until he was dismissed in 'fifty-five,' I said. 'I guess there are a lot of rainforests in the province. Ha, but if you know that, I expect you know what happened to him.'

'Disappeared.'

'Mm.'

I felt her gaze through my hair. 'I know that was a bizarre thing to bring up,' she said.

'It was pretty spicy.'

'It's just that . . . given your family history, I suppose I'm a bit surprised by your choice of career. Your time in Languages . . . it's all a bit, dare I say it, post-colonial. Are you hoping that the time-door will—?'

'Adela said that you can't change the past, you can only change the future.'

'That's wordplay. Changing the past *is* changing the future. Your girl just means that the past exists the way she says it exists. Have you managed to get your commander to stop calling me a negress, by the way?'

She was smiling as she spoke, but as Simellia often smiled, even when she was angry, I dropped into a crouch, spiritually.

'I'm so sorry.'

'What for?'

I thought it might be callow to say, 'For the existence of

racism'. I ummed and erred and eventually said, 'If it's any consolation, he has asked me, straight of face as you like, about being "half-caste".'

'Is that a consolation? No sugar, thanks.'

I put the tea bags on the sideboard. A pad of hardwater scum disported across the top of my mug.

'I appreciate,' I said slowly, 'that this project is more fraught for you than anyone else—'

'Stop hand-wringing,' said Simellia, still smiling, though increasingly looking as if the smile was being operated by winches inside her skull. 'God, Ministry bias training has a lot to answer for,' she said. 'I don't want to drop a piano on your head but believe it or not, I already know I'm Black. You don't have to roll over and show me your belly about it.'

I put the tea down in front of her.

'I'm sorry if I said something that upset you,' I said.

'You haven't upset me. You're just boring me.'

'Okay.'

'"Okay". I bet you had a Tumblr.'

That made me laugh, albeit nervously. Simellia's smile loosened a bit. 'Called it,' she said. 'I bet you put up a Black Lives Matter reading list.'

I sat down. I had, in fact, shared someone else's reading list, but she could have me lick the floor clean of germs before I'd admit it right then. 'Simellia,' I said, 'has something happened?'

Simellia rolled her shoulders. She seemed discomfited in her own immaculate costume.

'Yes,' she said finally. 'Do you remember when you told the Secretary that you were finding the whole proposed "readability" monitoring a bit MK-Ultra? It got me thinking about what we're doing with the expats. I'm a clinical professional. I'm supposed to be governed by a code of ethics.'

'What about the rest of us?'

She hadn't touched her tea. 'What *about* the rest of you?' she said.

'Hello, officer.'

'Stop it,' she said, far more sharply than she'd ever spoken to me. 'Take things seriously for a moment.'

I bristled – not visibly, not readably, but inside me I felt the spikes slide out. I should have ended the conversation there. Spikes under the skin, that angry internal prickle – I hated to have the lower hand, and I've never been good at managing it graciously.

'I'm not going to insult you by feeding you aphorisms about omelettes and broken eggs,' I said. 'But you signed up for this job. You thought, as much as I did, that what we were doing was world-changing. That's what you wanted, remember? Do you think the world changes by being asked politely? Or do you think there has to be risk?'

She took a deep breath. All the emotions I normally watched her purée into professionalism were churning on her face.

'I came here,' she said, 'because you – because – I thought you would understand. Don't you? Being the experiment. Being the pioneer they break the concepts on. The *first*. Are there any other Cambodians on the core team? Any other Southeast Asians, even? I can tell you exactly how many Black people there are, and I'd only need one hand to count them off.'

I leant back in my chair. She wasn't telling me off and yet I felt scolded. She reminded me of my sister, sometimes. 'Simellia,' I said, 'I'm not a victim. I don't give people an excuse to make me a victim. I'd advise you not to give them the opportunity either.'

Simellia stared. The emotion in her face spiralled away, water down a plughole. She stood up. 'Thanks for the tea,' she said coldly.

I let her leave without saying goodbye and sat in the pool of silence that followed the crash of the front door slamming shut. This was one of my first lessons in how you make the future: moment by moment, you seal the doors of possibility behind you.

V

'Your feet are swelling,' Goodsir observes.

Gore is back in the sick bay on *Erebus*. Stanley is tearing at his cuffs, bellowing for hot water. Gore's frostnip isn't close to the worst cold-induced injury the crew has seen — it isn't even the worst Gore has personally endured — but Stanley's panic is bracketed by the report Gore has just made.

'You're quite sure you shot him dead?' Lieutenant Le Vesconte, the second lieutenant, asks. He is a veteran of the Opium War, cool and soldier-like, and like all soldierly men, given to tenderness about bloodshed.

In the same dry tone, Goodsir says, 'Mr Gore never misses.'

Gore is grateful for the assistant surgeon's ironic calm. Goodsir is his friend, insofar as a commander and a lesser sawbones can be friends. No, that's not fair, they *are* friends. Goodsir is a career scientist. If they had figs on board, he wouldn't give them for the gold epaulettes on Gore's shoulders.

'I thought he was a seal,' says Gore. 'Poor devil. I ran over as soon as I heard him shout.'

'He was absolutely dead?' Le Vesconte asks again. He sounds like someone's peeled the skin off his voice.

'Yes. Send a couple of men out to the body,' says Gore. 'Take tobacco. Steel knives if we can spare any. Something we can leave that makes it clear we mean no further harm. Don't interfere with the corpse in any way.'

'I'd be hesitant to arm those people, Graham,' mutters Le Vesconte. 'In the circumstances.'

'Tobacco then. Mr Goodsir?'

'Sir.'

'Can I walk on these?'

Goodsir gives Gore's feet an appraising glance. He takes one swollen arch and chafes it briskly.

'I know it doesn't matter what I say,' he says. 'You're going to walk on them anyway.'

'Well done.'

Gore begins to cram his feet back into his boots. His gloves are by his thigh on the table. They have a brownish crust on them. The Esquimau had bled through his furs. By the time Gore had reached his side, his eyes were already cloudy.

'I shot him through the heart, Harry,' he says vaguely. Goodsir doesn't respond, but he squeezes Gore's arm. What for? Gore checks his inner machinery as he would a chronometer. Is that a feeling, sculling at the basin of his ribs? Does he need comforting?

Topside, the watch begins to stamp and shout. A tattoo of boots on the ladderway. Someone has sighted a party of Esquimaux, moving towards the ships.

Chapter Five

September found me in Pimlico, on a bench with Margaret Kemble. The air was bisected by an iron hinge of autumn cold. Sparrows gusted along the kerb, waltzing with the limp yellow leaves. Margaret and I were both wearing tartan scarves in fine Scottish wool, brought back from the Highlands by Arthur and Graham. Every so often, Margaret would stretch her legs to admire her new boots. She was dressed like a Southern belle cowboy, her reddish-blonde hair spilling over her collar. There was a gap as large as a spread hand between her scarf and her lapels which showed her décolletage. Margaret had large breasts, which I mention because she had not yet grown used to dressing them without stays and they tended to draw the gaze. They had a lively upward swell – they seemed to want to have a conversation – and buried deep in the cleavage were a couple of raised acne dots, resembling (charmingly) pink wafer crumbs. Her skin was very fair and bright, like an expensive moisturiser. I note all this because I think male writers are often mocked for their lengthy descriptions of women's breasts, but I do think some breasts provoke them, even from me.

She was due to retake the acclimatisation examination the following week. I was helping her revise.

'What do you think you'll vote in the next election?'

'Every man of them discourses on lies and petty connivery. I'd sooner vote for a mad dog.'

'You'll get into trouble for that, but I'm going to allow it. Do you have a boyfriend?'

'No. If I like the person asking, and if she be comely, may I ask her if she "has" a "girlfriend"?'

'You may.'

'Do you "have" a "girlfriend"?'

'Stop cackling, you horrid woman. Are you on Facebook?'

'"Facebook" is for folk who prefer to have their minds filled with soft oats and whey. When this bridge year ends, I will get an "Instagram".'

'Oh my God. Maggie, do *not* get Instagram.'

'Here comes Sixteen!'

Arthur was striding up the street, bent slightly against a wind which didn't exist. He was wearing a tweed jacket and looked like a period piece, but then again, so did Pimlico. I hadn't seen him since the men had got back from Scotland and I asked him whether he enjoyed his trip. He flushed and mumbled, 'Oh it was – lovely. Just – wonderful. Truly.'

He sat down next to me, his eyes on the ground. Margaret leant across my lap and said, 'Sixteen, do you "have" a "boyfriend"? May I "add" him on "Facebook"?'

While Arthur blushed deeper and muttered something about not teasing him, she looked up at me and said, 'How did I fare?'

'Great. You're a very modern woman. You've got your elbow in my crotch by the way. I don't mind but you really ought to buy me a drink first.'

'Behave, the pair of you. Before Forty-seven gets here. You know he'll tell you off.'

'He is there. With the canker of the Devil's own arse.'

'Oh, Cardingham?' I asked, and squinted.

Graham was wearing his motorcycle leathers. The first time he showed them to me – twisting his shoulders in the jacket, so that the leather creaked – I thought I was having an allergic reaction because my tongue went heavy and my fingers started prickling. I glanced at Arthur. He looked like he was also allergic to leather.

'Hello,' said Graham. 'Have you committed a heist together? You are looking very guilty.'

'You are looking like a frog who took a dip in ink,' said Margaret, the only one of us unmoved by the sight of a leather-clad Victorian.

'Good to see you too, Sixty-five. Thomas, you remember my bridge. I'm not sure if you've been formally introduced . . .'

'Ma'am,' said Cardingham, and it had such strong connotations of *bitch* that I was distracted from Graham, and Arthur and Graham, and Graham and Margaret.

'Hm. It's nice to meet you properly, Lieutenant Cardingham.'

Cardingham's features curdled. It occurred to me that Arthur (who was either gay or bisexual, had been marginalised in his own lifetime) and Graham (an explorer whose life had required flexibility and forbearance) had ill-prepared me for how a male 'historical figure' might react to me. Cardingham was disgusted. He thought I should be below his boots and ashamed to meet his eye. Where Margaret had gained ineffable ground, he had lost it. He burned with the anger of a child whose toys have been tidied away.

'Commander Gore's spoke much on thee. Thou strikes me as canny, goodwife.'

Or did he say *cunny*? I wasn't sure. His burr seemed awfully deliberate. Beside me, Margaret's delicate little hands curled into claws.

*

When I was eight years old, I developed a keen awareness of the non-human world. Mai, Daddy, Sister, Home, School, Teacher, Bath, Plate, Chair, Crayon, Dress – these were not, as I had thought, the building blocks of the universe, but discrete entities in a world we shared with worms, mice, sparrows, woodlice, squirrels, moths, pigeons, cats, spiders. I had a wretched sense of fighting for space. They were everywhere, the non-humans. They came from under things and out of shadows, they were higher than I could see in trees and deeper than I could penetrate in the soil. They could be in a room with me and I might not know it, though they'd know about me. A great, awful busyness was flourishing all around me. I didn't know how to process it. I became horribly afraid of spiders.

My parents, at the time, were trying to coax my five-year-old sister out of her fear of the dark, which she expressed in whimpers. Not me. I screamed and panicked. I climbed things, pulled down books and vases, sobbing hysterically. Some of the time there wasn't even a spider, I'd just had the idea of a spider.

My mother, who had witnessed the sort of horrors that changed the way screams sounded, first dealt with the panics by getting angry at me. Only now, as an adult, can I see that she was angry because I'd frightened her. It kept happening, and she tried to fix it, but she made it worse. You see, she thought she could kill the spiders that scared me and prove how invulnerable a human was before an insect – but she'd been

144

raised a Buddhist, and she was kind to animals, even the creepy ones. She'd botch it and hurt the spiders, which would then scuttle about half-maimed, raising more sobbing from me. And then she'd cry too, because she didn't want to kill a spider, not really. She didn't want to kill anything.

My father hit upon an eccentric solution. In the spring of the year I was eight, a fat tortoiseshell spider the size of a fifty-pence coin had built her web in our garden, taking over the front of a bush. I hated that spider. I wouldn't even step on the lawn once I knew she was there.

'What,' said my dad to me, 'you don't want to meet Missus Legs?'

'She got a missing leg now?' said my mother, exasperated. 'What did you do to her? You squash her?'

'Missus Legs,' said my dad, mugging frantically. 'The stately old lady who lives in the bush. Watching over her larder.'

'She got a ladder now, Cheesus Chrise,' muttered my mum. 'Next thing she got a screwdriver, building a house, I have to phone the council for planning permission.'

My dad was undeterred. He was determined that his bit was going to win over my mum's bit, which is at least half of successful co-parenting. He described Missus Legs as a fine old spinster, much respected by the rest of the insects – though she wasn't technically an insect, he added pedantically – a hard worker, a craftswoman, a doyenne of the kill technique. He invited me to witness the disembowelment of a pesky, antisocial fly, from a safe seat, but with full commentary.

It worked. Missus Legs slipped from non-human to almost-human – not a terribly pleasant human, of course, but a woman of means and not a little skill. 'Look,' said my dad, 'do you see how she's waiting in the corner? We can't see it, but she's filing her nails. She's already done the hard work of making up the web, she spent four years at architecture school to learn how to do that, and now all she has to do is sit back and wait and let the prey come to her.'

I took the lessons of the patient Missus Legs into my adulthood. I rarely hustled, was indifferent to grind. But I kept careful tabs and a great many secrets. When, at the Ministry, I found myself briefly professionally isolated – with Adela absent, Quentin missing, Simellia cold in the corridors, Control's focus on the 'readability' experiments run by the Wellness team – I sank back on my web. Something had turned somewhere, something was wrong, but as I didn't know what, I'd have to wait.

Though Quentin was AWOL, or possibly MIA, I kept filing my core reports with him in copy. I wrote to him: emails, texts, Teams chats, voice notes. I knew they were monitored; I counted on it, actually, because I wanted the Ministry to imagine I was open, affectionate and guileless. I let the messages ring with easy intimacies – nothing too personal, canteen gossip and remarks on what I was reading, mostly.

It paid off in the early autumn. When I came down for breakfast one morning, I found Graham at the counter with a dictionary and a tin of protein powder, performing exegesis on the label.

'Bite silk minotaur,' he said.

'Er. Good morning?'

He held up a card oblong – a violently prosaic postcard with a picture of Buckingham Palace, which could have been taken at any point in the last fifty years and sold at almost any shop in the greater metropolitan area. 'That's what it says on the back of this,' he said. 'A code, perhaps? Is that how billets-doux work in this era? Do I have to defend your honour? Good morning, by the by.'

Quentin risked a lot with that postcard, including that I'd

know that the truncated poetry on the back referred to a specific location available only on an app that assigned every square foot of earth on the planet three words. It was on the heath – a wide open space, brave to the sky and the passersby.

There was no time or date. I went out to the heath after work, for the post-emails constitutional that I'd often described to Quentin in my unanswered messages. I could see him from metres away. He looked so quotidian. He was wearing a baseball cap and the sheer ordinariness of the vision put my eyes on mute. A clever tactic, hiding in plain sight.

'Quentin. Nice drip. Why don't you call me any more?'

'That's confidential,' he said.

'How are you?'

'I'm being monitored.'

'Oh? Right now? Cheers for the fucking warning.'

'No. But. Where I sleep. Where I go. I have limited permissions. The Ministry—'

He broke off. Closer, I could smell sour breath and the alkali perfume of some kind of skin medication. He spoke to my collarbone. He was clearly unwell, or so I thought. I softened.

'Quentin. Are you all right? Do you need help?'

'Can I trust you?' he blurted out. I knew then that he was sickening, and the cumulative pressures of the time-travel project had crushed him. Quentin the former field agent would never have asked me if he could trust me, because he would have known I could lie. I had to talk him down, soothe him out, so I took the role I knew it was most comfortable to cast me in – Simellia had already given me the lines.

'Yes, of course you can. I'm worried about the project too. You've read my file. You must have assumed that I know what it's like to be the pioneer. The *experiment*.'

A sunrise of hope on his face. He nodded, eyes on that distant horizon where the genocide took place. What a strange character people make of me.

'Do you remember that sketch you gave me?' he asked.

'Yes,' I said – neutrally, this time.

'I think it's a weapon. I think it's a weapon that doesn't exist yet, except it's here. And – I'm pretty sure I've seen what it does. It is. Fucking awful.'

I reached out and took his hand, in a way that I hope he found comforting, but also in such a way that I could subtly slide two fingers down his sleeve. His pulse sped against my fingertips.

'That's worrying,' I said slowly.

He yanked his hand back.

'I know you don't believe me,' he said quickly. 'I wouldn't either. But I can prove it. This project isn't about scientific advancement. It's about a weapon.'

The idea that the Ministry were operating above board was simply silly to me – progress is not achieved by colouring inside the lines – but it struck me that Quentin was a risk to the bridge–expat environment because he was either a cadet whistleblower or else paranoid and delusional. Either way, because he was my handler, I felt him like a woodworm in my ark. If he was right, and if he squealed, then I'd be among the excoriated and punished, and my options would diminish to turning in the circle of lashes. If he was wrong, well, I'd let a madman walk away unhandled, and I doubted there were promotion prospects in that.

'Look,' I said to him, 'the bridges are integral to the project, and I'm the bridge of the most successfully adjusted expat. They can't touch me. Bring me the proof. And then I can take it from there.'

*

I forgot to tell you the end of the spider story. I started visiting Missus Legs. At the time I was working my way through *Alice in Wonderland*, and I'd go out to read to her, stumbling over Lewis Carroll's sinister lullabies. I liked the dignity with which Missus Legs appeared to listen, her cherubic stillness among the gossamer panes. And then – so fast I could only express it in plosives – kkkkk! bbbbb! – out from her corner to seize a stuck fly. I'd slam the book shut and watch her work.

I reached the lament of the Mock Turtle during the season of butterflies. A cluster of pupae on the branches of my dad's yellow rose bush split to reveal scraps of wing. As the butterflies dried and stretched, I noted the grotesque flamboyance of their colouring. Butterflies demand so much attention. A spider just wants to eat.

I reached out and pinched a half-finished butterfly. It felt almost furry – the microscopic scales, hours old, disintegrating under my fingers. A tug, a flick and I'd thrown it into the web. It struggled for a very long time before Missus Legs was done.

I'd tell this story when I was drunk, to friends at quiet dinner parties or to the men who'd called at my port in the years before I knew Graham. Invariably, they'd think it was a story about my little girl brutality. Who feeds a butterfly to a spider? But I always thought the story was about something else. Of course I was still afraid of spiders. I was eight years old. Missus Legs had a dozen eyes and sucked the life out of the living. Yes, I was still afraid of spiders. I had simply found the only way my child's mind could conceive of placating the fear. Join up. Take a wing. Get to work.

*

Autumn stomped on. The days mouldered and dampened, like something lost at the back of the fridge. No matter the weather, there were puddles of brackish rain slung across the pavements.

In early October, Margaret caught a cold.

Over the course of more than three hundred and fifty years, the common cold had mutated. Margaret's body was astonished into severe illness. She was removed from her bridge accommodation to a Ministry ward.

Adela called an emergency meeting in her usual meeting room.

'We need to infect all of them,' said Ralph. 'Get Sixteen-sixty-five to sneeze on them and then keep them under observation on the wards.'

'It could kill the Sixteen-hundreds,' said Ivan, who was Cardingham's bridge and whose voice was laden with the suggestion that this wouldn't be an altogether bad thing.

'The only time they've been on those wards was after the traumatic extraction process,' said Simellia. 'It could be triggering.'

'Oh, *triggering*,' said Ralph. 'And we don't want to trigger them.'

'No, we don't, Ralph. We want them to remain as mentally and physically robust as possible. It is quite literally our job to ensure that.'

It was a fractious meeting. Nothing exposes the seams of a group faster than the fraught world of care. More than death, care reveals too much about a personality to ever be discussed neutrally. Vaccines, palliative care, capacity to consent to treatment, what constituted serious illness, the use and abuse of a taxpayer-funded system: try them on a dinner party and watch the pack animal bite its way through the skin.

I suggested that, to assure Margaret she would be coming

off the wards and not pushed backwards through the extraction system, we could arrange for the other expats to video call and talk to her.

'Yes,' said Simellia distantly, 'I can arrange that.'

'Oh, I didn't mean that *you* should have to—'

'Thanks, Simellia,' said Adela wearily. 'If there's no AOB, I'd like to make my recommendations to the Secretary . . .'

Adela was of the 'never been to the GP in my life because I'm not a pussy' school of care and nothing changed. If the expats were dangerously ill, they'd be removed to the wards and never mind the trigger; if they could get a grip and deal with it at home, they should.

Simellia organised a group video call to Margaret's bedside, negotiating with the Wellness team as if they were hostage-takers. The four of us tried to comfort an upset, disorientated Margaret over Zoom. (The expats were disappointed by how clumsy the software was; they had not expected lags, pixellation or sound issues in this, the brave new future.)

'They have pierced me with needles! I fear 'twill dispatch me . . . were these not the very tools with which we were plagued at first?'

She held up her white arms, rattling with IV cannulas. Arthur and Graham both flinched.

'I remember those,' said Arthur hoarsely. 'But I didn't until now . . . Forty-seven, do you . . . ?'

'Yes.'

'That ward . . . Maggie, can you tilt the camera? Good God. Was I in that ward?'

Graham didn't respond, but he turned very pale. Simellia caught my eye, and for a moment we were united again, touching glances across a room. Then she took her face back and began to briskly discuss a schedule of calls with the on-site member of the Wellness team, who blurred the background as soon as they had control of the laptop.

Margaret only spent six days in the Ministry before she was well enough for release. Those six days were bitterly anxious and I rendered my nailbeds dogfoodish. But once she was out, I felt silly for my lack of faith in modern medicine. It was just a cold, I told myself. Of course she would recover from a cold.

Arthur came down with the bug next, but his temporal closeness to contemporary colds meant he was able to remain with Simellia for the miserable duration. Shortly afterwards, I caught it.

'Don't come near me,' I warned Graham.

'I'm fine,' he said airily. 'A mere catarrh in clement weather? I went snow-blind in the Northern wastes. I have no fear of a cough.'

I sniffed gloopily through a mask, a hangover from the coronavirus pandemic some several years beforehand. I was trying to cook borbor but the mere act of measuring stock for the rice was exhausting.

'Let me do it,' he said.

Through snot and eyeballs as hot as peppered eggs, I gave him instructions for cooking borbor, which I kept calling congee. I referred to the youtiao as cha kway and the spring onions as scallions, as I was too sickly to remember which languages I was supposed to be using. I left him to let it simmer and despite my idiosyncratic instruction, he produced something serviceable. He brought it up to my bedroom.

'Are you decent?'

'Literally never. Kkuugh.'

'Might you . . . attempt decency?'

'You won't be able to see anything, if that's your concern. Hkk. Gggh. Oh, that looks nice. Thank you.'

'You're welcome.'

'You seem tense. First time in a lady's boudoir?'

'I have sisters. Had. What's that?'

'Hairdryer. Hnnghh. Kkkgh. Yuck. Sorry. It fires hot air directly at your head.'

'How useful. What's this?'

'My alarm clock. It plays me birdsong in the mornings. Hkk. That half-moon lights up to resemble sunrise, so I don't wake up in the dark.'

'What a clever invention. What are these?'

'Contraceptive pills.'

'Contra . . . ?'

'I take one a day to prevent pregnancy. Ggggh. Not that I'm having any sex.'

He put the pills down hurriedly, flushing, and muttered, '"Having" "sex", what a revolting term. I hope I never hear it expressed again.'

For a day or so, things were, once again, misflavoured and uncomfortable between us. Graham's relationship to sexuality was a mystery. I had no idea if he'd ever had a sex life, or if he wanted one. The most his Ministry psychoanalyst had been able to get out of him on the comparative boisterousness and acquisitiveness of twenty-first-century sex was that he found it terribly eighteenth. I had a copy of his medical records from his extraction and he hadn't tested positive for, or been treated for, any STIs. Given the prevalence of prostitution in Victorian England, the non-existence of reliable barrier contraception in his era, and the fact that he was a sailor, this suggested he was either a virgin or very lucky. But then again, I knew enough about his biography to know that he was very, very lucky.

Inevitably, he caught my cold.

I was first alerted to this because I heard the muffled snap

153

of the bed frame at ten in the morning – by which time, he had normally been up for several hours. I knocked, received a coughing fit in response, and opened the door.

'I'm not dressed!' he croaked, sitting up.

'You are perfectly well-covered,' I said – a lie. The V of the T-shirt he wore – the first time I'd seen him in a T-shirt – came to a point on the flat of his sternum, revealing curls of black hair like a page of question marks across his chest.

'You . . . do not look well,' I added.

'Don't tell the Ministry.'

'If you get any sicker—'

'I am fine. I simply need a day or so to mimic you and remain indolent.'

'Don't sass me from your sickbed.'

I reached out and he drew the covers up to his throat in a parody of chastity.

'I'm going to check your temperature,' I said, and flattened my palm over his forehead before he could flinch out of my grasp. He looked up at me – cautious, watchful – and visibly tried to anticipate my next move.

His skin was shockingly hot to touch. 'You have a high fever,' I said, pulling my hand back. His sweat glimmered on my palm.

'I am fine. Truly.'

'I'm going to call—'

'*Don't.*'

'—Maggie and Arthur. They've had it already. They might be able to compare how badly gone you are.'

Margaret and Arthur arrived within half an hour.

'Forty-seven!' wailed Margaret, flopping onto the bed. 'You look beastly! Hanged be, this sack is soaked!'

'He's running a horrid temperature. Look. Feel his forehead.'

'Sixteen, get these women off me,' he said, a little desperately.

'Perhaps some tea?' Arthur suggested. Margaret and I traipsed out, with Margaret pulling at her sleeves.

'Oh, monstrous! His face is as soiled linens!'

'I can *hear* you.'

'You mun remove those vile garments,' Margaret called to Arthur. 'With a blade, should he resist it. Their vapours will worsen his malady.'

We went downstairs. Margaret suggested that an apple would be a welcome victual (her words), so I put the kettle on and started to cut an apple. Margaret told me that modern apples tasted both bland and unpleasantly tart, and I started explaining intensive farming. Upstairs, we could hear the low voices of the men.

There was the sound of heavy footsteps, then the domestic thunder of water: Arthur, presumably, was running a bath. More low voices, this time at a ricochet speed that suggested argument. Then, suddenly, Arthur said, or rather snapped, 'You can barely bloody sit upright. I'm not going to leave you to drown. For God's sake, Gray —' and then he said something else, soft and fast. I couldn't hear the words, but I raised my eyebrows in sympathy because I recognised the melody of pleading.

The voices stopped for a few minutes. Margaret and I exchanged glances. Then there was a hollow splash, which sounded very much like someone being dropped bodily into a tub of water. Margaret grinned. Upstairs, I heard a petulant, 'I can wash my *own* hair, thank you.'

'Maybe we should eat this apple and cut him another one,' I suggested. 'It'll just go brown.'

Margaret bit into a slice. She had bright, even teeth. I wondered what she was using to clean them in the seventeenth century that had left them so pearlescent. She swallowed and the white column of her throat contracted prettily. I got confused and went to make the tea.

'I have attended many "screens" of the season at the British Film Institute,' Margaret announced to my back.

'Oh yes? What are they showing?'

'Films from the land of Korea,' she said. 'They place the script in English at the base of the screen so that we might follow. I have seen many romances.'

'Have you watched much old Hollywood stuff? I think you'd really like it.'

'What is "Hollywood"?'

I smiled. It was so hard not to treat the expats like blank slates onto which I might write my opinions. I understood the adage 'knowledge is power' whenever I looked into Margaret's face, the sultry peach colour of her mouth and her acne glowing with unprinted newness. There was something hauntingly *young* about all of them, a scarcity of cultural context that felt teen-aged, and I didn't know if my fascination with it was maternal or predatory. Every time I gave Graham a book, I was trying to shunt him along a story I'd been telling myself all my life.

Margaret propped her chin in her hand and said, 'Is *Carol* a film of "Hollywood"? I took much pleasure in that.'

She twinkled at me and I twinkled back. She was just too charming; untwinkling was not an option. When she was alone with me, she pitched her voice slightly lower than she did around the men. Even for her, girlishness was a habit that was hard to break – for safety, for camouflage. I knew that. Sometimes, just under my tongue, I felt the exclamation marks I put into my speech, demarcating the sentences I didn't mind being broken off from my agency, as long as I was assured I would be protected from the outcome.

*

Graham was adamant about not informing the Ministry about his illness. It was the closest I had ever seen him to entreating. I thought about it a lot. I liked being entreated by him.

With the remedies of house and hearth, it took him a week and a half to get back to full strength. In this time, Arthur, Margaret and I plied him with care and got on his nerves. He didn't like to be touched or fussed over, and, after the first few days, became tense with irritation when we tried. Arthur and I took it personally (Arthur was once almost reduced to tears). Margaret didn't, so she was the only one who could get away with forcing him to accept help.

Despite how interesting I found Graham's pleas for secrecy, by failing to report a significant change in physical health or my meeting with Quentin, I was pushing my luck with the Ministry. I avoided going in for a couple of weeks, hoping to blend into the beige background of generalised bureaucracy. Towards the end of Graham's convalescence, the Vice-Secretary emailed me to let me know I'd been assigned a new handler and I assumed I'd gotten away with it.

I took the Tube in. The streets were beset with the cacophony of constant rain – enough that the local councils had started prepping for a flood.

Adela was sitting at Quentin's old desk, hands neatly crossed over a small pile of paperwork, with an air of a wind-up doll about to be set into motion. She was visibly waiting for me, and her demeanour suggested that I'd missed my cue.

'Adela. Good to see you.'

'Sit, please.'

'Er. Thanks. When will I meet my new handler?'

'I am your new handler.'

I goggled at her. I must have looked like a demented bowling ball, because she added, 'In light of Quentin's defection, the

Secretary and I considered it wisest if you and Eighteen-forty-seven were kept close to Control.'

The roof of my mouth abruptly dried. I unstuck my tongue from it like a strip of jerky.

'What do you mean, his defection?'

'He has attempted to make unauthorised contact with a man who claims to hold the rank of brigadier. Something to do with an irrelevant sketch by Eighteen-forty-seven.'

Time happened to me very quickly, and then very slowly. Panic as much as grief warps the way internal time works; I just had the wherewithal to wonder if this would be worth raising with the Wellness team.

'You know I gave the sketch to Quentin.'

'I do. I know you've met with him too.' She didn't sound angry. Not even expectant. But she left her sentence trailing for me to catch.

'Look,' I said, 'I think Quentin's – a bit delusional. I've been trying to persuade him that I'm trustworthy. I don't want him to lash out and leak things and endanger the project or Gra— Eighteen-forty-seven. You say he's been slipping stuff to Defence via the Brigadier?'

'The man who appears to hold the rank of brigadier, yes. And his associate Salese.'

'What does "appear to hold the rank of brigadier" mean?'

'He's a spy. Not for Defence. I mean that he does not work for the British government in any capacity, and never has. He works for one of our allies – technically an ally – certainly not a country we were expecting to send intelligence agents into our sovereign territories. We knew from the beginning, but I thought – that is, the Secretary, Defence and I thought – that it would be prudent to monitor him and establish the parameters of his mission before we alerted them, so that we could contain any fallout. Unfortunately he has since gone under-ground. As, it appears, has Quentin. You have been working with a traitor and aiding a saboteur. But you are . . . a good bridge.'

Even this, she said with brick-wall calm. I sensed retribution judiciously withheld, and I was bitterly grateful for her restraint. The way she watched my reaction reminded me of the stingingly intense way that the Brigadier had stared at me. As if they were both double-checking the whereabouts of my jugular vein. 'Jesus Christ,' I muttered, and lifted a thumb to my mouth to bite the skin.

'Don't!' said Adela sharply. I jumped an inch in my chair. She grimaced and bunched her hands into fists, so the knuckles bulged like marbles. 'You need to break that habit,' she said. 'It's a dangerous tell.'

*

You're angry, maybe, that I could have been this callow. You think you would have seized the lever here, swung the tram over the empty track instead of towards the row of bound prisoners. You ask me why I wasn't more suspicious. But nat-urally I was suspicious. Adela was shifting, elusive – her very face was inconsistent. Her reasons were bad, half-veiled. Then again, whose upper management am I not describing? Who trusts their workplace? Who thinks their job is on the side of right? They fed us all poison from a bottle marked 'prestige' and we developed a high tolerance for bitterness. I would have been more frightened if the pressure lifted, like an indoor cat struck by sudden rain.

*

Navy blue nights wrapped the glum and shortening days like a bandage. Fine capillaries of winter threaded through the autumn air.

Because Graham lived with me – because he was the parameters of my life – I ceased to think of him as a man who was supposed to be dead. He was real to me. He got me into very real trouble. Shortly after my meeting with Adela, he put Arthur on the back of his motorbike and they sped over the boundary lines into the countryside, where they spent the day picking sloes for sloe gin and treading in mud and I spent the day panicking about the Brigadier finding them. Adela gave me a dressing down for failing to ensure he had requested permission to leave. She was tonally indistinguishable from a parent reminding their bee-stung toddler that they'd told them not to shred the flowers.

I gave Graham history's squeakiest bollocking. He hardly paid it attention. He wanted to know how it was possible for the Ministry to know that he had crossed the boundary, or indeed where he was, and I was tongue-tied.

'Don't worry about it,' I muttered.

'I wasn't, but I will from now on,' he said.

Life is a series of slamming doors. We make irrevocable decisions every day. A twelve-second delay, a slip of the tongue, and suddenly your life is on a new road. I wonder what the winter of the bridge year would have looked like if I hadn't frosted Simellia, or if I'd been less sceptical of Quentin. I hardly dare linger on the ways I changed Graham, forcing him down strange tracks as I uttered a new word or concept with accidentally Edenic significance.

You can't trauma-proof life and you can't hurt-proof your relationships. You have to accept you will cause harm to yourself and others. But you can also fuck up, really badly, and not learn anything from it except that you fucked up. It's the same with oppression. You don't gain any special knowledge from being marginalised. But you do gain something from stepping outside your hurt and examining the scaffolding of your oppression. You'll find the weak joints, the things you can kick in. When I look back at myself on the bridge year, I see that I thought I was doing something constructive, escaping exploitation by becoming exceptional. In fact, what I was doing was squeezing my eyes shut and singing *la la la* at the gathering darkness, as if the gathering darkness cared that I couldn't see it.

*

One evening in early November I came home to the luscious mingled smells of cooking and smoking. Graham was sitting at the dining table with a cigarette between his lips, tapping at a laptop. He no longer needed several minutes to find the letter M, but he typed with his index fingers alone, pecking out sentences.

'Hello. That smells nice. What is it?'

'Hello. It's stock for pho.'

'Phở.'

'Fur.'

'Close enough.'

Graham had developed an interest in Southeast Asian food. He asked me questions about what my mother cooked, ferrying tiny melamine bowls under my mouth to check flavours. Sometimes I saw the same concentration on his face as when he sketched the alien shapes of the transmission towers. He took in anecdotes about my childhood meals as if they would contribute to a portrait of a whole woman. He ignored the fact that mostly I cooked assorted chicken pieces on rice. I could tell him things about galangal, and he found that very profound.

I glanced into the saucepan.

'Should it be boiling?'

'Oh – no – could you turn it down, please?'

'Done. What are you doing?'

'Some form of naval college examination,' he said diffidently.

'Oh,' I said, equally diffidently, and poked at the broth.

At the end of the bridge year, the expats had to begin the next stage of assimilation – they had to get jobs. He wanted to rejoin the Navy, despite its unrecognisable modernisation. I wanted him in a role that didn't require him to be at sea for months, possibly years, at a time. It was too soon, I told myself. Whatever Adela said he wasn't ready, he'd barely left London, let alone land. But I wanted him to stay for other reasons too. It was humiliating to know that about myself and to say nothing into his implacable placidity.

I wandered over to look at the screen and got a shock. On the laptop was a segment, not (despite what the browser's address bar said) from a Navy-issue proficiency test, but from one of the field agent exams. I recognised it – I'd failed it twice during my stint in Languages.

It occurred to me that a field agent who didn't set off scanners, who might be undetectable by modern technology, would be a boon to the field. I thought of the strange slack he'd been granted, his welcome on the shooting ranges, the indulgence he'd been shown as he wandered around the Ministry asking people what they were doing, and why, and how.

I didn't realise I was falling back in horror until I saw the wall become the ceiling.

'Here – what's wrong—'

He caught me and it was, immediately, the most he had ever touched me. My nails sank into his wool-clad upper arm.

'Nothing . . . dizzy spell . . .'

'Sit down.'

'No. I don't need to. It's all right. I'm all right.'

I wasn't all right. At close range, I could smell his skin, even through the cigarette smoke. His grip on me loosened. His hands hovered along my back, lighter than the passage of dragon-flies over water.

'I am going to ash on you,' he murmured.

'Put it out.'

One hand flattened between my shoulder blades. The other dispatched the cigarette.

'Can you stand?'

'Yes.'

'Might you . . . unhook your claws, then?'

'Oh. Sorry.'

'It's all right.'

This was also the most I had ever touched him and I wondered if he had noticed, if he had been measuring touch the way I had.

In the background, Graham's laptop had been providing an inappropriate soundtrack (Motown again). It clocked into its next track, which was the Beatles cover of 'You've Really Got a Hold on Me'. I started laughing – partly because it was the most ludicrous song that could play at that moment, and partly because it felt quintessentially Victorian of him to hate The Beatles, which he did.

'Oh, it's these awful caterwaulers,' he said, dropping his hands.

I laughed again. I wanted to think about anything other than Graham as a field agent at the Ministry.

'They're good! This version's better than the original. Better for dancing.'

He raised an eyebrow. 'It is impossible to dance to this appalling wailing.'

'It isn't. Here.'

I moved a hand up to his shoulder. He hesitated with his whole body, like a piece of paper lifting abruptly in the wind. It passed. He took my other hand and touched my waist with a heart-breaking vagueness.

'See?'

'This is not dancing. This is – swaying.'

'And even that you're doing off-rhythm.'

He sighed. God, he was a dreadful dancer. Stiff and keyless. Victims of hangings kicked with more vim. I'd never in my life wanted anyone as badly as I wanted him.

We drifted across the kitchen and he spun me, missing every beat in the song. When he drew me back in, he held me more firmly. The tips of his fingers tested the small of my back. I could see the green rings in his eyes, vivid and strange as aurora borealis.

'You're a musician. How can you have no sense of time-keeping?'

'You are a larger instrument than a flute.'

'I bet you say that to all the girls.'

He tugged me suddenly towards him and my heart jumped into my throat. I made a noise. In fact, I said, 'woof'. Later that night I'd lie in bed with my fists balled up by my temples, thinking bitterly, *fucking 'woof'*.

He was so close I couldn't make out the individual features of his face – just the curve of his mouth, softened by a small smile. He lowered his head and I felt his breath stir the hair by my ear.

'Behave yourself,' he said. 'Or I will put you in the stock.'
Then he let me go.

*

Christmas was coming in, the way it does in London – flat rain, flat wind and the folding down of the horizons. The city looked like it was painted by a lesser Impressionist. Things died in their usual way: the plants, the sunlight.

I was at the Ministry when we got the weather warning, running through the pornography protocols with the Wellness team assigned to Graham. We all had access to the expats' internet search histories. Arthur Googled so much ('macarena', 'brewdog', 'clubbing', 'ballroom', 'vogue', 'vogue dance', 'madonna', 'poppers', 'rimming') that Simellia had been referred to the Home Office deputation for their guidance on Adapting to Life in the UK. Margaret looked up naked women almost as much as Cardingham did, but she also looked at a lot of clothed women. She'd had a two-week stint as a 'Swiftie' but ran out of energy for the speed at which the discourse mutated and her basic disinterest in the music, much to Ralph's relief. She'd found out about film torrenting with alarming rapidity.

The reason that Graham was of especial interest to the Wellness team was that Graham had worked out that the laptop at his disposal was reporting to the Ministry. I'd been waiting with a mixture of dread and keen curiosity for his first pornographic search, which we'd been cautioned to expect and had material from the Wellness team to deal with the arrival of. It was a gruesome briefing. We had to notify Control imme-diately if the material contained children, animals or corpses, but were reminded that all the expats except Arthur came from eras in which the age of consent was twelve and marriage was not unheard of at fifteen. Violent pornography was not considered problematic (the Cardingham clause) but had to be accounted for alongside the ordinary behavioural reports and psych assessments. We did not have the option to have the contents of their X-rated browsing redacted – this defeated the purpose of monitoring them – but on-site counsellors, the Ministry assured us, were always available if we saw anything we found upsetting.

When Graham got online, as he did not call it, and learned to peck at the keyboard with the elegance and speed of a badly burned amphibian, I imagined what might turn up on my reports from the Ministry's search history database – *bosoms, tight-lacing, stockings* – and spasmed with embarrassment. I was sick on the anticipation that I'd learn he was sexually cracked in some way, or worse, only interested in blonde debutantes. One of his first searches was charmingly housewifely: *Most challenging recipes; How to make cheese soufflé; What is miso paste?; Where to buy miso paste?; How long has Japan been open to Europe?* A day or so after I'd read this report, I received another that listed the following search terms:

Hello horrible cat; Do you see all that I see?; Or do you read my mind for recipe ingredients?; Will you bring home coconut cream?

That the time stamp on these search terms suggested it had taken him a full six minutes to type this out did not undermine the sense he had slid his pawn to my queen. Yes – the evening I saw the first search, I'd bought miso paste on my homeward grocery shop, head empty as a scooped melon. I was so used to miso as a culinary concept that I didn't register my basket as subconsciously influenced; only Graham, dazzled by the Orient, noticed.

When I got home, he asked me, 'Well? Did you bring the coconut cream?' and smiled with real warmth at the way shame changed my posture. I could never eat miso anything again without tasting failure.

The psychoanalyst Graham worked with – or rather, withstood being asked questions by – was a Freudian. I found this charming and always made an effort to dress up nicely for debriefings with him, as I imagined that he had all sorts of crackpot ideas about women and I was hoping he'd diagnose me as a sexual sadist or something chic like that.

'Repression at this level can cause serious damage,' he was saying. 'More even than defensive othering, it could seriously inhibit Eighteen-forty-seven's ability to form meaningful relationships in this era.'

'Granted, but he knows we're watching.'

'Perhaps you haven't introduced him to incognito windows?'

'Of course I have. But we can still see those.'

'He doesn't need to know that. Frankly, I'm concerned that his methods for expressing need are *so* controlled. It suggests a profound trauma somewhere in his past, buried beyond processing. I'd like to go through the highlighted points in his biography . . .'

I thought of the Battle of Navarino – Graham would have been eighteen at the time, and would have witnessed such interesting sights as the cannon-disembowelled bodies of sailors hanging off the rigging – and then I thought about losing an entire life and home and family in less than a minute, and then I thought of my mother. Repression can be a useful tool for feeding your family, sending your children to school, *in spite of*—

'We've covered this material,' I said, at the same time as one of the operators stuck their head around the door and chirruped, 'Weather alert!'

'What's that?'

'Storm coming.'

'Shit. Thought we had until Tuesday?'

'They're saying it's coming now. You'd better get off home or you might not be able to get home. How're you getting home?'

'Bike.'

'Oof. I wouldn't.'

You don't become a regular cyclist in London without developing a carapace of 'fuck my haters', so I cycled home anyway. As the operator predicted, this was a mistake. The wind shook me like a beetle in a matchbox. After bashing myself against a number of surfaces, including the pavement, I hopped off and began walking my bike home.

It was full dark and starting to rain by the time I was about two miles from the house. Thunder sounded. The big cutlery cupboard in the sky had fallen off the wall.

Our street was in the early stages of overflow when I reached it. A lively river floor, applauding with raindrops, had replaced the road. I could make out the nauseous glimmer of high-vis jackets. There was shouting, some of it cheerful. The council had already delivered the sandbags – sent by trucks with wheels so big they looked like a rude joke – and people were fixing up domestic barricades. Blitz spirit, the newspapers called this sort of thing, as if either climate catastrophe or the Blitz was a national holiday. This stoic jollity was how we'd introduced the Second World War to the expats, by the way – Arthur had been so distressed to learn we'd gone in for global seconds that it seemed like the kindest option. We emphasised the scrappy heroism of Dunkirk, the selflessness of evacuee hosts, and, of course, the Blitz spirit. Still, we had not told them about the death camps.

Someone in the middle of the road, giving directions, had an outrageously powerful stormlight. I mermaided bad-temperedly towards the light. I was only really approaching this person so that I could be told off for biking and feel even worse. I was astonished when I heard, 'Oh! Poor drowned cat.'

'Graham?!'

He smiled at me from his private halo. 'Hello,' he said. 'I heard the storm warning on the radio and thought I'd better do something.'

'"Do something"?'

'Where'm I putting this lot, Mr Gore?' someone called from the truck.

Graham waded towards them. I followed – slowly, hampered by my bike.

'Where'd you get all this equipment?' I shouted to him.

'What's that?'

'The high-vis? That bloody great light?'

'Fantastic, isn't it? The walls need to be three foot at least, Anton.'

'Don't got enough bags for that.'

'Where's the driver? I'll speak to him—'

'Graham,' I said. He turned and smiled at me again, gallantry on automatic rerun.

'You'd better go inside,' he said. 'You'll catch a "cold" in those wet clothes.'

He swished towards the truck. The bike and I rattled after him. I felt like a compass experiencing a sudden shift in magnetic north.

'Graham. Is that Ministry gear? Why do you have it? *How* do you have it? Because I know very well you weren't issued it.'

'I thought it might be useful,' he said. That was all the explanation I got, because at this point a pipe must have exploded and the street turned into a waterslide.

*

We got through the storm with minimal damage to the neighbourhood. It was my first time realising we lived in a *neighbourhood*, not just in a Ministry former safehouse. Graham had been aware of the *neighbourhood* for longer than me – he knew, by name, several people in the street, our *neighbours*. He talked to them, which I thought was perverted. Between this and the number of unissued Ministry items I began to spot around the house, I realised I had not been keeping as close an eye on Graham as I should have been – or rather, I'd been paying attention to his affect and not his actions.

When Graham was theoretical to me and I'd been researching him as a dead man, I'd run across a blog post by a well-known Franklin expedition historian. It was about a missing chronometer, Arnold 294, which was listed as 'Lost in the Arctic regions with *Erebus*' in naval records despite having last been used on the *Beagle*, on the coast of Australia, in 1837. I knew Graham's service record like an alphabet, so I knew he'd been first lieutenant on the *Beagle* just before he was ordered to *Erebus*. The historian came to the same conclusion: Lieutenant (as he was then) Gore was the reason Arnold 294 vanished in the North.

There must be missing records, the historian suggested, because it would be very odd for Lieutenant Gore to have retained the chronometer. Early in our cohabitation, I asked Graham about the discrepancy and he put up a winsome smile.

'Oh,' he said, 'that was a terribly good chronometer.'

'So you applied for permission to keep it, or what? How did it work?'

'Well, sly cat,' said Graham, 'as you are always insisting, I *used my initiative*.'

I laughed so much that I forgot to push it. I should have learned my lesson from this conversation, but it seemed that no one else in Graham's life had, including his captains. People liked him and so they imagined that he agreed with them – all likeable people know how to be a flattering mirror – and he could make himself a perfect man of wax (I recalled, once again, Captain Fitzjames's pen portrait of *a very good officer, and the sweetest of tempers*). I had a vague sense that his belonging was conditional, and that it suited rather than behoved him to be allied with the Navy or the Empire or the Ministry, but I didn't think about this much further. He was allied to Graham Gore, he was pragmatic, and he seemed to like me. That was enough.

*

I was going to visit my parents for the week-long Christmas break – the only holiday the central bridge teams were granted. The expats, minus poor Anne Spencer, were repairing to a cottage on the Kent coast, with a couple of members of the Wellness team to oversee their festivities. To me, it sounded like a work social hastening to an apocalyptic event, but Graham visualised a cottage by the sea as a man who has walked through an abattoir visualised a scalding shower.

'It will be nice to see a fire made of fire. Walls made of wall,' he said.

'When men were real men, eh. What's this house made of then?'

'Plastic pipes and chipboard.'

A few days before we parted ways, he invited Margaret and Arthur over for dinner. He was making an extravagant seafood risotto, which called for both sparkling wine and brandy, when Arthur arrived.

'Hi, Arthur!'

'Hello, dear girl. I brought you a liquid apology.'

Arthur handed me a bottle of plum-coloured liquid.

'Sloe gin?'

'Sloe vodka! I'd never drunk vodka before. I thought it might be an interesting experiment . . . I *am* sorry Forty-seven and I got you into hot water when we went hawthorn-picking. I had no idea we'd crossed the boundary line. I just cling on and let him do the directions.'

I mumbled something vague and conciliatory, but fortunately Arthur was not nearly so curious as Graham about why the Ministry were able to track them to the three square feet they stood in; I think he was more embarrassed that he and Simellia hadn't ever hosted us, and probably never would.

Margaret arrived and collared me by the front door. She was dressed, with her usual eccentricity, in periwinkle velvet flares and a cashmere jumper embroidered with an angry-looking duck.

'Pledge you will not chide me,' she whispered, fastening her hand around my wrist.

'I'll pledge nothing of the sort. What have you done?'

'I have engaged "Tinder" on my "phone".'

'Maggie! You only *just* passed the acc exam.'

Margaret waved her phone at me. There was a slightly scuffed holographic sticker on the back, from some children's TV show aimed at stoned adults. It felt funny to live in a world where she knew what it was and I didn't.

'I'm wise enow to write love-letters,' she said. 'I have been so wise passing long. It is but a new medium.'

'What's the backstory the Ministry gave you? That you went to finishing school in Switzerland and now you're doolally?'

'Yes. I bestrode the mountains in my dirndl and carolled with the birds and sheep. Now the city miasmas have undone me and I am a scrambled egg in woman's casing.'

'Yeah, right, sounds plausible. Show me your profile, then. Huh. Well. That's a good pic. Quite . . . direct.'

'At least pledge not to mention to the men. You know well how those clodpoles mutter.'

I toppled her into the kitchen, still talking. Margaret was not looking forward to spending her Christmas in Cardingham's vicinity.

'Perhaps a pox will take him ere we leave the city. Or a "car" will snap his legs. Or—'

'That is very unchristian, Sixty-five,' said Graham gravely, handing her a glass of sparkling wine.

'I mark you did not offer to board with him.'

'Well, Arthur and I shared a room in Scotland. I know that his snoring is tolerable.'

Arthur blushed a bewildered pink and cleared his throat.

'I say, chaps, I brought along a fantastic little device. I think you'll find it interesting.'

He fumbled in his bag. He extracted two pieces of something which looked electronic, in a stolid 1980s sort of way, and connected them. A wireless whine filled the kitchen.

'Is that a theremin?' I asked.

'An adaptation,' said Arthur, proudly. 'Will you pass your hand along it?'

I waved my hand over the device's sensors. It squealed mournfully.

'Sixty-five, you try.'

Margaret stuck her hand into the theremin's sensor field. Nothing. I reached out and gently laid my hand over hers. The theremin sang wheezily. I pulled back, and it stopped.

'All right, Sixty-five . . . tell it you're there.'

Margaret tossed her shining hair over her shoulder and frowned at the theremin. After a few seconds, her hand trembled, and the theremin squeaked.

'I cannot master it so well,' she said, pulling back. 'Each time I reach for my "hereness" I fall back into my "thereness".'

Arthur hovered his hand over the charged space. The theremin stuttered between silence and song.

'You're controlling whether it can sense you?' I asked, amazed.

'Yes! It's not easy. As Maggie says, it's a bit of a bother to keep your "hereness" and "thereness" lined up.'

'How do you know how to control it?'

Margaret and Arthur exchanged glances. 'It's . . . hard to explain,' said Arthur. 'We didn't know we could feel it at all until we arrived here.'

Graham came over and stood between us. He ran his fingers through the air above the machine, as if dabbling them in a stream. The machine popped once but was otherwise silent.

'Is there any system to these noises?' he asked.

'It's just the C-major scale,' murmured Arthur. 'Starts on the left.'

Graham reached out with both hands and grimaced with concentration. He spread his fingers and bit his lower lip. Then, abrupt and cackling, came the opening notes of 'Greensleeves'. We burst out laughing and he treated the three of us to one of his rare, full-wattage, full-dimpled grins.

*

I took the slow train back to my family's house. The vague greys of the long London suburbs gave out onto tamed greenery and dual carriageways, to squat interminable supermarkets at the station edges and the bridges to towns without grandeur. The landscape abbreviated. Then I was home and the feeling of home closed in on me.

My sister had got back before me and she greeted me at the front door with a frown and soapy fists. 'The camping stove is leaking oil everywhere and I'm trying to wash the oil out,' she said, by way of explanation. 'Give me your bag. You look tired as hell.'

'Hello. Nice to see you too.'

On Christmas Eve, my family eat yao hon – Cambodian hotpot. The hotpot we keep warm at the table by means of an ancient camping stove; the discs of rice-paper for yao hon we soften in bowls filled with hot water, which more than one guest has mistaken for a finger bowl. From the dining room, I could hear my parents bickering over the camping stove's remains. I called, 'Hi Dad, hi Mai,' and there was only the barest modulation in their back and forth as they came into the hallway to hug me.

There were more piles of things around the house. The paperwork had started breeding in captivity. Plastic takeaway boxes stood on supra-cluttered surfaces, crammed with hand sanitisers, plasters, elastic bands, bottle openers and post-its covered in parental hieroglyphics. My sister jogged upstairs and underarm-bowled my bag into my bedroom. I heard the crash of a column of papers.

'How's the spying?' my dad asked jovially.

I flinched before I remembered: on my ascendance to the time-travel project, the Ministry had created a shell role for me in Languages, as a translator on a Top Secret project. My family assumed I'd been promoted to the role of Miss Money-penny.

'Yeah, good,' I said. 'Phone-tapping the innocent and that. Cleaning my gun at my desk and so on.'

'Do they give you a gun?' asked my mum, alarmed. 'Guns are dangerous, do you know?'

'It was a joke, Mai. I'm just taking the mick.'

'You make a mick with a gun?'

'Mai,' said my sister wearily. 'It's fine. She's just not very funny.'

'Okay,' said my mum philosophically.

My sister was ratty with me because, about ten days before, we'd fought, in the brief but explosive way that we did. She'd published, in a well-read online magazine, a story based on an incident from our childhood, of our mum accidentally leaving the handbrake off our parked car and the car rolling into a neighbour's Ford Astra. The neighbours came out to berate and threaten my mother in increasingly racially loaded ways – *dangerous, irresponsible, stupid woman can't understand me, what are you even saying, accent, gibbering, maybe it's different where you're from but here we have values*. My mother was distressed and her English deteriorated, which didn't help her case. When my sister and I ran out the front door to see what was going on, I started crying – I was nine or ten – and the neighbours claimed she'd pinched me to make me cry, for sympathy. They didn't let up until my dad, a white man, came ambling up the street, home from work. Suddenly they were happy to back off and see the insurance paperwork.

I hated this memory, had vaulted and bricked it up many years before, and I'd been horrified to see it written up, all our wounds open to the dirty world. I'd phoned my sister. 'Are you out of your fucking mind?' I barked. 'Do you think our

176

mother is material for your writing career? How could you be so selfish?'

My sister spiralled into aggressive defensiveness. Something something write what I want something something radical ugly truth something something vengeance in record something something our voices our narrative. 'You humiliated her,' I snarled back. 'You humiliated all of us.'

She'd hung up. This was our first time talking in person.

My sister maintained that her work was a sort of reclamation, a space-taking practice in protest of a childhood spent in squeezed spaces. That all she was telling was the truth, as if the Truth was a sort of purifier that turned mud and plasma into clean water by judicious application. I didn't know who read her writing, other than people who already agreed with her. To me, it felt like she'd chosen to hang a target around our necks. I didn't understand how anyone could find power in a show of vulnerability. Power was influence, was money, was the person holding the gun.

As I watched my family begin the complicated process of resuscitating the camping stove, I had a sense of terrific coldness, as if a wall had fallen away and left the room exposed to the December night. Perhaps I *should* have a gun? The Brigadier undoubtedly had one, maybe even Salese, and now I knew they were threats – or, at least, entirely unsanctioned. What had the Brigadier gleaned from his access to the Ministry? Did he know where my family lived? My mother, who had seen enough terror for six lifetimes? My father, so anxious about conflict he hoarded decade-old parking tickets? My sister, who thought herself brave, who thought rolling soft side up would shame the dominant animal? Was I safe? Wasn't I Ministry?

*

The expats texted me over the Christmas break. Arthur sent me multiple texts that he persisted in writing as telegrams (47 + BRIAN ON FLUTE + GUITAR STOP WOT A RACKET STOP ATTEMPTED CAYLEE STOP OBVIOUS MISSPELLING STOP ABSOLUTE DELIGHT END), and jolly, out-of-focus shots of the assorted company. Margaret rarely texted, but she sent me strange, seductive photos of things that had interested her: the sheen of the firelight on a broken tree bauble, a bowl of oranges, a speckled mirror that held a reflection of the moon.

I received only one text from Graham, who had turned his phone on for the occasion.

Dear horrid cat,
Being unused to and out of practice with this machine, I must make this brief. We are having a splendid, if somewhat pagan, time. I have strongarmed the company into attending the midnight service this evening. 65 cannot and will not behave. 16 and I have taken over the cooking of the trimmings but we dare not attempt the bird. I will telephone you on Christmas Day, to ensure you are in one piece. This missive took me half an hour to write.
    Believe me to be your affectionate friend,
    G.G.

He didn't call until late in the afternoon. I'd spent the day in a food torpor, playing with a pretty golden pendant in the shape of a striding hen that lay just under my collarbones. It was a Christmas gift from him. The note that accompanied it explained, in his idling cursive, that it was chicken necklace, friend to chicken bag. I'd given him a silk aviator scarf, and a copy of *The Spy Who Came in from the Cold*, since he was on his twelfth re-read of *Rogue Male*.

'Happy Christmas!'

'Happy Christmas. You sound rather languid. Did I wake you?'

'No, no. I always spend Christmas in a bit of a coma. Thank you for the beautiful necklace.'

'You're welcome.'

'I like the way the chicken is running.'

'She is on her way to an important meeting, as you so often seem to be.'

I heard the soft scratch of a lighter, then paper crackling with flame, then his inhale.

'Are you outside? I can hear you smoking.'

'Oh, can you? I'm sorry, how rude of me. But please don't make me put this cigarette out.'

'Wouldn't dream of it. You've got the hang of using the phone, then.'

I heard him draw on the cigarette. 'It's certainly less complicated than navigating you in person,' he said amiably.

'Oh yeah?'

'When you're standing before me with your – your – funny little mouth.'

That startled us both into silence. He cleared his throat and said, 'Well. It's pleasant to just – talk to you. Though it seems I can get even that wrong.'

'Oh no, you – I mean I'm – that is – er – are you having fun?'

'Yes. Are you?'

I breathed out, relieved and disappointed. 'Yeah, surprisingly. It's much more fun to argue with my family in person instead of in my head. Oh . . .'

He exhaled quickly. 'Ah,' he said. 'Don't feel awkward.

Everyone here has lost a family. We have jury-rigged a new one. It's almost like Christmas in the wardroom.'

'That's . . . good.'

'What sort of people are they? Your family?'

'Oh, very ordinary.'

'That's not true, I am sure. I wish you would tell me more about your mother's people. Do they have special traditions at Christmas?'

'Well, they're Buddhist. So, no.'

'Oh. Well. Is your family's home in the place where you grew up?'

'Yeah, we moved here when I was eight and they've been here ever since.'

'You must have been a strange little girl.'

'How dare you.'

'I can hear in your voice that you are smiling,' he said. 'What is it like there?'

'We're close to a forest. About a mile from a lovely lake I used to paddle in during the summer. I've been hissed at by several generations of geese.'

There were a few seconds of silence on the other end, and I thought he'd lost connection, until he said, 'I'm smiling too.'

'Oh? My ears aren't quite as good as yours, I can't hear it.'

'I will endeavour to smile louder.' He broke off, and huffed softly down the phone, a noise between a sigh and a laugh. 'You know, when you are out of my sight, I fear I've imagined you. And I—'

My heartbeat skittered. He coughed unnaturally and seemed to reconsider his train of thought. 'Tell me what it was like, growing up there.'

'Well,' I said, 'what do you want to know about?'
'Anything. Everything.'

*

Every time I told Graham something – about myself, about my family, about my experience of the world we shared – I was trying to occupy space in his head. I had ideas for the shape I should take in his imagination. I told him only what I wanted him to know and believe about me. But afterwards, I'd sometimes feel ill, like I was glutted on sweetmeats and dizzy with wine. It seemed a reckless indulgence: to have the appetite to admit, for certain, what I was and was not.

The great project of Empire was to categorise: owned and owner, coloniser and colonised, *évolué* and barbarian, mine and yours. I inherited these taxonomies. This, I think, was the reason I played fuck-about-Fred with my ethnic identity as much as I could. 'They' are still in charge and even when 'they' are saying *marginalised* instead of *mongoloid* they are still acknowledging that we are an issue to be dealt with. When would it be my turn to hold the carrot and stick? My sister had grandiose chat about dismantling the carrot-stick complex altogether, but this manifested in being upset all the time, tweeting enthusiastically about debut authors of colour who never seemed to publish second novels once the publicity cycle ended, and being underpaid.

Loyalty and obedience are fostered by stories. The Ministry and its satellites were staffed by people who believed they'd smoke one last jaunty cigarette in the eye of a gun. The truth was that we were shackled to the idea that the orders were good and the job was good. *Keep calm* is just another order like *Shoot that man* or *Delete the rest*. We carry on. Most of us would beg a bullet for kindness. Graham, I think, was one of the few people I'd ever met who could face death with that defiant cigarette, and that was partly because he was a nervous smoker.

Maybe I was tired of stories, telling them and hearing them. I thought the dream was to be post-: post-modern, post-captain, post-racial. Everyone wanted me to talk about Cambodia and I had nothing to teach them about Cambodia. If you learn something about Cambodia from this account, that's on you. When Graham was still in my life, I stared at myself in the mirror a lot, trying to see myself as a stranger. I had a non-internalised relationship with my face. It was not unusual for me to look at my face and think *What on earth is that?* It bored me not to look the same as whoever I was with – isn't that the whole point of being mixed-race? Oh England, England! The thing you do best is tell a story about yourself. Graham Gore went to the Arctic believing that a noble death is possible because of all those stories and then he became a story. Oh England, you wanted to make stories out of me.

When I first joined the Ministry and they'd pressed me through HR, a woman ran her finger down the column with my family history. 'What was it like growing up with that?' she asked. She meant it all: Pol Pot Noodle jokes on first dates, my aunt's crying jags, a stupa with no ashes, Gary Glitter, Agent Orange, we loved Angkor Wat, regime change, not knowing where the bodies were, Princess Diana, landmines, the passport in my mother's drawer, my mother's nightmares, fucking chink, you don't look it, dragon ladies, fucking paki, Tuol Sleng was a school, Saloth Sar was a teacher, my grandfather's medals, the firing squad, my uncle's trembling hands, it's on my bucket list, Brother Number One, I've got a thing for Latinas, the killing fields, *The Killing Fields* (1984), Angelina Jolie, do you mean Cameroonian? do you mean Vietnamese? will you say your name again for me?

I considered.

'I don't know,' I said. 'What was it like growing up without it?'

VI

The group's leaders — one old man and two younger hunters — request permission to board *Erebus*. At least, this is true as far as anyone can gather. Franklin's expedition failed to travel with an interpreter, and it is down to Captain Crozier of *Terror* to translate. He doesn't speak the same dialect as these Esquimaux, and hazards on fragments of shared vocabulary.

A party of ten natives come aboard. They don't act as the natives usually do — curious, self-possessed, roaming the ship, teasing the men, miming trade. They cluster on the quarterdeck and listen with blank faces while Crozier fumbles lugubriously through apologies. Gillies and Des Voeux have laid gifts of needles, tobacco, mirrors and buttons at their feet. No knives.

Eventually Crozier stumps back to the command of *Erebus*, who hover in a complementary cluster.

'Gore,' he says quietly.

'Sir.'

'The man's wife wants to look at you.'

'The man's——?'

'Wife. He was married.' He flicks his soft grey eyes up. Steel in the iris. 'No children, you may be relieved to hear.'

Gore obediently steps forward.

The wife — the widow — is at the front of the group. She is small, a bantam woman. Black hair. Brown skin, bright and clean. Cheeks vivid with last night's tears. Her eyes are dry and her lashes grow downwards, giving her stare a strangely veiled effect. Her mouth is very beautiful, a colour that Gore will remember and try to name for a long time afterwards. She looks at him. It's a look that puts him against the horizon: not insignificant, but like something that can be pressed up by thumb.

'I'm sorry,' he says, in English, because he forgot to ask Crozier how to say it in her language. She looks at him.

He should get to his knees. Offer his throat to the edge of her palm. Or maybe he should offer her his hand, to replace the hands of her husband. Brief wildness beats in his skull. Perhaps, after a manhood with no final home, fixing makeshift families in multiple wardrooms, killing and pinning land to maps, God has cast him on the shore by this woman. Years of his finger on the trigger to make sense of her expression.

'I'm sorry,' he repeats. She looks at him. After the group leave, taking their gifts, the stare will linger on his body. When he washes up in his cabin that night, he feels it slip under his shirt, growing into his skin.

Chapter Six

I returned home in the new year. Something had shifted in the narrow landscape of the house. The rooms felt connected where they had felt merely contiguous. Graham smiled at me sometimes, a vague confused smile as if I was a task he needed to complete but had forgotten the genesis of. One afternoon in the kitchen he took me by the shoulders and moved me so that he could get to the cups. He touched me so rarely that he might as well have wrapped my hair around his fist and cut it off with sewing scissors. I felt him on me all afternoon.

This increase in pleasant vagueness was a typically Graham response to intense internal pressure. The Ministry, in light of his repeated requests to rejoin the Royal Navy, was granting him admission into the field agent training programme, under close supervision. Cardingham, a career soldier, was also retraining for the field. We had to create identities and back-stories for both of them, generating a migraine-inducing number of fake files. Cardingham was forced to retake the acclimatisation exam. The whole set-up was a nervy compromise with Defence, details still being darned and sellotaped even as it was announced to the bridge teams.

'It's better that we continue to work closely with Eighteen-forty-seven,' Adela had said, 'given that he seems likely to survive the year.'

'So he's staying in London?'

'He'll have to live independently, of course. Out of bridge accommodation.'

'But he'll stay.'

I should have developed tinnitus from the alarm bells. Why were the Ministry so interested in making Graham and Cardingham field-worthy? Why weren't they expending the same energy on Margaret and Arthur? But all I heard was that Graham was staying. I'd been so thrilled I'd torn a flake of skin from my thumb with pinced nails. 'That's still a tell,' said Adela, but she did a DVD-player motion with her mouth and chin that was probably a smile.

*

At the crux of all the time-travel hypotheses was the question: how do you measure a person? Graham scored very highly on spatial reasoning tests and well on verbal reasoning tests. He was, according to his psychoanalyst, dangerously repressed; but then again, according to the acclimatisation examiners, he was gregarious and confident. He was the eldest of five children, after the death of his older brother at sea. He was an inch below average height, though in his own era he had been two inches above it. He had hazel eyes, a mass of curly dark hair, and a remarkable nose. He was thirty-seven years old and had been thirty-seven for nearly two hundred years. I expect, when you finish this account, that you will have a clear image of him, enough to pastiche and anticipate him. I'm glad of it. I need him to be alive to someone else.

Over the course of the bridge year, I amassed enough

statistical information about Graham that I could have pro-grammed a convincing Graham Gore AI. I dreamt along these lines, occasionally. My hands on silicone flesh. Keeping it somewhere where I could always see it, keeping it clean, forearm-deep in its motherboards. The dreams always went rancid when I tried to mimic Graham's voice, because I would dream him cool and martial, slur-saying and gun-shooting, Oxford English with a dash of naval salt, and he wasn't like that. It was some of what he was like, but not all.

I had *access to his file*, as we say. To have *access to a file* on someone is a simultaneously erotic and deadening experience. When you study a person, as I studied Graham, you enter a pornographic fugue state. All the things that should be intimate become molecular. Their body, which you have never touched, lies against the back of your eyelids every night. You begin to know them, except time always leaves you one moment behind, and so you have to know them more, more and more, chasing them through time, at the limit where their life meets their future, and you need to have it, 360 degrees of what they see and feel and sense, or else your file is incomplete. Who did they love, before you? What hurt them the most? What will cause the most useful harm?

I was obsessed with him. I see that now. I was doing my job and I loved my job. Do you understand what I mean?

*

'I'm going to take Maggie clubbing,' I announced one afternoon. Graham and I were in the kitchen. He was flicking through a cookbook. There was a shelf of cookbooks in the kitchen. I had never used any of them.

'Very good. I am not sure whether to warn her of your bad influence or warn you of hers.'

'Maybe you could just give us your blessing to misbehave.'

'I withhold my blessings. How do you pronounce this word, please?'

'Sichuan. Oh. Graham, you *know* you can't handle spice.'

'Bold new frontiers. You can play a mournful violin while I expire of the "explorer's disease".'

'The . . . ?'

'Indigestion.'

Margaret, alone of the expats, had tried to develop a circle of friends outside of the Ministry, mostly people she met through apps I'd never heard of, Lex and Zoe and so on. The Ministry had subtly and then overtly discouraged this. Margaret was too much of a liability – she sounded too bizarre and she ran her mouth. Besides which, she picked up anti-establishment lesbian anarchists (whatever she or they thought those words meant) with suspicious frequency. She was under flintily compassionate surveillance from the Wellness team.

Ralph was still her bridge, but he found her so challenging that I'd quietly suggested to Adela that I might cross-report on Margaret. This was partly because I wanted to impress Adela. Since our conversation about Quentin, she'd taken me under her armoured wing. It was eye-opening. I craved her way of seeming so steel-plated that it left no obvious vulnerability. Perhaps unsurprisingly for a woman whose mother's trauma had shaped so much of her inner landscape, I imprinted on my intense female boss big-time.

But, anyway, Margaret liked me. She might invite me to join her and Arthur – whom she adored and bullied lovingly – for a gallery visit or a game of mini-golf while Graham was away at the Ministry, preparing to retrain for the field. (Arthur loved mini-golf, and over the course of the expat year wrote a really rather funny series of reviews masquerading as assimilation test material of the mini-golf courses of London. I don't think Arthur understood the terms kitsch or camp, but they delighted him. I once witnessed him doubled over, tears of laughter sparkling on his cheeks, because a ball had to be putted inside a miniature Ferris wheel and travel all the way round, to drop into a hole.)

Margaret went to the cinema twice a week, religiously. She bounced around music venues looking for obsessions. She was probably London's last avid reader of *Time Out*. She would often invite me along. Not always – Margaret also liked to be a woman wafting through the city alone – she hadn't had much opportunity to live unstructured time back in the seventeenth century. But we might go out together and see a riot grrrl punk band whose drummer she'd been texting; and then I, Ministry operative, would have to supervise them both at dinner (Margaret had a mania for customisable pizzas with nonsense toppings); then Margaret might see that the drummer and I were one barbed sentence away from a fight about politics which she didn't understand. She'd say her goodnights and take me for a walk to point at neon signs and lavish window displays and bubble tea shops and demand playfully of me: How? but also, Why? She was work and play for me. I liked Margaret. Being around her made me want to run across zebra crossings without looking, that sort of thing, I found everything funnier than it was, et cetera.

We planned our clubbing outing with military precision. She sent me a dozen photos of different outfits. She'd learned the grammar of the mirror selfie. The crop top!!!!!!!! I texted, though I removed every exclamation mark but one before I sent the message.

We arranged to meet Arthur and Graham for a drink in Dalston first – a situation so twenty-first century I felt not a little proud of their progress. Margaret and Arthur were already drinking when we arrived. They had both ordered stupid-looking cocktails.

'I tried to stop her—' Arthur began.

'Look here! 'Tis known as "Sex on the Beach"! The spark behind the taps did take such care over its compaction, I must assume it is a potion to summon its namesake.'

'Well,' I said, sitting down, 'it's made with cranberry juice, which is supposed to be good for UTIs, which is what you're going to get if you have sex on an English beach.'

'"UTI"?' asked Margaret. 'Forty-seven! Sit down! Stop rubbing at your temples with that malodorous expression.'

'Everyone is so cruel to me,' said Graham, deadpan, 'even though I'm very handsome and brave and I have never done anything wrong. Sixty-five, where are the rest of your clothes?'

'Banished. I am never more bravely clad than when I go sky-clad.'

I started to laugh, a real, happy, unglamorous laugh. As true laughter does, it summoned smiles from the others. Margaret leant towards me, grinning, and I saw Graham catch Arthur's eye and roll his. It was a moment among moments, but everyone was held in it, captured in a small and easy joy. I return again and again to this memory. It's proof, you see. Not everything I did was wrong.

*

Graham's passage from petri dish to lab coat, as it were, was marked by a small, pretty ceremony that required No. 1 dress blues, alongside twenty-six other new agents who were joining, variously, from the Army, the Air Force, the police and the civil service. On the day of the ceremony, the sky was crisp cerulean, and the grass was rimed with silver. The entire city looked like an extravagant piece of confectionery, particularly in the Westminster courtyard where uniformed recruits were lined up. All around us, the buildings reared up and leant down. A breeze scrubbed the courtyard, made its colours fresh and raw.

At the bark of a man in epaulettes, the procession shifted, and I saw Graham – light glinting from the polished brim of his cap – standing to attention like a cat stretching for an upper shelf – his narrow hips and his faint smile – *there he is* – that magnificent topmast sail of a nose – *there he is* – I saw him in the highlights that the sun picked out – the sword at his waist, the shiny black shoes – *there he is, there he is.* I wish I could tell you how it felt to see him. He'd always lived inside me, years before I'd known him. I'd been trained to love him.

'Don't turn around,' hissed a familiar voice behind me.

I flinched so hard that my shoulder blades almost met. I blushed too. Internal rhapsodising makes people hold their heads funny. Probably I'd been giving it away.

'I said don't turn around.'

'I didn't,' I seethed. 'Jesus.'

'Quiet!'

'Quentin,' I muttered, 'where the fuck have you been?'

'*Shh.*'

This didn't come from behind me, but beside me – a woman about my age in a much more expensive coat and weirdly greenish blonde hair. Everyone in the crowd was intent on the ceremony, their faces locked forward.

'Put your hands behind you,' whispered Quentin into the back of my head. He'd moved closer. He bustled against me, as people in crowds do. It was just authentic enough to be annoying.

'Right.'

'Take this. Carefully. Do *not* lose it.'

He pressed what felt like a piece of card into my palm. Its edge dug into my lifeline. I shuffled it across my hips and tried to discreetly karate-chop it into my bag. It struggled to fit.

'Why is your bag shaped liked a chicken?'

'Don't.'

I punched and bullied the card into chicken bag. Poor chicken bag. It looked like a kebab by the time I was done.

Another imperceptible shift – easily dismissed as someone inching towards a better view – and Quentin was beside me. His cheek was streaked with what I assumed was psoriasis and his chin was grizzled with a strange, not quite organic patchy stubble.

'You look . . . tired,' I murmured.

'Don't try to speak out of the corner of your mouth like that. Too obvious.'

'Mm?'

'Just. Turn and talk to me. Like I'm a stranger in the crowd. Lower your shoulders. Look more relaxed. This stuff on my face throws off the recognition software.'

'Oh.'

I tilted my head towards him, polite as a cockatoo. I hoped it looked realistic.

'Quentin,' I murmured, 'what's going on? Has Genghis Khan broken through the time-door from the past or something?'

'Not the past. I don't think from the past. What have you been told about the time-door?'

'"None of your business", as far as I recall.'

I turned to look at him. He smiled – a real, rueful smile that made his eyes crinkle. Then there was a noise like a snapping wishbone and his head jerked.

'Quentin?' I muttered. He pitched forward and I caught him instinctively. Beside me, the woman with greenish hair started screaming, a single word, like a broken fire alarm:

'Gun! Gun! Gun!'

Blood was spurting from Quentin's temple, brilliantly crimson. Someone shoved against me and I lost my grip on him. He slid downwards and his body vanished like he was going underwater. Screams rose up all around me. If you've ever been in a terrified crowd, you won't forget it. People in real terror scream in a long, flat, oddly toneless way.

Another rough push and I was staggering sideways. My ankle rolled and I clawed at the nearest pair of shoulders for balance. The crowd was scrambling for the gates. Bodies bashed my ribs. I caught an elbow in the stomach and heaved. Everyone was running in a crouch, covering their heads. I righted myself, wiped red matter off my cheek, and lumbered forwards.

*

Time dilated. There were sirens and blue lights seemingly instantaneously, but I couldn't be persuaded to let go of a bollard for hours and hours (it transpired to be slightly less than a minute). I'd worn my black stilettos for the ceremony and one of the heels had snapped. I was standing lopsided in a farce of my very own.

'Can you tell me what you saw?' asked a uniform in front of me. In-house security, I think. The police of the police.

'Must have been a sniper,' I managed.

'Sorry?'

'Sniper,' I repeated, with difficulty. I was close to incomprehensible because my teeth were chattering so hard.

'Did you see the sniper?'

'No. Angle.'

The uniform turned away. 'Can I get a shock blanket for this lady, please?' she shouted to the paramedics. She turned back to me and said, 'Do you want to sit down, madam?'

I thought of Quentin going under. Had my foot rolled on the bony yield of his wrist? I bit my inside cheek and tasted iron.

'No. Thank you,' I said. 'I think it was a sniper on the roof. Based on the angle of entry. I was standing in Section A.'

I spat this out, gristle and bark, and she gave me a refrigerated reappraisal.

'Are you friends and family?'

'I'm Ministry.'

Over her shoulder, I could see Graham striding towards us, his face blank. A police officer jolted into his path and tried to stop him; he simply stepped around them. When he reached me, he clapped a hand on my shoulder and jerked me towards him.

'Are you hurt?' he asked flatly.

'No.'

'Excuse me, sir, it's medical personnel onl—'

'Give me your bag,' he said.

I gave him chicken bag and he slung the strap across his body. The chicken perched absurdly on his waist. He looked me up and down, then got onto one knee and grasped my ankle.

'Your shoe.'

'It's broken.'

'Step out of this one and I'll snap the other heel. Or else you will fall over.'

'Sir—' said the uniform heatedly. We ignored her. I kicked my shoe off and put my stockinged foot on his thigh. He broke the heel and then guided my foot back into the aftermath. On the top of his head was a patch, smaller than the base of a wineglass, where his riotous black curls had started to thin. When he looked up at me, I was struck by the starkness of his crow's feet. It unnerved me to see how human a body he inhabited.

'My hero,' I muttered.

He smiled coldly. 'Not this time,' he said.

*

Quentin died at the scene, I was told, though I knew that the moment I'd caught him; he'd had the slack weight of an abandoned thing. At least his death was instantaneous.

I was the last person to speak to him before he was killed, and so I was questioned for hours at the discretion of the police and the Ministry. Graham was sent home under supervision.

Graham took my bag with him. I didn't think to take it back from him because I was too busy blinking back the memory of Quentin's face dropping. I assumed the item that Quentin pushed into my hands would come up in my interrogation, until one of the officers let slip that there had been a CCTV malfunction, and the entire courtyard was unmonitored for the duration of the ceremony. I didn't mention it. I had enough to think about. The pretty way that blood fountains from a head wound. The way Quentin had smelled, hauntingly, of cologne.

When I got home, I was curdling with exhaustion. I'd stress-sweated and the sour smell had leaked through to my jacket. My stockings, apparently in sympathy with the rest of my mood, had laddered on both legs. I shut the front door and Graham came out of the kitchen, chased by whiffs of slow-cooked tomato broth, garlic and balsamic vinegar.

'Hello. Are you hungry?' he asked lightly.

I burst into tears. It seemed a proportionate reaction. I got onto the floor, very slowly, kneecaps first, and wept.

'Oh,' he said.

He stood over me for a few moments, then awkwardly squatted down beside me.

'Cigarette?'

He didn't wait for an answer, but lit two between his lips, then lifted my chin and poked one into my mouth. He settled back against the wall of the hallway and we smoked, me through tears, he through silence.

I wiped my nose roughly on my cuffs – he didn't comment – and I croaked, 'You've seen people die.'

'Yes.'

'In battle?'

'Or in the aftermath. On long voyages, too, but – I think you are asking me about violent death.'

'Am I supposed to feel like I've thrown up, but on the inside of my skin?'

He looked around for somewhere to ash. Chicken bag was by the door – he must have dropped it there, awaiting my attention – and he stretched out a leg to hook the strap and drag it closer.

'Very vivid,' he said, unzipping the chicken. 'No, you're not reacting wrongly or hysterically. It's understandable that you are distressed, especially if you've never witnessed sudden death before.'

'He just. Went. One minute looking at me. And then.'

'Mm. May I use this?'

He was flourishing a recyclable document holder, misshapen

from being mashed into chicken bag, which fastened with cardboard flaps. Its DO NOT BEND legend was creased into cryptic poetry. When I nodded distractedly, he tore a long strip from the flap and fashioned a small cup for the ash, which he caught just in time.

'Here,' he said – holding it up to me like a man trying to feed a cat a treat – but I was peering into the document holder. There was a distinctive manila folder in there, rattling with papers.

'You're going to burn your skirt,' he said, tugging the cigarette from my lips.

I wasn't listening. I was staring at the folder. It was an incident report, dated eighteen months before the time-travel project began. When I opened it and pulled out the papers, I found it detailed a 'disturbance' in a shuttered youth centre in south London. Five local teenagers. They'd been there engaging in *criminal activity* – poppers, breakdancing and a boom box in the main hall. They'd broken in through a window because the youth centre had been closed for six months. Neighbours had reported loud music and laughter, then a beam of blue light, and screams. The police had gone in, eventually, to deal with anticipated *gang violence*.

According to the incident report, what the police had found were bodies, serrated with massive, bizarre injuries, and a glowing blue door. The doorway was generated by some form of machine, which was visible through it. The police had assumed something involving capital-T Terrorism had taken place, and had called MI5, who sent field agents. A brave officer reached through the doorway and seized the machine, which they must have thought was a weapon. The door immediately collapsed, like a knot undone by a judicious tug on the rope. This, I learned, was how the Ministry received the power of time-travel. Not through invention but through the fine British tradition of finders-keepers.

At the bottom of the report was a handwritten addendum.

Field agent Quentin Carroll has raised several internal complaints about the disposal of the bodies of the deceased minors. Recommend that he be kept under surveillance.

I laughed miserably. Quentin had been right. What a way to prove a point.

*

The Ministry launched an internal investigation. The Ministry was cooperating with the intelligence services. The Ministry encouraged its affected employees to seek assistance from the on-site counsellors.

One of the things we'd abandoned on joining the time-travel project – in addition to annual leave allowance and choice of accommodation – was trade union membership. The Ministry wouldn't recognise any of the existing unions. There was some semantic trickery that meant we weren't technically managers and so couldn't join the FDA, and as time-travel was too newly established and too secret an industry we couldn't join the PCS. As a ministry we were small, we made consistent eye-contact with most of our colleagues. Our personal lives were our work lives. We were that awful thing: a *family*. One doesn't unionise in a family, because from whom would you be making demands?

It was bad, though, after Quentin. I had no one I could talk to who wasn't feeding my words to the paperwork. So I wrote report after report, sat through interrogation after interrogation, with my heart clear and grey, like rinsed fog.

Adela summoned me to headquarters four days after Quentin's

death. She spoke to me with a new intimacy. This was not the same as being spoken to with affection.

'There will be twenty-four-hour guards on the bridge houses,' she said. 'We're revoking movement privileges for the expats—'

'No.'

'Yes. We're still working to ascertain what relationship Quentin had with the Brigadier and Salese, but until we do, we must assume the expats are in danger. You need to keep Eighteen-forty-seven close.'

Adela's voice contracted on that last sentence. She wiped her gaze, concentrated in her one working eye, up and down my face, to see if I'd noticed, and continued, 'Our first priority is protecting the expats and the time-door. The time-door has been moved to a secure location. I suggest you retake the Physical Aptitude Assessment, and then we can work on your lateral reasoning scores—'

'I've failed the field exams twice,' I said slowly, but my finger was already curling around an invisible trigger.

'You will improve. You do not have a choice. This is a war,' said Adela.

'There's always a war,' I said.

*

The frost turned sloppy. Cold grey days drove down on the city. Between the sullen rain and the cloy of the street-slung cobwebs, I felt as if I was forever in a spit-filled, cavity-bogged mouth. I was listless with duty. Circumstances had pressed too hard on my head, and now I was part-sunk in a depression. I was, in fact, depressed – I would venture to suggest I was suffering from PTSD – although because I couldn't be signed off or share my workload, there didn't seem to be much point in acknowledging this.

One weekend morning I came down at half past eleven, having woken at eight and stared at the ceiling for hours. I had not dressed and I had not bathed. I bought packs of the same over-sized cotton T-shirt to sleep in and would wear them all day long. Over time the gelid touch of loose cotton on protruding segments of my body would come to feel like misery. Even now, if I brush against my breasts in the shower with the inside of my wrist, I feel abrupt unhappiness.

I thought I might have the energy to perform every action required to make a cup of tea, but I was surprised to remember how many there were: kettle-boiling, mug-fetching, milk-sniffing, teabag-choosing, teaspoon-handling. I poured a glass of tap water and sat at the kitchen table, staring into the soggy garden.

Upstairs, Graham was working on an arrangement for his flute but he stopped when he heard me moving around, and came down.

'Good . . . morning,' he said carefully.

'Mm.'

'Have you had breakfast?'

'No.'

'Are you feeling poorly?'

'I guess.'

He paused at the countertop. I waited for him to correct my 'I guess' for 'I suppose', which was one of his most picked-over points of vocabulary, but instead he said, 'How so?'

'Just. Not feeling good. Not contagious or anything like that. If that's what you're worried about.'

'I'm not.'

Later that afternoon, he came in from whatever errand he

had been on and handed me a small plastic bottle.

'What's this?'

'Vitamin D tablets. I think you should take them.'

'Oh. Thanks.'

'You're welcome. You should dress now. It's three o'clock.'

'Give it a few more hours and I'll be appropriately dressed for bedtime.'

He considered me, his expression as mild and unreadable as ever. If I'd had space for despair, my desire for him and his cool lack of desire would have triggered – like blood following a cut – despair, but I was at capacity and couldn't feel worse. I lay in my own body like a wretched sandbank and he went upstairs to practise the flute with studied, A-major good humour.

I didn't even tease him for his supplement obsession. Graham was a supplement fiend: his obsession had been brought on by discovering what caused scurvy and how small and fun Vitamin C gummies could be. I'd been living with him for months before I discovered his tendency towards small, charming, infuriating smiles was not only because he was a restrained, charming, infuriating man, but also because he was a bit self-conscious about a tooth he'd lost to scurvy, the replacement for which shone like a silver penny in a crematorium.

Two days later I pulled the abed-for-hours trick again, this time watching my digital clock flick through its cue cards to midday. As soon as the clock showed 12:00, as if he had been waiting for this to happen, he called up the stairs, 'Come for a run.'

'Have you not been yet?'

'No.'

I lay back and dozed for about quarter of an hour. I was woken by the sound of him saying, 'Come on!' at my bedroom door. He spoke briskly and clearly – not unkindly, but not with much gentleness or indulgence. I imagined he once spoke to the ship's company of *Erebus* like that. It was perhaps two tones away from a reprimand.

I dragged myself from the bed and went for a run with him. It was very pleasant, which I allowed with bad grace. I went at the pace of an unhappy thought, and when we reached the end of our route, he'd barely broken a sweat keeping step with me. He was almost certainly training for the Physical Aptitude Assessment himself.

As January stumbled on, I fell into lethargy, and he fell into caretaking. It was my job to take care of, and look after, him. He was not forced through time and space to play nurse for a depressed civil servant. Yet here we were, and I couldn't find the energy to remedy the situation. I was beginning to hate everything: the house, my job, the oily stink of my unwashed hair.

One afternoon, I made a cursory tour of the landing and the bathroom, then went back to bed. I lay there long enough that my parted mouth made a wet oval on the pillow. He knocked at my bedroom door. I rolled over so that I was face-up.

'Hi?'

He opened the door.

'I've wept the aubergines. I think dinner will be ready in about three quarters of an hour.'

'I'm not hungry, really. Thanks though. Sorry to make you cook.'

'I wasn't "made" to do anything. You ought to eat.'

'I'm just not hungry.'

He leant against the doorjamb. There was no expression on his face at all – just his features, neatly set.

'I understand that cats, culturally, enjoy spending much of their time in bed. Perhaps cat dreams are more dramatic than human dreams. Since I never remember mine, I can't compare. I certainly don't wish to interfere with your work or your busy napping schedule. But you will come down for meals.'

'I don't—'

'That was not a request.'

I blinked, slowly, then, finding that I preferred the part of the blink where my eyes were closed, I kept them closed. I heard the floor creak softly, and then he must have been close to me, because the smell of him made me ache – tobacco, soap, radiator-warmed wool, the mellow leafy scent of his skin. When I opened my eyes, he was kneeling by the bed, his face close to mine. I stared at the longbow of his lips.

'I think it would be better,' he said, 'if you did not embarrass us both by forcing me to drag you to the kitchen.'

His mouth had left me vulnerable. I felt shame, green and new, and it was more efficacious than any other emotion I'd experienced for weeks. I went downstairs for dinner.

He put on the radio to break the silence that had joined us at the dining table. A news announcer drily described the Australian wildfires. I say 'Australia' with cavalier non-specificity because most of the continent was on fire. Graham perked up when a journalist interviewed a citizen of Goulburn in New South Wales, who cussed out his Prime Minister with so many metaphors he sounded Homeric. Hundreds of people had been *internally displaced* by grass fires and the air was poisoned with smoke. I pressed the points of my fork into my tongue and waited to hear what Graham would have to say about this new example of egregious weather. But all he said was, 'I've been to Goulburn. It's where my family moved.'

*

I thought about Quentin all the time. It would be accurate to say I was blocked by Quentin – not the man but the corpse and its creation. Sometimes I knew I'd failed him and at other times I knew I'd fumbled a catch and failed myself. I missed him, mourned for him; and I hated him and the irrevocability of his death.

Margaret and Arthur visited me in my doldrums. At first they were dulcet and bedside-benign, but I sulked so acidly they soon stopped that. Purportedly they were in our house to see Graham. The regularity of their visits was such that I came to believe Graham was running a schedule.

Arthur was gentle, no matter how grotty my behaviour. He had found out about Scrabble and he sometimes brought his travel set along – my inner competitive bitch could stave off a black mood for half an hour or so. 'Simellia loves this game,' he told me once. 'She has introduced me to so many "bored" games. She ran a games club when she was at university, isn't that jolly?'

'Mm.'

'But her old friends left the country or started popping out sprogs so alas, the "bored" game gang is no more. She says our next step is "arcade" games. For a terribly long time I thought she meant the Games of Arcadia. Perhaps you'd discovered the lost text of Aristotle's *Comedy* and had used your spiffing machines to rescue the pages and write up his theory.'

'Nope.'

'She says that we will play Space Invaders.'

'Oh. Good.'

He smiled kindly at me. 'I had a lieutenant,' he said, 'who'd sit in the dugout chewing his pencil and drumming out metre on his notebook. With the mortars wheedling overhead. I said to him, "Owen, old chap, how can you think of poetry at a time like this? Your blasted trochees and dactyls and so on, when the Hun's trying to turn you to bully beef?" And he told me that poetry was the last thing that still made sense to him. And if you listened closely enough, you could still hear the birdsong.'

He shifted. We were sitting at the kitchen table, alone for a brief quarter of an hour while Graham went down to the corner shop to buy more milk for the tea. 'You think I'm ridiculous,' he said, in the same gentle voice.

'No, Arthur, I—'

'I don't blame you. I think I'm ridiculous too. But I am trying very hard to be happy. Though it's damned difficult to see what Owen saw. He didn't see it for much longer after I – er – left. The Marne, you know. This ring is his. He gave it to me after—'

We heard Graham's key in the door. Arthur looked very keenly at his letters. 'Forty-seven,' he called, 'do you know if "zigbo" is a word?'

Margaret, in her visits, was a bit more direct.

'You smell pestilent,' she might say conversationally. 'Have you bathed?'

Or: 'If you mun sleep, you mun play the good hostess and give me leave to join. Heave up!'

One Saturday we ate an entire triple-layered box of chocolates in bed, watching *The Simpsons* on my laptop. Margaret loved *The Simpsons*. She thought it was a much better cultural education than anything the Ministry could provide.

In her own era, Margaret had been under the protection of her older brother, a draper named Henry Kemble, whom she loved deeply. She was unmarried, though she'd had liaisons with other women (mistaken by the household, and some of the women, for friendships). She helped her brother's wife keep the house, helped her brother with the accounts. But after Kemble's untimely death from flu, the gilt rubbed off her star. She became a stone in a shoe, a hole in the road. She became, in that slow domestic way, hated.

When the Ministry had come through time to fetch her, they'd found Margaret locked in a tiny attic room with a chamberpot and a nest of rags for bedding. She was in recovery from the bubonic plague. As far as they could tell, her sister-in-law had sent a scullery girl to deliver food to the door until she too was struck down with the pestilence. It wiped out the entire house but Margaret in three days. Margaret, hungry and terrified, had tried to leave through the window, but the neighbours had thrown stones and broken bottles at her. Their house was a plague-house, and none were suffered to leave it. She'd caught and eaten sparrows. She'd drunk rainwater. And then when she was given a second chance, she caught the sword and came up singing.

*

Simellia came by, once. By then the gulf of experiences between us was universes deep, but she came nevertheless. She put the kettle on and made the tea herself. She badly harassed the tea bags, I think because she couldn't look at my face.

'I don't want to drop a piano on your head,' I said, 'but I know I'm traumatised. You don't have to be embarrassed about it.'

She smiled coolly at me, fathomless as always. 'You look terrible,' she said.

'So do you.'

This was true. Chic Simellia was no more. She wore leggings that concertinaed at the backs of her knees, and a hoodie so forgettable that I couldn't focus on its colour. It was like she'd hung up her sense of self in a cupboard somewhere.

'Do you want to talk about it?' she asked.

'Are you serious?'

'Yes. I'm a trained mental health professional.'

'Physician, heal thyself.'

She gave me tea, in my own mug – Alice peering up at the Cheshire Cat. She must have remembered from last time. That made me feel something, but too distantly for me to recognise what.

'Why are you here, Simellia?'

She took some time with that. 'Is there anything,' she said, 'you want to talk about? At all?'

I put my finger in the tea. It was too hot to drink, scalding. I left my finger in there for a couple of seconds.

'Control knew about the Brigadier,' I said. 'Did they tell you? That they were the ones to let him in? Enemies closer, et cetera.'

'Do you want to talk about him?' she asked quietly. 'Conversations you might have had with him?'

I was deep in the grey room on the bottom floor of my skull. I wasn't watching her face or hearing her voice when she asked. I didn't really notice that she wasn't talking to me the way psychiatrists talk; she was talking to me like someone desperate to talk herself. But I didn't catch what she was trying to draw out of me. I said, 'No,' and we sat in silence and watched my tea get cold until she remembered there was something she had to do somewhere else and left.

*

One early Saturday evening, when the sky looked like the underside of a sea-soaked barge and the cold was grimy and constant, Graham failed to make a cake. I heard him making domestic noises and the clack-thud of the oven. Half an hour later, he knocked on my door.

'Well,' he announced, 'I have ruined a cake.'

He was wearing a rare expression of irritation. He was trying to flatten it and it kept springing back into his face, as unruly as his hair. I don't know why but this cheered me up a bit. He was carrying a bottle of wine and two glasses.

'Would you like a drink?'

'All right then. What's wrong with the cake?'

'It's damp. And not cake-shaped.'

'What shape is it?'

'Puddle-shaped.'

He sat on the floor and leant against the chest of drawers, pouring us each a glass of wine.

'To failure.'

'To failure!'

'I have renewed respect for the *Erebus* cook Mr Wall, who produced our Christmas pudding under far less tranquil conditions.'

'I'm sure it's less terrible than you're letting on.'

'It is far worse. I'm trying to be charmingly self-deprecating but I am very annoyed.'

'I can see that. It's not like you to spend any time on my floor.'

'Hmm. I suppose there are other rooms in this house in which we could sit upright and drink, but I notice you rarely venture beyond the banisters these days.'

'We could go to your room.'

'Certainly not. You will destroy my virtuous reputation.'

'No one can see us.'

'God can see us,' he said, severely.

'Do you really believe in God?' I asked, without really

expecting an answer. He shifted his shoulders against the wood.

'What a peculiar thing to ask me. Of course I do.'

'Heaven and Hell and all that?'

'Of the life eternal I have no sense. I understand it is very fashionable, in your era, to suppose there is nothing but oblivion after death.'

'It's not "fashionable". It's just a lot of people don't see any rationale for believing in it. Seems like a fairytale.'

He shrugged.

'Belief has very little to do with rationale. Why demand a map for uncharted territory?'

I didn't have an answer for this, so I had some wine. It tasted vile, like chewing geraniums. Wetly, my brain connected action and consequence: he had brought up 'tonic' wine, since he regarded me as unwell, and was gamely drinking it with me so I would not realise how unwell I was. I'm sure if he could have sourced laudanum, he would have done.

'Remind me,' he said, 'of the religion you were brought up in.'

The neutrality of this request, from a man who until recently was still using 'heathen' as a genuine descriptor, made me realise he truly was a Ministry trainee. They must have put him through bias and sensitivity training.

I said, 'Why?'

'I'm curious. You mentioned there is a form of, how can I put this, reflective morality?'

'Eh?'

'A cruel action will be repaid with cruelty, a kind one with kindness.'

'Oh. Karma. Yeah. That works across lifetimes. If you're wretched in this life, you'll come back as a slug.'

He sipped his wine and barely grimaced. 'That seems cruel,' he said. I bristled despite myself.

'I don't think so. Actions have consequences. Every tiny decision you make, every choice of expression, affects someone else. We're all chained up together. Arthur stopped going to church, you know. He didn't see God in the trenches. Do you really have faith in a God who let the Western Front happen? Or Auschwitz?'

'Yes. I'm not telling you that I like it or that I understand it. God is a captain whose orders I must trust. He knows this ship better than I.'

'Is the world a ship?'

'Everything is a ship. This little house is a ship.'

He was so good at it: making his voice soft and pleasant and soothing me out of argument. It worked every time. We smiled unsurely at one another. Then he said, 'What is "Auschwitz"?' I thought, *ah fuck*. What a stupid thing to say, after my little speech about consequences.

*

After he left, I dropped into another doze, precipitated by the sudden exhaustion I felt when I imagined doing anything more taxing than rolling onto my side. I napped for hours. When I woke, my saliva had the scummy consistency of old tofu. It was coming up to midnight. I dragged myself to the kitchen for a glass of water.

He was sitting up at the dining table, curled like a pot-bound root over the laptop. There was a cigarette between his lips, and six more stubbed out in the ashtray. He looked up when I came in. His expression had a scraped-clean bareness to it.

'You're up late,' I croaked, fumbling for a glass. 'Wh—'

'You didn't tell me about the Holocaust.'

Tap water overflowed the glass and ran down my fist. 'Well,' I said slowly, 'the Ministry thought it might be detrimental to your adjustment—'

'I asked the machine to search for that word you used.'

'Auschwitz.'

'There were photographs—'

He broke off. I gulped down half a pint of water and watched him. What I had mistaken for unadorned expressionlessness on his face was hollowed-out horror. He must have been looking at the screen for hours.

'Children,' he says.

'Yes.'

'Piles of shoes.'

'Yes.'

He ground the cigarette out. 'How could this have been allowed to happen?' he asked.

I shook my head.

'People know,' I mumbled, 'and then they choose not to know. What happened to the freed slaves?'

'Pardon?'

'The slaves that you freed. From the *Rosa*. And the other ships.'

'Oh. Well, it depended. Some joined the Royal Navy or the regiments. Or they were apprenticed to places in the West Indies—'

'Apprenticed.'

'Yes.'

'Put to work, you mean.'

'What are you insinuating?' he asked, reaching for his cigarettes. Even from where I was standing in the dark kitchen, I could see the packet was empty. He crushed it, seemingly absent-mindedly.

'Plenty died on the return journeys, didn't they? Or while they were kept on those ships, waiting for their cases to be heard. You said yourself—'

'I know what I said.'

He got up and closed the laptop. Every move he made was slow, calm, unobtrusive. Nothing banged or scraped. We could have been having a conversation about what brand of bread to buy.

'The Preventative Squadron was intended as a moral service to humanity,' he said quietly. 'To consider its actions comparable to what was done at Auschwitz. That's impossible. If you believed that, how could you bear to live in this house with me?'

'I wasn't saying that *they* were comparable.'

'Really.'

'I'm trying to say that you were following what you thought were good orders.'

He stared at me. His eyes were unlit. He turned without saying anything, unlocked the back door, and strode into the midnight-coloured garden. Cold air barked at my legs. I came to the threshold and stared out after him, shaking in frigid winter wind. He was standing in the middle of the lawn, arms folded, and staring up at the sky.

*

When I was still a teenager, building my personality from the films and the books and the songs I later tried to give to Graham, the chief monk of one of Cambodia's largest wats announced that he could not rule out that the victims of the Khmer Rouge were not the final link in a chain of karmic cause and effect. If they had behaved with integrity in past lives, perhaps they would not have had to lie in mass graves at the end of this.

My mother never went back to our temple after that. She kept flowers and fruit on the shrine at home, but it became a place she put her thoughts to dry out. All her honouring she gave to her new country, which told her she was welcome as long as she worked. In terms of karmic cause and effect, that was far more palatable.

As for me, I was callow with youth and ready to commit to obsession. I picked up my first book about the golden age of polar exploration and I coalesced around it. I came to believe in the possibility of heroic death, and from there it was easy to believe in heroism. Heroism laid the groundwork for right-eousness, and righteousness offered me coherency. If I'd got really into punk rock, maybe I'd be a different woman. But I didn't.

One of the first comparisons we made on the bridge project was to the work of the Kindertransport. No one – not even Ralph, whose father had arrived on it – mentioned that though we rescued children, we'd refused to take their parents. Graham knew, at the end of his extensive Google search, what had happened to the parents. We frame the Kindertransport as an act of heroism, a coherent example of Britain's intrinsic charity and antifascism. It's not all untrue – those orphans were grateful, often, thrived, sometimes.

You think I was clumsy. You think I could have handled it better. No doubt you're right. It was a *teaching moment* that I fumbled; worse, it was a moment I'd created and my actions had consequences. But what could I have said? That the Holocaust was one of the most appalling, most shameful stains on the history of humanity, and it could have been prevented? Everything that has ever been could have been prevented, and none of it was. The only thing you can mend is the future. Believe me when I say that time-travel taught me that.

*

The next morning, he brought me a snowdrop in a glass tumbler and set it on my desk.

'First of the season,' he said. 'From the garden.'

I touched its sad white head. 'You've been here for nearly a year, then,' I said.

'Yes.'

'I'm glad you'll get to see this garden in the spring before you move.'

He touched the place on the snowdrop where I'd laid my fingers. 'Yes,' he said, and there was, as there so often was, nothing in his voice.

*

We entered the season of rains. A great graphite pencil inscribed the diagonal journey of water on the air.

In February, there was another violent storm, but the worst of it passed over southwest England. He didn't like what happened to Devon. He'd been born there, hung on to fond memories.

Our little house held up. He walked from room to room, peering out of the windows. When he came into the office, where I was hunched like a cooked prawn at my computer, he said, 'I will allow this. Your era's sewage system is a miracle of engineering.'

'It's all nineteenth-century pipes down there.'

'It's all nineteenth-century pipes in here,' he said, gesturing at himself. I smiled wanly.

My email made a chiding noise. Adela was the originator, and she'd put me in blind copy. It was a short email. Adela had a real gift for cramming apoplexy into a couple of lines.

'Bad news?' he asked. I coughed.

Anne Spencer had been shot dead attempting to escape the Ministry wards. She'd almost managed it. Towards the end, she had stopped showing up on CCTV cameras.

The email told us that her death would be reported to the expats as a suicide. 'This cannot be emphasised enough', Adela had written, with a double underline.

*

The funeral was a strange, sterile affair. It was held in a chapel in the Ministry, the first time I realised we had one. The coffin was closed and no one except the expats went near it. The service had the box-ticking air of an administrative procedure, except for the hymn, 'Bless the Lord, My Soul' in Jacques Berthier's arrangement. It was lusciously, shockingly mournful. I couldn't raise my head when it began. The sound of Arthur's clear, fine tenor and Graham's soft, coppery voice harmonising at the turn of every verse filled my lungs like floodwater.

Afterwards, I went to sit in a small courtyard that adjoined the chapel. It was waterlogged and smelled of mud. Nevertheless, I settled myself on the stone lip of a flowerbed, letting the cold seep through my black coat.

'Mind if I join you?'

'Oh. Arthur. Yes, of course. It's a bit wet, I'm afraid.'

Arthur smiled and sat down beside me, stretching out his long legs. Twisting the signet ring on his finger – a tell as clarion as my skin-biting – he murmured, 'We didn't know her as well as we would have liked. I wish we had.'

'Mm.'

'Perhaps she wouldn't have felt so – lonely.'

I didn't say anything, because there was nothing that I could say that wouldn't have been a lie. I touched my knuckles to the back of Arthur's and he took my hand in his. He said, 'When I first arrived here, once I got over the shock, I thought I had entered a sort of Purgatory. A second chance, you know. You can't imagine what it was like to be a man of – of my persuasion, in my time. Now it seems I've got another go of it in an era that suits me better. But, you know, you can make yourself feel lonely and miserable and out of joint just by falling in love with someone who can't or won't love you back. Perhaps they'll fix that in another two hundred years. Perhaps they'll come and get us and that's how we'll know we've reached Heaven. Are you and Graham lovers?'

My hand twitched in his.

'No.'

I looked at him. I mean I really looked at him: his sad handsome face, the vulnerability flying there at half-mast.

'Are you?' I asked.

'What are you two talking about?'

We both turned to look at the door. Graham was standing there, pausing in the act of lighting a cigarette. I had no idea how much he'd heard.

'We're plotting,' said Arthur, squeezing my hand and releasing it. 'We're going to try and get up to some really original sin.'

Graham blew a plume of smoke at us. 'I see,' he said. 'I'll be sure to keep a candle burning in the window for when you come home.'

*

217

The most difficult stories about the Khmer Rouge are the ones over which hover *almost* and *maybe*. She almost made it, but dysentery took her at the end. He is maybe buried in the mass grave at Choeung Ek, so we will pay our respects there. He almost walked all the way to Thailand, but the cadres found him in the forest. She maybe saw her infant son one last time before she was taken.

Anne Spencer almost made it off those wards. After I read the email, an ancient and exuberant terror blazed through me. It was partly the terror that had grown in me alongside my very bones, knowing as I did that I only existed because my mother had outrun *almost*; I don't know at what point you stop feeling the need to run, generation by generation, when you're born after that.

But it was also a wonderful, simple, human terror. The one where death brushes too close to you and you abruptly remember what an insane gift it is to be alive, and how much you'd like to stay alive even when death is laughing at your window, laughing in your mirror.

*

The Ministry's internal CCTV system was exempt from the laws of the Information Commissioner's Office. I couldn't access footage without filing for permission on behalf of the bridge team, which would mean everyone from the Secretary downwards would see me ratting around in the digital drywall. But I had security clearance to ask for a record of permissions requested, granted and denied; technical faults reported; tapes scrubbed after the requisite thirty days and tapes filed for archive use; and so on. I whistled for the paperwork.

I found half a dozen invoices for services to the system hardware in the weeks leading up to Anne Spencer's death. Apparently it took a while for people to realise the poor woman had managed to make herself invisible to surveillance cameras, and they assumed the system was malfunctioning.

Also intriguing were the maintenance files for the CCTV system that should have been monitoring the courtyard on the day Quentin was killed. The system had shut down when the power was automatically rerouted. Such rerouting was a standard emergency procedure in buildings with high security rooms. Simply speaking, if a very important item or person was kept under electrical lock and key and that electrical lock and key failed, the building automatically rerouted power from non-essential systems (like the CCTV on a public courtyard) until the back-up generator kicked in. It was a charmingly old-fashioned system that had proven bizarrely effective because it was hard to hack with contemporary malware.

What was unusual was that I couldn't find a corresponding record of breach or failure. The 'automatic' reroute had been manually input.

I filed an access request for a history of access requests. I found a record of external accesses to the reroute system, scrambled to protect the identity of the accessor. Username, clearance level, authority and permissions were all scrambled. But there was a digital record of the CMOS scanner – the fingerprint scan.

I pulled it and plugged it into the Ministry's database.

The result pinged.

I read my own name.

I lost my body for a few moments. When I came back to it, I was kneading my chest with the heel of my hand, at the place where my speeding heartbeat flicked the skin.

I was being framed, and of all the things it felt, *unfair* was right at the top. I still didn't even know who the fuck the Brigadier was or what he wanted and no one seemed inclined to tell me, even though I was the one who'd had Quentin's brains on my face.

I emailed Adela and asked if we could meet for a 'progress report', a term so meaningless she wouldn't be able to prep her evasion. As I cracked my nails on the keys, I thought how much easier it would be if I could just have a gun and a clear view of the Brigadier. The harder I kicked at it, the thicker the callus on my mind became. Yes, I thought, through a plaque of dead thoughts. If I had a gun, I could clean this all up.

*

I became ecstatic on spite. This firstly manifested as sitting at the kitchen table, eating an entire jar of pickled onions with a pair of chopsticks. I needed vinegar. After I'd given myself stomach cramps, I threw up and went for a post-puke run.

When I came back, I showered aggressively, painting the bathroom with soapy water. I wanted to bite a train, or maybe fuck one. I wanted to beat myself bloody in the burial chamber of the pyramid of Giza. As this sort of thing was prohibited by the laws of man and the Ministry, I decided to do the next best thing, which was go to the pub.

'Graham,' I said to my unfortunate housemate, who had bought the pickled onions.

'Yes?'

'Do you want to meet some of my friends?'

He gave me one of his rare, lovely, full-dimpled smiles.

'I would. I have been wondering how to ask.'

'Oh yeah?'

'Yes,' he said. He seemed to be about to launch into an

explanation, but arrested himself mid-exposition. The effort of stopping it made him blush a little. He contented himself with a prim, 'You've met mine, after all.'

'You've only got two.'

'Three,' he said pleasantly. 'We are friends.'

*

I organised drinks at a pub near to where I used to live, before the bridge year, and invited half a dozen of my closest pals. 'Closest pals', at this stage of the bridge year, was a bit of a proximity misnomer because I hadn't seen most of them in months. As I often glumly texted them, Work's so busy.

I told the group chat: My housemate's very posh and a bit weird. He used to be in the Navy. I hoped this would cover all bases. But he turned up on his motorbike and parked it with the rows of other scooters and bikes. I watched him take off his helmet, lean against his bike, light a cigarette and smoke thoughtfully at the sky, leather jacket gleaming and curls disarrayed. I didn't know how I could explain him to anyone, least of all to myself.

The pub was opposite a kebab shop which served hot tea and coffee and was frequented by east London's contingent of Uber Eats and Deliveroo couriers – hence the plethora of bikes and scooters. The couriers all seemed to know one another and could often be found splitting doner'n'chips while leaning against their vehicles.

'Hello, Graham.'

He ground out the cigarette and offered me a cautious smile. 'Hello,' he said. 'Shall we? What on earth is that caterwauling?'

'Ah. It's karaoke night.'

Inside the pub, a wisp of a woman, like a mouse with ambitions, was standing on the makeshift stage, sweetly lisping her way through 'The Best' by Tina Turner.

My friends were sitting at a table far enough away from the karaoke carnage that their conversation was audible. They turned like a crowd of parrots in a tree when they saw me approaching.

'So *you're* the famous housemate,' said one. 'We've heard so much about you.'

'Was any of it good?' he asked.

'Not a word.'

'Oh, I *am* relieved. I wouldn't want her telling lies on my account.'

I flexed my shoulder blades, forcing the tension out. He was an anachronism, a puzzle, a piss-take, a problem, but he was, above all things, a charming man. In every century, they make themselves at home.

*

It went well. My friends seemed to like him, and I think he liked them. He was good at side-stepping questions he didn't want to answer, and had a talent for whimsical humour that distracted them from the gaps he left.

The hours toppled past.

When I found myself considering a gin martini, in an establishment where the house wine was called Table and came in cardboard boxes, I knew it was time to leave. I stumbled over to the bar, where he was in conversation with one of my friends about his tattoos.

'What does this one say?' Graham asked.

'"Every love is an exercise in depersonalisation". Deleuze. Wrote my doctoral thesis on him.'

'How interesting. And what is this? A little crab?'

'Yeah. Got him after I took acid in Dungeness. I saw this crab on the beach and thought he was God.'

'Fantastic.'

'Graham. We should get going,' I said, and reached out. I was drunk, of course. My palm cupped several warm square inches of his ribs, through his clothes. He looked down at me.

'Yes,' he said. He moved in such a way that he had straightened up but not leant away, and my hand sweated into his jumper.

We said our goodbyes and ambled out into the street. It twinkled under the sodium papier mâché of the streetlights' cast. There were a few couriers drinking tea and eating supper from polystyrene boxes. I didn't see them until we'd almost walked into them: the Brigadier, and Salese.

I stopped short. My boots skidded on the pavement and Graham grabbed my arm to steady me. I was shaking. He smoothed his hands between my shoulder blades.

'Got,' said Salese, holding out a strange device. 'He's a free traveller.'

The device looked like a compass with pretensions to metal detection, and it projected a filmy white grid, on which flickered several symbols. It was, indubitably, the thing from Graham's drawing – not a weapon after all, but some kind of monitoring device. I thought *wonderful* in a monotone. The ghost of a pickled onion rose in my gullet.

'Good evening, Commander Gore,' said the Brigadier.

'Sir.'

'I am sorry to approach you in this way. But you need to come with us.'

'Might I ask what for?'

'I'm afraid not.'

'My bridge?'

'If you come with us, we need not harm her.'

He didn't like that. 'I don't think I will come with you,' he said. 'And I don't think you will harm her either. You will leave now.'

'Her read's off,' said Salese suddenly, squinting at the display. 'Time-odd. Rec a null.'

'Oh, very well,' sighed the Brigadier, and pulled what was unmistakably a weapon from his jacket.

Graham grabbed my wrist and dragged me out of the way just in time for a blue light to hit the pavement where I'd stood. It went *whump* and gouged a shallow hole. I screamed and lunged at Salese, raking my nails down that cold face. Salese screamed too.

'*Puso!*' shrieked Salese. There was a nasty clatter as the projection machine hit the floor. '*Puso, puso!*'

I may not have understood the word exactly, but I know when I'm being called a cunt.

'*Sake,* Sal,' snapped the Brigadier, his BBC accent dropping. Then Graham had him by the arm and I heard an unpleasantly biological snapping sound. Salese snarl-shrieked. I jabbed hard at an eyeball. Salese shriek-shrieked.

Graham had got the Brigadier to the floor, but the Brigadier was aiming the weapon again.

'Run,' said Graham quietly.

I ran. Behind me, there was another *whump*.

By the kebab shop, the couriers were scrambling. I stood wibbling by Graham's bike. He opened the back, briskly

224

slammed a spare helmet over my head – much too large, meant for Arthur – and dragged me by the collar onto the seat.

'Hold on!' he shouted through his helmet. There was another *whump* and a stream of cursing in a panoply of languages. I flung my arms around his waist and banshee-shrieked as the bike revved. Around us, like a hive of enraged metal wasps, the couriers were revving their bikes too. We went howling down the street.

'Which one are they?' I heard the Brigadier bellow.

We rode.

I had never been on the back of a motorbike before and I was not in a good place, mentally, for it to be my first time. Everything went too fast and was too loud. I sobbed every time Graham took a corner, the road rising up to threaten my knees. He sped through the city, running red lights.

The clamour of Friday night thinned out. Streetlights flashed past less frequently and trees began to lean out of the horizon. We were entering the neighbourhood that we lived in.

He slowed down enough that my hyperventilating was audible and parked near the house. He got off the bike and gently helped me down, handling me as deftly as if I was the weekly shopping.

'I think they're from the future,' I choked.

'Yes, I'd assumed as much,' he said, not unkindly.

He steered me up the front path. I fell inside and leant against the front door, panting in a thin way that incurred a steady whine from the back of my throat. He calmly began to remove his helmet, his jacket and his aviator scarf.

'You're fine,' he said in a low, soothing voice, tugging the helmet off me. My hair half unravelled. 'You're fine,' he repeated, unbuttoning my coat. I jerked my shoulders and it fell to the floor.

'They tried to kill us,' I croaked.

'Yes,' he said calmly. 'You should contact the Ministry. Here. There's a pin sticking out of your head.'

He reached out and I felt his fingers in my hair, gently disentangling a hair grip. His face was cool with concentration. I reached for his head with both of my hands and pulled him down to kiss him.

His whole body went rigid with tension. It arced away from me at every point except his mouth, which was slack with shock. For a couple of seconds, I felt him tremble as if charged with an opposite magnetism. Then, suddenly, it was like a rope had been cut. He flattened himself against me. He landed his fists on either side of my head and pushed against me so hard that I slid an inch up the door.

Objectively speaking, it was a bad kiss. Our teeth clashed painfully. He scraped my bottom lip. I scrabbled at the hem of his jumper and my fingers brushed bare skin. He gasped, and the gasp seemed to startle him, because he was abruptly off me, stumbling backwards into the wall. He landed in a globe of loose cream light shed through the door's glass pane. He stared at me, wild-eyed, tousle-haired, his mouth and chin wet.

We looked at one another.

'Graham.'

'Don't,' he said. For the first time that evening, there was panic in his voice.

I took a step towards him and he said, more urgently, *'Don't.'*

I stopped. He was breathing as hard as I was. It was as if the horror of the last half an hour had just caught up with him, or else that wasn't the *only* thing that horrified him – but I cut that thought off.

'I'm sorry,' he said, and reached out. I thought he would take my hand or touch my face, but he was holding out the hair grip. I took it from him. It was warm from my head, warm from his hands. I was still staring at it when he slipped past me and fled to his room. I heard him lock the door, which he never normally did. I would have found it funny if I hadn't found it so heartbreaking.

VII

A couple of weeks after the shooting incident, Gore leads a small party of men and two officers from the ice-bound ship to land. They march across the pack ice for sixteen miles and reach Cape Felix.

They have had unseasonably bad hunting, bringing home a scarce few hundred pounds of meat. All quarry is turned over to the common table, though the hunter may keep the head and heart of larger game. Gore shares his first heart (caribou) with Goodsir, who gives thanks by way of an impromptu lecture on parasitical animalcules that prey on warm-blooded mammals. '*Do you mean the darts of Cupid?*' one inveterate bachelor asks another. But Goodsir is only seven-and-twenty — he'll wed yet, once he's published his papers on Arctic insect species and made his name.

The camp at Cape Felix is intended as a magnetic observatory and a base for hunting parties when daily sojourns from the ship in search of game are no longer practicable. The journey to and from the ships exhausts all but the most determined hunters, and one can recognise the most determined hunters by their disfigured faces. Gore isn't sure what he looks like any more and that suits him fine. Perhaps frostbite will take a half-inch off his nose.

Lieutenant Hodgson of *Terror* is the chief magnetic officer at the base. Hodgson is charming as a lap dog and brave as a terrier, but he's young and not a scientist. His presence at the camp is a troubling sign. It suggests Crozier — a talented scientist and a Fellow of the Royal Society — sent his greenest lieutenant because he places no value in the work being done here. It could even suggest Crozier does not expect the fieldwork to ever reach England.

Earlier this year, in May, Gore led a party to John Ross's cairn to deposit a note from the late Sir John Franklin, intended for the Admiralty via wandering fur traders or Royal Navy chartists. Now, as reconnoitre (no one dares say 'rescue') fails to materialise — as it becomes clearer that no Hudson's Bay Company trapper has found the cairn and its message — a melancholy lethargy, rimed with hunger, crusts over the group. It takes all of his charisma, his good cheer and the unexpressed presence of the cat-o'-nine-tails for Gore to keep the Cape Felix camp lively, running, responsive.

Mornings are the worst. The sealskin sleeping bags freeze overnight, and then in the light of the dawn the frost evaporates, mists on the canvas ceiling and drips onto their heads. All their clothing is several exhausting pounds heavier, because they sweat into the wool and they cannot get the wool dry.

No, mealtimes are the worst. They put cold things into their mouths and the cold walks around their stomachs. The camp was running low on spirit fuel, and Gore gave his men a choice between no grog or cold rations. They all chose grog — Jack was ever a jolly tar. But water needs to be melted too, and they're even thirstier than they are hungry or tired. He's had to stop more than one man eating snow and scorching his throat. Des Voeux and the Marine Sergeant Bryant shot a hare two days ago and knelt to drink the blood from the welt in its flank.

No, what's worst is that there are no Esquimaux. This is their seasonal hunting ground. Last year they'd come aboard the ships to trade seal meat and furs for knives and wood. They'd patted sailors' faces and cheerfully resisted conversion to Christianity (Hell sounded too delightful — a land of eternal heat). This year, the natives are nowhere to be seen. They have leapt into the sky, sunk into the earth.

Gore thinks his trigger fingers might be going. They are swollen, sheening enamel-white. It takes him longer than he'd like to get his gloves on because he can't feel what he's doing. Still, he's dealt with worse than this. He'll give himself another week unless his fingers start to blacken. He still wants to bag an ox.

When it happens, it happens very quickly. Later, he will hardly be able to line the words up to describe it.

'The — flash of lightning, I thought it was. Then that — doorway of blue light.'

The horizon splits like a knuckle. A bright blue slit in the world. He raises his gun. He will wonder, some time from now, what would have happened if he hadn't, if he'd met his future another way.

Chapter Seven

I put the pad of my thumb to my lip and flattened it. Pulled it back. Stared. No blood, though it felt like there should have been. Not even the sensation of burning. The kiss had gone with the dawn.

'Don't,' murmured Adela.

'I wasn't biting.'

She made a conciliatory noise in her throat, the sort you make to ratty old cats who are trying to climb up the stairs. It was the closest she'd ever come to kindness and it bowled me over, literally. My forehead bounced gently off my knees.

I was sitting on a horrible, cheek-thin mattress in a Ministry safehouse. After I'd heard Graham's door lock, I'd shivered dumbly against the wall until a handful of brain cells formed a committee to remind me that the man my boss had identified as a spy had tried to assassinate us in broad lamplight, using a futuristic weapon that put the late Quentin's cryptic hint about 'not the past' into perspective.

I'd called Adela, who had answered immediately and stepped in to fix things. The night had teemed. There had been some logistical kerfuffle – vans with blackout windows, decoy vehicles, even a brief but impressive subterranean roadway. I was given to understand that the other bridges and expats were also being moved, into off-the-books safehouses in considerably worse nick than our original abodes. Graham and I had been placed in a knackered flat in the garret of an old government building, stifled from all sides by the city. The beautiful heath where I'd taught him to ride a bike was far away. The window in my room looked out onto a jungle of chimneys and vent fans, turning silvery in the proleptic dawn light. I could hear something dripping and I knew, with resignation, that I would always hear something dripping for as long as I lived here. The adrenalin high had worn off and I was feeling tired to my marrow.

Graham's room was along from mine, reached via a long corridor that had abandoned-asylum energy. Back at our old house he'd been bundled into a separate van with his motorbike and a shoulder bag of clothes. He'd glanced at me once, a quick searching look to check that I was being wrangled, and then he hadn't been able to meet my eyes again. As he ducked into the car, I saw how slight he was, how much shorter than the field heavies they'd sent into my now ex-neighbourhood. He was diminished in some way; he'd seemed to hold his charm close to his body, like a broken arm. I hadn't seen him since we'd been brought to the safehouse.

Adela was opening the top drawer of the bedside table. It was old and it stuck. She coaxed it out with far more patience than I had ever seen her exhibit.

'You trained on a Walther?' she asked.

I turned my head, on my knees, to look. She was holding a handgun. I noted this with the same resignation as I'd noted the dripping.

'When I failed the field exams, I was using a Walther, yes.'

'This is yours now.'

'Oh. Cool.'

'I'm putting it in this top drawer.'

'Okay.'

'But first I'd like to see you unload and reload,' she added, passing me the handgun.

It weighed as much as a gun did, neither heavier nor lighter than what I was expecting. 'I haven't done this for a while,' I said, but I did it anyway. Adela nodded approvingly and took it back off me to settle it in the drawer. My thoughts fired sluggishly – electricity through ooze.

'Ma'am. The Brigadier. I think he's from the future.'

'Yes.'

I didn't know what to do with myself, so I lifted my face to drop it into my hands – a childish urge to vanish my problems by shutting off my eyes.

'What do you mean, "Yes"? You knew? The Ministry knew?'

'We'll talk about this the day after tomorrow,' she said. 'I'll send a car. You'll receive a phone call from a withheld number to let you know when it's coming—'

'Day after tomorrow? After I've been shot at? Why not tomorrow? Why not now?'

'Because I said so,' snapped Adela, so quickly she can't have intended to say it. She sucked her teeth and her strange face wobbled. 'You need to rest,' she added, more neutrally.

'Yes, Mai.'

We sat in a rubble of silence. 'A joke,' I mumbled. 'It means "Mum" in Khmer.'

She rocked back like I'd spat at her, then got up quietly and left the room.

*

I slept deeply and briefly, a plunge pool of REM. I was not familiar with how people sleep after someone has tried to kill them, so I assumed this was within the bounds of normal. When I woke up, it was already the afternoon, and Graham was gone. The flat held his absence like a hole in the earth.

I reloaded the Walther, stuck it into a coat pocket, and sat in the mould-framed window of my bedroom like a gargoyle, staring at the view.

The local area felt hostile to human engagement. There was not much space for pedestrians and far too many cars. Every other turning gave onto the blank stare of concrete or glass buildings. It was the kind of area that makes pigeons extra-ugly. But it was crowded with people, living on top of one another, working around each other, some in suits and some in uniforms. I could see why the Ministry thought we'd be hidden here. There were so many unhappy people that a gun wouldn't suffice. You'd have to drop a bomb to ensure I was the right sad soul to die.

*

I knew he'd come back when the rich emerald smell of tobacco filled the hall. Something twitched in my chest – a muscle, a nerve, I wasn't sure, but it hurt.

He was sitting at the noisome kitchen table, staring at nothing. *Rogue Male* was lying splayed and face-down by the ashtray. The thing in my chest kicked again as I realised he must have grabbed it as we left our home. When I came in, he didn't move anything but his gaze, which swung up like a whip.

'Where have you been?' I asked sharply.

'I went out on the bike.'

'I don't know if this is some kind of shock reaction, or if

you're just completely bloody-minded, but are you aware two people from the future tried to kidnap you and kill me yesterday?'

'It did not escape my notice.'

'And you went on a solo road trip?'

He had the grace to look embarrassed, though the expression was half shielded by the hand that held the cigarette. 'I needed to think,' he said carefully. 'And I do not think so well when I am static.'

I walked four trembling, stork-stiff strides to stand in front of him. His gaze wavered again. I vibrated furiously. My knees were jumping like a pair of boxed frogs. I said, 'We were almost murdered, in cold blood, in the street, and you're acting weirdly because you regret kissing me. Is that right? Have I got it right?'

He cleared his throat awkwardly and ashed without looking, missing the ashtray. 'I rather think you kissed me,' he suggested.

'Whatever. You're about to tell me that it was an awful mistake, that it shouldn't have happened, et cetera.'

He pulled hard on the cigarette, so that its tip glowed like a warning signal, then plucked nervily at his packet for another. He used the burning cigarette to light the next one and glumly swapped them. At length he said, 'It should not have happened. And I'm terribly sorry for the way that it did.'

'Right.'

'You're angry.'

'No shit. It's humiliating to be treated like a child after being kissed like a—'

'Please—'

He coloured and blew a long stream of smoke at me. At length he muttered, 'I have been *trying* to court you.'

I blinked.

'What?'

He frowned at me over the cigarette. 'Evidently I mismanaged this. I don't have very much experience in courting.'

'I don't understand.'

'Neither, it must be said, do I. I don't understand what you want, nor what any woman of this era wants. I don't know what I have to offer you. You are perfectly independent. You're occupied to an almost violent degree by your own career. But, well, I thought, you *do* eat everything I cook . . . so perhaps . . .'

'You were planning on feeding me until I . . . what?'

He frowned more deeply. He looked as if he was having a bad time.

'I was hoping you might be able to explain that to me. If you found me suitable.'

'Suitable for what?' I exclaimed, exasperated.

'Well, I thought, maybe – I don't know. In my time, you know, things progressed very differently. I didn't know what you wanted.'

I gawped at him. I said, 'Graham. Not to labour the point here. But I kissed you. Very enthusiastically. Is that not maybe the tiniest hint about what I wanted?'

'We were in our cups, and you were frightened. I took advantage of your reaction, and the time it took to bring myself under control—'

'In this era, you don't have to go around controlling yourself if it's coming at you on a silver platter—'

'I am not *from* this era!' he cried – one of the very few times I ever heard him raise his voice. He leant forward, gesturing agitatedly with the cigarette. 'Understand that, as far as I'm concerned, you would have been in your rights to strike me, or chase me from the house, or vanish without a trace—'

'Well, I don't want to. I certainly didn't want you locking yourself in your room. What the hell? What were you doing in there?'

'Praying.'

'You've got to be kidding me.'

He leant back. He was wildly flushed, but he'd brought his voice under control, and his smoking hand hid the lower half of his face. 'Well, yes, "kidding" somewhat,' he muttered.

We stared at each other. The room was embarrassingly quiet after our joint outburst. I said, as levelly as I could manage, 'Tell me what you want. Not what might or could happen or go wrong. Just, right now. What do you want?'

I watched the smoke beckon the air. He took a slow, deep breath, like a man preparing to leap from a windowsill.

'Will you take off your gansey,' he said.

I pulled my wool jumper over my head. Its neck was narrow and on its departure it disarrayed my makeshift chignon. I felt my hair unsettle slowly down my neck.

'Your chemise.'

It was a T-shirt. I removed that too, dropped it to the floor.

He cleared his throat nervously and said, 'Your, uh,' then gestured at my bra with the non-smoking hand.

I took off my bra.

He'd only moved to pull on the cigarette. His head was wreathed in the smoke. I could just see that his eyes were bright and feverish.

'I wondered . . .' he murmured.

'Yes?'

'If they would be the same colour as your mouth.'

'They?'

He leant forward and quickly pinched one of my nipples,

hard, between the knuckles of his middle and fore finger. I made a noise like a slapped canary.

He leant back and took another drag on the cigarette, staring thoughtfully. The fingers that had pinched me trembled, almost imperceptibly.

'Take off your shirt,' I said.

He raised his eyebrows and for a moment I thought he was going to refuse. But he put the cigarette between his lips and began to unbutton the serge shirt. He shrugged himself out of it without looking at me.

'Put out the cigarette.'

He ground it into the ashtray.

'Stand up.'

I was talking very softly. I gave this last instruction at such a volume I could hardly hear it myself. But he stood. He was close to me. I didn't need to straighten my arm to touch him, which was the next thing I did. I flattened a hand on the middle of his chest. He was looking at me with the same mild, politely engaged expression that he always wore – as if this was a moment of no more import than any moment pulled from the pocket of our year – but his heart gave him away. Under my hand, it was pounding.

He had a cumulonimbus of black curls across his chest. I ran my hands over his ribs, white as bleached stone, scattered with brown moles. I scrubbed my thumbs across his nipples and he swallowed.

'Okay?'

'Yes.'

I moved my hands round and clasped the bookends of his back muscles, his winged bones.

'May I touch you? The way you are – like this—'

'Like—?'

'All over.'

'Yes. Please.'

He ran his fingertips up my arms, stroked my neck. His touch was frustratingly light. He let his fingers rest on my collarbones. We met one another's eyes. He moved his hands down, abruptly, over my breasts. It was such a blunt motion – so much that of a man who had really, really wanted to touch my breasts – that I scoffed, then grinned, and he lit up with a smile as sudden as the winter sun. He looked relieved.

'Is that—?'

'Please just – kiss me.'

He pulled me into him.

It was a much better kiss than last time. I clung to him while pinwheels dazzled and spun in my skull. His skin was hot.

He kissed me so hard and with such tempestuousness that it bore me back across the kitchen. I hit the fridge and he broke from me, breathing unsteadily.

'Oof. Cold.'

'Sorry.'

'Don't be. Kiss me again.'

He started to kiss me but then stopped to make a small, seared noise when I slid my thumbs under his waistband and curled them.

'Should we go somewhere else?'

'Yes.'

He didn't move, though. I was starting to tremble, out of need, which was thrilling and embarrassing. Also because the fridge was against my back.

'You may have some . . . expectations,' he murmured.

'Hm?'

'That I don't . . . that I have little experience in meeting. As I . . . as men of my time . . .'

'You're worried you won't make me come.'

'Good grief.'

'Is that it?'

'Yes. Is that how you would say it? "Make me come . . ."'

'God,' I mumbled, because even hearing him say it experimentally, like a vocabulary exercise in a foreign language, was a lot to handle. 'Yes. Don't worry. I'll teach you.'

'I would like that,' he said earnestly, and I covered my face.

'Take me to bed, then,' I said. He quite literally picked me up and carried me down our dreary flat. He chose my room and put me down on the bed, like a parcel.

'You have a very modern body,' he said.

'What does that mean?' I asked. I was wrenched by burst upon burst of tiny convulsions. I wondered if I was visibly shaking.

'I can see how you are put together.'

He didn't elucidate, just dropped his head onto my chest. I felt the rough paddle of his tongue then the edge of his teeth against my nipples. He pushed his face against my neck and found the place where the skin streamed with nerves. His head was heavy and warm.

'I want to "make you come",' he murmured, and it was exciting even with the inverted commas around it.

'You'll have to get your face wet.'

He laughed and blushed ferociously. Even his shoulders heated under my hands.

'Oh, I *see*.'

He stripped me of my skirt, tights and underwear in a few neat movements.

'Show me where.'

'Here.'

'Show me how. Slowly.'

He came down of his own accord. I tangled my hands into his hair. He worked well on both instinct and instruction. He learned fast. *A very good officer, and the sweetest of tempers.*

He lifted his head to say something to me. I was not in a state to hear it. I pushed him back down and I felt him laugh again. He worked on me, firmly and seriously, until my thighs started to shake. When I came, my back arched off the bed. I pulled his hair, I think, and I made a fair amount of noise, I think, though I am hazy on detail.

He cupped me gently and waited for the aftershocks to pass. When he saw me refocus my eyes, he nuzzled my stomach, smearing it.

'That was . . . pretty good.'

'Glad to hear it.'

'What did you say, when you were—?'

'I said that you taste like the sea.' He smiled up at me then added, 'I could feel you.'

'Oh?'

'Is it possible to make you do that when I – when I am with you?'

'"With" me, eh.'

'Don't be saucy,' he said, and twisted one of my nipples. I gasped and tugged him up by his arms.

'It's possible. Doesn't always work.'

'What needs to be done for it to work?'

'For a start, you'll need to take off the rest of your clothes.'

He rolled his eyes and started to fumble, one-handed, with the button and zipper of his fly.

'Don't stare,' he murmured.

'I want to see.'

He leant down and kissed me so that I couldn't raise my

head. The bed jounced under the movement of him kicking his trousers off.

I reached down, floundering a little because he still wouldn't let me lift my head to look properly, and wrapped my hand around him. He groaned before he could clamp his mouth shut.

'Will you—'

'Yes—'

'There—'

'Is that – yes—?'

He started slowly, watching my face. It was as if he was using a machine on me, and he was testing its efficacy by my reaction. That the machine was his body didn't appear to move him. But I tilted my hips and started to match him, meet him. His expression tightened.

'Please—'

'This – like this – you want this—'

'Yes—'

'Did you – think about this – tell me—'

'Yes – I wanted to – watch you – give in—'

He bit me sharply on the shoulder and some other animal noise escaped me. He started to dig his thumbs into tender places while he moved in me. I bucked insistently into the pressure. A certain thrilling pain, which lived in my body like another body, woke and opened its long series of tributaries through my ribs. He put his lips to my ear:

'I used to – hear you – tossing and turning – at night – I couldn't – sleep – your body – a wall away—'

'You wanted – to do – this – to me—'

'Yes—'

'Tell me – what you did—'

Into the wet heat between us, in jolts and gasps, he started to tell me about those nights, when God and the world felt far away and I felt so dangerously near, and neither prayer nor reciting the Articles of War nor squeezing his eyes shut stopped his mind from brimming with the thought of me, and he'd have to do to himself the only thing he could think of to help him sleep.

He said, softly, as if surprised by a sudden burst of rain, 'Oh. God.'

Later I examined my body and saw a line of thin crescent moons where he'd dug his nails in, flushed the same colour as my mouth.

*

Afterwards, we lay on our sides, facing each other. The clumsy metallic bonking of the radiators announced the arrival of the central heating. It was very dark – the sun had dissolved and I hadn't yet turned on my lamp – but I thought his eyes were twinkling.

'Well,' he said, 'that was interesting.'

'Ha!'

'Will you turn on the lamp, please?'

'Yes . . . There. Hello. So you're very . . . talkative.'

His ears – now visible – turned red. 'Yes, well,' he muttered. 'You make terrible noises. Like an alley cat.'

'You didn't seem to mind.'

'It's an amusing way to go deaf. Would you mind if I smoked?'

'Only if I can have one.'

'A fair trade. My cigarettes are in my pocket—'

I reached over the bed and fished his cigarettes and lighter out of his discarded trousers. He lit two and handed me one.

'Graham, can I ask you a question?'

'You may. I reserve the right to dodge it.'

'Do you – hmm. Trying to think of a way to put this subtly. When you said you didn't have much experience with courting . . .'

'I don't.'

'You don't strike me as . . . inexperienced.'

He shrugged and settled back on the pillows, ashing into the mug on the bedside table. I rummaged around the scant supplies of my diplomacy.

'What did you usually do when you, er, if you got interested in a woman?'

'I would break into a cold sweat and put myself on the nearest ship.'

'Were you – I mean, was there anyone . . . ?'

He continued to smoke reflectively. Then he said, 'You understand that, in my era, a man would have to be a villain and a scoundrel to do – any of this – with a woman he wished to court.'

'Are you a villain and a scoundrel?'

He raised his eyebrows. 'I am hurt that you have to ask.'

'*Was* there someone?'

'Not in a way that would have tarnished either of our reputations.'

'Ah. So. Right. Who?'

I puffed crossly on my cigarette. My heart had dropped two inches down my chest, or so it felt.

'It simply didn't progress that far—'

'What was her name?' I said, louder than I would be able to bear when I remembered this conversation later.

He frowned at me. At length he said, 'Sarah. Please don't feel the need to offer me the names of any of your ghosts. I don't want to know.'

He cautiously proffered the mug. I'd been drawing so hard

on the cigarette that there was a precarious worm of ash hanging off it. I tapped and it dropped into the thin scum of old tea still silting the bottom of the mug. These details were large and terrible to me. I said, 'The two of you never—?'

'Little cat. Please.'

'You're dodging this question very *strenuously*—'

'Because it's making you upset. No, we did not. At most I may have kissed her hand, and even that would have been rather giddy and ill-advised.'

I hated hearing this. I said, 'You strike me as someone who's done a fair bit more than that.'

'What a threatening observation.'

'Well?'

'I suppose so. Not with – women I would have wished to court. My experience with women generally is limited.'

I was almost at the filter and my throat hurt. 'And with men?' I said, more because I felt like being annoying than because I had noted his wary syntax.

To my surprise, he went quiet again, and regarded the end of his cigarette. Eventually he said, 'Well. One is a long time at sea.'

'What does *that* mean?'

'Enough,' he said, suddenly sharp. He flicked his stub into the mug and pinched mine, damp with the sweat of my fingers, out of my hand. I could see in the momentum of his movements that he was one twitch away from getting out of bed, leaving the room, pretending none of this happened – but then he jolted towards me, took me by the shoulders and pulled my head onto his chest.

'Put your arms around me,' he instructed.

He held me firmly. My nose was squashed against him, tickled by the black curls over his sternum. He smelled, attractively, of sweat. I folded the arm not crushed between us over his back.

'I'm not trying to keep secrets from you,' he said quietly. 'It's simply that – these matters – I have tried to separate from the rest of my life. Had I ever married, I imagine I would have kept up the fiction of a perfectly chaste life, if only not to humiliate my wife. You will learn nothing special or important about me from asking me questions that can only hurt you.'

'In this era, I think we'd call that "dishonest".'

'In my era, it might have been considered a kindness.'

I ran my fingertips over the white, curved place between his shoulder blades. I could just feel, below the skin, the toothy fragment of the microchip the Ministry had implanted in him when he first arrived, which had enabled them to monitor his movements with the closeness he'd found so inexplicable.

'Perhaps you're right,' I said. I kissed him. Axioms have us sealing all sorts of things with kisses. Vows. Envelopes. Fates. But parents don't always tell their children what the slurs and curses mean, for their protection. I thought it would be better, for now, that I didn't mention the microchip. To tell you the truth I tried not to think about it at all.

*

The next morning, when I woke up, I was alone in the bed. I lay there feeling bereft and sorry for myself until I heard a gentle knock at the door.

'Are you awake?'

'Oh. Hi. Yes.'

'Would you like a cup of tea?'

'Yes. Thanks.'

He brought the tea up and put it on the bedside table, rather than approach the bed and hand it to me. I wriggled upright. I was naked under the bedsheets. He didn't move to touch me, but he didn't leave the room or look away either.

'Adela's sending a car from the Ministry. I need to get dressed . . .'

'If you would prefer not to travel alone, I can come with you.'

'I'm all right, thanks. She and I need to talk.'

He nodded. He looked awkward. I was moved to wonder whether he had ever actually had a 'morning after', or whether he was improvising action and reaction, caught between his era's expectations and mine. If you are surprised that, so soon after a secret agent tried to kill me, I was wondering whether the man with whom I'd had sex *liked* liked me, remember that being in love is a form of blunt force trauma. I was concussed with love for him. I bent my head to the cudgel.

*

I was not such a fool as to imagine the Vice-Secretary for Expatriation had become my handler because she liked me. Adela had a plan that had something to do with Graham. Her brusque mentorship, its delineation uncanny but forcibly indicated, suggested that she wanted a workplace proxy, a daughter-in-casefile. It looked like she wanted me to be Graham's handler, and for Graham to be – what?

I arrived at the Ministry sweaty and vibeless. It was another dank toothache of a day, barely qualifying in its chromatic dullness for 'grey'.

Adela was sitting at her desk, hands stacked. She was so neatly posed that I found myself wondering what meme she was referencing. She didn't look at me, but through me. Instead of her usual abrasion, she spoke with cool diffidence. She acted like I was an ex she hadn't seen in a very long time, one engaged to a much younger woman.

'Ma'am. The Brigadier. Did he murder Quentin?'

'Enquiries are ongoing.'

'Why,' I said, 'does the Brigadier want Commander Gore?'

'He wants to go home.'

'Eh?'

The time-door, explained Adela, supported a limited number of what the Brigadier called 'free travellers'. That was why the Ministry lost two of the seven original expats – there wasn't enough capacity for them to be moved through time, it was like they'd tried to breathe through oxygen masks after other people had depleted the tank. But it was possible to make a space in the door – refill the tank, as it were – by taking a free traveller 'out of time', viz, killing them.

'How does the Ministry know that?' I asked.

'That information was extracted by the intelligence agents.'

'Torture.'

'You know we don't use that word.'

'That means there are other "free travellers" from the future around,' I said. 'If you found one to torture.'

Adela gave me a ghastly grin. 'Oh yes,' she said. 'Not just the Brigadier and Salese, I mean. They already know about the door's operational capacities. It was made in their era. Those two were never equipped for a long stay in the twenty-first century, incidentally. I believe they were part of a blitz assassination campaign.'

I tore a filet from my thumb with my teeth.

'The Brigadier used my fingerprints to access and disable the CCTV system at Parry Yard,' I said. 'That's why there's no CCTV footage of Quentin's assassination.'

Her one eye clicked into focus like a camera.

'That is a serious breach,' she said slowly. 'One that I had not anticipated. I'll deal with it. I've signed you up for a firearms refresher course. As a preventative measure. You ought to be able to bring your score up quickly. After all, you still have your depth perception.'

This was a macabre joke and even Adela seemed to sense that. She lifted her hand self-consciously to her eye-patch. I stared at her slender hand, its narrow ropes of vein. Her hand looked older than her face – around a decade older, in fact. She noticed me noticing.

'Botox,' she said drily. 'My jawline's been shaved. Nose job, that's a few years old now. Had my tear troughs and my cheeks done. This isn't my natural eye shape either. Brows are micro-bladed.'

'Oh,' I said. 'I always assumed it was reconstructive rather than cosmetic. Not that it's any of my business. Everyone should get to do what they want with their face.'

Whatever the test was, I failed it. Adela's face misted with disappointment.

'I'll handle the CCTV breach personally,' she said. 'Until I have lowered the security status, all bridge–expat teams are confined to their safehouses. Journeys to and from the Ministry must be taken in Ministry-issue vehicles, accompanied by an armed guard. Any communication or movement between safe-houses needs sign-off from both halves of Control.'

She gave me an almost maternal look and added, 'Though, as your handler, all of your requests need only be signed off by me. Don't worry about the Secretary.'

A Ministry car took me back to my new, horrid home. I heard Graham call, 'What are your orders?' before I'd even taken off my coat. I scrubbed at my face, pushed to fidget by his rare urgency.

'None. Sit tight. We're confined to the house, except for Ministry business.'

'Surely not. You are in danger!'

'Yeah. I'm taking a firearms refresher course. They know, Graham. They've known all along. They were trying to keep an eye on him.'

I flopped onto the sofa. He came to sit beside me, leaving a careful and charged channel of two feet between us.

'I am reluctant to ask you my next question,' he said, 'since it seems so comparatively trivial. But.'

I waited. He sighed.

'Well. Some time ago, I asked Maggie about "dating".' (He said this in the same disdainful way he once said 'housemate'.)

'You asked the lesbian from the seventeenth century about modern-day dating.'

'Yes. I am aware of the irony of the situation.'

'Wow. What did she say?'

'Well, she laughed at me for a while. But. My understanding of "dating",' he said, 'is that it is like trying on clothes for fit, except that the clothes are people.'

'That's a pretty brutal way of putting it, but I suppose so.'

'What happens if the fit is wrong?'

'Well. People break up. They stop seeing each other. And start over with someone else.'

'And if the fit is right?'

'Depends on what the people involved want, I guess.'

'At what point is that discussed?'

'There's . . . not really a set timeframe. You just feel your way along. Even as I say that I can see how deeply messed up modern dating must sound. But it's supposed to grant more of a sense of freedom and personal choice. No one has to commit to anything they don't want.'

He ran his hands through his hair. The curls flattened and sprang back. I was overwhelmed with the desire to touch him. So it was a shock, the psychic equivalent of biting down on bone, when he said, very quietly, 'I want to touch you.'

'Jesus,' I said, and surged across the sofa.

*

In addition to the firearms refresher course, Adela also insisted that I sign up for unarmed combat classes, Basic Cipher, and an international relations refresher for my 'region of expertise' that all field agents were required to attend every four months unless in-field. Graham and Cardingham, too, were granted special movement rights and dedicated transport to continue their field training at the Ministry. Arthur and Margaret did not enjoy the same level of freedom. I was relieved. My work with Adela meant that I soon had access to their safehouses' whereabouts – but I wanted them both stowed away safely until I had the mental wherewithal to work out next moves. In a game of chess, I reasoned, one does not rush the board with all the pawns and burn down the rooks. This analogy tells you everything you need to know about the level of depersonalised detachment I enjoyed after my attempted assassination.

I attended training sessions at the shooting range with Adela. There was an unofficial scoreboard tacked to a wall. It was updated weekly and I couldn't fail to notice that 'G. Gore' was always in the top four, clambering over and under the scores of two field agents and one of the quartermasters. It was inevitable that Adela and I were going to bump into the centre of our project at the range. Sure enough, one porridge-mild Wednesday, there was Graham and Thomas Cardingham.

'Poxy mommet weapons,' Cardingham was saying (loudly – he was wearing ear mufflers). 'Better to break a man with my yard than slay him with this scurvy arm.'

'You are a very bad loser, Thomas,' Graham said. I was amazed he hadn't told Cardingham off. Perhaps that was just how men talked to each other when women weren't listening.

'Marry, sir, with a musket in my hand thou wouldst find me a sweet foe indeed.'

'You're going to fall off the scoreboard. Oh, except you aren't on it this week. Or last week, I seem to recall.'

'Aye, my hand's not oft on such small pieces. Perchance thou art more familiar with the size. I ought to ask your bridge.'

At this, Graham coloured. He said, coldly, 'Mind how you tread, lieutenant.' Cardingham subsided and scowled with boyish embarrassment.

'Hello,' I said, because I wanted to see what would happen. The men turned around.

'We are graced,' said Cardingham with vicious irony, and bowed. 'Thou wast but lately on our tongues. With my full respect to the good commander, thou art often on his tongue.'

'I hope he has good things to say,' I murmured, eyeing Graham. But Graham appeared not to have heard me. He was staring, bemused, at Adela. I glanced at her and was baffled to see a sudden softness on her face. Though, knowing Adela, maybe her silicone fillers were melting.

'This is Adela,' I said. 'Er. My handler. Adela, of course you know Commander Gore . . . and probably Lieutenant Cardingham . . .'

'Yes,' said Adela hoarsely. 'I am aware of them.'

'It's an honour to be worthy of the attention,' said Graham politely. 'Will you be joining us?'

'No,' said Adela. Her voice was thick. Pallor strained through her cheeks. 'Regrettably, I must be going . . . but I expect your score to improve by twenty . . .'

'Yes ma'am,' I said, for want of anything else to say. Adela nodded, her stare landing between the three of us. Then she muttered something approximating a 'good day' and stalked out.

'She is *very* blonde,' murmured Graham. He seemed confused, as if he'd just been handed an egg and told to hatch it.

'Bottle blonde. I think she's naturally a very dark brunette, which accounts for the scruffly texture of her hair.'

'The women of this era have a certain constant cast,' said Cardingham. 'Perhaps it is the "chemicals" i'th'water. I have heard the ruling powers do filter in such poisons as emasculate men and pacify the weak. Perhaps they clone the womenfolk.'

'Aren't you both training for entry on the field agent programme? You're part of the ruling power now, lieutenant,' I said sweetly.

I glanced at Graham, and was surprised and put out when he didn't say anything.

*

But for the most part, Graham and I were locked in together. The state of emergency that sealed our doors also had the effect of truncating our thoughts and plaiting us together with an intensity I'd never before experienced. All we had was each other and the rooms we had each other in.

At the end of February, arriving with the abruptness of a

man walking late into a packed theatre, there was an afternoon of vivid light and heat. It was as if a wet towel had been taken off the bowl of the sky. I stood on the roof between the air vents and turned my face upwards.

'Yes,' I said, in a mad person's monotone. 'Ahaha. Yes.'

'Does summer start in February now?' he asked, standing beside me.

'No. We get these unseasonal hot days. Except they happen so often they're pretty much seasonal. Do you remember about global warming?'

'A fever of the earth.'

'Mm.'

'You look very pleased about this.'

'Terrible, isn't it?' I murmured. 'No, I'm not happy about the climate crisis. But I hate the winter so much.'

'You look livelier,' he said.

'Oh?'

'Shall we go back inside?' he suggested, in the vague way he spoke when he was about to put his hands under my top.

There were some things about sleeping with a Victorian naval officer that didn't surprise me, and there were others that astonished me. He kept trying to touch the edge of licence, but my parameters were so much more capacious than his. I didn't have the same sense of shame of it, but I don't think I ever had the same sense of holiness either.

Some things could have been him, or they could have been the era in him. He wouldn't go to bed with me if we were at all stoned or drunk (I went teetotal). He wouldn't strike me, even when I pleaded for it, even though I knew he wanted to – for various reasons I'm good at assessing this – and he worked off his desire to lay forceful hands on me in interesting ways – weird games with bowls of milk and thumb pressure in my hollows. He didn't seem to want his body involved in sex at all. He always undressed me first and undressed himself afterwards. He wouldn't let me go down on him for weeks after we started sleeping together, and even then I had to do it with the lights out, snuffling about like a randy anteater. '*You shouldn't*,' he whispered, both hands on the back of my head.

He enjoyed kissing more than any person I'd ever kissed – not as a precursor to other acts, but as an act in itself. He kissed me until my mouth burned. He locked my wrists in his grip so that I couldn't take my hands for a walk below his waist and kissed me until I was thrumming with need. I got to know his mouth very well. I was on warm terms with his shoulders, his neck, his chest, his arms, his shapely calves, his (very ticklish) feet. But he was shy about everything else, and guarded as a stray cat.

I became demented about his body in non-sexual contexts. If his shirt lifted and his trousers dragged when he was trying to reach a high shelf, revealing a crescent moon of hipbone, my heart would beat so hard I could basically chew it. The mole on his throat had me writing poetry. Watching him fumble for his cigarettes in his pockets was an incredible experience. By contrast, he liked watching me shower, and I just let him. He'd smoke while he watched and I'd come out of the bathroom with my wet hair stinking.

I could tell when he was coming, because he liked to talk to me when he was inside me, but he wouldn't make much more noise than a muffled groan when he climaxed, and so the volume would decrease the closer he got. He asked questions – how it felt, what I wanted, how I wanted it – for the sheer pleasure of listening to me respond.

And afterwards, brief demi-hours of peace. Holding me in his arms, the way that poems hold clauses. Smiling at me, as if to say, '*Well, aren't you glad we both survived that?*' Watching the sun go down over my shoulder, stroking my cheek with the back of his hand. His pretty dimples, because he was smiling so much, because I think he always felt that we were as divided by passion as propriety, and he was at his happiest when we were quiet and calm.

All this unfolded in what I now know to call our last weeks. Within the action of this story, these memories mean little. After the first time Graham and I went to bed together, they are symbolically all of a piece. I could have written to you without including them; after all, the things that happen between lovers are lost to the work of history anyway. But I wrote it down because I need you to bear witness to it. He was here, by and with and in my body. He lives in me like trauma does. If you ever fall in love, you'll be a person who was in love for the rest of your life.

*

March came in, mellow and pastel. The air felt washed. The scrubbed newness of the spring gave the rooftops and the street furniture a friendly polish. I was angry, every day, terrified of death at the hands of a burst of blue light, and I was also nursing fragile joy. It was disorientating. Sometimes I sat up in bed and stared down at Graham, in his coal-hot, silent sleep in the early hours of the morning, and I wanted to lick him all over. I wanted to put him in a locket by my heart. I wanted to get promoted fast enough that I'd always have enough firepower to protect him. And to be senior enough to stop him leaving, but I didn't like to think about that too much.

One evening, he made an impressive yao hon and then tried to eat his with a knife and fork.

'Listen. This is delicious, but I can't praise you if you're going to jab at your wraps with cutlery.'

'What on earth are you doing with that innocent lettuce leaf?'

'What I'm supposed to do. Put down the fork, for goodness' sake. It's like watching the Spanish Inquisition with the thumb-screws.'

'Your way seems very messy. Look. There goes your prawn. Goodbye, prawn.'

'Yeah, well, it's also the *right* way. Which one of us is "not entirely an Englishwoman" here, eh?'

'Which one of us can cook?' he countered.

Afterwards, I made a start on the washing up, but he cleared his throat and said, 'I thought we might go out. On the bikes. Take a flask of hot toddy with us.'

'We're not allowed to do that sort of thing any more.'

He took my hand, sudsy as it was, kissed a bubble on my knuckle, and said, 'Sometimes you wake me in the middle of the night because you are grinding your teeth so vigorously. I'd rather we break a rule than you break your poor molars. Come on. Let's "let off some steam".'

I smiled. Graham was an Age of Sail officer who had just witnessed the overture to steam-powered ships. Of all the idioms he absolutely fucking loathed, 'let off some steam' was right at the top. In using it, I suspected he was trying to charm me. In fact his next words were, 'Besides, there's something special I want to show you.' I love to feel special. Of course I was interested enough to break a rule.

*

I hadn't used my bike since we'd arrived at the new safe-house and I was electrified by the sense of freedom it gave me:

movement, in my chosen direction, from the happy effort of my body. After a half-hour of cycling down the bike super-highway, the city receded and the streets darkened. Soon we were having to pick our way along barely lit residential roads where the houses were squat and sleeping. Then we came to dark blue lanes grasped by the trees, the ground underfoot rustic with pebbles. My bike light bounced off his back.

'Where are we going?' I called to him.

'We'll come to a large field. Very soon.'

When we reached the field, it was a line of darkness scrawled on the deeper darkness. We stumped our bikes over the wet, breathless earth.

'There,' he said.

'Hmm?'

'Stars.'

I blinked at him, and then I looked up. It was true. Away from the grubby muslin of London's light pollution, in the fresh March night, the sky was full of stars. I turned back to him. As I adjusted to the dark, I could see he was staring upwards.

'I can't manage it exactly without a sextant,' he said. 'But I wanted to be able to orient myself.'

'So that, in the event of London flooding when the ice caps melt, you can sail to safer waters?'

'So that I will know where I was when I met you.'

I had always thought of joy as a shouting, flamboyant thing, that tossed breath into the sky like a ball. Instead it robbed me of my speech and my air. I was pinned in place by joy and I didn't know what to do.

'Come here,' he said softly, and pulled me into his arms.

I pressed my face against his neck. My body sparked and I couldn't move it, except to lean into him. I was filled with happiness, so enormous and terrifying it was as if I'd committed a crime to get it. No one had given me permission to feel this way, and I thought I might not be allowed it. He combed his fingers through my hair and I was frightened with happiness, harrowed by it. There was no way that anyone could feel this much without also knowing they were going to lose it.

VIII

April 1848. Commander Gore has been gone — presumed dead — for eight months. *It* is about to begin. He never sees any of *it*. He imagines *it* instead. He reads books about *it*, published decades, centuries after *it* happens. He takes the awful images conjured by scholars and hobbyists and palms out a story.

The companies of *Erebus* and *Terror* struggle through the winter of 1847. Their best sportsman is dead — not that there's much hunting to be had. A single storm on the ice wipes out another hunting party of two officers and three men, whose bodies are never found. Others succumb to the claws of the climate, to scurvy, to madness. Men starve and rave, dreaming of gravy. There isn't enough coal to heat the ships, nor enough candles to light the Arctic winter. Franklin's bold adventurers lie for hours in the dark, too cold and hungry to move, while the darkness looks like ink-soaked cardboard pressed against the portholes. The ships smell like carrion.

Spring comes. By this time nine officers and fifteen men are dead: the highest death rate of a polar expedition in hundreds of years. Crozier, whose soul barely inhabits his flaking, creasing body, orders the ships abandoned. Franklin's expedition — still, in 1848,

'Franklin's expedition' and not 'Franklin's lost expedition' — will march eight hundred miles with provisions to last barely half that, and hope that on the journey south, they'll find game and open water.

They fasten whaleboats onto runners and fill them with what they imagine they will need. Tents, of course; their sleeping bags of sealskin and deer pelt; their provisions, which are mostly tinned; one set of spare underclothes per man; guns, for hunting. Other things too. They pile the whaleboats with soap and books and candlesticks and journals and crockery. They are afraid they might be needed. They are afraid of everything, so they leave nothing. Their backs bruise under the weight of the boats. Their joints crack. They die by inches.

They haul the boats.

The officers pull alongside the men. Even Crozier and Fitzjames haul. The men are too weak to manage alone. There is no beauty in this, not after the first fifty miles. Just sore bodies, frostbite and dysentery. The surviving surgeons are granted a Marine guard each, to keep desperate sailors out of the medicine chests. The Marines have orders to shoot on sight. Goodsir is, for a time, one of the surviving surgeons, but he's seen off by a tooth infection and dies with poisoned blood. He is lucky; he is buried.

They haul the boats.

They start by burying the dead in shallow graves, then, further on, piling rocks over the bodies in makeshift cairns, but soon there are too many dead. They leave the bodies where they drop.

They haul.

They abandon empty cans, trinkets, clothing. They leave bizarre oases of clutter, civilisation in its larval form. The notion of *expedition*, of *England*, streams off them. They put one foot in front of the other and balance their minds on their heads.

They haul.

The landscape looks like something suspended in glass. It is like walking through a perfect, terrible illusion. Their tiredness is an omnipresent thing, God of the bones and the sinew.

Gore reads that thirty or so survivors from the hundred-odd crew make it to a final camp. 'Starvation Cove', later explorers call it. They are still hundreds of miles from the nearest European outpost.

Gore dreams about his friends. He sees Le Vesconte lying on the canvas of a collapsed tent. 'Henry,' he says in the dream. Le Vesconte does not respond. He has no legs and half his pelvis is missing. His hipbone pokes through torn meat like the gunwales of a shipwreck. The bone is not white, but ivory and speckled grey. Le Vesconte's mouth is slack and open. The dark purple fruit of his tongue lolls from his lips. His eyes are white and slimy. They have rolled back in his head.

Gore dreams he sees Lieutenant Little of *Terror*, creeping towards the body. Blood is tracking sluggishly down Little's face. His eyes are clouded. Gore understands, in the dream, that Little can no longer see people, only flesh. 'Edward, listen to me,' Gore says. Little creeps along the stones. 'Edward. That was a man. Not food.'

Surviving testimony suggests the Inuit tried to help, where they could. But more than a hundred poorly prepared Europeans, already dying, in a land where the Inuit lived at a level of strict subsistence, in a year where summer never came, were too many souls to save. Franklin's expedition hadn't been invited to the Arctic. Why did they insist on leaving their bodies so far from their native earth? This is the rational response.

Gore knows better. He thinks of the face of the woman whose husband he killed. He wakes up with the taste of dead flesh in his mouth. It is God's love, or God's vengeance, that he survived in this impossible way, that he has to remember them all and her besides. He will not be responsible for another death, another friend lost. He dreams with the bitter determination of a man who must reach camp before dark.

Chapter Eight

The days flickered between catastrophic rain and unseasonal heat, flashing dark and bright as starkly as a chessboard. We played at domesticity, rearranging our strange new home around the belongings the Ministry had thought to seize from our old one.

The Ministry, meanwhile, locked down. The administrative team began the unwieldy, bug-polluted process of moving data and confidential information onto another secure server. Internal comms were a mess. Emails bounced or sent with hysterical duplicates. The phones bluescreened. Even our key cards stopped functioning properly. Simellia got herself trapped in a mystery vestibule because her key card caused the lock to melt when she touched it to the pad, showering her with a terrifying rain of fat green sparks and setting off the alarms.

I was in the building at the time, on my way to a meeting with Adela. The alarm was curiously nasal, like a complaint just at the edge of articulation. Someone from the ops and maintenance department staggered full-pelt past me and I followed in their wake. When we got to the fused door I could hear Simellia loudly reciting the hollow crown speech from *Richard II* on the other side, bashing rhythmically on the door with the iambs.

'We can hear you!' I called. 'We're getting you out.'

'"We" are, are we?' muttered the maintenance woman. Back-office ops loathed the bridges. I'd never understood why but I was paid too much to care.

Simellia, once she emerged, was back in her uniform of chic, though she'd lost some weight and moved sepulchrally inside her deconstructed blazer. She'd also let her hair out into an Afro, which I'd never seen her do before. It suited her, though I wasn't sure whether I was allowed to say this, and so I didn't.

'You,' she said.

'Me. Hello.'

'And baby makes three,' said the maintenance woman. She snorted when we ignored her and cantered off. The Ministry suffered a maintenance emergency more or less every half hour during the lockdown; she'd be needed elsewhere.

'Technically Ivan made three,' I said, 'but you know he's in the process of being stood down.'

'What?'

'Adela thinks Cardingham's development is better left in the hands of the field agent programme. We can make a solider out of him, but probably never a modern metrosexual.'

'And I heard Ralph is under house arrest?' said Simellia.

'Protective custody,' I corrected. 'He's ex-Defence, likely high on any anti-Ministry hitlist.'

'Do you know where his safehouse is?'

I shrugged. I knew where everyone's safehouses were. Adela had made it known to me that Graham and I were considered, by the Ministry's bellicose hierarchy, the senior bridge–expat team. We deserved more access, *required* more access, as Graham's adjustment was so pivotal and promising. If it was unfair, it was also useful. Certainly Adela's insistence that we were special in some way tallied with my experience of being in love.

'My key card has stopped working on Ministry property and Adela has cancelled our last three meetings,' said Simellia. 'I've been trying to get Arthur's benzodiazepine prescription re-evaluated and his own Wellness team is blocking me. Do you know why this is all happening? All we've been told is "emergency procedures"—'

'Someone tried to kill me,' I said. 'The Brigadier.'

Watching what happened on Simellia's face was like watching a papercut fill with blood. I saw the shock of impact, the brief beat of perhaps-nothing, the welling. She reached for me and, I think, would have embraced me, but her hand brushed the gun beneath my jacket. She pulled back.

'I can speak to Adela about Arthur, if you like,' I said, holding her gaze. 'I'm going to see her now.'

'Thank you,' said Simellia, very coldly. 'That would be kind. Look after yourself.'

*

One pleasant spring afternoon, I arranged to go with Arthur, Margaret and Graham to a Turner exhibition. The expats played a game that they called ghost-hunting. They would visit a place – a pub, a monument, a stately home – or a gallery or exhibition, to see if they could spot anything or anyone that they recognised from their own era. In this instance, they expected Graham would see the most ghosts, as the exhibition was devoted to Turner's marine paintings. In fact, I'd organised the jolly little trip – haunted by plainclothes agents and signed off by Adela – partly because I wanted to test the limits of my special status, but also because I felt responsible for them. After the move to the safehouses, it became abundantly clear that Arthur and Margaret were not enjoying the same *meaningful cultural integration* as Graham, or even as Cardingham – by which I mean, the Ministry simply found them less interesting. Fewer and fewer meetings were devoted to their adjustment, their long-term goals. Only the 'readability' experiments continued to run with any degree of consistency. Besides that, I knew Graham – who kept up a supervised and frequently curtailed programme of visits – had told them something about what was happening behind our doors, in our beds – I didn't know what – Graham was vague and evasive when I asked him – but he must have found a word for 'lovers' that didn't make him feel excessively Victorian and ashamed, and now I had no control whatsoever over how Margaret and Arthur might be receiving this knowledge about me. I had to fix it.

Margaret, who understood how to sneak soft-drink cans and snacks into cinemas, was not impressed by the idea of the gallery trip. Consider how much she'd had to learn: negotiating supermarkets, brands and flavours, the invention of the aluminium can, the basic untrustworthiness of the popcorn counter, the invention of film.

'We're hence to look at pictures of boats?' she asked, exasperated, in the car.

'Ships, Sixty-five, *ships*,' said Graham. 'The finest of the line.'

'Big boats,' Arthur supplied. Graham's shoulders stiffened.

The exhibition was divided into several rooms, which charted Turner's developing practice throughout his life. I stared listlessly at detailed and virtuosic paintings of 'big boats' at sea, tilting horribly in the wind.

'Were you ever sea-sick?' I asked Graham.

'Not since I was a boy. A Gore stomach is a nigh unturnable one.'

'I feel sick just looking at these.'

'You could not be a ship's cat, poor little cat.'

It wasn't until I walked later into Turner's century – the 1830s, the 1840s – that I started to see what all the fuss was about. The forensic detail of the early paintings was gone. In their place, the sensory drama of the rain, the wind and the waves was portrayed in sweeping, fuzzy strokes, more suggestion than depiction. I stood and gawped stupidly in front of *The Fighting Temeraire*, irradiated by its impossible orange sun. I felt a gentle hand on my jaw. Arthur was closing my mouth.

'You'll catch flies,' he said.

'Ha. It's very impressive, isn't it?'

'Very. Even Maggie has stopped complaining. Forty-seven is transfixed – over there—'

I glanced over. Graham was staring hard at a canvas I'd recently pulled away from, *The Slave Ship*.

'Ah right. Let's – let's leave him to it.'

'He's told me a little about his time sailing with the Preventative Squadron. Is that the correct terminology, "sailing with"?' Arthur added, embarrassed by the affection he'd loaded his voice with.

'Beats me. "Floating around with" is about my level of expertise. Here. Let's sit down.'

Margaret was already sitting on the padded benches in the middle of the room. She gave us a wave.

'I caused the sounding of the bell,' she said.

'You set an alarm off?'

'Yes.'

'Well done!' said Arthur. 'How long did it take?'

'I felt my "hereness" readily! The guard was most vexed. I'faith, I would not steal these pictures. I am not so fond of boats.'

'*Big* boats,' I said. Arthur laughed and settled between us.

I was shy of Arthur. Most friendship quartets don't function in squares but in lines, and Arthur and I were the furthest away from one another. I liked him, and in any other circumstances it would have been impossible not to adore someone with as good a heart as he had. But he was in love with Graham. It was all over him like chickenpox. I felt myself going harridan and crooked when Graham looked longer than usual at Margaret so I couldn't imagine what it cost Arthur to be around me. Still, he was the most forgiving soul I ever met. I suspected he blamed himself: his gender, his era, his heart.

'Have you come to a decision on your film schools, Sixty-five?' he was asking.

'Prague,' said Margaret promptly. 'It is not so far. You may visit me.'

Margaret's primary skills were of the household-running variety, chores she had barely engaged with since arriving in the future and which she had no intention of picking up again. She 'had her letters', as she put it, but she was still attending adult literacy classes. She'd fixated on the notion of film schools – that she lived in a world where she could be trained to create cinema, her favourite thing in the twenty-first century. The Ministry did have a budget for retraining the expats. But there was no way they would let Margaret out of London, let alone Britain. Perhaps Ralph had been wringing out some daydreams for her.

'Where will you be apprenticed, Sixteen?' asked Margaret.

'Do you have any sense of what, in this brave new world, you'd like to do?' I asked.

'Have a rest,' said Arthur.

'Ha. Yeah, wouldn't we all. You could try something scandalously outré instead. Joining the circus? Professional go-go dancing? Accountancy?'

Arthur smiled. He was twisting the signet ring on his finger. Margaret reached out and took his fidgeting hand.

'Speak it,' she said.

Arthur sighed. Then he said, 'I think the suffragettes did bally well. I can see there are famous *career opportunities* for a bright and ambitious young lady. But I can't help noticing that the exchange has not been all equal. I rarely see chaps taking care of old folks or scrubbing the floors. People still look at a man ferrying a child without a wife alongside with something like suspicion. Or pity.'

'You want to work with children?' I said, alarmed. We didn't have material on how to deal with the expats if they got broody and I wasn't much good at it with normal people either. Arthur gave me a despairing look.

'You see? You're surprised. Maybe disappointed.'

'No, that's not what – Arthur, of course that's possible—'

'Is it? I've read all sorts on the liberation of the queers – do you say it like that, "the queers"? – anyway, and the working woman and the feminist revolution and so on and so forth. But . . . You know, I'm not Forty-seven, I stay awake through everything I watch, and I can see what your era likes. You use the same patterns as we did, as Gray's people did and Maggie's too. You just expect women to do more of it, that's all.'

'But you're not a woman, Arthur,' I said.

He threw me an amused look – not in oneupmanship, but playfully, for me to catch – and said, 'But I'm not the blueprint for the perfect man, either.'

'You are the print of a perfect egg,' said Margaret.

'Thank you, Sixty-five.'

'I love you very well, egg.'

'Love you too. That's a fine example of what I mean, by the way! I am supposed to hatch into *something* – very useful and effective – to make all of this palaver with bringing me over here worth its salt. Even back home – excuse me – back in my era, there was always a sense that money and effort had gone into mixing my preparation, and I'd jolly well better bake and set in the right mould and not go off my onion in any way. The *reward* is, well, all the finer things – children, a family, some peace of mind – but the *cost* is matching the recipe. And I am a little off my onion, you know.'

'So you – want children?' I asked, audibly floundering.

Arthur tossed me another look, but this one was opaque. I'd feel terrible shame about that, in the weeks and months and years afterwards. I couldn't find the right words to answer him, couldn't even imagine – high-achieving poster-child of an immigrant preserved by the benevolent British state that I was – what the answer might be, but I was saved by Graham's arrival at the bench. Arthur turned his face up to him.

'Hallo, Gray. Have you finished looking at the big boats?'

'Ships. I am done with this room, yes.'

'Did you see any nice boats?' asked Arthur pleasantly.

'*Ships*,' Graham said, and stalked off.

We got up and adjusted our clothes. We were all wearing sheepish, excitable expressions, like children caught drawing on walls. We followed Graham into the next room and crowded around him, clucking annoyingly.

'This sail has the aspect of a cloud! 'Tis wondrous fair. Did you ever mistake an enemy sail for mere weather, Forty-seven?'

'I like this guy's cool little bandanna. Did you ever wear a cool little bandanna? Something . . . groovy?'

'This one is rather good. With the burst of light. As if the big boat is coming to collect passengers to Heaven. God's own dear little ferry.'

'You are all tedious people,' he said calmly. 'I should have you flogged for insubordination.'

'Did you ever order floggings?' I asked. He ignored me to

read the painting's legend. Quite suddenly, he straightened up, eyes blank, and moved off without speaking.

'Oh,' said Arthur, distressed. 'Do you think we went too far?'

I read the legend:

Hurrah! for the whaler Erebus! Another fish! (1846) *Turner seems to have borrowed the name of this whaling ship from HMS Erebus, which with her companion vessel, the Terror, had sailed for the Arctic the previous year. In one of the greatest disasters in polar exploration, neither ship nor any of their company returned.*

'Ah,' I said.

*

He brushed off all attempts to comfort or question him, of course. He arranged the conversation so that his momentary lapse of face was obscured. It was a trick of his, as expertly wielded as his perfect cogency with his 'hereness' and 'thereness'. He would build sentences around the rooms where burnt and broken things squatted, and I would never be able to see the damage for the bars.

Cars took us back to our separate safehouses. Margaret and Arthur wilted as they retreated into the vehicles. Their days of free wandering were over. The twenty-first century was a thing that was happening outside their windows. Of course I felt sorry for them. They'd been at the mercy of the Ministry since they arrived. Every in-breath and shed tear was monitored. But the Ministry had saved their lives. It had some small say in how those lives continued.

At home, Graham, his jaw set and his eyes dull, pushed me against the door.

'Do you remember,' I said, 'that this is more or less how we first kissed?'

'Don't ask me about the things that I remember,' he muttered.

I put my hands through his hair and he put his face in my neck.

'Please,' he murmured.

When he was inside me and his breath was dewing my throat, I wondered what was going through his mind. I kissed him until my lips hurt and I tried to hear his thoughts. What was it like, to be the only one who came back? The only one who still had a body to touch, to hurt, to yearn with? The last one still able to die?

*

The crumble and leak of our new lodgings were as uncomfortable as wearing ill-fitted clothing. I became acutely aware of the vulnerability of my body, as if it were a rented house with locks I hadn't had the chance to change. The field agent programme included a course in unarmed combat and, at Adela's insistence, I signed up to see if it would make me feel any better. After I'd attended six sessions, Adela appeared one day, in expensive athleisure.

'Spar with me,' she said. 'I'd like to see what you've learned.'

'Mainly that it's almost always better to run away.'

'That's a start,' said Adela, then kicked my feet out from under me. I hit the mat with an embarrassing grunt-woof.

'You didn't say we'd started!'

'Attackers generally don't,' said Adela placidly. I rolled out of the way just before her heel came down on my stomach and scrambled upright.

'No, if it's the Brigadier, he'll just shoot me with— He's got this weapon that makes blue light and—'

'You've escaped once. There, why did you strike so slowly? Now I have your wrist.'

I wrenched free and skittered backwards. 'What does that mean, I've escaped "once"?' I panted. 'Is he coming back? Do you have information on that? Where is he? Ow! Jesus!'

'I was merely remarking upon it. You are more capable than you realise. How is Commander Gore?' Adela asked, easily blocking two weak punches. 'I understand the quartermasters filed permission to train him on long-range weapons. You are telegraphing your punches.'

'I don't want to hurt you.'

'You're not going to,' she said, and landed a meaty blow into my shoulder.

'Ow!'

'Block.'

'Ow! I'm trying! Yeah, he's at the Ministry almost as much as I am. Not just for training either. For historical context too, I think. Aah! Like. No one explains the Cold War better than the archivists. Fuck! Ow! Also a while ago I dropped some big history on him with no context and he's working his way backwards through declassified missions.'

'Blitzkrieg and 9/11.'

'Ha. Ouch! The trenches and Auschwitz, actually.'

Adela froze, the edge of her hand arrested mid-strike.

'What?'

'I said the word "Auschwitz" out of context and he spent all night looking up the Holocaust.'

'You didn't tell him about the attack on the Twin Towers?'

asked Adela. She seemed genuinely confused. Her hand hovered in mid-air. I hesitated, then decided this must mean the sparring was over, and relaxed.

'No. God, can you imagine? He'd already spent 1839 blowing up the sultanate at Aden. I'm not sure how much I'd trust him to keep the whole war on terror thing in, like, non-racist proportion.'

'Yes,' said Adela, in a flaking voice. 'If he'd come to the news abruptly, he would have converted to the Ministry on the spot.'

She met my eye and added, 'I imagine.'

Slowly the look went rancid.

'I had my guard down. It would have been sensible to attack then,' she said, and punched me in the face.

*

Beating the shit out of me put Adela in a good mood for several days. I wrangled permission from her to take Graham for a monitored bike ride to Greenwich, to see the Franklin expedition memorial. 'We can't expect him to adjust without closure,' I'd said. 'And it might improve his grip on his "hereness" and "thereness". I know he's already scoring highly on voluntary readability but there's no harm in reinforcing it.' She'd looked at me as you might a cat who, with unusual perspicacity, has brought home a ten-pound note instead of a dead mouse.

The day I'd chosen was, in fact, fair. The light was even and soft, like carefully sifted flour. Deranged by the heat shift, unseasonal roses were bursting and shedding luminously in front gardens and public squares. A cool breeze ran alongside us as we cycled; it resembled nothing so much as a handshake. As with every time I experienced clement weather, I was overcome with the sense that my troubles and pains had been put on hold, and would resume after an interval break in which I could, spiritually speaking, use the bathroom and get a drink and generally fix myself.

Under the March sunlight, the buildings of the Old Royal Naval College looked scrubbed and canvas-clean. He stared out over the long green lawns, frowning.

'It's a monument to itself.'

'Yes. But a very beautiful one.'

'How curious that I have survived to watch my obsolescence grow old enough to be celebrated as legendary.'

He walked slowly up the path, looking around as if he'd never seen a building in the wild before.

'Little cat,' he said, and I obediently trotted to his side. There were at least two other people in sight distance, which meant we were in public, which meant he wasn't going to kiss me or embrace me, but he reached out and quickly squeezed my hand. For him, this was a scandalous display of affection.

We walked side by side to the Chapel, at a chaste and proper distance, and up the steps.

'Oh,' he said.

'Mm.'

'Somehow I did not think it would be – right there.'

The Chapel's memorial to the Franklin expedition, under which the body tenuously identified as assistant surgeon Harry Goodsir was buried, was in an alcove near the entrance. I was embarrassed by the sight of a half-rolled poster display for a recently closed exhibition and a small herd of black queue barriers which had been left nearby. The moment should have been grand, heart-rending, important. I felt sure there should be mournful organ music. Instead the memorial looked forgotten.

He stood and stared for a long time at the engraved muster roll of officers.

'They promoted Edward then,' he said softly. 'Good.'

'All the mates got their commission too.'

'Oh, as it ever was. One often had to wait for someone to die in order to ascend the ranks. It's just unusual for the person dying to be oneself.'

I smiled unsurely. He was very pale. A trick of the shadow had swallowed the green in his eyes. They were an opaque, flat brown, like a spring tree that had failed to regrow.

'And – Dr Goodsir is—?'

'Yes.'

'He was in fine, bombastic form the last time I saw him. He came out to the magnetic observatory and went into rhapsodies about the lichen. He told me moss is a sign that God has a sense of humour, and fungi that he has a sense of awe. He was very eccentric. You would have liked him.'

'Yeah. I've read his letters home. He seemed like a funny man.'

'I forget that we are objects of study to you. That you can read our private correspondence.'

'Sorry.'

'No, don't be. At least they are remembered and cared for still.'

I didn't know how to respond to this. I touched my fingers to his palm. He made a soft, gear-adjusting noise in his throat and said, 'Would you mind if I had some time alone here?'

'Of course not. Uh. Should I wait—'

'You may wish to find something to occupy yourself.'

'Ah. Yes. I'll go to the Museum.'

I regretted saying that, because part of the Museum had relics dug up from the collapse of his expedition, but he was already in a different place in his mind. He didn't look at me, but he reached out and brushed my cheek, as he might have absent-mindedly petted an animal. 'Thank you,' he said.

In the end it was an hour before he sent me a carefully composed text, arranging to meet me near the entrance to the Greenwich foot tunnel. We got lunch at a food stall and I could see him trying to work out the recipe for the Nutella-covered pisang goreng. I joked that we'd have to buy a fire blanket and he accused me of having little faith, then asked why I'd never let him have Nutella before. I said that I tried not to let myself have it otherwise I ceased to partake of the other food groups.

He said, 'On the subject of which.'

'Yes?'

'Cannibalism.'

'Uh.'

'I knew those men.'

'Yes.'

'And they wouldn't have done that.'

He looked at me, as if debating how much I would weigh if I were hundreds of beans and poured in a bottle.

'Would they?' he added.

'I'm sorry. If you know about that then you know how we know. The Inuit had no reason to lie. And, well. We found the remains, eventually. The British, I mean, and the Canadians and so on. The bones had knife marks. There's this thing called pot polishing—'

He held up his wooden fork and I broke off. His lips were pale. So was the rest of his face, but it was the lips that startled me. Finally he said, 'Do you believe the natives were telling the truth?'

'Graham. It's what happened. There's archaeological evidence.'

'But then you believe that it could have been true of me.'

'It would have been true of anyone. They were starving.'

'And the Esquimaux didn't help.'

'We say "Inuit". They crossed paths here and there. I know

there's at least one record of a successful joint caribou hunt after the ships were abandoned. But. I mean. You must remember what King William Island looked like. There's just not enough game to support that many men.'

He gave me a strange, blurry look, like he was burying something in the back of his skull. 'Do you know the names of the last men?' he asked.

'No. About thirty men made it to the final camp at Starvation Cove. But we don't know who. Some people think the very last survivors were Captain Crozier and Dr McDonald, based on Inuit testimony, but really we have no idea.'

Relief crept through his face. I wondered who he had imagined, starving and blank-eyed, picking calf muscle from their teeth.

*

The next morning, when I woke up, he was in my bed.

We'd taken to sleeping together most nights. He slept as if a plug had been pulled on his brain. He looked sweetly boyish when he was asleep, and it made me afraid. I adored him and it was robbing me of a layer of skin.

But he was rarely still in bed in the mornings, as he rose some two hours before I did. When I saw him there, lying still on his back and staring at the ceiling, I felt a shiver of wrongness.

'I'm never going back, am I?' he said. His voice was low and conversational, as if we were picking up a chat we'd been having five minutes beforehand.

I wriggled closer and settled my hand on his chest.

'No. You can't.'

'I don't think I really believed it. But it's true. They're all dead. Everyone I ever knew is dead. Everything I had in my life is gone.'

I rubbed my thumb on his chest. *'Be present and calm,'* the Wellness team had advised. *'Focus on action. Accept confusion; do not demand explanation.'* He stared at me, vague and empty, the way an animal looks at a book.

'There is no one left in the world who has known me for longer than a few months. I am a stranger in a strange land.'

'I know you.'

'Do you?'

'I'm trying. I'd like to know you better.'

Something softened in his face, enough that I caught a glimpse of the ocean of sadness he had dammed and kept damming, every night, every day.

'Come here,' he said.

*

People sometimes asked me if I'd ever been 'back' to Cambodia. I told them I'd 'visited'.

On one such visit, with my parents and my sister, my mother arranged a trip to the seaside resort town of Kep. There, women manning market stalls cooked mudfish and baby squid over charcoal and cheerfully fleeced us – my mother's Penh accent as poor a passport as her family's Western faces – and we ate fish and rice with prahok and bitter melon on a raised wooden picnic platform. A wandering drinks vendor with sak yant tattoos told my mother that nice Khmer girls didn't drink and my father had to buy the beers and sneak them to her, holding up a fan each time she took a sip, an operation they managed with increasing hilarity.

When we were fed and had made a memory of it, she took us further up the coast. Eventually we found what she was looking for in an abandoned, weed-choked plot smelling outrageously of animal behaviours. She pulled up something red from the floor.

'Look.'

It was part of an intricately carved floor tile, bearing the rubbed remains of a mandala pattern. We started to look, amazed, around our feet.

'It was my family's holiday home,' said my mother. 'Your grandmother chose the tiles.'

When something changes you constitutionally, you say: 'the earth moved'. But the earth stays the same. It's your relationship with the ground that shifts.

The time-travel project was the first time in history that any person had been brought out of their time and into their far future. In this sense, the predicament of the expats was unique. But the rhythms of loss and asylum, exodus and loneliness, roll like floods across human history. I'd seen it happen around my own life.

I knew Graham felt adrift on treacherous waters. He desired me – that much was obvious now – but either he wished that he didn't, or he wished we could have done it his way. He was in an uncertain relationship with everything in our era, but he knew how to make love to me and he knew it was what I wanted. If I'd let him have his choice, he would never have touched me, but would have courted me chastely in that little house until the Ministry made him enough of a man that he could create an honest woman out of what he had to work with.

I suppose I mean to say that I'd betrayed him, because he'd been told I was his anchor, and instead I insisted he become mine. Betrayed him in other ways too, of course, by keeping secrets from him and reporting on him. But that was all in the original job description.

*

He sat with his back against the headboard and held me in his lap, rutting unhurriedly into me. My mouth and breasts stung pleasurably where he had kissed me and rasped me with the shadow of stubble on his chin. He rolled one of my nipples like a rosary bead between his knuckles, and clasped my hips in one arm, pinning me in place.

'Let me—'

'Be good and take it slowly.'

Twice I'd wrenched myself off him and tried to provoke him into rough movement with my mouth and my hands. Our bodies were slick with sweat and when I moved away from him to do this, the cold air in the bedroom lapped at me with a peculiar frigid eroticism. When I came back to him, he licked my mouth clean.

'Let me—'

'No,' he said, and bit me lightly on the throat.

On my bedside table, my work phone started ringing.

'Oh—'

'Ignore it.'

'It's – uh – it's – work—'

'So far as I understand it, *I* am your work. Thus, you are working. Do you like it – when I am very deep – like this—?'

The phone rang out. A few seconds of silence, then it started again.

'Oh – Godsake – I should—'

He sighed, then lifted me up and dropped me onto my back. I hooked an ankle around his hips. Soon he didn't even need that urging. The bed thudded ferociously against the wall. I came, one foot scrabbling at his calf, to the sound of the headboard thumping and the phone ringing. It was very stressful. He climaxed soon after, gasping in my ear. I stroked his back, touching the bump of the microchip.

All the tension streamed off him and he flopped onto me.

'Hhhuk. Heavy!'

'I think I put my back out trying to hold your hips at the right angle,' he said peacefully. 'For which you are welcome, by the way.'

'Gerroff. Phone.'

'Hmm. I'll stay here until I can feel my spine again.'

I waggled about, trying to dislodge him.

'You're going to get it all over your thighs,' he observed. 'And then you will be so annoyed.'

'What happened to the blushing virgin I married?'

'Well, we did not marry. You took me out of wedlock. Now I'm ruined.'

This worked, however. He rolled off me and pulled the bedsheets around his hips.

'You weren't a virgin either,' I said cheerfully. He ignored me.

The phone lit up with a text message. It was from Adela.

Come to the Ministry immediately.

IX

May 1859. Captain Leopold McClintock's search expedition has spent eight months locked in the ice by Bellot Strait. Frostbite, scurvy and the long Arctic winter have ravaged his crew. Now the sun is back and sledging is once again practicable.

McClintock's Lieutenant Hobson heads south along King William Land. Some Esquimaux have told him that, nine years before, they saw a straggling group of thirty starving, ragged white men — the purported remnants of Sir John Franklin's expedition to discover the Northwest Passage. Franklin's two ships, *Erebus* and *Terror*, have not been seen since July 1845. None of the officers and sailors who sailed with him have been found.

The Esquimaux hinted at other things too. Dismembered bodies at makeshift campsites. Boots boiled in pots, boots still filled with human flesh. Knife-scores on tibia, finger bones sucked clean of marrow. A last camp in a harbour on the mainland, where they found a corpse who had passed watch chains through gashes in his earlobes, perhaps for safe-keeping, perhaps clinging to the idea that he might yet return to a place where the watch was worth something. Hobson spoons his rations and wonders what his own biceps would taste like.

At the place the Europeans call Cape Felix, he finds the remains of a camp. There are tents still pitched, filled with bearskins and canvas sleeping bags. He finds two sextants, wire cartridges, snow goggles, brass screws. He concludes that this was not a camp of last resort, but a scientific observatory, set up for the milder summer months. The only strange thing about it is the speed with which it was abandoned, leaving behind valuable property of the Royal Navy.

Sledging further south, he discovers a cairn of piled stones. Inside is the only piece of communication from the Franklin expedition that will ever be discovered: a note on Admiralty notepaper, written over twice.

The first message, in strong, confident handwriting, reads:

H.M.S ships 'Erebus' and 'Terror' wintered in the Ice in lat. 70° 05' N., long. 98° 23' W. Having wintered in 1846–7 at Beechey Island, in lat. 74° 43' 28" N., long. 91° 39' 15" W., after having ascended Wellington Channel to lat. 77°, and returned by the west side of Cornwallis Island. Sir John Franklin commanding the expedition. <u>All well.</u>

Party consisting of 2 officers and 6 men left the ships on Monday 24th May, 1847.

(Signed) GM. GORE, Lieut.

(Signed) CHAS. F. DES VOEUX, Mate.

The second, wavering in the margins:

25th April 1848 H.M. ships 'Terror' and 'Erebus' were deserted on the 22nd April, 5 leagues N.N.W. of this, having been beset since 12th September, 1846. The officers and crews, consisting of 105 souls, under the command of Captain F.R.M. Crozier, landed here in lat. 69° 37' 42" N., long. 98° 41' W. This paper was found by Lt. Irving under the cairn supposed to have been built by Sir James Ross in 1831 – 4 miles to the Northward – where it had been deposited by the late Commander Gore in ~~May~~ June

1847. Sir James Ross' pillar has not however been found and the paper has been transferred to this position which is that in which Sir J. Ross' pillar was erected — Sir John Franklin died on the 11th June, 1847; and the total loss by deaths in the expedition has been to this date 9 officers and 15 men.

(Signed) JAMES FITZJAMES, Captain H.M.S. Erebus.
(Signed) F.R.M. CROZIER, Captain & Senior Offr.
and start on tomorrow, 26th, for Back's Fish River.

The note revealed two important things.

Firstly, that the expedition had abandoned their ships in April 1848, after two consecutive summers so cold that the sea had remained frozen. Twenty-four men had already died and the lauded Franklin was among their number. Francis Crozier and James Fitzjames, captains of *Terror* and *Erebus* respectively, had led the ships' companies in an overland march of eight hundred miles. None, as far as Hobson could tell, survived the effort.

Secondly, that Lieutenant Graham Gore — who had been granted a field promotion to Commander — was dead before the march began. History had swallowed him, closing over him as the sea does over a luckless sailor.

Chapter Nine

At the Ministry, Adela stared at me with wild eyes. She looked like her edges had been improperly filled in and I realised it was the first time I'd ever seen her without make-up. A palm-sized clump of hair frizzed out from her head.

'There's a mole,' she barked.

'A—'

'I thought it was Quentin. It was last time. That's why he was neutralised.'

'Neutra—'

'You're in danger, do you understand?' she said, seizing my arms. I stared at her, hot with shock. Adrenalin slimed under my skin. I felt like overhandled putty.

'I *know* I'm in danger. The Brigadier—'

'Someone inside the Ministry is feeding him information,' she said. 'And I don't know who.'

I had a feeling like I'd always assumed I was a real girl, but someone had flicked me in the eye and it had produced no pain, only a glassy click: I was just a doll, with no more inner intelligence than a bottle of water.

'How do you know there's a mole in the Ministry?' I asked. Adela threw her hands up.

'There was a breach!' she said. I'd never heard her talk in exclamation points before. It took a decade off her. 'The time-door's location was leaked! And I still can't find the Brigadier! I've looked everywhere he ought to be!'

We were looking at one another, neither with much of a grip on our expressions. Something was washing over Adela's face. I thought, at first, I was witnessing a rare example of high emotion, but the longer I looked, the more I became convinced that the weird battlements of her chin and cheekbones were moving again. She looked viscous, recently shaken.

I stared, fascinated, at her expression's bending scaffolding. 'You said the mole was Quentin "last time". What did you mean?'

Adela combed her fingers through her hair. The big kink at the side of her head began to flatten, in an oily, exhausted way.

'One day,' she said, 'you will have to stop asking stupid questions for the sake of conversational presenteeism. It endears you to no one. You know exactly what I meant.'

*

After my meeting with Adela, I went back to our wretched dripping flat and sat in our miserable kitchen, trying to read a report – though really I just stared at the same page for twenty minutes. Graham was out on the motorbike, a permission that hadn't yet been rescinded. I heard him pull up in the forsaken courtyard that hid the entrance to the flat, and then, a few minutes later, I heard the key in the door. He stumbled over the doorstep, and called my name in a strangled voice.

I was on my feet with my heart blistering with panic. He almost never used my name, my real name, not 'little cat' or 'my bridge', but my name, which he pronounced right, which

288

he'd known from the beginning. I slammed into the hallway. He looked awful. His face was white and smeared with sweat.

'Something has happened to Maggie,' he said.

*

He'd been feeling concerned, responsible, since our gallery trip. A good officer takes care of his crew. He had been out to visit her. When he'd arrived at the door of the shrouded ex-shopfront that concealed her safehouse, he'd been puzzled by a line of darkness at the edge of it, like a pole of paint. A curious optical illusion. The door had been kicked in and left very, very slightly ajar, so that a single inch of the dark hallway beyond was visible. He walked in and called out for Margaret. His voice landed strangely in the penumbral air.

He'd found stairs. He'd gone up the stairs, which he would never normally do. Something felt rotten, shattered. In the bathroom, crazed with part-uprooted floor tiles, a filled bath. Ralph under the water. A semi-submersible thing that had once been Ralph. Eyes wide, unseeing. Already the face was beginning to bloat. He backed out, took the landing to the splintered door of the bedroom. He saw the figure on the bed. A dead woman. Strangled. For a few seconds, the chewy purple of her face made her features indistinguishable. Then he realised: not Margaret, but another woman. Ash-blonde and taller. Someone she'd been dating, illicitly kept in touch with. A now former lover. The room had been knocked about by unkind hands. Margaret herself was nowhere to be seen.

'Oh God,' I croaked.

'I know where she would have gone,' he said.

'Where?'

He told me there was a tunnel system, half collapsed, near

Greenhithe, in Rainham. Industrial estates had burrowed their foundations into it, the Thames had drowned a significant portion of it, but his investigations over the past year, biking at the very edge of the boundary lines, had proven it was still there. It was in use when he was in the Navy, he explained, when it was not so secret, but it appeared to be a secret now. He had always told Arthur and Margaret to go there if anything went wrong and he would come for them.

I was scratching at my throat, compulsively marking it with white lines of breaking skin. 'Why did you tell them that?' I babbled. 'What did you expect would go wrong? When did you plan this? Why didn't you tell me?'

He only answered the last question.

'I assumed you would be with me,' he replied. 'And that I would take care of you. We must go to Arthur's first. He won't know what's happened. Then we will move to the tunnels.'

I wanted to say something but I made a noise like a tin whistle being crushed underfoot.

'Pack,' he said. 'Warm clothes. Waterproofs. Wear them if you can, to save space. We need water and emergency rations.'

'Right. Okay. Okay. I can get access to spartan supplies at the Ministry. I – yes – if we take the bike I can—'

'Box hidden in the toilet cistern,' he said. I gasped so abruptly I choked on my own spit. When I'd stopped coughing, I rasped: 'Did you plan this?'

'I planned *for* this. You told me you were in danger. And I wouldn't be much of an officer if I hadn't. Hurry. We only have the tank bags and the top box for storage, so be prudent.'

I moved in shock. I found the box in our cavernous Edwardian cistern, uprooting the valves as I dragged it out. It wouldn't matter, because if the Brigadier and Salese knew where Margaret lived, then they knew where we were. They probably had access to the microchip data – if not the live feed then certainly the summary data reports. We wouldn't be coming back here.

If Graham had asked the expats to gather in one place, that made it easier for me to herd them into protective custody. I just had to be fast – faster than the blue-light weapon, faster than the speed of information from a mole. Good God. I kicked the box of iron rations into my room so I could grab my gun. Holster, box, quickmarch to Graham's bedroom. Adrenalin fuzzed all my edges.

He was loading a handgun. He had pulled the bottom drawer out of his bedside table, scattering its meagre contents. I assumed it had been hidden beneath it.

'Why the fuck do you have that?'

He raised his eyebrows but didn't look over. I edged closer.

'Jesus, Graham, it's Ministry-issue.'

'Yes.'

'The quartermasters—'

'Do not know that I have it,' he said briskly.

He stamped his foot through the discarded drawer. The board at the bottom splintered, and I saw a flash of dark blue. Passports. I was prepared to bet my emergency rations that they were under fake names.

I recalled the amount of time he had spent at the Ministry, charming people with his chatter and his questions. I thought about how well he played innocuous, how utterly opaque he could render his eyes. I remembered that he didn't set off alarms, he didn't register as a human presence when recorded by modern technology. I stared at him and I wondered if I knew him at all.

He met my eyes at last. He didn't say anything. But he did kiss me, quickly and urgently, which was something.

*

I spent the bike ride flush against Graham, near-tearful, rattling with an internal ticker tape of questions, ribboning through me in an abundance of disorder.

What had Simellia said to me? *'I'm being blocked by Arthur's own Wellness team.'* Ivan stood down – what had become of him? Ralph dead. Ed 'removed' after Anne Spencer – why hadn't I checked on him? I hadn't seen the Secretary in weeks. I worked exclusively, even conspiratorially, with Adela. Had the Secretary had an agreement with Defence? With the Brigadier? Was the 'mole' not a mole but a series of mole tunnels undermining the project, an anti-project, a final lobby from Defence to collapse us and absorb us in the name of national security? Had I, in fact, backed the wrong institution? Nausea, panic, the crushed-velvet crump of a migraine.

I'd never been to the safehouse (a former doctor's office, porcupined with scaffolding) that Arthur and Simellia shared, and I was in no state to take it in, except to note that the front door was slightly open and the lock was broken.

'Simellia?' I croaked, at the same time Graham called, 'Arthur?'

Graham went ahead of me into the building, along a series of chemical-redolent, grey-carpeted corridors that gave onto hardly furnished rooms walled in chipboard. I saw a large mirror leaning against the wall, casting a bilious slanted reflection, piles and piles of books for which Simellia had not yet found a case. I imagined the blue-light weapon in every shadow and alcove. Kicking open another anonymous, pock-marked door, I mistook a Basquiat print, a coat stand and a curtain for the Brigadier, my gun arm swinging round each time.

Upstairs, I heard a noise like a sudden down-stroke on violin strings. It took me a few seconds to realise it was a human cry.

'Graham?'

I ran up the stairs and went gun first into the nearest room.

Graham was crouching down. The expression on his face was one I've never been able to forget.

Arthur was lying on the floor, his eyes clouded and open. His head was turned to one side – he was facing me as I entered the room. Blood and vomit pooled from his lips. It looked almost like a speech bubble on the carpet. The air had an acrid, sickly tang.

'No—'

This can't be happening, I thought. I squeezed my eyes shut and opened them again. Graham was running his hand down Arthur's face, closing his eyes. *'Careful, you'll startle him,'* I wanted to say.

'Is he—'

'Yes.'

'Oh my God.'

'We need to leave,' said Graham flatly. 'Wait downstairs.'

I backed out of the room. I saw Graham lean down and press his forehead to Arthur's temple. Then I turned and walked back down the stairs, legs trembling.

There was a table by the front door, stacked with umbrellas, flyers, keys, small change and other by-the-entrance ephemera. There was a small notebook, which I picked up and opened. I flipped through it. Arthur's handwriting. I put it in my pocket. I'll give it back to him later, I thought. I recognised the thought as one of a person in shock, but I couldn't stop myself thinking it.

Behind me, Graham came quickly down the stairs. He was pushing Arthur's signet ring over one of his fingers. As I watched, he pulled his bike glove over it.

'Let's ship out,' he said. His voice was toneless and his eyes were dry.

*

The ride to the tunnels passed in a blur. We took the motorways, which were thundering and anonymous. This is what the road to hell is like, I thought. Not paved with good intentions, but tarmacked and screaming with vehicles driven by people who don't know and don't care that Arthur is dead.

Greenhithe, like a long grey throat, regurgitated us by the docks. We abandoned the motorbike and our helmets behind a warehouse, taking the bags.

'It's not far,' he told me. 'The entrance is concealed by the marsh.'

I reached out and clasped his shoulder, to steady myself as much as anything. He turned and dragged me towards him, curling fists into my waterproof coat. He squeezed me so tightly that it hurt. I could feel him shaking, he who never moved without a perfect clarity of intent. The whole time, I was thinking: the microchips, the microchips. They found Arthur because of the microchips. Let me out of your arms: I need to think about what to do about the microchips.

*

The journey into the tunnels felt like a descent into a nightmare. Brine and rotting seaweed smells filled the air, which contrived to be both clammy and frigid. We had to wade through a flooded room, holding the bags over our heads, before the passage sloped up again. We began to pick our way through neater, more carefully paved catacombs, ribbed with iron struts. I squinted at the walls, lit by the pocket torches we each clutched. As far as I could tell, these were utility tunnels for the dockyard.

We came out in a crude bunker, drier than the rest of the tunnel and divided by stone walls.

'Maggie?' whispered Graham.

'Gray!'

Margaret burst from the ceiling. She had been hiding in a disused vent. She was covered with slime and her eyes were wild. She fell, landing heavily, scrambled upright and threw herself into Graham's arms. He swept her off the floor, his face in her filth-thickened hair.

'I fled,' Margaret sobbed. 'I abandoned her – I fled – not knowing – if you'd come—'

'Of course I would. I told you that I would.'

'I was – so – afraid—'

I lurched towards them. My limbs felt like they'd been boiled for too long. Margaret saw me and cried out. She kicked free of Graham and embraced me ferociously. I kissed her forehead and spat the mud onto the floor.

When Margaret had got her sobbing under control, she twisted to look over my shoulder.

'Arthur?' she asked.

I looked at Graham. He took a breath. His shoulders jumped.

'We were too late,' I said, so that he didn't have to. 'He's gone.'

*

We didn't have long to grieve. Graham and I changed from our soaked clothes into fresh ones. He explained the layout of the room, such as he understood it. There were three entrances, one of which was underwater. The other two were the long catacomb walk that we'd just come through, and a significantly more damaged and dangerous crawl space, whose entrance was set into the hollow of a dual-carriageway bridge.

With narrative inevitability, we heard scuffling and grunting somewhere in the roof.

Margaret and I instinctively crouched. Graham straightened up and cocked one of the handguns.

There was a black square cut into the wall near the ceiling, on which Graham's gun was now trained. Something appeared in and filled the square. It dropped to the floor, like a laid egg, at the same moment that Graham fired. The gunshot echoed so loudly that Margaret and I both shrieked.

'God's blood, commander, 'tis me!'

A grey canvas bag – the egg – lay beneath the square. Cardingham's face appeared in the hole. He looked sick to his stomach.

'You!' shouted Margaret. 'How were you privy to this place?'

Cardingham clambered gracefully to the floor.

'Our commander told me of it, i'faith. Though I had much trial finding this den. How wouldst thou have me be? Killed, like the captain? Lower thy weapon, sir.'

'How did you know Arthur was dead?' asked Graham.

'My bridge has been absent for too long. I hied to his dwelling, as I thought that Moorish woman wouldst know best where my keeper hid. I discovered his body. Lower thy weapon.'

At last, Graham brought his arm down.

'You saw nobody else there? A tall man with dark grey hair and a military bearing? Goes by the rank of brigadier—'

'Nay, sir. Thou thinkest this the work of professional men? May this not be a lover's revenge? Didst thou know he was a sodomite, commander?'

Graham silently thumbed the safety catch and put the gun away. Then he said:

'Sixty-five's friend was murdered too, probably accidentally and in her place. Two months ago the Brigadier and his companion attempted to kill my bridge and take me. We're safe for now, but we must plan our escape—'

'You're not safe,' I blurted out.

They looked round at me.

'You're microchipped,' I said. 'Er. There are tiny machines implanted in your backs, just under the skin. It doesn't matter that you don't show up on modern scanning equipment. You're like the Invisible Man holding a flaming torch. The Ministry know exactly where you are, all the time, and there's someone feeding that info to the Brigadier.'

For a second or so, there was nothing but the renegade slap of the distant water on stone. I could almost feel the chill of his blood retreating from his face before Graham quietly asked me:

'How long have you known this?'

'You were all released to your bridges microchipped. So. I suppose. The whole time.'

Margaret and Cardingham just stared, dumbstruck, but Graham's face twisted. His mouth convulsed with fury and contempt. He got it under control, but not before I felt its impact bruise me. He said to Cardingham, 'Thomas, do you have a blade with you?'

'I have a "first-aid kit", among the instruments of which is a scalpel, a curved needle and a catgut. We are of accord, I wager.'

'Do you know where the "microchips" are?' he asked me, without looking at me.

'Yes.'

'You'll cut mine out and sew up the wound. I'll cut Lieutenant Cardingham's and you'll do Margaret's. Then I'm going to take them and drop them in the river. Thomas, give me the scalpel.'

*

297

He led me into an alcove on the left of the room, separated by a rotting wood door. It was dry and pitch-black. Some quirk of its construction stifled noise and when I spoke or moved, the shadows swallowed the sound.

He stripped to the waist, facing away from me, and knelt. I wedged a torch into a crack in the wall and reached out. As soon as I touched him, he shuddered. I wondered if he was thinking, as I was thinking, of all the times my hand had lain here, on his naked back.

'What did you want from me?' he asked softly.

'What?'

'Why did you bring me back from the dead? Why did you come into my life like this?'

'We – we saved you. I wanted to know you.'

His head tipped forward into his hands.

'Well,' he said. 'Did you satisfy your curiosity?'

'Graham.'

'For a while, I really did believe that you— What were you planning to do with me? Put me in a filing system, I suppose. Where you could keep me boxed up.'

'I never wanted to—'

'Yes you did!' he shouted. It was loud enough that it burred with echoes. He scrambled around to face me, enraged, eyes flashing. 'Yes you did. You had a very clear idea of who I was *supposed* to be. You've been going hammer and tongs to get me there.'

I was breathing fast and hard. It wasn't quite hyperventilating, but it wasn't far off. 'That's not fair,' I said. 'I made you my life.'

'And in the heat of your obsession,' he said, 'did it occur to you to remember that I am a person too?'

His colour cooled. Whatever was burning in his eyes, he tamped it down. He turned away.

'Scalpel,' he said. 'Stop crying. You won't be able to do it properly if you are crying.'

*

Margaret wept the whole way through her operation. When I'd sewn her up, she turned to face me and grabbed my wrist. Her skin was perfect and opalescent under the dirt of the tunnels. She held my chin and forced me to look into her eyes, still jewelled with tears.

'Mark me,' she said, 'and never forget it. *I forgive you.*'

I bent and put my face in her neck, pulling her – tiny and warm and trembling – into my arms. 'I'm sorry,' I said wetly to her throat. 'I'm sorry, I'm sorry.'

*

Graham took the microchips out somewhere, with the intention of letting them float downriver, I think – he'd stopped telling me what his plans were. On his return, he divided us into three-hour watches, to be taken at the furthest edge of the catacomb corridor. Cardingham went first. Graham would follow him, then me, then, by morning, Margaret.

'Why can't we leave now?' I asked tremulously.

'Tide,' he said brusquely, without looking at me. 'Until it's further out, tomorrow morning, our escape channels are so limited that stirring would be suicide. At this moment there's only one safe route we can take, along the river, and I'm sure they're monitoring the banks.'

Margaret and I folded spare clothes under our heads for pillows and hunkered down under coats for blankets. We lay in one another's arms, wakeful and anxious. Graham, in the side room, worked on something by torchlight – something to do with the passports. He hadn't looked at me since I'd cut the microchip from his back.

'How did they dispatch Arthur?' Margaret whispered.

'Poison, I think.'

'Did he suffer overlong?'

I thought of the vomit, the blood. But Arthur's face had been glazed and loose. Perhaps it had been quick. Each time I thought about it, my body was filled with insectile chatter, a desperate urge to get up and shake and move and fix the situation. But there was no fixing to be done. Arthur was dead.

'Should I e'er find this Brigadier,' whispered Margaret, 'I will break him, bone by bone. Sixteen would have wanted me at peace, but I cannot obey it. He was as a brother to me. A man of marble where all others are of clay.'

She started to weep again, sluggish little tears like liquid mercury, her face barely moving. I touched one and watched it spread against her skin.

'He was a good person,' I said.

Eventually I felt her twitching as her body succumbed to an uneasy sleep. I must have slept too because the room withdrew from me. I dreamt, inevitably, of Arthur. I dreamt in layers of dreams where I woke in the dream and he was there and I said, 'Oh, thank God, I dreamt you'd died', and I'd wake again in the dream, and know him dead, and wake again in the dream, and think him still alive. My consciousness split like chapped skin, worried to the point of blood.

I was woken by rough shaking. I came to with a belligerent yelp.

'Your watch,' said Graham, above me.

I sat up in fits and starts, like a balloon animal inflating.

Everything ached, especially my neck. I wasn't quite awake and so I reacted to Graham's presence as I would have done a day before. I flopped against him and buried my face in his shoulder. He stiffened but otherwise didn't move.

'Happy anniversary,' I muttered.

'What?'

'It's one year today. That you came here.'

He was still and silent for a moment longer. I breathed in the familiar scent of him, felt the familiar passage of his breath. Then he pushed me away.

'Your watch,' he repeated.

*

When I'd first interviewed for the bridge role, Adela had said to me, 'Your mother was a refugee'. But my mother never described herself as a refugee. It was a narrative imposition, along with 'stateless' and 'survivor'.

My sister and I grew up, as many children of immigrants do, half parented and half parenting. Our mother needed our help to navigate her new country. Her need pinched us in different ways. My sister became invested in cataloguing, in retelling and remembering, in what she called the truth. I became obsessed with control, which I suppose is another way of saying I wanted command of the narrative.

Graham hadn't been all wrong when he said I'd been trying to shape him. How could I resist it? He came to me as a story. Now I'd let the story slip out of my grip. I'd panicked and he'd had to look after me. I'd let slip something I shouldn't have and now he was angry at me. I should have taken charge of the situation, and instead here we were: hiding in a cellar and expecting to take on the Brigadier and the mole by ourselves. But someone had put a gun in my hands, a platform beneath my feet. Where was she, to add the final underline?

*

In the catacomb corridor, swinging my pocket torch, I turned my phone on. Six missed calls from Adela. I texted:

> help

She responded within seconds.

> Where are you?

> dockside service tunnels rainham
> can u track phone?

> Accept phonecall when it arrives do not speak do not
> move even a foot

In five minutes a track call came through. I accepted it and waited. I even held my phone in the air to get better signal, although experience had taught me this was a futile gesture.

> I have location
> Weapons? Any sign of Brig?

> 2 guns w 47 no brig
> what should i do low battery

I can get them into protective custody. Will send a
SWAT team. Meet me here. NO FURTHER CONTACT
mole still loose dont know if theyre tracking

She sent me a location – about half an hour's walk away, right
by the river. Probably the microchips Graham had disposed of
were tracked that far down the water.

I pulled Arthur's notebook from my coat pocket. There was
a tiny gold pen in the spine. I held the torch in my teeth and
wrote:

*I know what this looks like, but please don't be afraid.
I've gone to get help.*

I tore the page out and left it on the floor, held in place and lit
by my torch. Then, using my phone's light, I made my way to
meet Adela.

*

I began my trek across the marshes in the thin, frost-tipped
light of pre-dawn, but the sun soon leaked into the air. The
birds went wild for it. I'd never realised how psychotic the dawn
chorus sounded – its scrabbling high notes, its melismas of
desperation. Then again, I'd never been that exhausted or frightened.

Adela was standing in the debris-strewn mud at the bottom
of a stone staircase streaked rot-brown with rusted metal posts.
The Thames churned behind her.

I was all the way down the stairs and at Adela's side before
I realised that the Brigadier and Salese were also there, and the
Brigadier was pointing the blue-light weapon at Adela.

'Oh,' I said.

'"Oh" indeed,' said Adela drily.

'You will not move,' said the Brigadier, 'or I will shoot.'

'I'm wearing a reflector,' said Adela. 'Good for at least five shots. How much power do you have left in that thing? I know you emptied half the battery on Eighteen-forty-seven's attempted capture. And you haven't managed to get back to your era to recharge.'

'I don't need to shoot you,' replied the Brigadier. 'I will shoot her and that will be the end of both of you.'

'Wrong again,' said Adela. 'She's already on a different time-line. She told Eighteen-forty-seven about the Holocaust instead of 9/11 and I think it's sent him down a different path. The link's broken.'

'Why would shooting me kill you anyway?' I asked. I didn't mean to blurt it out. It was just that I was so frightened I could feel my heart in my bowels. Cold sweat was dripping down my ribcage, tickling me unpleasantly.

Adela sighed. 'I knew I was naïve when I was a young woman,' she said. 'But I didn't realise I was *this* naïve.'

'You're one,' barked Salese. 'Future-self and past-self.'

I was too intent on the weapon to turn to Adela, but I said, 'You're me?'

'Don't parrot. Yes. I'm amazed you hadn't worked that out already. I'm from, let's see, twenty-odd years in your future. These two are from the twenty-two hundreds.'

There was blood in my nose and in the back of my throat. In my panic, my body was putting beats in all the wrong places. 'Arthur's dead,' I said, just to stop her talking.

Adela's face dropped horribly for a moment – a truly incredible sight on her mobile features. Then she arrested its slide and pinned a blank expression in place.

'Arthur Reginald-Smyth. Yes. And Margaret Kemble.'

'Maggie's alive,' I said.

This time her face opened, and she didn't stop it.

'She's alive?' Adela croaked.

'This timeline's Ministry being less efficient than the original,' the Brigadier broke in. I realised the hand holding the weapon was trembling slightly. The more I looked, the more I noted signs of exhaustion, sickness and filth about the futurists. Whatever mission had brought them here, it wasn't going to plan.

Adela was gawping at the Brigadier. '*Less* efficient?' she said. 'You didn't kill Sixteen-sixty-five this time – the Ministry saved her.'

Salese gawped back.

'*We* didn't kill her?'

'Yes,' said Adela. 'You murdered my friends. Last time it was Arthur and Maggie, both. But this time round, you only got one.'

'No. You types nulled. We breathed a paper.'

'There are declassified records,' the Brigadier translated, 'that show the Ministry had the non-combatant expats killed once they realised the door only supported a limited number of people.'

I did goldfish faces for a few seconds, then managed to say to Adela, 'The Ministry killed them? Did you do this? Did you know about this?'

But she was staring back at me, shivering oddly. 'Arthur's the name of my son,' she said.

'What?'

'Arthur John Gore.'

I was about to say something cravenly stupid, such as, I'm not even sure if I want children, when Adela stepped forward and stabbed Salese in the throat.

The impact wasn't smooth. A greenish screen fizzled and flickered over Salese's body – some kind of shield. But Adela grunted and pushed past its vivid static, driving the knife home. I hadn't seen the knife appear, but now it was centre stage. Blood sprayed, hit the casing of green, dripped lushly down the inside. Salese gagged, eyes rolling back. This all took less than three seconds.

In that time, I'd thrown myself at the Brigadier with my brain all grey. He was a big man, but hollow with it. He'd been hungry for some time, I could feel that in the baggy give of his flesh when my knuckles connected. He wasn't afraid of pain. I kicked his shins and heard a crack and I punched his mouth and felt a tooth turn in his livid gum and he took it all grimly, without breaking attention. He had his hand on my hand, and my hand was wrestling his for the blue-light weapon. Then he turned his head, just for a moment, and he must have seen what had become of Salese, because his grip unflexed. I wrenched. When I was done, I was holding the blue-light weapon, two of my fingers appeared to be dislocated and the Brigadier was backing away.

'You killed Sal,' he said. His voice was raw. To my horror, there were tears tracking down his face.

At Adela's feet, the corpse that had been Salese bled out onto the sand, turning it not red, as I'd expected, but a colour that was closer to black.

*

The Brigadier ran. I lifted the blue-light weapon. It was very like a gun, or what a gun might dream about becoming. I understood, instinctively, the sight and the trigger. So I fired.

There was a brief cyan flicker, then the weapon made exactly the same noise a vacuum cleaner makes when you turn it off.

After that it was completely unresponsive, which is just as well really, because my brain caught up with what I'd just done and tried to do and I threw up.

When I straightened, Adela was looking at me sympathetically.

'I used to puke every time. You get used to it.'

'Why did you—'

'Reflectors are designed to screen the wearer from plasma bullets. They weren't designed with metal knives in mind.'

She reached out and, without ceremony, snapped my dislocated fingers back into place. The birds sang over my screaming.

*

We walked back towards the hideout. I stared at her, and she stared at the way ahead. She looked like her organs had been removed and placed in cold storage; worse, like it had happened when she was on her way to what she thought was a birthday party.

Eventually, she said:

'You want to ask me about the future.'

'Well. Yes.'

'What do you want to know?'

'What's it like?'

'What an anodyne question. The United Kingdom has been at war with the Tiger Territories for about a decade. Mai almost got deported right at the beginning. The Ministry stepped in, though. She's dead now. Mai and Dad are both dead. Did you want to know how they died?'

'No,' I said, shocked. 'Why would you tell me that?'

'I'm still processing. It wasn't that long ago. If that's any comfort.'

'Jesus fucking— What are the Tiger Territories?'

'Stupid media nickname, I shouldn't have used it. Countries that used to have tigers, more or less. China, India, Thailand, Cambodia, Vietnam, Nepal. Couple of others. They want us toppled. US and Brazil are on our side. Russia's in the middle of a civil war – they started using chemical weapons in the early 2030s without rationalising what it would do to crops. Tigers are extinct.'

'And where did you say the Brigadier and Salese come from?'

'Further ahead. The twenty-two hundreds. We believe they made the time-door. Apparently the planet is not in a good way, climate-wise, so they're trying to change history. Targeted assassinations, mainly, a bit of intelligence gathering. I don't think they have the resources or infrastructure for much else. They got stuck here when we seized the door.'

We walked in silence. I'd become so hot and tearful that my personal radius had expanded several inches from my body.

'Why "Adela"?' I asked her.

'It was really close to the top of the baby name book and I was in a hurry,' she said.

'Ah. Did you really lose your eye in Beirut in 2006?'

'No. Battambang, 2039.'

'And your – face?'

Another grim hiccup. 'Ah. It turns out time-travel *does* come with side effects. Even your body forgets your "hereness" and "thereness", if you do it often enough. We thought it would be a tactical advantage, but I suppose the same claim was made for crop-destroying chemical weapons. You were right when you called my surgery reconstructive. I would venture to call it life-saving. Failure to correct for "hereness" shifting was how we lost Agent Cardingham, back in 'thirty-four. Poor man. I never liked him but that was a dreadful way to go.'

'And you said that. Well. We have – or – you have a son?'

'Yes.'

'With—?'

'Yes.'

We rejoined the road. Two sets of boot heels thudded martially on the tarmac. The manic scrubland loomed around us.

'We married not long after all this happened the first time round,' Adela said. 'After the – funerals. It was – hard. Graham put Arthur's ring on my finger. That was – too much. I gave up wearing it. I think he understood but it was – difficult. I really thought I might be able to spare you all that, if I got the mole this time.'

'What about all the stuff you said about not changing history?'

'People aren't history,' said Adela scornfully. 'Good grief, why didn't I listen to anything anyone told me when I was young? As long as the Ministry rises to power, then history happened the way we said it did.'

'And, your, uh, our—?'

'Arthur was born a year later. He's a teenager now.'

That threw me off. When I'd heard 'my son', I'd imagined him in mystical terms – a pink-cheeked, wide-eyed kid of three or so, radiating his innocence like a plutonium rod. To know that Arthur Gore was a person, with opinions and articulated thoughts, was unnerving.

'What's he like?'

'Oh, he hates us. As teenagers do. He's a gobby little shit,' she added, and I noted the pride in her voice. 'Of course, it's not easy being a twenty-first-century teen with a Victorian patriarch for a father.'

'Is he a patriarch?'

'He's not as bad as he could be. But he has very high expectations and requires that they are met. And he expects obedience with good cheer. Filial devotion and all that. Honour. Achievement.'

'He's an Asian mother.'

'Ha. Yes.'

Adela checked the futuristic weapon, which she had wordlessly taken from me. 'I miss Mai,' she said, quietly. 'You should spend as much time with her as you can. Dad too.'

'I will. Um. Does our – does your husband know you're here?'

'Who do you think ordered this mission?'

I stopped short in the road. Adela turned to me.

'That's why the Brigadier was here – for me, and for him, as early in our timelines as possible. I understand that, in their era, the Ministry and the British government as a whole are considered culpable for what *their* Britain looks like. I suppose we invested in weapons and manufacturing that were not what you probably still call "carbon neutral". Charming term. It fell out of fashion – will fall out of fashion. Anyway, the situation was desperate. You're not long off your first resource war. Or the first Special Branch Coast Guard. Graham was closely involved in that. He finally made post-captain,' she added, with a phantom smile.

'What the hell is a Special Branch of the Coast Guard?'

'Defensive patrols. The migrants, you know. Boats. There were too many. They started trying to enter by force.'

I stared at her. She shrugged tiredly and said, 'I was worried when you said you hadn't told Graham about 9/11, because in my timeline, that immediately converted him to the Ministry. Highly trained mercenaries attacking civilians. The necessity of belligerent tactics to prevent another attack. Neo-Crusades following the collapse of the Empire. And so on. You were right about the way he reacted. I remember him bringing up the Aden expedition. Though I'm sure he'd deny it was "racist", you know he's funny about that word. The Ministry promoted him quickly. Much quicker than they promoted you. He's *good*. He was in the field for a few years but he was fast-tracked into leadership. He's – how can I put this? – *extremely* senior.'

'But why did he send you?'

'I insisted. I knew this mission better than anyone.'

'But *why*?'

She looked me up and down. Her expression was a bit squishy. Not with her usual facial strangeness. I think it was nostalgia.

'When you are my age,' she said, 'you will realise just how green you were. I had to make sure this all happened the right way. Most things don't happen. Mostly the universe is parking space.'

'But—'

'The world is at war. We are running out of *everything*, and everyone thinks they're owed what's left. But as long as the Ministry exists, as long as the Ministry *comes to exist* in the shape it does in my era, then we have the technological advantage. That isn't nothing, having weapons other people don't, the kinds of soldiers other people don't. Some other countries get left behind, but that's how progress works. You really didn't pay attention to anything that's ever been said about history, did you?'

I said, 'Did you kill Quentin?'

She lifted her thumb to her mouth and bit the edge of the skin. 'Technically,' she said, 'we both did. Since you are me.'

'I thought the Brigadier did it. Someone with my access credentials shut off the CCTV—'

'You are aware we have the same fingerprints.'

'Oh. Right. But why did you do it?'

'Because last time, Quentin was the mole, and I thought that he was the reason Maggie and Arthur were – were murdered.

And he *did* pass information about the Ministry to the Brigadier and Salese. That was extremely fucking inconvenient. You can't imagine what Britain looks like in my era. Coming back here was a shock. It's so decadent. Like stepping into Rome before the barbarians sacked it. I seem to remember the boomers had a real hard-on for food rationing as an ideological exercise when we were your age. Let me assure you that no one enjoys food rationing.'

'You didn't know the Ministry had Maggie and Arthur killed?'

'No. None of us did. Well. I wonder. Graham is so senior now.'

'Do you think he knows?'

'Hmm. There was a period when things were bad between us. Lasted a few years. Dad was very sick, and Mai was struggling to care for him, and Arthur was having a lot of trouble at school, and our workloads were . . . Anyway. We were . . . distant. I assumed he was having an affair.'

'You didn't ask?'

'We tried to put those years behind us. Besides, when have you ever known Graham to answer a direct question?'

Her voice was strained when she said this, but I remember the way affection luminesced under her skin. I still love him, I thought. Even after everything that happens, at least I still love him. I asked her, 'Are you happy?'

Adela considered this. 'No.'

'Oh.'

'Not being in the middle of a war makes you happy. Not grieving. Not being so profoundly fucking loathed by your son. Not having to kill people for your salary. Speaking of which—'

'You aren't going to kill Graham!'

'No, I'm not going to kill him. I love him.'

'I—'

'You hardly know him. It's going to be two years before you even see him cry.'

'He cries?'

Adela's mouth quirked at that. She fell into an agitated reverie. I felt her pulling away from the moment as the tide pulls from the shore – I mean I could feel the suck of it as her attention retreated to some inaccessible socket of 'elsewhere'. It was horrible. Her 'thereness' at work against her, I assume – or two decades of regret, piling up with such force it changed the shape of her thoughts. I wondered how it felt, realising the version of history she'd lived for years was a lie. Because of the choice she made next, I never got to experience it myself.

'Here,' she said. I looked down. She was holding a palm-sized tablet and a memory card. I attempted to take them with my dominant, recently damaged hand. She shook her head and I took it with the other. 'Ministry passcodes,' she said. 'For this project.'

'Why are you giving me these?'

She dragged her hand through her brittle bottle-blonde hair and the black roots flashed up with a wanton, impossible pride.

'Because I've been a company woman all my life and look where it's got me. The Ministry had Arthur and Maggie killed. No one ever told me. *He* didn't tell me. If I'd known—'

I said, 'Maggie's still alive.'

Another origami of emotion creased her face. 'Oh, Maggie,' she murmured.

'Can you go back again and save Arthur?'

I thought I might get another *'You're a stupid girl'*, but Adela just looked sad. 'Time,' she said, 'is a limited resource. Like all of our resources. You only get to experience your life once. And you can travel through time, a little, though it's like smoking cigarettes: the more you do it, the greater risk you're at from death by its effects. And yes, you can go back and change the details, a little, but there's a limit to how often. Every time you dig a new pathway into time, you exhaust a little more of it, and if we go back too often and mine too deeply in the same place, again and again, pulling history from the same coal seam, it will collapse. It will obliterate us, like a black hole. You have to get it *right*.'

'What – good grief – what is right? In this context? Adela?'

'I should get the surviving expats. I'll keep them safe. The Defence S.W.A.T. team are on their way, with heat scanners and infra-red goggles, emergency protocols being what they are, so I can at least stay ahead of them and their tracking techniques. But you need to go to the Ministry, with those passcodes, and you need to end this project. I'm one half of Control – I do still have that authority. If we're going to get it right, then we're going to have to ensure I am *all* of Control, and for that, the project needs to be wiped.'

'If I leave now, Graham will think I betrayed them.'

'I'll explain. I'll bring them to you, to the safehouse, and we can plan next moves. Just trust me. We'll get it right this time.'

She smiled suddenly, the first real smile I'd ever seen on her face. I saw myself in her then – her mouth, her cheeks, her eyes.

'He is wonderful, isn't he?' she said. 'I'd forgotten how handsome he was when we first met. And how happy. It's been a long time since I've seen him as happy as I saw him that day in the shooting gallery. I've missed him so much. You have no idea.'

'Hands in the air, please,' said a clear, calm voice.

I whirled around. There was no one to be seen. The dense emerald vegetation of the scrubland surrounded the road. He could have been hiding anywhere. His voice carried strangely.

'Easy, little cat,' Graham said, his voice still calm. 'You have some explaining to do. Madam, put your hands in the air. We have you in our sights.'

'Plugged thine ears, sir,' I heard Cardingham snarl. 'Refused my counsel and now see — these whores do conspire. Thou rolled i'bed with death.'

'Shut up, Thomas.'

'Commander Gore and Lieutenant Cardingham,' said Adela, scanning the scrub. 'Rest assured that we mean you no harm.'

'I suppose this depends on your interpretation of harm,' said Graham from his hiding-place, quite pleasantly. 'Perhaps you don't intend to kill us. But to survey a man, to rob him of his freedom and use him like a tool — would you not consider this harmful?'

Adela leant towards me. 'If I were you, I would run before the S.W.A.T. team gets here,' she whispered. 'Things are going to get very *crowded*, very quickly.'

I look back on this moment, and I do wonder: should I have done something else? Stayed? Argued? Pleaded? Thrown myself towards the sound of his voice, onto his mercy? Would it have changed anything?

As I ran, a gunshot rang out. The bullet passed close enough that I heard its whistling song. And I thought, that wasn't Graham. It wasn't Graham who just tried to shoot me. It can't have been Graham. Because if it was Graham, he wouldn't have missed.

X

The people he persistently thinks of as his captors take him along a corridor. He's learned, through delirious trial and error, that the lumps beneath their brief jackets are guns. It has been a difficult few weeks.

'You were in the Discovery Service, weren't you?' one of the white-robed attendants had said. 'Think of this as a *mission of discovery.*'

Thus this brave new world is reframed for him as a job he can do well or badly.

At the end of the corridor is a door. Through the door is a room. In the room is the officer who will be his 'bridge' to the future.

When he enters, he sees a little ghost shifting her feet on the carpet. Black hair. Brown skin, bright and clean. The marquee sweep of her black lashes. The indescribable colour of her mouth. She looks at him. He can't meet her eyes. He drags his stare off her, his blood thin and acid in his wrists. Do they all see her? Everyone is so still, he can't tell. Perhaps she manifests for him alone.

There is a man who he thinks must be the officer, and he tries to fix his gaze on that face. But the little ghost steps forward.

'Commander Gore?'

'Yes.'

'I'm your bridge.'

Later (and he will have many days and weeks and months of later) he will see that the resemblance to the Inuit woman is a weak one, fuelled by guilt and fancy. Her hair is less lustrous, her skin is paler, her face more feline. Her eyes are a different shape. She is several inches taller and narrower besides. Nevertheless, nevertheless.

God's ways, as Lieutenant Irving had once observed, are not our ways. His methods can be mysterious. His intentions, however, he carves on the flesh.

God gave me to you, little cat. It is His will that I am yours. In His infinite mercy, He has offered me redemption.

Chapter Ten

I ran for as long as I could and then I stopped. I'd sweated through my clothing and the sweat encased me like cheap plastic. I stank and I was thirsty. I was still in bastard, bastard Greenhithe and I didn't have enough battery on my phone to call an Uber.

I had to take a bus, trains, another bus and eventually the Tube to get into the Ministry. The day cracked open around me. I waded through its rancidly vivid yolk, feeling damaged by the sheer colour and depth of normal vision. In a spy movie, this would have been done in a montage. Instead, I had to clamber to my narrative conclusion, step by staggering step.

*

I took the escalator to Adela's office. I did not, however, make it all the way there. Simellia was waiting at the top.

'Oh my God. Simellia. Oh God. You have to help me. Arthur—'

'Come on,' she hissed. I jogged obediently after her. I caught sight of myself in the glass of the doors as she pushed through to unfamiliar rooms, tapping in unfamiliar passcodes. I was the colour of a recently hatched baby bird, and just as ugly. Panic has never become me.

Finally, Simellia seemed to have found a suitably private room.

'Oh fuck,' I croaked, flopping into a chair. 'Simellia. Arthur is dead.'

I started to cry, big messy sobs which had been gathering in the reservoir of my lungs since the day before. I was so busy snotting and heaving that it was a full minute before I wiped my face on my sleeve and realised that Simellia was pointing a gun at me.

'Is that a gun?' I said, stupidly.

'Yes.'

'Oh.'

I looked around. We were in a beautiful little room, with soothing cream and mustard furniture and what looked, to my eyes, like reinforced walls, wallpapered exquisitely. There were no windows.

'Where are we?'

'The vestibule.'

'The—?'

'Before the time-door.'

'I thought bridges weren't allowed near the time-door.'

'We aren't.'

I blinked gummily. 'Oh. Hell. You're the mole.'

Simellia grimaced. 'Yes.'

'Jesus.'

Heat and rage barrelled up through my chest, enormous as a sun, shrank to a tennis ball by the time it gained my throat, and came out as another 'Oh'. Eventually, I managed a further syllable: 'Why?' When she didn't respond, her forehead gathering and ruching with the effort of not crying herself, I said, 'But you must have known what would happen to Arthur?'

'They told me what happens to sub-Saharan Africa.'

'What are you talking about?'

'Two hundred years from now. It's finished. South America's mostly gone, except Brazil and its satellites. Half of Britain's underwater. Europe dropped bombs on any ships in the Mediterranean coming from North Africa. No refugees. They died there or they turned back and died of disease and starvation and the heat. Billions died, *billions*. Then the backlash, when water started running scarce, against immigrant communities. Salese told me—'

'Did you believe them?'

Simellia smiled sadly. '"Did I believe them",' she echoed. 'How hard did you try to be a white girl that you're asking me whether racism exists?'

'That's not fair.'

'Isn't it? Do you know what you become?'

'A Ministry employee. Which you are as well.'

'You're a murderer.'

'A civil servant.'

'They showed me. What the Ministry did. Does. Will do. In the future. Once I knew, I had to help them. Of course I didn't want Arthur to die, but if I'd blocked the Ministry in any way then they'd have known it was me and they'd have detained me and done God knows what to me and found Salese and the Brigadier and—'

She broke off, her lips shaking. She rolled her eyes upward quickly but she could no more have shovelled a waterfall than she could have stopped that tear falling.

'You are pointing a gun at me,' I said, carefully. 'Why have you brought me here? If it's to kill Adela by killing me, it won't work. We've changed history, apparently. Or the details, anyway.'

'I'm not shooting you unless you make a break for it. I just need you in my sights.'

She shifted from one foot to the other. She was wearing a bias-cut skirt in muted yellow linen, which fell elegantly around her calves. Its grace was noticeable because it contrasted so dramatically with her uneasiness holding a gun.

'You really think all that stuff about me?' I said at last.

'I believe it could happen.'

Of all the things I felt, weapon in my face, life fraying at its end point, I felt hurt. I gave Simellia a bitter little frown, like I was handing it to her on a plate with a cake fork. She sighed and sniffed enormously.

'I think you think you're doing the right thing,' she said. 'You've always been so careful round me. Worried about what you'll say or how I'll take it. You really thought you were onto something with Eighteen-forty-seven, didn't you?'

'I—'

'You let him off the hook again and again. I watched you. He came up through the Empire. He *believed* in it. And you did too. I read your file. The things that happened to your family. That's why you joined up. Getting behind the biggest bully in the playground.'

'You know what,' I said, 'I really held you in high esteem, Simellia.'

'*You* know what? No you didn't. You liked me and you couldn't work out why, you little freak. You kept wondering when we would start competing. Or when I'd test you. I never wanted to test you.'

'What did you want?'

'To not watch you become a fascist in slow motion.'

During this conversation, I'd been thinking about Ministry

training. Specifically, the firearms training and unarmed combat training. Simellia's training was in psychiatry and psychopathology, not field work. I could see from where I was sitting that she hadn't taken the safety catch off the gun. So, rather than attempt repartee, I kicked her hard enough in the knee that I heard her patella crack.

'Fuck!'

'Aaa—'

'Give me—'

'Let go—!'

At the end of this ungainly little tussle, I was holding her gun, and mine, and bleeding lightly from the mouth, and Simellia was sitting on the floor cradling her leg.

'You little bitch,' she said, seemingly both amused and enraged. 'Are you going to kill *me* now?'

'No. Ministry'll do that, probably. Or fire you.'

'Oh, fired from the Ministry. Fate worse than death.'

'God! Will you just— I'm going to put a stop to this, okay.'

'We are on the path to total climate destruction.'

'We can change it. I'm starting to suspect history changes all the time. How do I get to the time-door? I'm asking as the person now holding the guns.'

Simellia dragged herself upright and limped across the floor. She touched a panel in the wall that was seemingly like all the other panels in the wall, and it brightened into a screen. She tapped at a keypad then slid aside.

'The Brigadier's in there,' she said. 'So I'd take the safety catch off, if I were you.'

I managed a sour little chuckle. I put her gun away in my holster and seized her hand. It probably looked like an allegorical picture for Friendship for a moment, but then I wrenched her arm up behind her back and put my gun between her shoulder blades. Part Two in a triptych: Friendship Weaponised. Arthur, after all, had died on her watch. That he had also died on mine, I didn't really want to contemplate.

'Shall we?' I said, and Simellia, who never laughed, laughed.

*

In the middle of the room was a metal frame. It was the height and shape of a door. When I first saw it, I deflated. Had I really gone through the past twenty-four hours of horror, pandemonium and violence to be faced with a low-production cliché?

Then I took in the squat, awful machine on the far side of the frame.

I could try to describe it but words flex and disperse when I think about it. It had a mouth, I think. Around it, colour was not. Around it, shape was not. Threat radiated from its carapace, which itself appeared both constructed and grown. Though I cannot pretend to know how the time-door worked, I could imagine what it would look like when it was switched on. That monstrous machine belched its belly-deep cosmos outwards, and the doorframe captured it and channelled it to a particular time and place. The machine fired time as a rifle fires bullets. No wonder, when it was seized, they thought it was a weapon. No wonder every time it was switched on, it had accidentally killed people. That must have been what Quentin actually saw: not a handheld weapon, but the time-door itself, slicing a path through time out of the air and the bodies of those teenagers.

'Beautiful, isn't it? Our finest work, with our last resources.'

The Brigadier was crouched near the time-door – the actual machine, not the frame. He was touching it, though the nature of the time-door made it hard to understand exactly what he was doing. He looked awful. He was probably the only person I'd seen all day who looked as bad as me.

'You will kill me now,' he said, simply.

'Mm,' I said, as 'no' seemed like it might knock a few inches off my advantage but 'yes' was just rude. 'What happens if I let you go home?'

'Home,' repeated the Brigadier quietly. 'In my era we say "bunk". From "bunker", which in this era I know you imagine are frightful, spartan, war-time things. But –' and here his BBC accent dropped, and he sounded like Salese – 'better bunk than airside when the air's full tox. If I'm back to bunk, I'll fight again.'

Simellia said, 'The atmosphere around his part of England is full of toxic waste from chemical weapons experiments. Ministry-authorised in the twenty-one hundreds. So he's saying he'll just keep fighting—'

'Thank you. I had gathered.'

'The war won't *stop*,' she said, her voice squeaking on the last word. She swallowed. 'History will repeat itself, literally. The door means we just keep going back and forth, back and forth, again and again and again—'

I gave her a rough shake and she stopped. In my defence, I meant it kindly. I wasn't sure if I could bear to see Simellia start to break down. If I strained my ears, I could hear synchronised boots, hitting the floor with belligerent intent. The heavies were arriving. Adela had either escaped with the expats and triggered a martial response, or else she was under arrest and I was about to be as well. I'd find out when they got here. The Brigadier glanced up.

'You killed Sal.'

'No, Adela – well. Yes. Was Salese your—'

'Was mine. We don't use the words you use in this era. Sal was mine and I was Sal's, that's all.'

'I'm . . . sorry. Though you did also try to kill me.'

'You don't know who you become, to us.'

The Brigadier stood up slowly. The sound of boots was getting closer.

'At least we saw London,' he said. 'I had read so much about it. Teenaged goths in Camden Market. Office workers with their shoes off on the lawns of the parks. Big Ben. All the life here.'

'Why, what's London like in your era?'

The Brigadier shrugged. Outside, I could hear shouting.

'It's gone,' he said.

The trouble with private, singular power is that it narrows the world to an arrowhead. Your heart beats at the tip, an encased and uncommunicative sole reference point. Falter for a moment from a forward trajectory, consider for a second the myriad pressure of outside forces, and the arrow will slow, wobble, begin to fall. Your heart will wind up nailed to the dust. If you wield power for yourself, the only way is outwards and onwards, away from the ground-bound world of shared concerns.

I hope you will forgive me, or at least that you will understand me. I was the only person in the room with a gun. The Brigadier was finished, defeated. Simellia too. It had never been my duty to save them. As for Adela, if I thought of her, it was only to remember what she'd said about getting it right – which she hadn't, poor wretch. And I thought of Graham. I thought, I will never let them take him away from me. My beloved portable object. As if only I had choice.

So I unloaded the clip of the gun at the machine.

The room flooded with red light. An alarm tore through the air: *ee ee ee ee ee*. The floor vibrated infinitesimally and I imagined that, all over the building, bulletproof metal gates were slamming down on exits. Around the time-door, colour *was* and shape *was* but neither were colours or shapes that I recognised. The sight of a brand-new colour terrified me. I dropped the gun.

'Good God,' I said. 'Fucking Christ. What happens now?'

'You don't *know*?' shouted Simellia, above the noise.

'No! Is it going to kill us?'

'I don't bloody know!'

Just as abruptly as it started, the alarms, the clamour, and the shaking stopped. The machine made a noise like a sinister burp. The Brigadier scrabbled at it. There were a series of questioning beeps, a burst of red. I saw a screen – an operating system, I assumed. Then something absolutely godawful happened to the Brigadier, a form of implosion-explosion, a rip in the air as if the whole room was scenery and a knife had been plunged into it. If a black hole could sneeze, it might have looked like this. Then – something – small, and yet peculiarly filled with stars – hung in the air. The Brigadier was gone.

While I was staring at this pendant galaxy and wondering if I would be sick again, Simellia dived for the other gun in my holster.

It had been an enervating twenty-four hours. I'd slept on a stone floor with my heart broken and my friend dead. I do, therefore, try to forgive myself, that Simellia simply snatched the gun off me and put the muzzle to my temple. The heavies burst through to find a hostage situation among the machinery.

'You let me out of here, or I'll shoot her,' Simellia rasped. 'Do you know who she *is*? Do you know what might happen if she dies? Because I don't, but I'm the only one desperate enough to find out.'

'What?' I squeaked.

'You're uniquely duplicate in space-time,' hissed Simellia. 'They've probably got orders to keep you safe, in case your death damages the time-door. Now shut up.'

Someone shouted to *'stand down'* from behind a mask. Automatic rifles pointed at the ceiling. We edged into the vestibule, into the corridor. The air was filled with stinging smoke, which we, without masks, struggled horribly to negotiate – I recognised the tactic from my basic training. It was the most bungled, choking, excruciating escape attempt in the Ministry's short history. And it worked.

*

In a car park near the Ministry, Simellia released me but kept the gun pointed at me. She was shaking and the muzzle weaved in the air like a drunken bee.

'I'm going now,' she said.

'Where?'

'I'm not telling you. Be serious.'

I looked into her grey-tinged, exhausted face. 'You don't know, do you?' I said. 'You think you're going on the run. Where will you run *to*, Simellia? Where can you go where they can't find you? And if they can't find you, they'll find your brother. Your sister. Come on. Give me the gun. We'll go and find Adela and—'

Simellia shook her head, hard. 'No,' she said. 'No more compromises. I'm not going to be a part of this any more.'

'Then what will you *do*?' I shouted, exasperated. 'Who do you think will help you now, except the Ministry?'

'I'll tell the truth about what happened here. There will be so many more of me. So many more, you won't believe it. Your problem always was that you'd given up on other people.'

'Simellia, be sensible,' I said, but she was backing into the shadows, gun raised. The yellow of her skirt licked at the darkness.

'Go home,' she said. 'Just go home. We end here, you and me. Go home.'

So I did.

*

I got on the Tube. My hair was tangled, my clothes were dirty and rucked, I smelled powerfully of sweat, and I wasn't even the weirdest-seeming person in the carriage.

When I got home, I unlocked the door, stepped through, took off my shoes. I was breathing as if I'd forgotten how and kept having to manually restart myself. I went into the kitchen to make a cup of tea, because why not make a cup of tea at the end of the world?

Graham was in the kitchen.

He was sitting at the table, and he had a gun trained on me.

'Oh,' I said. A pity I hadn't yet come up with a new line, given the frequency with which people had been pointing guns at me.

'Keep your hands where I can see them.'

'What are you doing?'

'Be quiet. Were you followed?'

'I don't – think so? I tried to destroy the door. I thought if I destroyed it, then this would all be over. Graham, why are you pointing a gun at me?'

'Because I don't trust you.'

He stood up and I flinched. His arm was perfectly steady. Arthur's ring glinted on his finger. He didn't even look angry. He was just, indisputably, unutterably, holding me at gunpoint.

The safety catch was off – of course. I said, 'You'll kill me if you shoot that thing at point-blank range.'

'I know.'

'Oh my God. What are you doing? I tried to help you.'

'You hid things from us. All the Ministry's plans. Adela told me everything before she died.'

'*Died?*'

'I assume that's what happened to her.'

'I don't understand.'

'I am not especially interested in what you do and don't understand.'

'Where's Maggie?'

'Safe.'

'Can I see—'

'No. I am keeping her safe from *you*.'

The panic erupted, blossomed in my chest.

'Graham, I – you have to understand – I was just doing my job—'

'How can you think that?'

'I had orders – I thought I could fix it—' I said. In fact, I wailed it. I was learning that I was a snivelling wretch when I thought I might die.

'You had orders,' he repeated. 'How fascinating that you should have been born and raised in the twenty-first century and not hear how you sound. All that ambition, all that manoeuvring, and it amounts to "following orders". I used to find you so extraordinarily subtle, a tactician, a magician. To think it was because you were a coward. Do you understand that Arthur is *dead* because of you?'

'Listen—'

'Shut up. Adela said you had the passcodes.'

'Yes—'

He jerked his chin to the laptop on the table. Mine, not his. I had a painful mental image of him taking it carefully from my room, setting it up on the kitchen table, gun tucked in his belt.

'I want you to delete everything,' he said.

'I will, I will. Please put the gun down.'

'No. Sit.'

Shaking, I lowered myself into the chair.

'Graham – listen – did Adela tell you who she was?'

'Delete everything related to this project.'

'Yes – look – I am – but – do you know who she was? In the future, you and I—'

'There is no "you and I",' he said sharply. 'There was you, and there was a hobby that you had. Stop talking. Destroy all trace of this project. Or by God I will pull this trigger and send you to Arthur to make your apologies on behalf of the Ministry directly.'

I rattled at the keyboard and watched files flash up, one after the other. Sweat and tears rimmed my eyelids. He shifted position and the gun grazed my hair, very lightly. I cried out in terror. From the corner of my eye, I saw him flinch. I looked at him quickly and, for a moment, we held one another's eyes. His mouth trembled.

'Just do it quickly,' he whispered.

'Graham—'

'Stop saying my name!'

I typed and clicked and shivered uncontrollably. The little device Adela had given me unscrambled access codes, but I was so terrified I kept seeing fives as sevens and almost locked myself out. I saw, for a few seconds, my own psych files – the Wellness team had kept tabs on every bridge – and it felt like a death sentence when I rubbed myself out. The screen kept pulsing a sickly eighties green. I could hear him breathing – erratically, and trying to keep steady, like a man working through appalling pain.

'There! It's done! Put the gun down and let me—'

'I'm leaving,' he said. 'I'm taking Maggie with me. You will not attempt to track us. I know when I became your lover you used me as you liked and now you hold me in contempt, but I think you still care for Maggie. If they capture her, they'll kill her. If you love her, you won't help them.'

'Did you ever love me?' I asked, helplessly.

'Stay here. Don't follow me,' he said. He backed out of the kitchen, keeping me in his sights. He bolted up the hallway, ducked quickly out the front door. Slammed it.

I sat quite still at the kitchen table. There was a clock above the door and I watched it tell five minutes, ten minutes, fifteen. Half an hour passed. Forty-five minutes. It was only when I saw the small hand tick relentlessly onto the next number that I realised: that was it. There would be no dramatic prime-time-movie turnback, no changed hearts and reconciliation kisses. He was gone.

*

I was still sitting at the table, watching the clock face blur as tears rose and fell, when Ministry officers arrived to place me under arrest. Since I was already at the far edge of the scale of misery, I said to the arresting officer, 'Oh, hello,' as if he was the postman. He looked at me like I'd peeled my own face off to reveal a Scooby Doo villain. It was such a bizarre expression that, despite myself, I started to laugh.

*

It turned out that surprisingly few people knew that the late Adela Gore was from the future. Revealing that to the wrong interrogating officer got me placed under house arrest in a new safehouse. I was there for less than a week. I cannot describe how long a day feels when you think you might have to sit with it indefinitely. It's a form of torture, I realise that now. Holding someone in a cage against their will is like fisting your hand in their hair and directing their every motion. And I'd been so busy – so worker bee, so good drone – that not hearing from me for six days would hardly register with my family and friends. I'd made myself an island of one, and now I was going under the waves.

On day six, a car arrived to take me to the Ministry. It had blacked-out windows. A woman with a discreet gun bulge in her violently unchic trouser suit sat opposite me for the journey.

I was taken to Control's floor, into a light, lovely room with rich green curtains. The Secretary sat behind a spy-thriller-villain desk. He poured me a whiskey. It was three in the afternoon. I looked in vain for a fluffy white cat.

'Oh dear,' said the Secretary, sympathetically.

I put the whiskey to my lips and let it burn the nail-sized patch I'd bitten into them. It was the same whiskey that Graham drank – of course – the whiskey was Ministry-provided – and it tasted like talking to him. I wanted a cigarette, very badly.

'You knew I was Adela,' I said into the glass.

'I did. She told us.'

'When?'

'Long before you joined us. Before the project began, even. I think it was about a month after the time-door was seized. Oh, that wretched door. We had no idea how to work it. We put it in the experimental weapons facility in Defence.'

'Is that the exploding pens department?'

He gave me an indulgent smile. 'It's mostly chemical and biological weapons,' he said, 'and malware development, but we all like a good Bond, don't we? Anyway, one afternoon, a lab technician came screaming down the corridor with his entrails down his trousers, poor lad. He'd stood in the line of the beam at just the wrong moment. She'd come through.'

'She?'

'The woman you knew as Adela Gore.'

I put the whiskey glass down hard. The Secretary had a flighty fountain pen arrangement involving a stand and a brass holder and I upset the lot.

'I was in Defence before this,' he said, picking his fountain pen up. 'Advisory board to Westminster. She chose me herself.'

I saw glass rupture and blossom outwards, a momentary amber-and-crystal firework by the bookcase. A couple of seconds later I realised I'd thrown my glass at the wall. The Secretary hadn't moved and I felt very tired all of a sudden. I sat back down, having not been aware of standing up.

'So she came through,' I said, 'and explained that she was from 2040 whatever and you had to make the history happen, using the time-door. Pick up the right expats from the right eras to get the right future, like making a cake. Is that about it?'

'You are correct.'

'Why kill them, then? Why Maggie and Arthur?'

The Secretary waved grandly at the window, in a gesture that apparently took in the whole city.

'My dear girl,' he said, 'I'm sure you've worked out how valuable the expats are to us. But only if they can be trained. Alas, Sixteen-sixty-five and Nineteen-sixteen were valuable data sets but would have made useless agents. Don't blame yourself – present or future. Adela Gore didn't know. She ran the future-making project competently, but that's all she ran. She was never, so far as I understand it, a leadership-level decision-maker, though she was an indubitably efficient field agent. And you, I'm afraid, are not even Adela Gore. You have failed, in every permutation, to achieve her. Which brings me to the matter you have been brought here to discuss today.'

I felt two cold circles open in the palms of my hands.

'Your redundancy package,' he said.

'The way Maggie and Arthur were made "redundant".'

He gave me a puzzled look and pushed a closely typed piece of paper across the desk. There was a startlingly large number near the top, cherry-topped by a pound sterling symbol.

'Wait. You're actually making me redundant?'

'The expats are either dead, missing or in custody. I don't know who you're going to become, but it doesn't look like Mrs Graham Gore, agent of the Ministry. Regardless, due to your *unique* relationship to the time-door, it is prudent to leave you be. For now.'

My wrist jerked up about an inch. The urge to chew my thumb skin was as bad as the craving for a cigarette. I sat, as subtly as I could, on my hand.

'So. You're *not* going to kill me?'

The Secretary sighed. 'Come with me,' he said.

He led me to the far wall – it was a big enough office that I can describe one of the walls as 'far'. A wood panel made a very unwooden beeping noise and swung open. I was beyond surprise at this point. I trotted after him down a reinforced steel-and-glass corridor, passing armed guards and diverse alarms. Eventually, I was brought to a spare, enormous room, like a recently plundered laboratory. On an autopsy table in the middle was—

'That *was* Adela Gore,' said the Secretary. 'We think it happened when Simellia tried to sabotage the door. I'm told by the men on the scene that it looked like she exploded, but in reverse, and with light instead of viscera. Nevertheless, her passage into – whatever this is – functioned as quite a distraction, which allowed Eighteen-forty-seven, Sixteen-sixty-five and Sixteen-forty-five to flee.'

'Yes, that's what happened to the Brigadier too . . .' I said, slowly. There were some covered pits ahead in the conversation which I needed to negotiate. 'So. *Simellia* destroyed the door?'

The Secretary looked thoughtfully at me. 'I understand she attempted to. The SWAT team found bullets matching a Ministry-issue firearm embedded in the floor and wall, and it seems that she absconded with another.'

He waited. I edged out into the conversation again. 'Yes. She did . . . have a gun. What do you mean, *attempted* to destroy the door?'

'It's an extraordinary machine. It can pierce the very fabric of space-time. I don't think it can be destroyed by something as prosaic as a handheld gun. It is . . . damaged. I am not at liberty to say more. I would advise you not to pursue this line of questioning, in case I find I am interested in a new line of my own.'

'And all the expats are missing?' I asked hurriedly.

'Gore and Kemble are. Cardingham has been found and detained. He is co-operating. I understand he's always co-operated with us, whatever the timeline.'

'Simellia,' I said, suddenly.

'You know what will happen to her when we find her,' he said, quite gently.

'Jesus. You *can't*—'

'But I can. Not only that, I must. I've often heard you people use the term "solidarity". A word which describes the unity of a group with a common interest. A group which protects itself from external dangers that threaten its safety. I am describing citizens, and a country. Do you see that?'

I was still holding the piece of paper with my redundancy terms on it and I began to twist it into a sweaty cone. I still think about this little speech, by the way. I think about how annoyed Simellia would have been by the term 'you people', and by the illegibility of describing us both under the same umbrella term, even an offensive one.

'You're evil.'

'I am happy that you have the luxury of thinking that. It means your life is so safe you are pleased to play with the notion of individual morality. Individuals are not important. A country is.'

I stared at the boxable galaxy on the table, or rather, hovering slightly above it. It didn't seem to have all its planes in the dimensions I was used to viewing and it made my eyes water. I wondered if I'd killed Adela, or if her timeline had simply ceased to exist.

I imagined Graham somewhere in the future, waiting for his wife to come home, sinking into grief as the years racked up; a teenage boy growing into a young man, regretting not hugging his mother more often. But maybe I'd vanquished them too, wiped out their timeline. My son, who I never got to meet, conquered by atrophy before he ever existed.

'We don't know what happened to her,' said the Secretary, 'and so we have to make sure nothing happens to you, because she was a version of you and who knows what effect you might have on the future. You have so much *potential*. Isn't that nice? But if you come within five hundred feet of this building again, security have orders to open fire.'

*

I had no job, I had no home. I got most of my belongings back from the Ministry reclamation centre but for weeks I would discover I was missing a belt, a dress, a keepsake that must have been lost in the Ministry's rapid-fire stripping of the house. Half my books were missing, *Rogue Male* among them. Chicken bag came back to me bent into un-avian shapes. Most frustratingly, they returned my electronics but none of the requisite chargers. It felt like a final, petty little fuck-you.

They kept everything that belonged to him. Technically, his belongings were bought on the Ministry budget, and so were Ministry property. But I would have liked to have something of his.

My work laptop and work phone were confiscated. As I never used my personal phone – an ancient model with half a screen – to take photos, this also meant that I had no pictures of him. All I had left were the internet's reproductions of the 1845 daguerreotype, just as I did before he came into my life. I wore chicken necklace, warming it between the pads of my fingers, and tried to recall his hands. But the image faded. One morning I woke up and I found I could no longer remember exactly what colour his eyes were.

I left the city and moved back into my parents' home. The Ministry's agreed narrative was that I'd been made redundant in a Languages department reshuffle, and that was what I told my parents: the Ministry's fist up my rectum, puppeting my jaw.

Coming home hurt. They were right there, my parents – the authors of my blood and neuroses – and they were just people. Incredibly ordinary people, the sort no one writes novels about. I thought about the bargains I'd made with power, for power, paying with personhood, when all they really wanted was for me to be happy and to have a decent job.

My dad reassured me that my 'redundancy' payout was a

very good one and tried to jolly me into positivity; my mum took my hardship personally and promised to put 'a curse' (unspecified) on my former employer. She'd never shown any inclination towards hexing and hedge magic before but it was nice to see her energetic. I slumped, mostly. I became a child again, reduced to a sorry smallness against the impassivity of the adult world. He was gone, and he'd taken the woman I could have become with him.

*

For several weeks I was either crying or not-crying. The latter state was a numb space where I should have been crying but couldn't summon tears. I might be walking up the stairs and suddenly feel so overcome with numbness that I had to stop and sit and lean against the wall for an hour. I might be washing up and lose myself so utterly to the numbness that I would stand with my hands in the water until it turned cold and my palms were pale and puckered like the skin on milk.

One day, I read Arthur's notebook, which the Ministry did not think to remove from me – probably because Arthur had never been a threat and was even less of one dead. 'Day' is pushing it – it was 3.30 a.m., which was a normal waking hour for me at the time. Most of the notebook comprised lists of questions: *What is a VPN? Who is Mussolini? Swinging Sixties – meaning? P.C. Brigade – who and where based?* Usually, on the opposite page, there would be scribbled answering notes. I surmised that Arthur and Simellia would have regular meetings to go through his questions strategically. I never did that with Graham. I was, in so many ways, a bad bridge.

There were two other things in the notebook, and I almost mistook them for one another. Some were hurried, jotted nota-

338

tions of song lyrics. Arthur, unlike Graham, seemed to like modern music, and tried to keep track of what he was listening to. The other was poetry.

His poetry was terrible, and I think that he must have known that – he could never have been Rupert Brooke or Siegfried Sassoon – but he couldn't stop himself from writing it. There was something impossibly noble in that, quintessentially Arthurian. I read one of his poems and I heard it in his voice. There was a wound in me that kept unknotting its own sutures. I missed all of them so much. Now that they were gone, I felt I knew them better than I had when they were with me. I'd thought Graham was a scion of Empire and he'd thought I was a radical nonconformist by dint of my very existence. If only we'd seen each other clearly—

I stepped outside and stood on my parents' immaculate lawn. In the sky, like the glyphs on signal flags, were the stars. Maggie saw these same stars, and Arthur, and Graham too. But the stars aren't eternal. Most were already dead, and I was looking at ghosts. At some point in our planet's future, the skyscape will change. There might not be people left by then, not if the Brigadier's world was anything to go by. These stars were a temporary, beautiful gift of our era – the era that we all shared, a human era. I'd die one day, just like everyone else, so I had better try to live.

The next morning, I rolled myself out of bed for breakfast, fizzing oddly with four hours of sleep. I asked my parents if they'd like to go for a walk in the woods while the weather was nice. Their relief was visible. I remembered Adela's plea: *'You should spend as much time with them as you can.'* I tried to remember who I was before he arrived in my life.

*

Spring turned to summer. Summer burst and bedded down. My sister got me some freelance proofreading work, which meant I started getting emails again, but at least I wasn't required to kill anyone or spy on my friends. I'd stopped crying every day, though I did still cry. I was still living with my parents, though I was mulling over moving back to London. The Ministry's hush money gathered moss in my bank account. It was more ready cash than I'd ever had in one place and I didn't want to touch it.

One afternoon, my dad called me downstairs while I was avoiding emails in my sister's old bedroom, now my de facto office.

'Bit of an eccentric parcel for you.'

'Oh?'

'Been at the depot for a couple of weeks. They've been trying to work out where the house was. Got your name, though.'

'How can they have missed the house? It's numbered.'

'Well. See for yourself.'

He handed me a small parcel. I instantly felt as if the ground had erupted with crevasses. In the top corner was a US stamp, but the rest of the packet was scrawled over with Graham's languid cursive. There was no address. Instead, he'd written a description of approximately where he thought the house was and what it looked like, based on my stories about my child-hood, and put my name at the top of it.

I tore the parcel open. Inside was the missing copy of *Rogue Male*.

There was something wedged between the pages. I opened the book and plucked out a glossy photograph. In the foreground, there were spruce trees, thrumming emerald green, and trampled, wild earth. I thought I could pick out a lake in the background, gleaming promisingly. It was anonymous in its loveliness.

At the left-hand edge of the photograph, there was a glint of something. I tilted it, squinted and bent my neck. There were strands blowing in the wind – copper-flushed gold, gossamer-light. Hair. There was also the barest vertical sliver of fuchsia. I was looking at long, strawberry-blonde hair and the edge of an arm in a hot pink jacket, far enough away from the lens that someone else must have taken the picture. This was a photograph that showed two people, then: one just out of view, and one behind the camera. They were alive.

I started to put the photograph back into the book, when I realised that it was marking a page with an underlined passage. I read:

She knew, I suppose, that in our mixture of impulse and intelligence we were alike. Her emotions governed her brain; though she would support her side with devastating logic, logic had nothing to do with her devotion. I should never have suspected that of myself, yet it is true. I have never taken sides, never leaped wholeheartedly into one scale or the other; nor do I realise disappointments, provided they are severe, until the occasion is long past. Yet I am ruled by my emotions, though I murder them at birth.

At the bottom of the page was another note, written in the same scrambling penmanship as he'd signed the note in the cairn in 1847. It said:

Of course I love you

'You all right, kiddo?' asked my dad. He looked bemused. Who knows what face journey he'd just witnessed.

'Uh. Yes. Dad. Do you know what trees these are?'

'Hmm. Sitka spruce, maybe?'

'Where would you find those?'

'West coast of America. Probably taken in Alaska.'

'What's the biggest city in Alaska?'

'Anchorage,' said my dad promptly. I could see he was pleased that I was engaging with his pub quiz knowledge and also not crying on the sofa. 'Got some pals up there, have you?'

'Yes,' I said slowly. I was thinking about the hush money I hadn't touched, the emails I didn't feel like answering. I was thinking about approximate whereabouts I could locate from a single photograph – if I was careful.

'Yes,' I said, a bit more clearly. 'Do you know, I haven't had a holiday in over a year. I think I might take a trip.'

*

This is how you change history.

As far as you know – or as far as the you that is me knows – the time-door is broken. You may never receive this document, which tells you what you will become if you follow this version of yourself. But if this falls into your hands, then I want you to know how it happens, step by step, so that you can change it. I exist at the beginning and end of this account, which is a kind of time-travel, but I hope you'll find a way to contain me. I know how much you've longed for your future to lean down and cup your face, to whisper *don't worry, it gets better*. The truth is, it won't get better if you keep making the same mistakes. It can get better, but you must allow yourself to imagine a world in which *you* are better.

I don't mean to sound pessimistic. I only do because I can see how wrong my choices were. Don't do it like this. Don't enter believing yourself a node in a grand undertaking, that your past and your trauma will define your future, that individuals don't matter. The most radical thing I ever did was love him, and I wasn't even the first person in this story to do that. But you can get it right, if you try. You will have hope, and you have been forgiven.

Forgiveness, which takes you back to the person you were and lets you reset them. Hope, which exists in a future in which you are new. Forgiveness and hope are miracles. They let you change your life. They are time-travel.

This daguerreotype by Richard Beard is the only existing picture of Graham Gore. It was taken in 1845, just before Gore left on his last expedition to the Arctic.

The illustrations used in this edition are watercolour and pen sketches by Gore himself, made on the outward journey to the Arctic. The one at the front of the book is titled 'HMS *Erebus*, 22 May 1845, 3AM, off Aldborough' and the one at the back is titled '*Blazer* taking HMS *Erebus* in tow, 31 May 1845, 6PM'. Gore sent them to Lady Franklin (wife of expedition leader Sir John Franklin) from Disko Island in Greenland, where the crews of the *Erebus* and *Terror* wrote their last letters home.

Afterword

On 19 May 1845, two ships, the HMS *Erebus* and the HMS *Terror*, departed from Greenhithe in Kent to find the Northwest Passage, a (then) hypothetical route through the North American Arctic which would connect the United Kingdom with the trading kingdoms of Asia. In late July 1845, two whalers saw *Erebus* and *Terror* in Baffin Bay, off the west coast of Greenland, awaiting good conditions to enter the Arctic labyrinth. The expedition was never again seen by Europeans. After seven years of searching, on 1 March 1854, the entire expedition was officially pronounced lost, and all its members dead. It was not until 1859 that William Hobson, a lieutenant on another Arctic expedition, found a cairn containing the Victory Point note – the text of which is reproduced in Chapter IX of this novel.

The expedition had been under the command of Sir John Franklin, veteran Arctic explorer, known as 'the man who ate his boots' after the disastrous, murderous and possibly cannibalistic 1819 Coppermine expedition. *Terror* was captained by Francis Crozier, an exceptionally able sailor and scientist who had participated in five prior Arctic and Antarctic expeditions; *Erebus*, the flagship, was captained by James Fitzjames, a charismatic and ambitious man with no polar experience whatsoever.

Fitzjames's next in command on *Erebus* was First Lieutenant Graham Gore, one of only six officers on the expedition with Arctic experience.

There is very little material about Graham Gore. We have no record of his birth, nor his will, nor any letters he wrote from the expedition itself. We have his service record but almost no information about his personal experience of his career. His father, John Gore, captained the HMS *Dotterel* and entered the eleven-year-old Graham as a 'young volunteer' on the ship in 1820, so we know he must have been about thirty-five years old when the Franklin expedition sailed. His most enduring pen portrait is by James Fitzjames, in a letter to Fitzjames's sister-in-law Elizabeth Coningham:

> *Graham Gore, the first lieutenant, a man of great stability of character, a very good officer, and the sweetest of tempers, is not so much a man of the world as Fairholme or Des Vœux, is more of a Le Viscomte's [sic] style without his shyness. He plays the flute dreadfully well, draws sometimes very well, sometimes very badly, but is altogether a capital fellow.*

Footnote though he was, it is possible to work out a handful of things about Gore. He was a popular and well-liked officer; he was in continuous employment from the very start of his career, which was unusual for an officer in the peacetime Royal Navy, and many of the men who served with him remarked on his kindness. He played the flute and enjoyed drawing (he contributed a number of illustrations to John Lort Stokes's *Discoveries in Australia*, after serving as Stokes's first lieutenant aboard the HMS *Beagle*). He was a keen sportsman, and often turns up in other people's letters and memoirs shooting things (caribou, seals, rabbits, cockatoos, egrets, you name it, he's shot it). And, based on the single daguerreotype that exists of him, he was a very attractive man.

I extrapolated a great deal about Gore for this novel. Fitzjames mentions seeing Gore fishing over the side of *Erebus* with a cigar clamped in his mouth: I turned that into a smoking habit. Stokes remembers Gore coolly remarking, 'Killed the bird . . .' after a gun exploded in his hands with such force it threw him onto his back: I turned that into a personality of preternatural calm and amiability. I reasoned he was probably a good shot, given how much practice he'd had at shooting. In the only surviving letters by Gore, digitised by the website Arctonauts. com, he comes across as a humorous, self-possessed man, who said, of his career in the Navy:

but (it may be very foolish) I have always had a presentiment, I shall one day arrive at the top of the tree whether I like it or not

So I put him – in one version of his future – at the top of the Ministry. Whether he likes it or not.

The earliest version of *The Ministry of Time* was written to amuse some friends. I never intended for it to have more than about five readers. But I'm glad that *The Ministry of Time* emerged from that project. If anything, it's taught me that it's always worth reading the footnotes.

Kaliane Bradley
London, 2024

Acknowledgements

It took a wardroom's worth of people to launch this vessel. Thank you to Federico Andornino and Margo Shickmanter, my brilliant editors, who brought effervescence, strength and precision to the text – it is a more beautiful thing than it was because of them. Thank you to Chris Wellbelove, my agent, for his faith in me and his clarity of vision; both he and his assistant, the wonderful Emily Fish, read and re-read and re-re-read *The Ministry of Time* and yet never lost sight of the heart of the book.

Thank you to Lisa Baker, Laura Otal, Anna Hall, Lesley Thorne and the whole team at Aitken Alexander Associates, who have found so many new harbours for *The Ministry of Time* – it's been such a dream to work with them. Thank you also to the team at Sceptre: Maria Garbutt-Lucero (my hero), Holly Knox, Kimberley Nyamhondera, Alice Morley, Melissa Grierson, Helen Parham, Alasdair Oliver, Vicky Palmer and Claudette Morris; and to the team at Avid Reader Press: Alexandra Primiani, Katherine Hernandez, Meredith Vilarello, Caroline McGregor, Katya Buresh, Alison Forner, Clay Smith, Sydney Newman, Jessica Chin, Allison Green, Amy Guay and Jofie Ferrari-Adler.

Thank you to Anne Meadows, whose generous feedback and affectionate encouragement at a crucial point in the early rewrites changed this book for the better.

I am indebted to, and thankful for, the friends I made because we all became unhinged about various antique lads who died in the polar regions. I am especially grateful to the friends who read the first version of *The Ministry of Time* as it was being written, without whom the book would never have existed: Isaac Fellman, Lucy Irvine, VP James, Theodora Loos, Kit Mitchell, Waverley SM, Allegra Rosenberg, Sydni Zastre, Arielle, Berry, Ireny, Jess, Kate, Leo and Rebecca. I'm also deeply grateful to have watched AMC's TV series *The Terror*, developed by David Kajganich, without which I would never have met Graham Gore at all.

My friend Rach, a Wilfred Owen fan, came up with Arthur's Lieutenant Owen and the origin of the signet ring. We leave it to you to decide in what happy circumstances that ring might have been given.

This book is informed by a wealth of scholarship. Thanks especially to Edmund Wuyts at Arctonauts.com, who was an invaluable resource on all things Graham Gore; and to Russell Potter, whose blog 'Visions of the North' was where I encountered – among other things – the discovery that Gore was almost certainly behind the chronometer Arnold 294 (last seen on the *Beagle* in Australia) being listed as 'Lost in the Arctic Regions with *Erebus*'. I have cast this discrepancy in a more nefarious light than may have been the case – sorry Graham.

In the final chapter of this book, I quote from *Rogue Male* (1939) by Geoffrey Household. My edition (and thus Graham's) is the 2007 New York Review of Books reissue.

To inform the Arctic segments, I drew on *Frozen in Time: The Fate of the Franklin Expedition* by Owen Beattie and John

Geiger; *I May Be Some Time: Ice and the English Imagination* by Francis Spufford; *May We Be Spared to Meet on Earth: Letters of the Lost Franklin Arctic Expedition* edited by Russell Potter, Regina Koellner, Peter Carney and Mary Williamson; *Discovering the North-West Passage: The Four-Year Arctic Odyssey of H.M.S. Investigator and the McClure Expedition* by Glenn M. Stein; L.H. Neatby's translation of *Frozen Ships: The Arctic Diary of Johann Miertsching 1850–1854*; *Narrative of an Expedition in H.M.S. Terror: Undertaken with a View to Geographical Discovery on the Arctic Shores, in the Year 1836–7* by Sir George Back; the unpublished Arctic diaries of Sir Robert John Le Mesurier McClure, which are held by the Royal Geographical Society; and the expertise of my polar exploration friends. Any inaccuracies or blunders you encounter in *The Ministry of Time* are my own.

Thank you to my family – my parents, Rany and Paul, and my siblings Brigitte, Pauline and David – for their unwavering love and support. Thank you to Becky, Narayani and Anna for their bolstering, their kindness and their willingness to let me talk for hours on end about some dead guy.

Thank you, above all, to Sam. There would be no point to any of this happiness without you. Thank you for believing in me from the beginning.